**A train ride to triumph and tears—
unforgettable men and women
whose destination is
a place forever in our hearts**

∎

**SAM HOUSTON HAWKEN.** An iron-willed young Texan, this intrepid Union officer would risk his life to stop the Confederate train speeding toward Atlanta—and reach the beautiful Southern belle he loved.

**MIRANDA KEMBLE.** Feisty daughter of one of Georgia's wealthiest families, this stunningly beautiful woman would have to take on a man's job when her father died—and watch her lover fight against her country.

**NOAH BALLARD.** A man of the New South, his vision of a glorious future depended on one vital mission—to beat both man and nature to get the Confederacy's last train from Mississippi to Atlanta.

**FANNY SHAW.** A sophisticated and sensual British actress, her outrage against slavery derailed her marriage to powerful Pierce Kemble, but joined her heart with another Kemble—one as dangerous as he was rich.

**LAMAR KEMBLE.** Proud son of the Southern aristocracy, this handsome cavalry officer was sent to stop the Yankees' train—in what would become a violent confrontation between friendship and loyalty to the land he loved.

∎

# THE
# RAILROAD WAR

*Also by Jesse Taylor Croft*

\*

THE TRAINMASTERS

Published by
POPULAR LIBRARY

# THE
# RAILROAD WAR
## THE TRAINMASTERS BOOK II

## JESSE TAYLOR CROFT

**POPULAR LIBRARY**

An Imprint of Warner Books, Inc.

A Warner Communications Company

# THE
# RAILROAD WAR

## THE TRAINMASTERS BOOK II

# ◆ ONE ◆

"I am *trying* to speak to you, *Miss* Miranda Kemble,"
Ariel Kemble, eighteen, said to her sister, who was three
years her junior. "I have spoken to you four times, Miranda,"
Ariel went on more insistently, "and you didn't even look at
me once, much less answer me." Then with a louder voice:
"Miranda! Miran*da*!" But Miranda kept her face turned to
the open window. Her gaze had been unwavering since the
moment the train had left New York City. Though Ariel was
less cross with Miranda than exasperated, she feigned serious anger because her sister's attention was in fact important to her.

The sisters, together with their father, Pierce, and their
uncle Ashbel were journeying on the Hudson line to Garrison's Landing, the hamlet that served as the station stop for
West Point, which was across the river. The United States
Military Academy was located at West Point, and their
brother, Lamar, was graduating this week from that illustrious institution. Ariel, Miranda, and their father had traveled
all the way from Georgia to participate in the ceremonies.
Uncle Ashbel had joined them in New York City.

The two men were seated just ahead of the girls. Unlike

1

Ariel and Miranda, they were engaged in vigorous conversation. Pierce Kemble was usually excited and voluble, his head nodding with energy and enthusiasm, his face flushed as he spoke. Ashbel was atypically the listener.

Pierce's excitement had much justification. He was more than $350,000 richer than he had been only a week before, although much of that $350,000 was already spoken for since Pierce Kemble had incurred substantial long-term debts. Nevertheless, $350,000 was a vast sum, and it was his.

The train was only a few miles from Garrison's Landing. Ariel needed to speak to Miranda soon if she were to get her business over with before the excitement of their arrival. It was, however, a delicate situation.

"Miranda!" Ariel repeated, for what she was sure was the millionth time. Then she reached over and shook her sister's shoulder.

After a long moment, Miranda, lazily turning her gaze from the window and the rugged, lovely landscape beyond it, fixed her eyes on Ariel, who was in the aisle seat next to her. Ariel's lips were pressed tight, her brow was rigid, and her eyelids were lowered to a most ominous half-mast. Seeing this, Miranda let her own face brighten into her most radiant, most charming, most winning smile.

"You were saying something, dear?" she said sweetly.

"I've been trying to say something to you for *hours,*" Ariel said. "And you have pretended not to hear me."

"Oh, that can't be true, Ariel. We've not been on the train for hours, and I've only been admiring the view for a short while."

"Must you be so literal?" Ariel said, her exasperation growing. She hated when Miranda played the innocent. In Ariel's opinion, her sister was never, *never* innocent. For Miranda, tricks and mischief came more naturally than sleep, especially when Ariel was the target. Which was the main reason why Ariel wanted to conclude her business with Miranda before they left the train. In the restricted setting of a passenger car, Miranda was on her best behavior. Heaven only knew what deviltry she'd find to wallow in once the ferry brought them to West Point, with its dozens of unattached young men for an audience.

"Isn't the river beautiful?" Miranda was exclaiming, changing the conversation to her liking. As she spoke, she lifted her hands high above her lap, where they had been resting, and opened her palms reverently to the scene outside the window. "The hills, and cliffs, and bluffs . . . I've never seen anything so achingly lovely, have you, dearest?"

The train was passing through one of the most delightful scenes on the river. Just north of Peekskill, near Bear Mountain, the river narrowed into a rocky gorge. Rough, bouldered hills strained against one another, then tumbled down sheer flanks to the river edge.

"It's so fierce looking out there," Miranda continued, attempting, Ariel was convinced, to use the beauties of the landscape to avoid hearing what her sister had to say. "And yet it all seems to be moving—almost to flow. And we seem to be standing still."

Ariel glanced sourly out of the open window. It was the noise and the jolting discomfort of the train and the grit and ashes drifting inexorably in more than the scenery that excited her attention. And distaste. The train's rattles, creaks, and metallic cracks and bangs made the trip feel to Ariel more like a punishment than a purposeful and speedy progress toward a destination. Even the breeze from outside was no pleasure to her. It destroyed her hair. And infinitely worse, it grimed her gorgeous new clothes, which were a small portion of the glorious abundance of new things their father had during the past week bought for them at the most fashionable clothing emporia of New York. Their luggage was all but overflowing with the newest New York and Paris fashions.

Miranda, contrarily, indifferent to the dirt, adored the breeze; she reveled in the wind rushing against her face and through her sherry-colored hair, lifting it, making it fly.

"If the train weren't lurching and jostling," Ariel grumbled, "and if it weren't so filthy, and if I weren't so uncomfortable in it, I could perhaps look with pleasure at the countryside." As she spoke, she dabbed with her hand-kerchief at the soot on her face.

Miranda gave her a sharp stare, followed shortly by a darling smile. She didn't like her sister to contradict her when she was off on one of her imaginative flights, but since at the moment she was playing innocent, she decided she shouldn't step out of character.

And then the train plunged into a tunnel.

"Oh!" she yelped.

"It's only a tunnel," Ariel explained without either concern or patience.

A moment later they were out of it, and Miranda was smiling again. "You were saying?" she said, as if it were her sister and not Miranda herself who was keeping Ariel from getting on with her urgent business.

"I want you to do something for me," Ariel said, catching her sister's eye. Miranda's irises were a devious yet penetrating green, with yellow catlike flecks.

"Just tell me what it is," Miranda said guilelessly.

Ariel gave her a long look. "While we're at the Academy," she said finally, carefully, "I'd like it that . . ." She turned her eyes away for a second. And then: "It's about my engagement to Ben Edge."

Ariel was scheduled to marry Ben Edge of Virginia early in September. He was a fine, and very wealthy, young man. It was a good match, as Ariel well knew.

"Your engagement?" Miranda repeated, urging Ariel to continue, her mouth slipping into a somewhat less innocent smile. Miranda could guess what was on her sister's mind.

"That's right," Ariel said. She looked into Miranda's eyes again. "I think it might be best if we . . . kept the knowledge of it out of . . ."

"You don't want the boys at West Point to know you are about to be married?" Miranda said.

"That's right, Miranda," Ariel sighed, relieved she didn't have to actually say the words, for she was in fact a bit ashamed of herself. She *did* love Ben Edge, but she was not going to deprive herself of a few pleasant days with other handsome young men.

"Oh, my," Miranda said innocently, "I don't know if I could do that!"

"Why not?" Ariel said in a rush.

"Well," Miranda said, "what about Father and Uncle? And what about Lam?" Lam was their brother Lamar's nickname.

"I've already talked to Father and Uncle Ashbel, and I can deal with Lamar."

"You've already talked to Father? And he is going along with your"—she smiled sweetly—"lies?"

"Oh, come," Ariel said. "It's no lie. It's simply a"—she searched for the word—"a little piece of 'practical diplomacy,' as Daddy himself calls it."

"That's what he said when you told him?"

"That's right."

"Sounds like him," Miranda said with a shake of her head.

"And then he said, 'We aren't lying when we don't report the truth fully. We're just being smart. Only a fool tells the whole truth.'"

"And what if Lam has already told all the other men at the Academy?"

"I told you that I would deal with Lam later. Now I'm dealing with you."

"All right," Miranda said with a quick, decisive nod.

"What do you mean, 'All right'?" Ariel blurted. "Do you really mean yes, you'll do it?" She was astonished that Miranda might have been won over without a longer fight.

"Of course I'll do it for you, darling. There's no harm done in something like that"—she lifted her head and glanced sideways at Ariel—"is there?" When she finished these words, Miranda leaned over and kissed her sister on the cheek.

"Thank you," Ariel said, returning the kiss. "Thank you *so* much. That will be *such* a relief to me. I just want to make my stay at the Academy . . . uncomplicated."

"I'm sure you do," Miranda said. Then she laughed. "And what did Uncle Ashbel tell you when you told him what you wanted to do?"

"Uncle Ashbel? Oh, you know him," Ariel said, giggling nervously.

Uncle Ashbel could be counted on to have a witty, sophisticated opinion on every subject under the sun. Unlike most sons of the South, he was a traveler. He'd journeyed everywhere, from Shanghai to Cape Town, from Patagonia to Vladivostok, and up every river that the girls had ever heard of.

He was full of shocking and delicious tales about the nearly naked and very willing girls of the South Pacific and the equally willing and even more naked girls of West Africa. He told them about the golden idols of Peru, the elegant and amusing thieves in Morocco, the ruthless British opium traders in Hong Kong, and the jungle-shrouded pyramids in the Yucatán. The two nieces only half believed his outlandish claims.

Their skepticism was in fact mostly justified, although there was more than a grain of truth in Ashbel's tales. He was an international trader who owned enough ships to make him quite wealthy and allow him to travel to exotic ports.

Besides, it wasn't the truth of Uncle Ashbel's stories that counted, it was his style.

Then Ashbel Kemble himself, craning over the seat back ahead of the girls, was facing Ariel and Miranda. "I heard my name spoken in vain," he said with a warm look. He liked his two nieces very much.

"We'd *never* speak your name in vain, Uncle," Ariel said.

He laughed. "I suppose not," he said. "At least not when I can hear you. You both want too much from me."

"Uncle!" they both said as one.

"Well," he said, "I did hear my name. What do you hungry tigresses want now?"

"Nothing at all, Uncle," Ariel said.

Miranda, grinning, looked at him and then at Ariel. "She was just explaining to me," Miranda said, "that she intends to put her engagement out of sight during her time at West

Point. And," Miranda's eyes flashed, "I am sort of curious to hear what your reaction was to her plans."

"Me?" he said, laughing. "What's so fascinating about my opinions of a young lady's deceptions?"

"Uncle, please," Ariel said, her face flushing bright rose, "can we talk about something else?"

He looked at Miranda. "You know I can't say no to a girl so lovely as you, especially when she is my niece."

"Uncle Ashbel!" Ariel said, blushing even more. Then turning toward the aisle, she covered her face with her hands. "Please! Don't embarrass me any more!"

"Few things give me greater pleasure than embarrassing you, dear child," he said. "Shame becomes you."

Suddenly Miranda screamed—a long, wailing cry of pain and terror.

Ariel instantly jerked around to see what was the matter, for with her eyes covered, she hadn't seen what had happened to her sister.

Miranda cried out again, and her hands were brushing at her breast. It was smoking!

"Oh, my Lord!" Ariel said to herself with a heavy shudder. She was otherwise frozen with shock. Flames and smoke swelled out of a patch of Miranda's blouse. The patch was not large, covering only the space over her heart, but she was on fire nonetheless.

A plum-sized ember from the locomotive had been sucked through the open window onto Miranda's breast. Miranda had by this time managed to shake it off, and now the horrid-looking thing was still glowing on the floor of the train. As soon as Ariel was able, she ground the flame under her shoe.

Miranda screamed again. "My blouse!" she cried. "My new blouse!" Now Ariel used her shawl to smother the place where the cinder had landed. When she stopped and pulled back, Ashbel, with no thought of decency, ripped away the front of Miranda's blouse. Ariel hardly noticed that he was cursing like a sailor all the while. "Jesus Christ! Goddamn! Bastard railroads! Goddamned pine burners!"

Pierce Kemble looked on, standing with a pained but

helpless expression on his face. Ariel knew better than to count on her father in a crisis.

The train conductor was by this time present in the aisle next to Ariel, and several of the passengers had joined him. A pair of elderly woman who occupied the seat behind the girls were now bent over Miranda and Ariel in order to get the best possible view. The conductor drew a gold watch from its pocket and worriedly flipped it open, as if he feared that the incident might delay his schedule.

"Is she all right? Can I be of assistance?" he said.

"For God's sake, just move back," Ashbel shouted, "and give the girl room!" The conductor and the passengers obeyed, all except the elderly women, who looked more eager to see the spectacle than the rest.

What they saw on the girl's breast was a flame-blackened piece of undergarment framing a blistered and raw-looking coin of flesh.

"Do something about those two women," Ashbel said to Ariel in a commanding voice. Ariel did as she was told. She placed a palm on each old lady's shoulder and forcibly shoved them back into their seat. They started to protest, but Ashbel wouldn't let them finish. "Close your mouths, ladies, and keep quiet," he shouted. "And don't either of you make a move. The world would be a better place minus you two." And then to Miranda, much more softly, "How do you feel, darlin'?"

She groaned. "Dizzy," she managed to say. "Hard to breathe. It's ruined, isn't it? The lace? The embroidery?" And then she looked at Ariel, her eyes wide with apprehension. "And . . . *Mother*! she whispered hoarsely. "She will be at the hotel! She'll kill me for ruining my new . . ."

"You're right, I'm afraid," Ashbel said. "You won't be wearing that blouse again, darlin', I'm sorry to say. But I don't think you should be concerned about your mother." As he said that, he looked at Ariel. Her expression confirmed that he was right. The girls' mother wouldn't be unhappy if all the new things Pierce Kemble had purchased for them had burned. The marriage of Pierce Kemble and Fanny Kemble—now once again Fanny Shaw—had been dissolved ten years earlier in a famous and acrimonious divorce. Time had not healed the bitterness.

Then Ashbel spoke to Ariel. "I don't want this girl going into shock. Let's make her more comfortable." And stretching out his hand, he began to unfasten the buttons of the high collar of her blouse. He also very gently plucked away the scorched undergarment from around the burn.

"I don't think that is proper," Ariel said, putting her hand up to restrain him.

"You may have noticed, or you may not have," he said, ignoring her hand, "but the girl is already showing a fair portion of naked breast. Not that anyone would bother to notice the shame of it, not in the condition it's in right now."

"Oh!" Ariel cried, realizing he was right, for Miranda's left breast was almost entirely exposed. Hastily Ariel draped her shawl over it.

Miranda moaned deeply when she did it.

"Idiot!" Ashbel said. "She *hurts*! Don't let anything touch that!" And he flung the shawl aside. Then he unfastened several more of the blouse buttons. "Can you breathe better now, darlin'?" he said to her. "What about your waist? Is that too tight, too? Damn women's clothes. I don't know who decided to bind up so ferociously a machine God wanted to make loose for dropping babies."

"Uncle Ashbel!" Ariel protested, shocked.

"Yes, Uncle, I can breathe better," Miranda was saying. "It hurts, though. Mightily."

"Of course it does." He gave a hard look at the charred and blackened flesh. "It's ugly," he said, "but maybe not as bad as it looks." Then he raised his head and looked around. "Where's that damned conductor?" He turned to his brother. "Well, Pierce, move. Quick. Go to the conductor and make him give you some cold, clean water. I'm going to clean her up."

"Do you think you'd better?" Pierce Kemble said. It was his first contribution to the incident. "Don't you think there will be a qualified doctor at West Point? Shouldn't she be greased or something?"

"You go do what I told you, Pierce, and we'll argue later about further treatment."

Pierce did as he was told. Soon he returned with a pitcher of water. While he was away, Ashbel tore Ariel's shawl into strips, and then he asked Ariel if she would wash the wound, which she did—gently, lovingly.

Even so, Miranda cried out a number of times. Ariel soothed her as best she could. While Ariel was cleansing the wound, Ashbel offered Miranda some whiskey from his hip flask. She refused it.

When Ariel was done, she and her uncle both carefully inspected the result. "You'll live," he announced, "though you might end up with some kind of a scar. But don't worry, girl," he smiled. "It'll give you a story for your husband. In fact, if I were you, I'd work up more than just one story about it." His smile broadened, and he once more surveyed the burned spot. Then with an amused roll of his eyes, he said, "You could have picked a lot worse place to have a scar."

"Uncle!" Ariel admonished.

But Miranda, lowering her gaze, giggled a little. Then she raised her face and sought first her uncle's and then her sister's eyes. After that she touched each of them lightly on the cheek. Without speaking, she reached across Ariel's lap to where her shawl was lying, and, arranging it carefully so it wouldn't touch her wound, she drew it over her nakedness.


There was a bustling, noisy crush of people on the South Dock at West Point after the ferry from Garrison's Landing arrived: the train from New York had carried a large number of those who planned to attend tomorrow's commencement. There were, additionally, officers in blue and cadets in gray who had come down to the dock to greet families and guests, and a number of army enlisted men who had been called in to act as porters.

Over the dock, festive pennants and streamers had been strung on lines connecting lamp poles, and on taller poles flew the national ensign and the flag of the Academy. Off to one side, on shore, a small band played snappy tunes. Beyond the band, on the wide graveled lot that flanked the dock, carriages and wagons waited to take the arriving guests and their baggage up the hill to the Academy. To make everything perfect, there was a blue sky and warm sun.

The Kembles were among the last to alight from the ferry, in order not to cause Miranda any additional strain.

When the two girls appeared at the head of the gangway and started to cross, there were quick, concerned glances from those passengers who had already reached the dock. And the glances were followed by whispered comments and explanations. No one who'd been on the train, of course, was ignorant of the accident the young beauty from Georgia had suffered, but the West Point officers and cadets on the dock needed to be informed. Then there came a shout from someone near the end of the gangway, and a moment later the crowd parted so a way could be made for the stricken girl.

Though her chest still pained her, Miranda was not displeased with her sudden celebrity. In fact, she was delighted by it.

And so she lifted her head high, and with straight back, steady step, and resolute bearing moved through the crowd toward the other end of the dock, where her brother Lam waited for her with two other cadets. She was followed by her sister, her uncle, and her father, and she achieved the effect of a royal procession: she was a princess followed by attending lesser nobility.

As she walked, various people on either side of her remarked on her courage, beauty, and grace under adversity, and she tried to give to each of these kind and friendly souls an inclination of her head to acknowledge how grateful she was for their attention. This slowed her progress toward her brother and the two cadets who were with him, one of whom, she had not failed to note, was especially tall and good-looking.

And then, about halfway between the gangway and the landward end of the dock, her progress was brought to an abrupt halt. A plump woman with a bright smile took Miranda momentarily by the hand and drew her to her ample bosom. "How brave you are, you dear girl," the woman said. "How perfectly lovely and adorable. I hope that I'll get a chance to see you at the ball tonight. I trust you won't be completely indisposed." She glanced behind her, and Miranda noticed a short and slightly less plump version of the woman who held her hand. "Freddy," the woman said, "wouldn't you like the first dance with this bravest of girls?"

"I'd be most pleased," the cadet said.

Miranda drew back, searching vainly for an excuse to pull herself away from this woman and her son. He had a face that would sink ships, but she was too nice a girl to do anything so impolite as to let him know that.

A moment later, however, she was saved. "I'm sure she'd love a dance with Freddy," said a loud male voice. "But I'm afraid she's already promised the first dance to me." The man, Uncle Ashbel, of course, had moved up beside her. He then contrived to slip her away from the grip of the woman. "Come on, my dear," he continued. "We must bring you to the hotel. It's a warm, close day, and with your recent wound, you might feel suddenly faint." He looked meaningfully at the plump lady, all the while dragging Miranda toward her brother.

"I hate to disturb your moment of glory, precious, but we really should move on," he said softly but imperatively, once they were out of earshot of the lady and her son.

"I'm afraid I don't understand," she dissembled with high, arched brows. "I'm sure I wasn't . . ."

"It's a great pleasure to be noticed," he interrupted. "But life is short." Then he pulled her to a swifter pace. "You'd like to be all day promenading down the dock, but I have better things to do. And so, I hope, will you."

Momentarily serious, she said, "Well, thank you anyhow, Uncle dear, for saving me from the woman back there—and her son." After the word "son," she made a grunting sound deep in her throat.

Ashbel laughed, and then Lam rushed up to them, trailed by his two cadet friends.

"Miranda! Uncle Ash! Ariel! Father!" Lam was shouting joyfully and expansively. In one smooth and dramatic movement, he pumped Ashbel's hand and kissed Miranda many times on the cheek, for Ashbel had managed to hurriedly warn him about embracing her. Then he kissed and embraced Ariel and flung his arms around his father. All the while a stream of greetings issued from his lips.

Her brother was an excitable young man, but Miranda had never seen him so ecstatic. Still, she could understand his excitement. He was nearly at the moment of his greatest glory: he was about to become a second lieutenant.

Uncle Ashbel, meanwhile, was busy introducing himself to the two other cadets, who had held themselves apart from the family ceremonies.

"Oh, my!" Lam laughed. "I'm completely forgetting my duties as host. These are my roommates and friends. I should be making proper introductions."

In a flash Lam was standing next to the shorter of the two cadets. The boy was eight or nine inches taller than Miranda, who was then a shade over five feet. He was a fleshy young man, though not unattractively overweight. His fleshiness was boyish, leftover baby fat, and indeed, Miranda realized, he was still smooth faced. There wasn't yet the shadow of a beard on him, but he had a great curly nimbus of dark hair on his head, which gave the boy considerable presence, even if it did not change the fact that he was scarcely older than Miranda herself. "This young officer and gentleman . . ." Lam said, his hand resting on the boy's curls. Then he laughed, "Correction: future officer, but as a gentleman, hopeless."

The other young man threw a playful punch which grazed Lam's arm.

"Anyhow," Lam continued, dancing away, "this young man is a fellow Georgian from Atlanta, and his name is Noah Ballard. He's from the railroad Ballards." The older men bowed and the girls curtsied and spoke the proper introductory phrases. Then the men glanced knowingly at one another. They both knew of Noah's father, John Ballard, the president of the Atlanta and Western Railroad.

Miranda glanced at her father. His mind was working hard, she could see. And she could see what he was thinking: The boy's from Georgia. His name is Ballard. He's from a good family, and he has a future.

The boy, she saw when she returned her attention to him, did not seem as young looking as she had at first imagined. He had a steady, penetrating expression which was becomingly military, she thought.

Then Lam moved to the other cadet, the tall, especially good-looking one, whom Miranda had noticed earlier. "This other . . ." Lam paused significantly, after which he cleared his throat as conspicuously as he could manage. Finally, he allowed, in a stagy whisper, ". . . man." More laughter, more punches. "No," he went on, "I'm being much too generous. This beast has a name. *It* was called Sam Houston Hawken by the poor wanderer who found this thing as a young child, living with a pack of coyotes on the wild Texas plains."

More bows, curtsies, and nice phrases followed.

His hair is long and shaggy; he does look a little wild, Miranda thought to herself as she made her curtsy. I like that.

"Lam is actually right about one thing," Hawken said after the preliminaries were complete, "I'm truly from Texas."

"A Texan, imagine," Ariel said, as though Texas were as exotic as Kashmir.

"As your name demonstrates," Ashbel said.

"Yes, it does," the young Texan said with a shy smile.

"I sense a tale in that," Ashbel said.

Hawken kept smiling modestly without replying. For an instant his eye caught Miranda's, and the smile grew wider.

"And *you*, you little enchantress," Lam said, approaching Miranda. "You've had a misfortune. You must tell me all about it."

"Well I . . ." she said.

But her father interrupted. "You'll hear all about it, I'm sure, soon enough. But first we have luggage." He pointed to a pile of baggage that had been deposited on the dock. "That," he announced, "is what two young ladies require in order to survive for five days in the wilds of the Hudson Valley. What I myself need I carry in a small valise."

"Father!" the two girls protested. "Really!"

"That's not fair," Ariel said. "Father took us shopping in New York City."

"And after that shopping expedition," Ashbel broke in quickly, "there'll be nothing left for the natives to wear for months."

"Uncle!"

"The luggage! The luggage!" Pierce Kemble said. "We must take care of the luggage." He paused and his face grew darker. "And your mother," he asked Lam, "has she arrived?"

"Yesterday, Father," Lam answered.

"Well, then," Pierce said, "we must face what we must face."

"The luggage," Ashbel said, pointing—and of course diverting attention from the discomforting nearness of Fanny Shaw.

"Servants, follow me," Lam said to Noah and Sam. "Make yourselves useful. You owe me more than you can ever repay after I've allowed you this sight of spectacular female pulchritude."

"You do have most especially delightful sisters, Lam Kemble," Sam Houston Hawken said with a twinkle in his eye and a smile.

A darling smile, Miranda thought, hoping that the wild-looking and handsome Texan was being sincere and not just polite.

In a moment the men were off to attend to the baggage. Soon after that, the little party was embarked in vehicles that climbed the steep and winding road that led from the landing to the plain high above the river. Flanking the plain were the various buildings of the Academy, including the hotel where they were headed.

\*     \*     \*

A number of portraits of the young actress Fanny Shaw had been painted before she made her unhappy match with Pierce Kemble. Two of the most notable dated from the time she was close to her daughter Ariel's eighteen years. The portraits, by Thomas Appleton and Sir Thomas Lawrence, revealed a radiant, breathtaking beauty, unusually slim of waist yet opulently bosomed and delightfully wide of hip. The Fanny of the Lawrence was a young lady of the city, dressed in a daringly low-cut gown. Here was a sophisticated, highly cultured girl, tall necked, proud, with an exquisite oval face and large, dark, magnetic eyes. In the Appleton, she had become a country girl with a frank, open, and sweetly rustic look. She was wearing a loose and gauzy, though equally low-cut, white cotton blouse. In the first her appearance was more controlled, more determined, more finely detailed. She was clearly confident and utterly at her ease. In the second she was less restrained, less conventional, and yet no less commanding. In both, the observer was attracted irresistibly to her dark, glowing eyes with their promise of mysteries and fulfillment. She was at once splendidly lovely and soft, captivatingly feminine and magnificent, unyielding and dominant.

Miranda and Ariel were both clearly daughters of that swan, but Miranda, at fifteen, was still gawky and angular and unsure of herself. Ariel, though, was a near mirror image of her mother at the same age.

As the carriages moved up the long road from the South Dock, Fanny Shaw sat on a wicker love seat on the veranda of the West Point Hotel, surrounded by admirers. Standing somewhat apart from these was a tall, haggard, nervous man who was at that time the Secretary of War, Jefferson Davis. Her fame as an actress and beauty had been diminished neither by age—she was now in her midforties—nor by divorce. She was no less captivating, magnificent, and exciting than the slender girl of the portraits. But over the years, she'd filled out, matured, grown statuesque, grown (it must be admitted) stouter than she'd been back when Pierce Kemble had recklessly pursued her from city to city, throwing roses at her, pouring seemingly endless champagne, and making a total fool of himself to show his love of her.

Fanny and her father, Charles Shaw of the distinguished British theatrical family, had been on a tour of the United States. And Pierce was in the front row at every performance, just as he was waiting by her dressing room after every performance was finished. And she fell in love with him.

On the face of it, her marriage to him made sense. Pierce was good-looking and wealthy, and he came from a family of planters that owned hundreds of acres of rice land in the islands below Savannah and thousands of acres of cotton land north of Atlanta. All this he inherited, while his younger brother, Ashbel, received enough of a capital stake to give him a start as a merchant trader.

Yet, though his wealth and property was in Georgia, Pierce Kemble lived in Philadelphia, where he was born and grew up. So the reality of his ownership of hundreds of slaves had not impressed itself upon Fanny until she had actually visited the Kemble plantations after her marriage.

Their union collapsed after Fanny had borne Pierce three children.

There were many reasons for the break: his irresponsibility, his indolence, his infidelities, his great and mounting debts, for he gambled at both the card tables and the stock exchanges. His unpredictable and uncontrollable temper was loathsome to Fanny, as was his ownership of slaves. But the greatest source of discord between them was her refusal to do as she was told.

She could not submit her will to his, as wives were expected to do. She could no more be subservient to him than she could approve of a slave's subservience to his master. It was her belief that a wife was not a chattel, and that marriage was a joint arrangement between two equals whose relations with one another would be on equal terms and governed by mutual consent.

Her views were not shared by her fellow southern ladies and gentleman.

And, in fact, these convictions did her no good either

with the public, who followed her divorce proceedings with enormous and eager appetite, or with the judge. For Fanny was branded a radical, and worse a "manly woman."

In truth, Fanny was sometimes her own worst enemy, for she allowed herself to be seen in public all too often in "manly" garb, doing "manly" things. She would, for instance, ride horses alone in manly dress, and she would ride into lonely places where good women did not ride. She had even been known to put on breeches and go fishing.

When the divorce came to trial, most of the sympathies of the public—who were kept fully informed of the case by the press—understandably went with Pierce. The judge sided with him, too, declaring that he was the wronged party: Fanny had deserted him.

Thus most of the disgrace of the divorce landed on Fanny, and as was customary, Pierce was granted custody of the children.

Fanny was not left empty-handed or childless, however. She was to be given a yearly income of $1,200 by Pierce, and she was to have the children each year for two months during the summer. In addition, she had significant income from her acting and her stage readings as well as from her published writings.

In fact, she made more money than Pierce did. Which was just as well, for he was only good for the $1,200 for three of the years following their divorce.

After the commencement, Ariel and Miranda were to return with their mother to Lenox, Massachusetts, where she maintained her permanent home. The two girls would spend the summer there.

When the carriages from the dock started to pull up at the hotel, Fanny rose and, excusing herself from her companions, walked to the edge of the porch so that she could get a better view of those alighting. She missed her girls; she was eager to devote her full attention and energy to them.

And then there they were!

"Miranda! Ariel!" she cried out, her face brightening,

her eyes shining as she raced down the short flight of steps to the drive.

In a moment Lam was helping his sisters down from the open carriage they'd been riding in, and Fanny was embracing her daughters with all the fervor ten months' absence from them could inspire in her.

Miranda, unable to help herself, recoiled in pain when her mother's breast crushed against her own, and a thin film of sweat covered her brow.

Fanny, misunderstanding, instantly feared that Miranda was recoiling from her. Fanny's fear mobilized her to crush her daughter even more tightly.

"Oh, my darling," she cried between kisses and through the tears that had begun to flow freely. Miranda, stoically, made no sound. "Oh, my dearest one, it has been so long, so very long . . . *too* long since I've held you like this."

"Mother," Lam was saying, but Fanny ignored him.

"What is the matter with you, my darling?" Fanny said with increasing passion and anxiety. "Why are you so pale?"

"Mother!" Lam repeated more loudly, and tried to split Fanny and Miranda apart.

"Don't do that, Lamar," Fanny ordered, but at least she was giving him her attention. "Can't you see that I'm . . ."

"Mother," Lamar said before she could finish her sentence, "Miranda is in pain. You mustn't hold her so."

"In . . . what?" Fanny said, withdrawing from her daughter with visible reluctance.

"In pain, Mother. She was burned on the train. A flaming cinder lit on her."

"Oh!" Fanny cried, then sobbed and choked and fell silent.

"I'm sorry, Mother," Miranda said, wishing to comfort her mother in her anguish. "I . . ."

"Oh, no, my dearest," Fanny said. "You have nothing at all to be sorry about." Fanny's hands were clenched tightly together at the level of her bosom. It was her way of restraining herself from touching Miranda, which was what she longed to do more than anything else in the world. "But where?" she asked. "Where is the injury? You must tell me all about it. And then I must minister to you. I will be your angel of mercy."

Miranda lifted the edge of the shawl she was wearing so that her mother could catch a glimpse of the area of the burn. She did this carefully, so that the exposed flesh would be visible only to her mother.

"Oh!" Fanny said, leaning closer to have a better look. "Oh, my poor, poor darling. Is the pain severe?"

"Not any longer," Miranda said, forcing a brave smile.

"It must still ache, though, doesn't it?"

"Yes, it aches."

"Then we must take you into the hotel and do something about it."

"I'll be fine, Mother. I'm sure of it."

During the commotion over Miranda, Fanny had momentarily lost sight of the approach of Pierce Kemble, who had not ridden on the carriage with Fanny's children but had taken a wagon with his brother, Ashbel, Lam's two cadet friends, and the sisters' baggage.

While she had been at West Point, Fanny had been as apprehensive about the arrival of her former husband as she'd been eager to see her daughters, but—happily for her—the immediate presence of the girls had allowed her to ignore his approach.

But now Pierce was walking toward her with Ashbel on his heel. The two Kemble brothers were followed by the two cadets, Noah and Sam.

Sam, she noted before she placed the full, withering force of her attention on Pierce, had his eyes exclusively on Miranda. That did not displease Fanny. Though Miranda was only fifteen and too young to be courted by young men, it never hurt to line up likely prospects. Sam was a nice-looking boy—though a bit shaggy and disheveled, especially for one about to graduate from the United States Military Academy.

As it happened, she didn't notice that the other cadet, Noah Ballard, was as intent upon Ariel as Sam was on Miranda.

When Fanny turned her gaze back toward Pierce, she saw that he had held back. That trace of cowardice in Pierce caused Fanny to stand that much taller and to brace her legs, as though she were going to launch a physical onslaught against the man whom she'd once loved.

It was quite clear to all present that Fanny Shaw was enormously energized now, for the mighty engines of her emotions had already been worked up to full throttle by the force of the compassion she'd just expended on her daughter. It was only a short step for the era's greatest lady of the stage to turn from compassion to hostility.

But first she had to greet Ashbel, whom she liked, and who liked her.

"Hello, Ash Kemble," she said with a wide smile, extending her hand for him, "and how is my children's favorite uncle?"

"Hello, Fanny. I'm doing passably well. And you?" He took her hand and squeezed it with genuine warmth.

"Profoundly chagrined," Fanny said, "if the truth can be told, to learn of the accident my darling girl has suffered." On the "chagrined," Fanny's eyes began a slide away from Ashbel that ended upon Ashbel's brother, who was now dawdling as near the edge of the little group as he could manage.

"Ahh . . ." she said after a deeply dramatic—and deeply satisfying—pause to take Pierce in with her ravaging eyes. "So there you are." She laughed a chill laugh. "The seller of souls." Her voice had dropped to a whisper now, a whisper that could be heard easily by anyone on the hotel veranda who cared to listen. Which is to say all who were there. No one at West Point on this lovely June afternoon was unaware of the imminent collision between these two one-time lovers. And not a few had contrived to be on hand for the spectacle of their first encounter.

"The seller," she repeated, a little louder, "of souls. The *ven*-dor of men's and women's and children's"—she looked toward her audience, her face a mask of horror and revulsion— "bo-o-o-dies." It came out a long, agonized gasp. "How splendid you are, Pierce Kemble!"

"Don't you think we might avoid parading our differences before this crowd," Pierce said with a jaunty, cavalier tone that was far from his true attitude. Fanny frightened him when she was like this, but it would never do for him, a man, to betray his fear. "These people have no interest in our disagreements," he continued. "Nor do I have any interest in reigniting the hostility that you find so easy to bring to combustion."

"I was not speaking of the mere trivial differences between a man and a woman," Fanny announced. "I was speaking of the brands, the moral stigmata, the chains of guilt and shame that you have placed upon your own corrupted soul."

"Really, Fanny," he went on lightly, still trying to avoid being drawn into her dramatic web. "Could you, for once, come down from your marble horse. Your self-righteousness does not become you, my dear. Can't you instead think of the children and of the import of the moment? Can't you remember that we're here for the sake of a joyful time? For the commencement exercises, for God's sake, of our son?"

He had a point, she knew, and besides, she didn't want to make a fool of herself. On the other hand, she refused even to appear to be persuaded by anything Pierce Kemble said to her. And besides, she had one more point to make, in case the audience on the veranda happened to have missed the true force of her words.

So Fanny started her next speech slowly, gently, as though she had banked the fire in her soul. "I've been reading in the newspapers, Pierce," she said, "that you have come into considerable money during the past week or so. Is that true?"

"Very true," he said with a pleased smile. He was proud of his recent good fortune.

"I read that it was in the neighborhood of three hundred fifty thousand dollars that you have obtained."

"That's right."

"Would you like to tell the people here how you obtained it? Or, shall I say, can you hold your head up and without shame admit where your three hundred and fifty thousands came from?''

"That's easy enough, Fanny," he said, still lightly. "It came from the sale of some property that I no longer had a use for."

She closed her eyes for the space of a few breaths. Then, opening them, she glanced first at Pierce, then at the audience on the veranda which had been growing during the exchange. Then she spoke: "That money, that soiled wealth, came from the sale of human beings at one of the largest slave auctions ever held in the state of Georgia. That's where it came from."

He shrugged. "Property," he said.

"More than four hundred men, women, children, and even infants auctioned at the Ten Broeck Racecourse. I can't think of an act more shameful and more evil, Pierce Kemble."

Then she, having made her most important point, slipped a glance at Ashbel, who was standing in the background, studiously avoiding involvement in Fanny and Pierce's current conflict. Taking his cue, Ash moved up.

The audience on the veranda, he noted in passing, seemed more sympathetic to his brother than to Fanny. The gentlemen of the military tended to be conservative, and many of them, of course, were from the South. As for Ash himself, the question of slavery was a matter of relative indifference. He owned no slaves, since slaves were in no way useful or practical to him. And he believed that in time slavery would die out, for slaves would cease to be either useful or practical to the planters of the South. But on the other hand, he thought of himself as a realist. Some men would always dominate and control other men. This would happen no matter what name was given to the practice. It was true on his ships. It was true in an army. It was true in the fields.

"Let's end this discussion now, shall we?" Ashbel said brightly, leading Fanny away by the hand. "Ariel, Miranda, come. We must see about rooms. Pierce, Lam, would you be so kind as to see about the baggage?" And remembering Miranda's burn, he turned to her. "How is your wound, my dear?"

"I can scarcely feel it any longer, Uncle."

"Lovely," he said. He was glad to see that Pierce had taken the hint and was making himself scarce.

"She must rest now," Fanny said, her interest in her daughter's welfare rekindled. "I must tend to her."

"I'm fine. Really I am," Miranda said. "I'll just clean up and change. You needn't bother yourself over me, Mother."

"No, no, no. I won't hear of anything like that." She lifted her hands for all to see. They were somewhat large and were her one unattractive feature. "These are healers' hands. I have the healing touch."

"Actually," Ashbel said, "the girl may be onto the right cure for what ails her, though she hasn't actually articulated it."

"What do you mean?" Fanny said. Her hands were still raised, opened and with palms out. She liked the effect she made with them. "This girl needs rest and quiet and a mother's care. There's dinner and a ball tonight, and endless ceremonies tomorrow."

Ashbel continued, "If I may be permitted to disagree with a woman so beautiful and forceful as the great Fanny Shaw, I'd like to suggest an activity for Miranda and the other children rather different from what you have in mind."

"I can't imagine what," Fanny said, though she was willing to listen to his proposal. She was not immune to his flattery.

"There are about four hours before nightfall and dinner. During that time, I'd like to see the three cadets and the two young ladies off doing something pleasant together—if young men and young ladies still find pleasant things to do with one another in these benighted times. There must anyhow be cool, dark paths to walk along in the primitive forests that surround this place. Or shady clearings to sit and converse in." He laughed. "I wouldn't find it hard to be persuaded to sit with a lovely young lady on some soft and grassy knoll." He turned to Miranda. "Well?" he asked her.

"I'd love that," she said, beaming.

"You see?" Ashbel said.

"But your *burn*?" Fanny said to her daughter.

"I can scarcely feel it."

"But will the boys be free for the rest of the afternoon?" Fanny said, unwilling to give in completely. "They must have to prepare for tomorrow."

"I'm sure they will find a way to be free, Fanny. They are resourceful young men." Then to Ariel: "You'd like that, wouldn't you, dear?"

"I'd like to spend time with the cadets very much," she said.

"It's a good thing to be free, isn't it?" he said with an exaggeratedly straight face and laughing eyes. "You must be delighted, now that you are here at West Point, that you haven't been spoken for already."

"But she is engaged to Ben Edge," Fanny said.

"Mother," Ariel said, "I...um...I've..." As she stammered, she shot a glance back over her shoulder to make sure that Sam and Noah were still out of earshot.

"Ariel has chosen," Ashbel broke in, taking her off the hook, "to keep that knowledge a secret during her stay at the Academy."

"Oh, she has, has she?" Fanny said, laughing. She threw her head back and laughed some more. "Well, I won't be the one to tell on her—on you," she said with a sharp but amused look at her older daughter. "Does Lamar know of this...prevarication?"

"Yes, Mother. I took him aside and talked to him earlier."

"Well, then," Fanny said, rubbing her hands together in a washing motion, "off with both of you. Clean yourselves up and change into something appropriate for a walk in the woods."

"Oh, thank you, Mother," the girls said as one. And both of them rushed up and kissed her on the cheek.

"You'll tell the boys?" Fanny said to Ashbel.

"I'll pass them the word about their good luck," he said. "I only wish I could go with them."

"So do I," Fanny said with a grin.

"Well then, *Miss* Frances Shaw, let us not let the children exhaust the available pleasure. You and I will also go for a stroll in the woods.''

"Oh, no, Ash," she said with a laugh and a shake of her head, "I couldn't possibly. I have much too much to do to get ready."

"Put it off, Fanny. Come with me."

"I can't. I really mustn't," she said, and mounted the steps of the hotel porch. At the top of the steps, she turned back to him. "You know, Ash, I think I married the wrong Kemble."

"I knew that twenty years go, Miss Frances Shaw."


Ashbel Kemble's scheme for the afternoon outing was the splendid success that he wished it to be, which is not to say that all went smoothly for the cadets and the Kemble sisters. Even so, the rough moments did not detract from the pleasures of the occasion. If anything, they added to the excitement and gave it seasoning. By the time the outing was over, Miranda and Ariel knew they'd spent a perfectly glorious time with their brother and his two friends. And for reasons that they did not immediately recognize, both girls would remember this afternoon for the rest of their lives.

It was Sam Hawken and Noah Ballard, of course, who most occupied the two girls. For they were both vivid, fascinating, and handsome—and wonderfully unlike the other young men Ariel and Miranda had yet encountered.

There were vast worlds of difference between the two cadets and the witty and amusing yet so wilting boys the girls were condemned to dance with in Philadelphia at the cotillions sanctioned by Miss Lancaster's Atheneum, which was the boarding school the sisters attended in that city. The boys of Philadelphia were full of charm and airy words, but not one of them had ever felt the slightest temptation to taste a meaty thought.

Miranda liked to laugh, but she liked to think, too.

She was pleased that Noah and Sam were not strangers to charm, but she was just as pleased that they were also smart. Their minds had strength and intensity and were without the gloom or moroseness usually associated with high seriousness. While Miranda never once heard silly, airy words from them, still, everyone in the little party laughed a lot and talked a lot. Noah and Lam, especially, had opinions upon every subject imaginable. Since the rites they would go through on the morrow would never happen to them again, a measure of conceit and cockiness, and even pompousness, could be easily forgiven.

Sam, more private and reserved than the other two, kept his thoughts shrouded. He wasn't diffident or shy, however, only watchful. Yet for all his silent, enigmatic dignity, he was equally full of himself for the same understandable reasons. Tomorrow they would become men.

Miranda was much intrigued by this quiet mystery of Sam's. The less forthcoming he was, the more she wanted to find out all about him.

But it wasn't just as separate individuals that the three cadets fascinated the sisters; it was also together, as a team. Powerful bonds of comradeship joined Sam, Noah, and Lamar. And Miranda, who was perceptive about such things, was deeply impressed that the three boys were so sensitive to each other, so alert to each other's moods and changes of internal weather.

Yet, oh, how good-looking they were in their uniforms! Black shoes, white duck trousers, short gray jackets with high stiff collar and three rows of brass buttons down the front! The buttons looked like brass cherries, Miranda thought, a resemblance she didn't fail to make light of when the chance presented itself.

After the party set out from the hotel, the boys escorted the sisters on a tour of the Academy gounds and buildings. And these, despite their sad gray stone and gloomy crenellation, seemed graceful and faerielike in the dazzling midafternoon light. Then the boys led the sisters on a slow stroll up the two-and-a-half-mile path to the Crows Nest, which was a scenic picnic spot favored by the cadets.

When they arrived, the place delighted the girls. It had a view like nowhere in Georgia, and Lam suggested that they rest there until it was time to return to prepare for supper.

When no one objected, the little party arranged itself, chatting and laughing all the while, about a soft and shady but sun-dappled spot.

Though Ariel and Miranda were both flushed after the exertion of their climb, the effort only enhanced the glow of their pleasure and high spirits. Miranda was having such a glorious time that it was only in the act of stretching herself out on the carpet of grass that she grew conscious of her recent wound. She hadn't once thought of the burn or of her pain since she had left the hotel.

But she was quickly able to put the pain out of her mind again, because now, for the first time, she had a chance to really observe the cadet who had most caught her fancy.

Sam Hawken was taller than the other two, but he was no giant. Hawken, Miranda guessed, was close to an even six feet, for he was just over half a head taller than Lam, who she knew was five feet seven. Noah, like her brother, was also of medium height, a couple of inches taller than Lam.

And yet, though her brother was the shortest and slightest of the three, he was the only one with flawless military bearing. Lam sat there on the grass, calm, confident, straight-backed and impeccably tailored.

Sam's appearance was not nearly so perfect—not that he was sloppy. Miranda knew it was hard for careless men to graduate from West Point. But Sam was not so carefully composed as Lam, nor so scrupulously groomed. Sam's thick thatch of sandy-red hair seemed to have been combed no more recently than the previous week. And as soon as he was out of sight of watchful officers, he had unfastened his collar and the top buttons of his jacket.

Noah, as in much else, seemed to find a median between Lam and Sam. Where Lam was stiff, Noah was easy and casual. But he was not as loose and free as Sam was, not by a long shot.

Yet it wasn't his appearance that chiefly set the young Texan apart from the other two; it was his manner. He didn't say much, and he was powerfully self-possessed, but he wasn't calm or cool. Far from it. Rather, he was restless, intense, charged with energy. Even sprawled on his side with his head propped up on his hand, it was easy for Miranda to imagine this young man leaping into combat at the first note of the bugle. This was no parade soldier; this was a warrior. Or at least so her imagination wanted to picture him.

And he had delightful eyes that were a lovely shade of hazel. The eyes were calm, still, but they didn't miss a thing, and they were focused on Miranda often. The look he gave her was frank and penetrating. Yet never during his glances did Miranda feel discomfort or shame. Nor did she bashfully avert her face when he looked at her, as most fifteen-year-olds of her class would have done. She looked right back at him.

In this she was her mother's daughter, curious, open, and direct. Ariel, however, took after her father in much of her style and most of her attitudes. She was not nearly so bold as her sister.

The conversation on the walk up to the Crows Nest had been witty and amusing. But as the sky grew dimmer and more golden and the shadows lengthened, the conversation turned serious, even grave. The pressure of tomorrow's events superseded the cadets' mirth. Of course, they each had new assignments to accept, and they were each exhilarated and hopeful about their new duties.

But they could not help but feel uneasy about the world they were entering. The times were difficult and perilous. The peace and order that they were swearing to preserve and protect were dangerously threatened, and not by an external enemy. The threat came with within. The states of the Union were growing ever more out of balance—so out of balance that the nation might become disunited and split in two. And if that happened, the two halves would almost certainly battle for dominance.

And then where would the soldiers and officers at West Point be?

They'd have to choose sides, and that would mean they'd have to fight men whom they'd come to love and revere. And there were darker possibilities. What if the three friends split just as the country threatened to do? Could one of them actually choose the side the other two opposed?

The long and heavy fears about the future made the three cadets anxious and apprehensive. But the prospect of imminent leave-taking filled them with more immediately pressing feelings of sadness and loss. They were about to separate from each other, which was bad enough, for many cadets, West Point was the closest family they had ever known. Leaving it was harder than leaving their mothers and fathers.

These moments on the Crows Nest on the afternoon before graduation—with the two delightful girls as attentive and pleasant listeners—might be for Lam, Noah, and Sam the last chance to speak intimately with their closest friends for God only knew how many years.

They talked first about graduation and about the sadness of the leave-taking. But they didn't dwell long on that subject. None of them had experience or age enough to find words adequate to the depth of feeling it raised. Conversation swiftly flowed toward the hopes and dreams each of them had for their new assignments.

Miranda and Ariel already knew that Lam had been ordered to report to Fort Leavenworth, where he would serve with the First Cavalry. Sam and Noah each described for the sisters his own coming assignment.

Sam, like Lam, would see his fill of horses. He was going off to San Antonio and the Second Cavalry.

Sam's assignment, Noah told the girls, was more than a nice piece of good fortune that would put him close to his home. It was a great opportunity, for Sam was being sent to the Second Cavalry at the request of its commander, Colonel Robert E. Lee, and Lee was known to be a man who was going places. He was also known as a man who took good care of his friends. Lee had been superintendent for the first three years Sam and his friends had been at West Point. During that time, Lee had grown fond of the Texan, for Sam had qualities Lee appreciated in an officer.

The First and Second Cavalry, Lam went on to explain, were both newly formed, elite units, and it was quite an honor to be assigned to one or the other of them. They'd been created at the instigation of Mr. Jefferson Davis, the Secretary of War. Davis, himself a West Point graduate, had distinguished himself for bravery in the War with Mexico. He was also, as it happened, delivering the commencement address the next day.

The job of the Second Cavalry was to protect the settlers of the Texas frontiers from the raids of the Comanches and other hostile Indians. And the original intention had been that the First Cavalry would perform similarly in Kansas, but other kinds of violence had outrun plans in that·tragic territory. Over the past months, Kansas had become a battleground between Free-Soil settlers and proslavers. It looked likely that the First Cavalry would have to do what it could to keep the peace. And this was going to be no easy matter, for the army was at least as sharply divided over the issue as other Americans—though the division would presumably still not prevent the soldiers from taking the orders of their officers. Meanwhile, Kansas was turning into a lake of blood.

And that was exciting Lam. He wasn't pleased about the bloodshed, but he was pleased that he might have a chance to display his own soldierly virtues while restoring the peace and preserving order.

Noah Ballard had been assigned to the Corps of Engineers, and was being sent to Charleston, where he'd be one of a team working on improving the fortifications at Fort Sumter.

"He's a damned fine engineer," Lam said to his sisters in praise of his friend. "So fine that I'd be willing to wager he never sees battle. He'll be so busy building things, he'll never have the time or inclination to burn them down."

Noah laughed at that. And then he added, "I very much hope so—not that I would shrink from a battle," he quickly added apologetically.

"Of course not," Lam said.

"But Lam's right," Noah said to the sisters. "I'm more engineer than army officer."

Ariel stared at him for a long moment. Her brow was

deeply furrowed, and her hand was on her cheek, tugging at a long ringlet of hair that hung there.

"Do you really mean that?" she asked with a vague, perplexed smile. "You would seriously prefer being an engineer to being a commander of men?" she went on, her voice growing darker and her fingers pulling more nervously on the lock. Ariel's face was innocent and open, but Miranda knew her sister. She knew what lay behind Ariel's expression. Ariel was disturbed by what she was learning about Noah Ballard. Miranda waited to find out what exactly was bothering her sister. The explanation was not long in coming.

"I will command railroads," Noah answered briskly.

"Really?" Ariel asked with a curl of distaste on her lips.

That's it, Miranda suddenly understood. She *likes* him—or at least she's attracted to him and wants to like him. Yet she doesn't approve of men who build things, especially who build railroads—which, after all, are dirty, smelly, and uncomfortable.

Miranda knew that in this opinion, as in most of her opinions, Ariel echoed her father. Pierce Kemble was convinced that things mechanical and practical, and the men who dealt with them, were beneath the attention of any man of taste and judgment. It was the business of gentlemen to fight and ride, to drink and hunt, to appreciate fine wine, fine horses, fine women, and fine surroundings—and to rule. All the more utilitarian and functional matters were to be left to those who were less than gentlemen.

Lam was already fast turning into the perfectly finished embodiment of the man his father expected him to be. Lam was handsome, arrogant, dashing—half bold cavalier and half sensitive poet. Ariel was quite evidently disturbed that Noah might aim his life in other, less respectable directions.

"Really?" Ariel repeated still again after Noah did not favor her with an instant response. Miranda could see her sister's eyes flash.

"Yes, really," Noah said at last, carefully. "I'm proud of what I choose to be," he continued, his voice sharp, his eyes angry.

And *he* likes *her,* too, Miranda thought, glad to see him fight back and show his mettle.

"Well, I'll say," Ariel drawled haughtily, "I'm sure that if such things please you, then far be it from me to try to stop you. But," she tossed her head, "you clearly do not intend to be a gentleman. No gentleman occupies himself the way you intend to occupy yourself. Why, engineers are no better than shopkeepers."

"Then I am proud not to be a gentleman," he said with forced calmness.

"Ariel," Miranda warned in a quiet voice, "don't make a fool of yourself."

"I'm not making a fool of myself," Ariel said with a shrug. "I'm simply making the very same observation that father makes. 'There are men of character,' he says, 'and there are men of utility. Men of character are called gentlemen. Men of utility are called servants.' "

"And you believe that?" Sam Hawken asked quietly. His voice was as soft as Miranda's had been.

"Yes," Ariel said. "I do. I certainly do."

"We'll have to get you out west," he said to her.

"What do you mean by that?" Ariel said.

"I don't have time to explain now," he replied in a voice that was again soft. "But someday I promise I will."

"He means you're spoiled," Miranda said with a smirk.

"That's not true!" she cried.

"Of course it's not true," Noah said. Ariel gave him a piercing look. "You're not spoiled, Miss Kemble. You just don't know what the hell you're talking about."

At that, Ariel's face fell. Lam laughed when he saw her crushed expression, and Sam smiled, too.

"You don't need to insult me," Ariel said.

"I didn't insult you. I told you you were misinformed, which is hardly a shameful thing."

Miranda was liking Noah more than she'd imagined she would. When she first met him, he seemed soft, unformed, and boyish, while Sam was lean, tough, and leathery. But she was seeing an attractive toughness now in Noah, too. And a fervor that approached zeal.

"I don't take it as a kindness when you tell me I'm dumb and ignorant," Ariel pouted.

"You are neither dumb nor ignorant, Miss Kemble. Anything but. You're as breathtakingly lovely a creature as I've met, and your head is by no means hollow, either. But you've got attitudes that are misguided."

"I don't think . . ." she started to say, but he held up his hand to stop her.

"There's no blame in you for what was never taught you. When somebody gets older and makes no effort to learn, then there's some blame in that. It's older people who've been telling you the things that you've got wrong."

"Everything I've told you I've learned from Father," she said, bristling.

"I know that," Noah said. "And I like your father, and I respect him. But he's wrong, and he's taught you wrong."

Miranda glanced at her brother, for she was afraid that he'd take umbrage at Noah's negative words about their father. And since she wanted to hear what Noah had to say, she didn't want Lam to interrupt. But Lam simply sat there, stiff as ever, taking in all that was happening.

"First," Noah said, "you're wrong about gentlemen."

"All right," Ariel said, managing to produce a sullen pout.

"A gentleman," Noah said, choosing his words carefully, "is a man who puts a mark on the world. A visible, palpable mark that anyone can see or know about. And then when he leaves the world, he leaves it better than when he found it.

"Before the coming of machines, you put a mark on the world by mastery of the land, by mastery over the people that worked the land, and by mastery over the men that fought the battles.

"But there's a new mastery. It's the mastery of the machines and of the industries that the machines make possible."

Ariel was shaking her head. "No. You're wrong," she said.

"How so?"

"If you're right, then a factory owner is as good as a landowner."

"That's exactly what I'm saying."

"No," she said, shaking her head more vigorously. "No factory owner can be a man of character. It's just not possible. Factories are all clockwork. Factory owners spend all their time wringing their hands over schedules and output. They have no time for graciousness and hospitality and . . ."

"Isn't she eloquent?" Lam interrupted. "Pay attention to her, Noah. She's not just beautiful."

"But she's still wrong," Noah said. And he continued, "Don't farmers worry just as much about schedules and outputs? Of course they do," he answered his own question. "In fact, in the future farms will turn more and more into factories. And the gentleman farmer will lose his position to the farm engineer."

"No!" Ariel cried softly. "Never!"

"I'm telling you what's happening," Noah said, aware that he was winning the debate. "Not what people in the South want to happen. They want time to stand still. But it won't."

"Why do you hate the South?"

"I don't. I love it as much as you do. But the South must change."

"And become like Massachusetts and its thousands of machines all click, click, clicking, and its tens of thousands of men and women all click, click, clicking in time with the machines?" She caught Noah's eye. "Slaves live better than that."

"I agree," he said. "Most factory workers are slaves by another name. But," he insisted, his eyes holding hers, "the masters of the factories and the railroads will win the future."

"No," she said, tearing her eyes away.

"And that's where your father, and everyone like him, has blinded himself."

"No," she said again, but with much less force.

"But that's what I aim to change."

"You?" Ariel asked.

"If anyone can do it, Noah can," Sam said quietly.

"How can you change the South?" Miranda said brightly, with a sparkle in her eyes. "I thought we were perfect the way we are."

"Don't you be sarcastic," Ariel said.

"I was just asking," Miranda said sweetly, "out of pure curiosity."

"I'll give you an example," Noah said. "Take Atlanta, my home."

"I love Atlanta," Miranda said. "The Kembles have land near there."

"If you love it the way it is, then you'll love it more the way it can be—the way it *will* be."

"You'd make it a dirty, smelly factory town," Ariel said. "That's what you'd do if you have your way. No thanks. I don't want any of that."

"Four railroads meet in Atlanta. And more will come there in time. Atlanta will become a great city—when we so choose. It will be the Chicago of the South. And there are factories there already: rolling mills, machine shops, arsenals. But it's railroads that have made Altanta. The town didn't even exist before railroads, and now there must be fifty thousand people living there."

"That's plenty of people," Ariel said. "More than enough for me."

"Atlanta even got its name from a railroad man," he continued, ignoring her in his fervor. "Did you know that? A man named Edgar Thomson christened her back when he was chief engineer at one of the Georgia railroads. Now he's president of the Pennsylvania, the richest railroad in the country."

"I don't want Atlanta to turn into Chicago. I want it to stay Atlanta," Ariel said. "I don't want any more machines. There are enough machines already."

Noah shook his head in exasperation. Then he looked at Lam and Sam. "I'm not just saying this because it would be nice for the South to have factories and railroads. I'm saying it because the South won't survive without them."

"In a war?" Sam asked, uttering what the others would rather have left unspoken.

"Yes, in a war," Noah said. "I think it will come to that."

"Then the South will lose," Sam said, almost casually.

Ariel's mouth opened, but then she closed it. Miranda glanced at Noah and then at Lam. There were chill expressions on their faces—expressions that pointed out to Miranda a problem in what she had at first thought was a perfect friendship.

If Sam had shouted, "There is no God!" at a revival meeting, he would have got the same look that Lam and Noah were giving him.

Lam laughed nervously. "That's the first time you've ever said anything like that."

"I didn't mean to suggest that the South might lose," Noah said to Ariel, disassociating himself from Sam. "Only that we will have a tougher time than a lot of folks think."

"I thought Texans were all wild men who love to fight," Ariel said to Sam.

"I'd gladly fight for you," Sam said. Then he looked at Miranda. "And your sister."

"I thank you," Ariel said coolly. "But that's not what I meant."

"If you meant to ask if I'm looking forward to a war, no, I'm not. The *gentlemen* of the South are spoiling for a fight, but I'm not."

Miranda looked at him with even greater interest.

"What *do* you mean?" Ariel asked, which was a question Miranda very much wanted answered, too. But they were both to be disappointed.

"I won't add to what I've said."

Lam, meanwhile, quickly moved to cover over the chill Sam had produced.

"Don't mind Sam," he said to Ariel and Miranda. "He doesn't count. He doesn't love the South."

"Then how can you and he be friends?" Miranda asked.

"Because he doesn't hate it," Lam laughed. "And besides, the South won't lose. We've got the bravest and wisest men. In a contest between machines and brains, the brains will win every time.''

Sam shook his head and smiled. His silence only made him more fascinating to Miranda.

"You were about to say?" Miranda asked him.

"No," he said. "I've truly said more than I want to say. And besides," he added as he started to rise, "it's time to get back down the hill. We've got a dinner to eat and a ball to dance at. And I'd be most pleased to have a few dances with you, Miranda. And you also, Ariel."

Miranda and Ariel both blushed. "I'd be happy to dance with you as often as you'll have me," Miranda said. "But I'd still like to hear why you think the South will lose," she insisted. She was deeply curious about Sam Hawken, and she was not a girl who easily buried her curiosity beneath maidenly propriety. "I'd really like to know more about you."

"About me?" he laughed.

"That's right."

"I don't think I'll find it difficult to oblige you." He was now standing in front of her, offering her his hand.

The other two cadets had also risen to their feet, and Noah's hand was extended toward Ariel.

"Walk with me on the way down to the hotel," Sam said softly to Miranda, as she raised herself up. "We'll follow the others. Will you do that?"

"Yes, of course I will," she said.

A few moments after that, the five had set off again toward the Academy. It didn't take long for Sam and Miranda to lag several paces behind the others. Sam pointed to Noah and then grinned at Miranda. Ariel's hand was resting comfortably in the crook of Noah's arm. Lam was walking on Ariel's right.

"Noah likes her," Sam said to Miranda, offering her his own arm. She rested her hand on the proffered spot.

"Yes, I know," Miranda said. "And she likes him quite a lot. If she didn't like him, she wouldn't have fought him so hard. She would have tried to please him and make him want her."

"Oh, God," he said. "Girls! Always doing the opposite of what they really want."

She laughed and tilted her head back. "That's not true."

"Isn't it?" He looked down at her, catching her eye, liking the new cock of her head. "Do you always do exactly what you want?"

"Whenever I can."

"How about your sister? Does she, for instance, really want to marry that fellow from Virginia she's engaged to?"

"How do you know about that?"

"Lam told us all about you before you came."

"He told Ariel he hadn't done that," she said.

"He told her that so that she'd think she had the freedom to chase after one or the other of us."

"And you were willing to go along with the game?"

"I'm happy where I am now. And I think Noah is not unhappy, either."

"Not one of you three is a gentleman."

"On the contrary, we have done the perfect gentlemanly thing. We've let ourselves be graciously blind to the pretenses and untruths that a lady has chosen to clothe herself with."

"You sound like Uncle Ashbel," she said.

"From what little I've seen of him, I think that is a compliment."

"It is a compliment."

"Well, then, I thank you."

"But I'm still curious about you."

"In what way?" His eyes were hooded, she noticed.

She was just about to answer him with, "In every way," when Miranda spotted an opening that led away from the trail. It was a narrow path, and for some reason it sparked her curiosity enough to leave her momentarily silent. The path was positively inviting not only because the woods that way looked lovely and dark, but more importantly because Miranda at that moment wanted more than anything else to be alone with Sam Houston Hawken.

She paused and stared down through the trees. "Where does this path lead?" she asked.

"Through the woods and along the heights above the river," he said, stopping alongside her. "Eventually it rejoins this trail."

"It's so inviting," she said. "Will you take me on it?"

He reflected on that. "It's very steep," he said after a moment. "And there are the others to consider. . . ."

"All the better!" she said, smiling.

She could tell he was thinking that they would be alone and unescorted, so her smile grew wider. "I'm just a child," she said innocently. "I'm only fifteen."

"I should be getting back to the hotel. There's dinner and . . ."

But she did not hear him. Or more likely, he thought, she was ignoring him. For by then she was already moving briskly, well along the path. "Come on, Sam," she cried, "or I'll be alone."

"Well, we can't have that, can we?" he muttered. But then he called out, "Lamar? Noah? Can you still hear me?"

"Sam?" a distant voice called.

"We'll be joining you a little later," Sam yelled.

"Where are you going?" Ariel called out. But Miranda was not listening. After a moment, Ariel's voice came again: "You shouldn't go off by yourself like that!" But Miranda still did not bother to hear her. "Don't you be late, Miranda," Ariel called out, finally admitting defeat, but only Sam heard her.

He had to hurry to catch up with her, and by the time he did, she had gone a considerable way.

"Well," he said when he was near enough to her to talk normally, "you handled that maneuver with considerable skill."

"Handled which maneuver?" she asked, looking back over her shoulder; the path was too narrow for both of them to walk abreast.

"Splitting me off from the others."

"Oh, *now*," she protested, but not vigorously.

"But I'd be lying if I told you I was displeased."

She looked at him again, and then she smiled.

"Now you can tell me all about yourself," she said, "and there'll be only me to hear it."

"Does that make a difference?" he said.

"To me it does."

His eyes brightened with mirth, and he broke into a smile. But he did not answer her. And then he laughed.

"What is there to laugh at?" she said.

"At inquisitive little girls."

"I'm not a little girl."

"You just said not five minutes ago that you were a little girl of fifteen," he laughed. "You can't have it both ways."

"Oh, you knew what I meant."

He laughed again.

"Quit teasing me," she said.

"I wouldn't dare treat you with anything but the utmost seriousness and respect," he said with a grin.

"Then why do you refuse to tell me about yourself?"

"Do I look like a man with dark secrets?"

Her face showed that he indeed did, and his smile grew wider because he had guessed right. He was enjoying this sparring with her, and she wasn't liking it at all. She wanted to get through to him—to make him see her as a woman and not as a child.

They had been walking through trees, but now they emerged into the open. Sam's face grew worried.

"Look where you're going," he warned. She had been looking back over her shoulder at him as she walked.

When she made no move to comply, he repeated, "Look where you're going. I mean it."

"Oh, really?" she said, thinking he was still playing with her. But she did turn and look ahead. And when she did, she made a little frightened cry, for she was standing on the brink of a steep grassy decline. It wasn't a cliff; yet it only failed to be a cliff by a few degrees.

She stepped back a little dizzily. But then she felt his hand on her shoulder, steadying her. "Why didn't you tell me it was so close?" she snapped. "I could have gone off the edge." His hand, she was aware, had remained on her shoulder. She shrugged it off and stepped away from him.

"I did tell you," he said reasonably.

"But you almost let me fall off," she persisted.

"There was no danger. I was right next to you."

She moved close to the edge and looked down. At the bottom of the steep grassy slope was a rocky spring. Then she heard him laughing again.

"I hate teases," she said without looking up at him. In fact, she wasn't peeved at him because he was teasing her, but because he was so successfully fending off her efforts to direct the conversation toward himself. She was also growing aware of an aching pain from the burn. The exertion of her brisk walk and the heat and the chafing of her underclothes all contributed to her discomfort. The ache made her both nervous and lightheaded.

He didn't respond directly to her remark about teases. "Am I correct in understanding that you and your sister are very similar?" he asked.

"How?" she asked, giving him a look that said that she thought she and her sister were quite different.

"Do you both fight the people you like?"

"I fight the people that tease me and play silly games with me," she said.

What happened next neither Miranda nor Sam afterward remembered clearly. Miranda was certainly giddy due to the pain of her wound. At any rate, she lost her footing near the edge of the decline and pitched forward, reaching out helplessly toward Sam. He grabbed for her but missed her hand and failed to stop her progress downward. What he did instead was fall with her.

They both spilled head over heels down the precipitous grassy hillside.

"Jesus Christ!" he said at the moment his balance deserted him.

Miranda hit the grass first and rolled over and over. As she turned and as the sky and earth reeled crazily around her, she realized that the hill wasn't as steep as it had looked from the top.

The truth was that she was having fun.

She laughed, then let out a whoop of joy and pleasure.

She bounced and rolled and reeled crazily. There are my feet and legs and pantalets! she thought to herself. They're sticking straight up into the sky! How silly!

Twigs and small leaves brushed her, and moments later she felt her shoulder graze a hard place, but she scarcely felt any of these things. And then she was sliding through soft wet dirt, and she thought of her dress—her fresh and summery daffodil-yellow dress which would now be permanently soiled with indelible grass stains.

She glanced at Sam tumbling down behind her. She was glad that he, too, was in the same fix she was.

And then she was at the bottom, sitting in a shallow pool of muddy spring water. Sam Houston Hawken was on top of her, with his arms and legs tangled in hers.

He groaned, gingerly extracting himself from her. "Spending time with you is more than an adventure. Are you all right?"

At that moment she realized that she could have pulled or broken something. She shook her head to clear it. Then she took quick stock of herself. "I don't think so," she said. Her breast, she quickly realized, had started to sting from her burn, but she ignored that as best she could.

He was free of her by now, but he was not yet standing. Instead he was sitting on the bank of the spring and staring at her—shaking his head, his eyes sad and accusatory. Does he think I did it on purpose? she thought.

"I must look horrible," she said. "Am I a wreck?"

"That pretty well sums it up," he said.

"Well you're not fashionable yourself, Cadet Hawken. Your trousers are torn and there's mud on your face."

"I can well imagine," he said, rising to his feet and taking several deep breaths as he did. "Here, take my hand." He leaned over toward her, holding his hand out. She took it, and, pulling her to her feet, he helped her onto the bank.

"Now that you've caught your breath, tell me again whether you're all right," he said.

She took a few steps, then raised and lowered her arms a

few times. "I'm fine," she said in spite of her painful breast.

"Thank God," he said, then raised his eyes to see how far the two of them had tumbled down. He shook his head in amazement at their good fortune. "It's a long way," he said, still shaking his head.

"We're just like Jack and Jill," she said, smiling and tilting her head back.

He smiled along with her, to her relief, but it was a sober smile. "You're right," he said. "Jack and Jill, imagine that." He paused. "I wonder if *she* pushed him."

Miranda decided not to pursue that thought. He looked at the sky, which was growing darker by the minute. "We should get back. We'll be in trouble enough as it is."

She looked at him and at the sky. "All right," she said. Then she stooped down and cleaned herself as best she could in the spring. He stooped down beside her.

Sam was pensive and quiet as they returned to the hotel. The fall had darkened his mood and left him much less inclined to be playful.

She imagined that his change in mood was due to apprehension about the consequences of their tumble. He must be worried about what people would think about them when they appeared so messy and disheveled.

But when words at last returned to him, she learned that he wasn't thinking about their appearance at all.

"I'm bothered," he said. Her hand had found its way into his as they walked. Neither was especially conscious of their contact—it simply felt right.

"Bothered?" she asked.

"Uh-huh," he said. "We all are—Lam, Noah, and me. We're all in for a fall. The whole country will be in it. Half will fall one way, and the other half will fall the other. And the three of us . . ." He stopped.

"You're suggesting," she said softly, carefully, "that you may not fall with the South?" He looked away from her. "I don't know," he said. "I truly don't. I'm a Texan, and I love my home—don't get me wrong about that—but I truly don't know."

"It doesn't matter to me what you choose."

They came over a rise. On the plain below them lay the Academy. She stopped and turned to face him, taking both of his hands in hers.

"Will you dance with me often this evening?" she asked.

He laughed. "I won't let another cadet touch you. You can bet on that. However, they might lock me in the guardhouse and you in your hotel room for what we've just done."

"No, they won't. I won't let them."

"I'm glad you're so sure."

"Come on," she said, her face shining. She started to move forward. Her step was brisk, happy. "I must change. I want to dance with you."

"And you will!"

Miranda Kemble had been in bed a long time, for the graduation ball had ended more than an hour and a half earlier. But she was nowhere near sleep. Ariel was sleeping deeply next to her in the double bed, her arms flung across the pillow about her head. Miranda wanted to recreate in her mind the lovely and exciting day she'd just lived through, even if that meant losing sleep.

So she ran through the happenings of the day over and over, dwelling at length on the ones that especially moved her.

She continually let her thoughts turn to the ball itself. It had turned out to be every bit as dazzling and delightful as she had expected, despite the grand battle between her mother and her father, which, it must be said, she had half expected; the two of them loved to fight their wars in public. The ball was held outdoors. A dancing floor had been set up on a corner on the plain under the stars, and it had been lit by Japanese lanterns strung out along the sides.

She had danced a hundred dances—a thousand dances! —with Sam Hawken, as he had promised. And she would have danced a million dances with him, except that her mother intercepted him and took him aside for close to an hour. Then Miranda had danced with a number of unmemorable boys—and Noah, when Ariel would give him up, and Uncle Ashbel, whom Miranda adored.

The grand battle had not erupted until near the end of the evening, her mother and father having a well-developed sense of timing honed to a fine edge over years of experience.

Of course they had behaved horribly, and of course she was embarrassed—she had cried and cried. And of course she was angry. Her father and mother had been divorced for years, so why did they still need to inflict pain on one another, and on their children, and on everyone else nearby?

After they had more or less worn themselves out with their screams and their shouts, Lam had managed to put himself between them. He had taken his father away in one direction, while the two sisters led their mother off in another.

The girls had to take Fanny to her room in the hotel, so Miranda barely had time to say good night to Sam Hawken, Noah, and Uncle Ashbel. And Lam was nowhere to be seen—which was probably just as well. He was doubtless still with their father, who was always impossible after one of his battles with their mother. But Miranda consoled herself that she would have time with Sam over the next few days.

As these images played through Miranda's mind, the door between her room and her mother's opened a crack, and dim yellow light glowed through. Then the door opened wider, and Fanny Shaw, in a dressing gown, tiptoed across the floor and kissed Ariel on the forehead. Ariel stirred and mumbled something unintelligible. Then Fanny came around the bed and bent down to kiss Miranda. She paused when she saw Miranda's open eyes, but she finished the kiss. Then she whispered, "You're awake, darling, aren't you?"

"Yes, Mother," Miranda whispered back. She raised her head a little, unsure what she wanted to do. From her expression, she could tell that her mother would like to talk, but Miranda herself did not know whether she wanted to talk to her mother. Should I be angry at her? she wondered.

Or should I forgive her? Or do I still want to be by myself and think about the day I've just had?

Then she noticed in the dim light that there were tears on her mother's face. And while Miranda didn't want to let her mother off the hook so easily, she melted nevertheless.

"I'm sorry for my outburst against your father," Fanny said. Her voice had now risen above a whisper.

Miranda sat up. She would talk with her, she decided, but she didn't want to wake her sister. She began to rise from the bed, but her mother laid a restraining hand on her.

"No," Fanny said, "stay where you are."

"But Ariel," Miranda said. "We'll go to your room."

"I'll only be a moment."

"All right," Miranda said. She remained sitting while her mother sat down next to her. Miranda looked at Ariel again.

"Don't worry about her," Fanny said, wiping the tears from her face with the edge of the sheet. "Ariel will sleep through doomsday.

"Your father and I . . ." Fanny said. But Miranda stopped her before she could continue.

"Don't talk about Father," she said with a hard edge in her voice. "I know what you will say about him. And I know what he will say about you."

"I'm sorry," Fanny said, and then her quiet tears began again.

"But the tears aren't for me."

"They aren't?" Miranda asked.

"They're for you." As Fanny said this, she placed her arm around Miranda.

"Why should you cry over me, Mother?" Miranda asked.

"I see you so little, my darling—a few months of the year during the summer, now and then at other times. And the last time I was with you, you were a girl. But now you've grown. You've almost become a woman.

"And that makes me sad, darling, sad enough to cry." She punctuated the statement with a tear. "But I'm proud of you as well."

Miranda looked at her, waiting. She loved her mother

very much, but she was not always sure whether her mother was being open with her or acting.

"You're becoming a fine young woman," Fanny said.

"Thank you, Mother," she said after concluding that her mother was truly moved. But she could tell that Fanny was leading up to something, so she waited a little longer for her to come to the point.

Fanny's face grew rapt and intense—she took on the look of a prophetess. This was not an act, Miranda knew. Her mother was passionately serious when her face had that look.

"You like that boy, don't you?" Fanny said. "Sam Houston Hawken?" She drew out his name slowly.

"Yes, Mother."

"I could tell. I've never seen you look at a man that way before."

Miranda smiled, remembering.

"And I take it you will see him again?"

"Tomorrow."

"Yes, of course, tomorrow," Fanny said with a wave of her hand. "But not only tomorrow—after that?"

"I hope so, Mother."

"Good," Fanny said. "Do that. He's a fine young man."

"Really, Mother?" Miranda said. Somehow she had expected opposition from her mother as well as her father, simply because her parents *always* opposed romance.

"Yes, absolutely," Fanny said. "Even though he's a strange one, perhaps a tad unpredictable . . ." She caught Miranda's eye. "Your father, you know, is quite predictable, but I just didn't predict him correctly."

"Don't talk about Father, please, Mother."

"All right," she sighed. Then she turned her attention back to Sam Hawken. "I had quite a long talk with your Sam. I've decided that he will become something. He has drive and brains, and beneath his hardness he is sensitive and tender. So, my darling, write to him. See him when you're able. I have good feelings about him—there is depth to that young man."

At that, Miranda stopped breathing for a moment. Then she said, "I *do* want to see him again."

"You are not a girl who allows barriers between yourself and your goals," Fanny said softly.

Miranda gave her mother a wide, happy smile.

"Now," Fanny said, "tell me how the burn is healing."

"It stings a little," Miranda said.

"Move into the light. I should examine it."

"All right, Mother," Miranda said. Unfastening the top buttons of her nightdress, she exposed the burned place.

When she saw it, Fanny sighed audibly and pressed her lips together, for it pained her to see her daughter hurt. But in a moment she had pulled herself together.

"It's not so raw looking as it was when I first saw it," Fanny said, "despite your roll down the hill. That," she added parenthetically, "made an enormous impression on your Sam Hawken. But you will have an evil-looking scar, darling." And then she smiled wickedly. "*That* will give you quite a tale to tell your husband."

"Oh, Mother!" Miranda protested. But the wicked smile remained until Miranda softened, and she leaned over and touched her lips to Fanny's cheek. "I love you, Mother," she whispered.

"Yes, darling, I know. And I, too, love you."

Fanny Shaw rose, returned to her room, and shut the door. Soon Miranda was asleep.

She did see Sam Hawken several times over the next few days, twice alone. It was over seven years, however, before she saw him again.

# ◆ TWO ◆

Lieutenant Tom Stetson had been waiting a long time before he caught sight of the man he was expecting. The man was tall and lean, with unkempt sandy-red hair and a closely cropped beard. He was threading his way through the crush of people surrounding the train dispatcher's tent. He wore the uniform of a major in the Army of the Confederate States of America. The name on his papers was Walter J. Rusk.

The lieutenant was standing on what was left of the station platform of what was left of the Jackson railway terminal, and he was keeping an eye on his and the major's horses. In the major's saddlebags were a set of dispatches that had originated in Texas and which were destined for Richmond. The major's ostensible purpose had been to acquire space on a train out of Jackson for himself and the lieutenant, and that was what had apparently taken him so long.

Some three months before, Union General William Tecumseh Sherman, during the course of General Ulysses S. Grant's siege of Vicksburg, had captured Jackson, the Mississippi capital, from General Joseph E. Johnston, the

50

area commander of the armies of the Western Confederacy. In the brief two days he had spent in Jackson, General Sherman had managed to demolish most of what was militarily useful in the town: the arsenals, the penitentiary, the cotton factory, the Confederate Hotel, a government foundry, a gun carriage establishment, and the railroads.

A large part of the population of the town had left with Johnston in May, but most of them had returned after Sherman's departure. They and Johnston's soldiers had repaired as much of the destruction as they were able. Of special importance was the crucial railway line to the east. That line was now back in satisfactory working order. Trains were even now being formed up in the yards beside the station.

Sherman was again besieging Jackson, and again Jackson was defended by Joseph E. Johnston. This time, however, Johnston had thirty thousand men under him, to Sherman's fifty thousand, where previously he had only commanded six thousand. He now also had a fine set of fortifications built in a great arc around the west of the city, and his flanks were well secured by the Pearl River, which bordered the town to the east. It was a strong position, and Sherman would have a hard time rooting him out of it, despite his superior numbers and the current high spirits of his men. For the Union armies had only ten days earlier, on July Fourth, accepted the surrender of the great Confederate fortress of Vicksburg not many miles to the west of Jackson. And on that same day, a thousand miles to the northeast, the battle near the Pennsylvania town of Gettysburg had ended, and Robert E. Lee's Army of Virginia began its long retreat back toward Richmond.

The guns on this scorching-hot morning in Jackson were silent, which was one reason so many people were about— the women with their bundles and their children, the old people with just their bundles, and the men in bare feet and ragged clothes, with their old rugs for sleeping and their toothbrushes stuck like roses in their buttonholes. Most, like the major and the lieutenant, were either waiting for passage or trying to obtain it. No one had much appetite to be in town when Sherman entered it for the second time.

The question was whether Joe Johnston intended to fight. The answer might lie in the numbers of soldiers who seemed to be waiting for trains. But that was not a conclusive answer; more evidence was needed.

Because of the heat, the major had left open the top of his collar and uniform blouse. His wide-brimmed gray hat shaded his face, concealing his expression from Lieutenant Stetson. Tom Stetson was from Kentucky, and he, unlike the major, had left his collar tightly fastened, and he was suffering mightily for his propriety.

The lieutenant stared up into the sky, where thunderheads were piling up. There'd be thunderstorms later in the afternoon, a welcome relief from the heat and dust. Then he looked again at the major, trying—and failing—to tell if the other man had been successful in his quest. Even if his face had not been darkly shaded, Stetson knew he'd have a hard time making out the major's expression. He was a close one, behind his veils were curtains, and behind the curtains were walls of iron. But Stetson liked him for all that. He was good to work with. He was fair and he watched out for you. And more to the point, they got sent on assignments like this one, assignments that brought with them considerably more than the usual excitement—and danger. He and the major risked hanging for what they were doing now.

When the major was close enough to address, Lieutenant Stetson gave him a salute. "How'd it go," he asked, then added, "Major?" The "Major" didn't come easily to him. He was used to addressing the other man with another title.

"Fine, Lieutenant," the major answered, returning his salute casually as he scanned the rail yards in front of him. The yards were a hive of activity. An empty train was just arriving from Meridian; it was pulling across the recently rebuilt bridge over the Pearl. Another train was forming up nearby, and yet others were being loaded. The area was surprisingly organized and orderly for a city under siege. The major was not used to seeing Confederate operations so well managed.

The major turned his attention back to the lieutenant. "They can put us on a train that leaves here at one o'clock," he said. Then he made a come-on motion with his hand, to take the lieutenant away from the other people who were milling about the station platform.

When they were a few feet out of earshot, he pulled to a halt. "So, Tom," he said, pointing a finger at the train that was loading, "what are they putting on that train over there?"

"Mostly looms, as far as I can tell. And tents."

"Joe Johnston doesn't want Sherman to get them this time."

"I guess not."

"I'm surprised he missed them when he had the chance before," the major said.

"We had only two days to do the job."

"Don't say 'we,' Tom," the major warned softly. "It's 'they' for now."

When Sherman occupied Jackson in April, he found the looms of the factories still producing tents for the Confederacy. Johnston had pulled out so quickly and Sherman had pulled in so rapidly that no one thought to shut them down. Because Sherman was in town just a few days, he only managed to destroy some of them. The next time he entered Jackson, the major and the lieutenant both knew, Cump Sherman intended to make up for what he had missed the first time.

"Sorry, sir," Tom Stetson said.

The major gave the lieutenant a tight little smile of acknowledgment, but his eyes were on the area next to the train that was now forming up. The train was all flatcars. In the area beside the flatcars were big field cannons. If General Johnston intended to defend Jackson from his well-fortified positions, he would need those cannon.

"See those?" The major nodded toward the train.

"Yes, sir," Tom Stetson said.

"What do you make of that, Tom?"

"The cannon?"

"Right, the cannon," the major said. "I wonder if

they're in the yard now because they're on their way to the lines. Or are they here because they're on their way to Meridian?''

The lieutenant thought on that for a moment.

''If they're sending them to Meridian,'' Tom said softly, ''then . . .'' He paused to take in the sharp look the major was giving him. After a moment, he resumed, making the correction the look demanded. ''Then *we* would not have them for a battle with Sherman.''

''Right.''

''*We'd* never be able to fight a battle without them.''

''Right.''

''So *we* aren't going to fight a battle?'' Stetson offered.

''*If* the cannon are waiting shipment to Meridian,'' the major said.

''Son of a bitch.''

''On the other hand . . .'' the major said, leaving the thought unfinished.

He then let his gaze swing around the yards again, taking as much in as he could. He needed all the information his eyes could record, but it would not do to be obtrusive.

What seemed most in evidence, though, were women, children, and old people, the flotsam and jetsam of the battles that had raged for months all across northern Mississippi and western Tennessee.

''Yeah,'' he said to himself softly, pitying them all, ''get moving again, you people. The bad times are coming soon and this won't be a good place for you. But where will you be safe?''

''What's that?'' Tom Stetson asked, unable to catch his words.

''Never mind,'' the major said, shaking his head sadly. ''There's no help for it.''

He rubbed his chin for a moment, reflecting. Then he looked at the lieutenant. ''Tom, here's what we need to do before we catch that train. You stay here and keep watching our horses. There are people here who believe they need them more than you or I do. More important, I want you to keep an eye on the rail yards. Make a note in your mind of everything that's going onto those trains.

"Meanwhile," he added with a smile, "I have an appointment with a lady."

"A lady?"

"That's right."

"A real lady? As in lace and fine clothes and servants."

"That's right: auburn hair, a voice like an angel, fine clothes and servants, and no man to whom she is officially and legally attached."

"You lucky bastard. I thought every woman who called herself a lady had found some reason to absent herself from this part of Mississippi."

"Evidently not. Count trains, my son. I'll return for you in due course."

"So long—*sir*," Tom Stetson said, managing to make it sound like a curse. His eyes, however, were twinkling.

But the major, having already turned and set off, ignored him.


As it happened, since the major had never previously met the lady in question, he was not telling the truth when he described her to Lieutenant Tom Stetson. The woman the major went to see turned out to be quite different from the fine but imaginary lady he'd left in Tom's mind.

Her name was Jane Featherstone, and she looked to be somewhere between thirty and thirty-five. She was pleasant but ordinary of face and figure, and her appearance was livened by quick, probing, though somewhat nervous eyes. She had one servant, and she lived in rooms above a dry-goods store two blocks from the state capitol.

As it also happened, the major needed to see her not because she was an attractive woman, but because she was a Union spy. For nearly a year she had been one of the agents operated behind Confederate lines by General Grenville Dodge, a railroad man from Iowa who ran an extensive espionage network all through the South—when he was not rebuilding the railroads in Tennessee for General Grant or protecting those railroads from the ravages and depredations of Confederate cavalry raider General Nathan Bedford Forrest.

Miss Jane Featherstone was one of his top agents.

When the servant, a quadroon from New Orleans named Francoise, ushered Major Rusk into the parlor, Miss Featherstone rose from her chair and extended her hand. There were two windows in the room, both thrown wide open, and they cast harsh light on the dark and heavy furniture and the frayed rug. A big upright piano abutted almost one entire wall, and over it, in a frame, hung a diploma from the Boston Conservatory of Music. Until very recently, Miss Featherstone had made her living providing musical instruction to the children of Jackson's better classes.

She was dressed in gray and brown, and there was a great stillness about her, even as she moved toward him.

"Major Rusk?" Jane Featherstone said mildly, and let him take her hand. "I don't believe we've met. But I'm pleased to make your acquaintance, I'm sure." She looked at him with caution and interest.

"Forgive me for intruding on your peace," the major said.

"There's no peace in this town," she said simply.

"I reckon not," the major said with a small movement of his lips that could have been a smile. "But I do trust I'm not disturbing you. I don't normally arrive unannounced to ladies I don't know. Under the circumstances, however, there was no other way to see you except to appear at your door."

"So then, here you are," she said with a wry smile. "What can I do for you?" As she said this, she motioned him into a dark red plush love seat next to her own upholstered chair. With another gesture she ordered Francoise to withdraw.

"General Dodge," the major said, coming immediately to the point, "sends his greetings." He noticed that Miss Featherstone took a long breath and raised her brows in the slightest flicker of movement. Then she held her gaze steady on him. "And his thanks," the major continued quietly.

"He is most grateful for the information you've provided him during the past two months."

"General Dodge," she said. It was a statement, not a question.

He nodded.

"Please continue," she said.

"I've been instructed to tell you that the general has caused two thousand dollars to be placed on deposit in your name at the Wells Fargo Bank in San Francisco. Your passage to that city will be arranged whenever you choose to avail yourself of it."

She nodded slowly. "And what would a Confederate major know of General Dodge?"

"I'm not a Confederate major, Miss Featherstone," he said, then handed her a paper he'd kept hidden in the lining of his tunic.

"You've come from General Dodge?" she asked cautiously after she'd glanced at it.

"No. From Sherman. General Dodge doesn't normally divulge the names of his"—he paused, searching for the word—"associates, even to General Sherman. But for various vital reasons, he did this once." He looked at her. "You're in no danger from me."

She nodded again. "So what can I do for you, Major?" she asked quietly.

"It's Captain," he corrected. "Captain Hawken. I'm an aide to the general."

"But you're a southerner?" she asked, noting his accent.

"I'm a Texan," he agreed.

"And you are fighting for the North?" She looked at him closely, cocking her head slightly to one side. He remembered another woman holding her head that way long ago, but he did not remember when or where. It was a gesture that he found attractive.

"You are also a southerner?" he smiled, answering her by asking her the same question. "And you are fighting for the North as well—a conspicuously dangerous choice in this place."

She shrugged, her shoulders scarcely moving. She is so

*still*, he thought. And yet she was not a helpless woman; she had produced a great deal of valuable information.

"But, yes," he said, answering her question, "I'm a southerner, and I've chosen the northern side for reasons that satisfy me—as I would think you have reasons that satisfy you." He wanted very much to ask this lady why she'd become an agent for General Dodge, but he thought better of it.

"Thank you," she said, lowering her head, then throwing it back again. That quick motion amid her stillness became her.

Where have I seen *that* before? he asked himself.

"What can I do for you?" she asked. "Why have you come to me today?"

"General Sherman is most interested," he said, "in learning whether General Johnston will fight or whether he will slip away. And if he plans to try to slip away, when. General Sherman hopes that you will be able to give us answers to these questions."

General Joseph Johnston was more famous for retreats than for assaults. This was not to say that he wasn't a fighter, only that he thought of himself as a spider rather than a tiger. He lured his opponent into a net of his own making.

But Hawken knew that Sherman wanted to fight Johnston sometime during the next couple of days. Hawken's job in Jackson was to discover ways to prevent, or at least delay, a Joe Johnston movement to the east or south.

"I've just come from the train yards," Hawken went on. "But it's not clear whether there is movement away from here. If there is to be a withdrawal, we must know about it. And we must know when it will come."

She looked at him for a long while without speaking. Then she turned away. "Johnston won't fight Sherman in Jackson," she said in her small voice, still facing away from him. "He plans to move out. He had hoped to complete his move tonight, but that has proved impossible. There aren't enough locomotives and cars to acomplish the job, even with pack animals and wagons moving whatever they can handle. He is now hoping to accomplish his action by early tomorrow morning, but it appears that noon tomorrow is the earliest it can be done.''

"Amazing!" he whispered, more at her accomplishment in obtaining the information than at the information itself. "And you're sure of that?" he asked, as he considered the implications of her information. It was not good news.

"Of course," she said quietly. "Have my other reports proved accurate?"

"In every detail," he acknowledged after a time. Then he shook his head angrily. "Damn!" he said. "I don't like what you've told me. Johnston's acting too soon for us! And that makes problems for me." Problems that might require him to take action on his own, he thought, and he had no idea what actions he could possibly take.

He caught her eye.

Her expression was altering now. Her face was sadder, grimmer, with a touch of pleading in it.

"But tell me," she asked, louder, "why do you need to know when Johnston is making his move? Isn't it enough that he is leaving at all? Does General Sherman require another battle? Poor Jackson doesn't require another fight, nor another occupation by the Yankee army," she added.

"I'm not sure why these things matter to you," he said carefully.

"I think it should be obvious why these things interest me," she said. "You see where I live. And you can understand my interest in my own safety." She smiled a peculiar little smile as she said this. "So it very much behooves me to know when General Sherman plans his major assault."

He looked out the window, gaining time. He didn't want to tell her what she wanted to know. Even though there was some risk to her in ignorance, she had no need to know what General Sherman's purposes were. At the same time, he needed her—as long as she had information that General Sherman desperately needed. It would not do to set her against him.

"I can well understand that you are reluctant to speak to

me of military matters,'' she said, beginning to look pitia-
ble. ''But I am anxious about my own position in Jackson.''

''We will, of course, arrange for your safety,'' he said.
He took a breath and continued, ''This war will drag on as
long as the South has armies that are capable of putting up a
fight. At the same time, the South is outmanned, outgunned,
and outproduced. And that means that the southern armies
will eventually lose just about every fight they engage
in—as long as the North can catch them. If the Confederate
armies keep moving and avoiding battle, then the hope is
that the North will grow tired of chasing them and will give
up. We have to try to catch and beat the southern armies until
they are not capable of fighting anymore. That's what
Sherman is trying to do now.'' He paused. ''Or else we have
to destroy their capability to fight in ways that do not
require battles.''

''I don't understand.''

''We destroy factories and railroads and food.''

''Even if ordinary people are hurt by that, not just the
soldiers?''

''Even if all the people are hurt by that.'' He leaned
closer to her. ''That's the way of war, Miss Featherstone.''

She nodded.

''That's why what you have to tell me is so important.
You could conceivably make the war shorter.''

Her mild look seemed a reproach. ''But when will Sherman
enter Jackson?'' she asked.

''I have no idea,'' he answered. ''That's why I'm here
now talking to you—in order to find the information that
will make that decision possible.''

A most curious woman, he thought. He was beginning to
see what made her a successful spy.

''You must be very thirsty,'' she said, breaking the
uncomfortable moment. ''I'm afraid all that I can offer you
is plain water. But I can promise that it will be cold.''

''Then I will take that gratefully,'' he said.

''Francoise?'' she called out. When Francoise appeared,
she instructed her to bring a pitcher of water and glasses.

After Francoise had returned with the water and then left,

Hawken began asking Jane Featherstone particulars about the military situation in Jackson, about the disposition of General Johnston's troops, and about his timetable for departure.

As he and she discussed these things, he came to a conclusion about what he had to do to prevent Johnston's departure—or at least to hinder it for a couple of days, long enough for Sherman to complete the flanking movement he had already begun.

Sherman's Thirteenth Corps, under Ord, had taken the rail line that ran south toward New Orleans. And his Ninth Corps, under Parke, had done the same for the line that ran north to Memphis. So Johnston would have to move east.

A cavalry attack, if it could be mounted, would probably do the job. But the question was whether there was time to return to Sherman's lines and arrange that. Hawken doubted it.

The railroad line to Meridian had to be cut.

It was well past noon when Hawken finally stood to leave.

When Jane Featherstone rose to lead him out, she said, "Will I see you again?" Her face was as expressionless as usual, but now for the first time Hawken caught flickers of vivaciousness—and steel—in her eyes.

"Yes, if it's possible, I'd like to see you again," he said, meaning it. She excited his curiosity. But there was also an undertow of passion and recklessness beneath her mildness.

"And I, too," she said with her half smile and soft voice. In addition to the glimmer of gaiety in her eyes, there was something else—eagerness? "You're quite handsome, you know. And interesting."

He nodded.

"Until we meet again?" she said, offering her hand.

"Until then," he said, and turned to leave.

Once outside in the blazing heat, he sighed. Jesus! he said to himself. That's one hard lady. Never mind her softness and her silence. I've never been kept so off balance by a woman. At least, he added, not since Miranda Kemble.

And then he remembered where he had seen a cock of the head like hers before. It was at West Point, the day before

he graduated. And the woman—the girl—he'd noticed doing
it was Miranda Kemble herself—so very different from this
strange women. She was so much more open and direct and
spirited. And yet . . .

He wondered about Miranda. He hadn't heard from her
since the start of the war. Before that, there had been letters,
but he had not seen her since she was fifteen.

He shook his head sadly. *Damn the war!*


A Confederate major—a genuine Confederate major—was
directing and organizing the trains at the Jackson, Mississippi, train yard for General Joe Johnston. Major Noah Ballard
stood on the edge of the yard where the tracks converged
toward the bridge over the Pearl. A few yards away a
locomotive had just been attached to a fourteen-car load.
And while Noah was waiting for it to start, he glanced up at
the sky. It was a few minutes after one o'clock by his
watch, and already huge summer rain clouds had started to
pile up in the west. How long will they hold off? he thought
to himself, grim-faced, worried about his already desperately
perilous schedule.

Though he was an engineer and not a railway manager, he
did what he was told, and he went where he was sent. And
of course, railroads were in his blood. His father was still
president of the Atlanta and Western, a line that the war had
made more vital than ever.

Noah had been at this job for ten days. Before that, he
had planned the fortifications around Jackson, then directed
their construction.

A leather pouch slung around his neck and perched on his
hip was stuffed full of papers indicating where and what had
to be moved, and what he had available to move it in. But
the information in the papers scarcely began to approximate
the reality he was facing in the job General Johnston had
given him: to move an army of over thirty thousand with all
its baggage and equipment and impediments out of Jackson
by noon the following day, and to do it under the noses of a

larger Federal army that had every intention of stopping them.

If he failed, and if Sherman defeated or captured Johnston's army, then there would be only one weak Confederate force, Braxton Bragg's army in eastern Tennessee, between Grant and Atlanta.

And meanwhile, Noah had 18 usable locomotives, and somewhere between 130 and 150 cars, depending on luck and the always precarious final stages of wear and tear. Each car might carry as much as sixteen thousand pounds of baggage or equipment, and each locomotive could pull, with yet more luck, trains of up to 15 cars.

And he had hundreds of thousands of tons to ship.

The railroads of northern and eastern Mississippi showed on their books three to four times that number of engines and cars. Noah had no idea where the hell they had gotten to. And he didn't have time to find out.

How many angels can dance on a pinhead? he asked himself, shaking his head. That's an easy one compared with, How can I in one day move an army of thirty thousand with 18 locomotives and 130 cars?

It was an impossible situation, and he knew it. On top of that, he had only one way out by rail: the rickety Southern Line that ran between Jackson and Meridian, ninety miles to the east. All the other lines out of Jackson—the New Orleans and Jackson to the south, the Great Northern to the north and Memphis, and of course the Vicksburg and Jackson to the west—had all been taken by the Federals.

He became aware of the engine he'd been waiting for. It was puffing mightily, straining to move its unaccustomed load.

"All right, Noah, we're moving it," a voice called out. The voice belonged to Gar Thomas, the superintendent of the Southern Line. As with many other short rail lines in the South, the Southern's superintendent for all intents and purposes ran the line, handling all the work usually performed by both the president and the general manager of other, longer roads. Thomas was in his early forties, round faced, balding, mustached but beardless, and like most southern railroad superintendents, he was not especially effective at his job. Still, Gar was a good sort, friendly, eager, pleasant, and Noah was glad to have him around, for his companionship if not for his competence.

All the same, Noah sorely missed having someone with skill and experience to help him manage his task. It wouldn't take much of a mishap to bring the whole operation to a halt.

He made this last observation as, with considerable effort, he manhandled the tall lever that brought a switch into its closed position. Slowly the rails swung and closed, and the locomotive Noah had been listening to started to move. Groaning and struggling, with huge gouts of black smoke surging out of its great, bulbous smokestack, it strained and jerked forward.

Noah moved back as the train approached, and he waved in response to the waves of the engine driver and the fireman. But he didn't watch as the train crossed the narrow, single-track bridge over the Pearl. He didn't have time.

He drew a pencil out of the pouch and searched until he found the paper he wanted. After that he checked off the number of the train that had just passed, and then he lifted his head and searched for Gar Thomas.

He now had nine trains running on the single track between Jackson and Meridian. Three should have recently arrived in Meridian, and six more were loading. They'd move out of Jackson during the next hours. Once these trains reached Meridian, a six-hour trip if all went well, they'd be turned around and sent back to Jackson. The last train out of Jackson was due to leave at four this afternoon. That meant the first trip out of Meridian back to Jackson could not leave there until at least ten tonight.

"What's next?" Noah said to Gar when he found him.

"Over there," Gar said, indicating the spot with a tilt of his head. A hundred yards away three horses with riders were waiting. One of the horsemen was shouting at Noah and Gar and making a come-hither motion with his arm.

The smallest of the riders was General Joseph Johnston. The other two would be his aides.

"Let's go, then," Noah said, and started moving toward the general.

When Noah and Gar drew near, General Johnston dismounted. Standing near his horse, he waited for Noah to approach and salute.

Johnston, a West Point graduate, was then almost fifty. He was a small man, but every inch a general. With his well-fitting gray cloak, his well-tended pepper-and-salt mustache and goatee, and his intense personal magnetism, no one would mistake him for anything but the commanding officer.

He was popular among the troops. Few generals watched more carefully over the safety and well-being of their troops, and fewer still were as ready to help with the labor. There was a famous story about Johnston dismounting and wading—polished boots, gold braid, and all—into a mud hole to help push a mired cannon back onto solid ground.

Johnston's popularity, however, did not extend to Richmond—or at least to that part of Richmond occupied by the President of the Confederacy, Jefferson Davis. Davis, though himself a West Point graduate, had no use for Johnston. As far as Davis was concerned, Johnston wasn't the fighter he needed. He wasn't aggressive enough to suit the President. He was too afraid to lose men. Even more important, Johnston refused to keep Davis informed of his plans and actions. He kept his own counsel, executed his own strategies, and gave scarcely more than lip service to Davis's wishes.

Davis was passionate, erratic, and impulsive, and at times perhaps less than completely sane. But he was the chief executive. And so, inevitably, the conflict between Davis and Johnston would soon come to a head.

At any rate, Davis had no other choice for his Western Area Commander than Joe Johnston. There was no other general officer besides Lee of sufficient rank and stature for the job.

The strife between the Confederate Commander of the West and his commander in chief had not yet affected Noah Ballard. He and Johnston got along famously, so Noah was a little surprised to note, as Johnston returned his salute, that the general looked miffed with him.

"I thought I told you, Major, that you were to leave the work of corporals to corporals," Johnston said. "I just saw you pulling a switch. Why does the Confederacy require majors to pull railway switches? Next generals will be driving locomotives."

"I'm sorry, sir," Noah said. "There was no one else to do it."

"Because you looked for no one else," Johnston said. "I don't mind majors working, you understand. It never hurt any major to work hard, even with his hands. But a major is a major because he is supposed to be able to tell less intelligent, knowledgeable, or experienced men how to do things so that he doesn't do the work of a hundred men all by himself."

"Yes, sir," Noah said.

"Having said that," the general continued, appearing to mellow, "I'm still pleased with you, boy. So pleased that I've found another load of manure to place on your back." He remounted. "You will come along with me, Major. Lieutenant," he said, addressing one of his aides, "would you be so kind as to dismount and allow the major to borrow your horse? You can rejoin us at my quarters." And then the general addressed Gar Thomas. "Mr. Thomas, do you think you can manage matters until Major Ballard returns. I'll try not to keep him for long."

"I'll do what I can without him, General," Gar Thomas said.

The general maintained his quarters in a house at the western edge of Jackson a half mile from his armies' lines. A man in the uniform of a captain of the Quartermaster Corps was waiting for the General and Noah in the parlor of the house. Desks had been set up in other rooms, and various clerks and staff members were busy at them. But the parlor had been left for the general's personal use.

The captain had been pacing the floor impatiently when Johnston and Ballard arrived, trailed by the general's aide. But he came to a halt to greet them when they entered the parlor. He was a bulldog of a man, tall and barrel chested, florid and meaty faced, thick of limb and body, with a noticeable paunch. Though he wore the elegantly tailored uniform of a bureaucrat and his face was flushed and roughened by rich food and drink, his movements were surprisingly agile and graceful. His name was William Hottel.

It didn't take Noah long to realize that it was Captain Hottel's arrival that was the source of the general's current displeasure. The captain, it turned out, belonged to the Railroad Bureau in Richmond. He had been sent by Colonel Sims, the head of the Bureau, to manage the vital rail lines in eastern Mississippi and western Alabama. Before he began his stint with the Bureau, he had been manager of the Tennessee part of the Louisville & Nashville Railroad.

Noah was acquainted with the work of the Railroad Bureau, though this was his first encounter with one of its officers. It had been set up by the government in Richmond to take overall control of the railroads of the South. It had the authority to manage the lines, if it so wished, and allocate what scarce resources and equipment were available to wherever these would be most effectively used.

The idea hadn't worked, not because it was a bad idea, Noah believed. On the contrary, the North had a similar organization in place that did everything it was intended to do. But in the South, the setting up of structures of command and organization did not necessarily lead to obedience and organized, purposeful activity.

Confederate commanders in the field never failed to overrule the wishes of the officers of the Railroad Bureau, unless of course these wishes actually coincided with their own. And the officers of the Bureau had no better luck trying to manage the operators of the various southern railroads. In the South, each railroad was seen as a feudal fiefdom whose territory was inviolate.

Joe Johnston was no more eager to relegate his control of the transportation in the area under him to Richmond bureaucrats than was any other general. In fact, his own railroad officer, Noah Ballard, was not in the Quartermaster's Department. He was an engineer. Even though Noah was only a few days on the job, he was well aware that Johnston had been satisfied with his decision to put the young engineer in charge of his railways.

On the other hand, Johnston did have his troubles with Richmond. He might be willing to sacrifice Noah on the altar of administrative peace.

Or at least that was the worry that filled Noah's mind as he took the measure of Captain William Hottel.

"The captain comes to us with a great deal of experience running railroads in Tennessee and elsewhere," Johnston told Noah as he completed making his introductions. "And he has come to *represent*,"—he said the word quite slowly— "the Railroad Bureau in our part of Mississippi. Therefore, you will be working with Captain Hottel as you complete your current duties."

And then Johnston addressed Hottel. "Captain, perhaps you would be so kind as to show Major Ballard a copy of your orders from Colonel Sims?"

"Happy to," Hottel said, and handed Noah his papers.

What the orders said was that Captain Hottel would, upon his arrival at General Johnston's headquarters, take charge of the entire operation of those railroads of western Alabama and eastern Mississippi then currently within the control of the Confederate States of America.

What the orders meant, finally, would of course be up to the discretion of General Johnston.

After Noah finished reading the orders, Captain Hottel retrieved them, then handed them over to General Johnston, who passed them to his aide.

"You will also want to see this, I think," Hottel said to Noah, offering a folded piece of notepaper. "It's something personal for you from your father."

Noah's father had scribbled:

> I've known Will Hottel for a long time, Noah. He's a good man, and you can work with him. The work you and he do will be of much use to me, and to all of us. Forgive me for having to be so brief, but the time pressures, on all of us, are severe.
>
>                                    Your loving Father.

\*   \*   \*

Noah refolded the note and placed it in his pocket.

"My father likes you, Captain," Noah said.

"I've gathered that," Hottel said, "and I'm grateful for his kind words. Your father had a large hand in getting me here."

"You've come a long way, Captain," the general said, moving to end the conversation. 'You'll want to rest, I'm sure, before we ease you into your new responsibilities."

"Thank you, General," Captain Hottel said. "But I'm as fresh as I'll ever be. And as long as I have you and the officer who has been handling your railroad matters together, we might take advantage of the moment to get some work done."

"Some work?" the general asked, looking displeased.

"I think that we should all be clear as to our particular areas of responsibility," Hottel said.

General Johnston shook his head. "You may not have noticed, Captain, but this city is currently under siege by a force of fifty thousand men. I aim to extract our troops from that siege during the next twenty-four hours. And that means I don't have time to thrash out areas of responsibility with you." And then, before Captain Hottel had a chance to reply, the general began moving toward the door as he placed his hat on his head. "Major," he said to Noah, "would you take care of Captain Hottel for me? See that he is fed and housed—and otherwise taken care of?"

"Yes, sir," Noah said, forcing himself to speak evenly. This is all I need today! he thought. Even though Father has good words for him.

"I'd hoped that the general could find time to stay for at least a few minutes," Captain Hottel said. But Johnston only smiled blandly and continued on his way.

"I'll take care of the fighting while the two of you take care of the moving," he said. As he stood at the door, he turned and caught Noah's eyes. *"Major,"* he continued, "you have my full authority to do everything in your power to make life as easy and comfortable for the *captain* as you can. I'm sure, I need hardly add, that you will both be of great help to one another."

When he finished that, he looked meaningfully at Noah. Then he winked.

"Yes, sir," Noah said.

One thing Johnston meant, he knew, was that Noah was to use his rank to insure his authority over Hottel—no matter what Hottel's orders from Richmond were.

Then Noah turned to Captain Hottel. "Well, Captain," he said, "since, as you say, you're ready to get down to business, what spark of reason do you have in mind to illuminate this swamp of darkness and confusion?"

Captain Hottel smiled blandly. "I'm not sure I understand what you mean."

"What I mean is that we're up to our knees in trouble," Noah said. "And I was wondering if you had any immediate ideas about how to help pull us out. I have thirty thousand men, with all their baggage and equipment, and I have eighteen locomotives and maybe a hundred and thirty cars, give or take twenty, to move them with on worn-out rails and roadbed. So you would be a large help to me if you could come up with a way through that. Can you?"

"Not immediately. No," Hottel said, looking pensive. "Not immediately. But . . ." And then he paused.

"But I'm surprised that you have so little rolling stock," Hottel went on.

"Are you aware, Captain, that there's a war on?"

Captain Hottel just smiled at the rebuke. "Are *you* aware, Major," he said after a moment, "that, according to my records there are well over fifty workable locomotives in northern Mississipi and a like number of cars—perhaps two or three hundred of them?"

"I've seen the inventories," Noah said. "But I can't use what's on paper."

The captain shrugged. "There are a *minimum* of fifty locomotives." He gave Noah a self-satisfied look. "In other words, there may be even more."

"Like I said, I can't use paper machines."

"Why haven't you looked for them?" Hottel asked.

"Because I've been on the job for only ten days, there's a war on, and I have other things to do," Noah said, barely holding on to his patience. Captain Hottel rubbed Noah the wrong way, John Ballard's endorsement of him notwithstanding.

"But they are all still out there," Hottel said, "in northern Mississippi. And they're waiting to be used."

"But they're completely worthless if I don't have them. You must know that." He looked at Hottel. "God only knows where they are, and God only knows how we could go about getting them."

"Still, it does make you pause to think, doesn't it?" Captain Hottel said with a smile. "Working locomotives and railroad cars—the very things that the Confederacy needs more than anything else right now—have been sitting nearby under your very nose. Wouldn't you love to have them?"

"Sure," Noah answered. "They'd be a gift from God." He stopped. "But you know something, Captain?" He stopped again. "Tell me," he said, "are you thinking of trying to find all that equipment?"

"The thought passed my mind," Hottel said.

"Don't bother."

"Why not?"

"I can manage—not well, but passably—with what we've got now. And after we pull out of Jackson, all that other machinery won't do us a damn bit of good."

"How's that?"

"There's no way we can move them east where all that equipment is going to be needed."

There was only one completed railroad line in the South between the Mississippi River and the East. It ran from Memphis through the northernmost parts of Mississippi and Alabama to Chattanooga. There a line branched north toward Richmond and south toward Atlanta. Since the Federals now held all the western portions of that east–west line, the South had no through east–west train service.

Another line running east from Vicksburg through Jackson and then to Montgomery and Atlanta was uncompleted. The section between Selma and Mongomery, the section bisected by the Tombigbee River, would not be completed for some time.

If the Confederacy wanted east–west rail service during the summer of 1863, they had to travel down to Mobile, ferry across the bay, the connect with the lines that went to Atlanta.

"You don't think that equipment will be needed here," Hottel asked innocently, "after Sherman and his people leave?"

"After Johnston withdraws from Jackson, Captain, you can write off Mississippi from the Confederacy."

"That's writing off the entire West, then," Hottel said, as though the thought came as an utter surprise to him.

Noah gave a short, sharp nod in answer. Then he made a move for the door outside. "Meanwhile," he said, shaking his head again, "we've got to do what we can with the eighteen we have."

Hottel just looked at him with curious, probing eyes.

Noah gave him a to-hell-with-it gesture. "But I take it you'd like to track down that equipment?"

"I'd like to locate the locomotives," Hottel said. "Yes, I'd like that very much."

"Go ahead if you want. Find out where they are." And get out of my hair, he thought.

"I just might do that," Hottel said. "Meanwhile, let's get ourselves organized."

"What do you have in mind?"

"Let's you and me sit down to a leisurely lunch, where you can explain your procedures and methods and I can elaborate on the information I've brought with me."

"If it's like the information about that equipment you say is ready for plucking, I'd be very interested in hearing it. But not now. I've no time, I'm sorry to say."

"You must eat."

Noah shrugged. "I can't. I have too much to do. But why don't you come along with me and see what's happening?"

"Well, at least take a drink then," Captain Hottel said. "I have some decent brandy in my bag." He pointed to a large leather bag on the floor.

"You're tempting me," Noah said. "But I really must get back to the yard. I've been away too long already."

"Don't you have people who can handle things themselves?"

"Funny, but the general asked me that same question. The answer is no. There's Gar Thomas, whom you'll meet soon, I'm sure. And there's me. And now there's you," he said meaningfully.

"All right, then," Captain Hottel said. "Let's go to the yard."

At that, Noah realized that what he really wanted was to be rid of Captain Hottel. "Wouldn't you rather I found you some quarters first?" he asked. "Someplace to clean up and change?"

"No," Hottel said. "Not at all. My bag will be safe here."

"All right, Captain. Come on, then."

Damn it to hell! Noah thought. Fire and Blazes!


Though it was well after midnight, Jane Featherstone was wide awake. She sat in a rocking chair with an unread book in her lap, and stared out of one of her windows, listening to the melody of the rain. In the distance shells were falling again. But the noise didn't disturb her. On the contrary, she liked the shelling, even when the occasional round fell near the building where she kept her rooms.

The lamp beside her on the table was burning low and needed tending, but she did nothing about it. She was comfortable with her private thoughts.

And she wished her solitude was not soon to be broken. She was expecting a visitor, and she wasn't looking forward to the visit.

All evening she'd been thinking about the Yankee captain who'd paid a call on her that morning. She'd liked him, and she'd liked the effect she'd had on him—she'd made him so delightfully off balance. And she'd done it not by anything

that she had said, but by what she thought of as her
sphinxlike manner. Yet he'd handled himself well and carefully. He was not about to fall on his face over her, and she
admired that. She liked the thought of the challenge he'd
pose for her. Did he laugh much? she wondered. She hoped
so.

The visitor she expected was less controlled. He was
ardent and passionate and earnest. These were not unendurable
qualities, but they made a man easier to manipulate. And at
the moment, her manipulation of him made Jane Featherstone
feel a little guilty.

The truth was that, beneath her mask of mild softness,
beneath her pose of feminine helplessness, she enjoyed
being a spy for the Union—not because she admired the
Union cause, but because she enjoyed the excitement and
the danger.

Her parents—high-toned, slavery hating, and quite strict
disciples of Christ—had not provided her childhood with
much excitement. Her father had first been a merchant in
Nashville, at which he had succeeded, and then an insur-
ance salesman, at which he had not just succeeded but
prospered. Jane Featherstone had grown to despise the life
where all risks—both here and in the hereafter—were covered.

Now, having abandoned her parents and all the silliness
they had tried to impose on her, she felt more vital than
she'd believed possible. And yet she wasn't completely
comfortable or satisfied with every situation she found
herself in. For instance, as much as the Yankee captain
fascinated her, she didn't like betraying her coming visitor's
confidences to him.

Footsteps sounded on the stairs, and then someone knocked
softly at her door.

"Coming," she said. She rose and started to draw her
dressing gown about her, then thought better of it. She wore
nothing beneath the dressing gown because of the heat, but
she was not unaware of the effect glimpses of her bare body
would make on her visitor.

When she reached the door, she paused. "Who is it?"

she called softly, knowing perfectly well who was on the other side.

"It's Noah, Jane," the man on the other side said.

"Oh, Noah, my darling," she said as she opened the door. "I had so hoped that you would come. But I feared that you wouldn't be able to get away."

"As you see, I did," Noah Ballard said. Smiling, he stepped through the open door and took her in his arms.

"My dear, you're drenched," she said, stroking his hair, which was plastered to his head by the rain. Even though Noah was soaked, and even though her dressing gown instantly took on his dampness, she pressed her body close against him. "But I'm so happy to have you here," she went on in a whisper. "It must have been difficult to get away."

"Well nigh impossible," he said. "I've been running the trains for the general since . . ." He stared at the ceiling, trying to remember how long he'd been on his feet working. Failing, he threw his hands up and went on, "But the general passed by and saw that, in his words, I was about to fall on my face and drown in the mud. So he ordered me to go and get some rest." He pulled himself away from her, leaving his hands gripping her shoulders. "I knew that I would only get rested when I was with you," he said, smiling broadly.

She ran her eyes up and down his body. "But look at you! We'll need to clean you up! Give you a change of clothes! Make you comfortable!"

"But I have to leave soon," he protested mildly. "Don't bother."

"I will not have you in my bed before you are dry," she said imperatively, moving her fingers to the buttons of his tunic to confirm her point. "Come into my bedroom," she said.

He laughed, followed her into her bedroom, and helped her remove his clothes.

"Wait," she said when he was stripped to his underwear. She left him for a moment. When she returned, her hands were holding towels. Soon Jane was rubbing and stroking his back and shoulders, then his chest and stomach with one of the dry cloths. She was doing it slowly and with great tenderness, while he stood there quietly, enjoying her attentions.

"If I had aromatic oil now," she said, "I would anoint you with it, the way the women of the Bible do for their men."

"Oil? My God, no!" he said. "What you are doing is perfect just as it is. And you are perfect just as you are. No need for you to become a woman of the Bible for me." Then he added, "And this is all I'll have time for."

"You're not leaving so soon?" she said with a show of alarm.

"No. Hardly. It's all I'll have time for because I want to have more time for you. . . ."

When he said this, color came to her cheeks and she felt her breasts grow warm and flushed.

"Take your clothes off," he said. "Let me take you into your bed."

"No. Wait. Not yet," she said with a hint of coy delay. "I will brush your hair."

At first he shook his head, but after she went to her dressing table and returned with one of her hair brushes and proceeded to stroke Noah's dark, curly, very fine hair, he relented. Her attentions were too pleasant to resist. She drew the brush slowly from his hairline across the top of his head and down toward the back of his neck.

Finally she laid the brush down.

"Now," she said.

He brought his hand up to her throat and gently drew her dressing gown away from her shoulders, letting his eyes drink in her breasts and her smooth belly. Soon after, both of them were naked and in bed. This time he had a dry cloth in his hands, and he was stroking her breast and flanks with it, for she was moist, not from the rain, but from the hot, humid air.

Then it wasn't the cloth but his hands that were stroking her. She opened her legs and he slipped inside her, filling her. They began to move against and with each other, until she and then he cried out.

\*   \*   \*

Noah was standing before one of the windows in Jane's parlor, still unclothed. But since it was still as dark inside as it was out, he was sure his nakedness wouldn't be observed. No one was about, as the hour was late and the Union troops had stepped up the shelling. Meanwhile the rain had stopped, and there was a mist about. The shelling was indiscriminate, to make sure no Rebs slept, Noah guessed. There was no special effort to aim for specifically military targets; the entire city of Jackson was fair game for the Yankee gunners.

For a time shells were falling a block or two away on Yazoo Street. And then some were falling closer, close enough for him to think of taking cover.

He was aware that Jane had slipped beside him from the bedroom. He glanced at her. She was as naked as he was. Her presence next to him that way was unsettling.

"Aren't you frightened?" he asked with a gesture toward the outside and the shelling.

"Aren't you?" she answered with a sly, playful smile.

He took her hand and drew her close to him. "A little," he said, "to tell you the truth.

"I don't worry so much when they drop here and there, haphazardly. I don't take cover then. If one of those catches me, well, that's the roll of the dice. But when they start bracketing where I am . . ."

There was a large flash a few houses down, and both of them jerked back from the window.

"Like now?" she asked, still smiling.

"Like now," he agreed, and peered cautiously out.

But then, whatever governed the Yankee gunners turned their attention to another target and the shells started falling elsewhere.

Noah looked at her face, which was beaming excitedly.

"Am I right in thinking that you like this?" he said.

When she returned his look, he saw passion in her face. "I love it!" she said. She lifted her lips to his and kissed him. "I *adore* it!"

He shook his head. "Why, in God's name?" He was amused at her, but also perplexed. "It's not right, Jane—and it's not feminine."

"Why is it that only men are permitted to enjoy a battle?"

"I don't enjoy a battle," he said. "It's . . ." He didn't finish the sentence, for her hand had covered his mouth.

"Hush," she said. "You're about to tell me a piety, and I despise pieties. You're about to tell me that war is evil or hell or some damn thing like that. And then you will go on to tell me that some chosen men are born to sacrifice themselves on the altar of war for the sake of the common good. Blah. Blah. When the truth is that you love what you're doing now. I've never seen you so happily engaged as you have been during the past few days. Or so alive, Major Ballard."

"But . . ." he sputtered through her fingers.

She playfully inserted her fingers into his mouth.

She laughed and then withdrew them. He shook his head and laughed along with her, more out of perplexity and wonder at her than because he shared her amusement.

Exploding shells had lit fires in some of the buildings down the street, and in their light her body shone red gold.

"You *are* beautiful like this," he said, continuing to wonder at her. "But truly, my love, I'm not happy to see the city under siege and the shells falling. I suppose there's excitement in it, but the product of the excitement is the waste of women and children—and of good men, too. And of their livelihoods."

"Then why have you been standing so long by my window, my love?" she said, tossing her hair. "What's so fascinating?"

He thought on that a moment. Then he answered, "You know why I've been standing here—at least before you joined me. It wasn't because I'm fascinated by anything out there. I wasn't fascinated by anything until you joined me." She smiled at that. "It's because I'm worried. I'm worried about how many locomotives can dance on the head of a pin."

"What?" she asked, smiling.

"I have to move cannon and ammunition and tents and food and mules and fodder and God only knows what else—including a good portion of the men themselves. And I have one remaining rail line, with roadbed that's either partially destroyed or run down to near uselessness and equipment so ancient and worn out that it isn't worth repairing."

But I'll do it, he continued to himself, thinking thoughts that he did not feel he should express openly to her. And I'll do it well. I've put bridges up in a week after the Yanks destroyed them, bridges that originally took six months to build. And I've got locomotives running that everyone else said should have been scrapped.

"And now on top of it all, they've sent a captain of the Richmond Railroad Bureau who has orders to take over everything I'm doing."

"You don't like that?"

"Of course not!"

"You like doing what you think can't be done?" she laughed. "You wouldn't rather be back working on the fortifications?"

He laughed with her. "No, I like the trains," he said. "They've gotten in my blood. They almost seem alive."

"Like me?" she whispered deep in her throat, rubbing her breasts back and forth against the hair of his chest.

"Not like you," he said, reaching down and pinching her buttock.

"Oh!" she cried, flinching away from him. "You beast!"

"They'll never make a machine as bold and playful as you," he said.

"They better not," she said, closing in on him once again.

"You know?" he said, seeming not to notice her move. "I spent all day with the man—his name is Hottel—and at first I thought I'd despise him, I thought he was a fool. But after several hours with him I began to wonder. Maybe he isn't such a fool as I thought. And that makes it even harder for me."

"How so?"

"If he's a fool, I can treat him like a fool. But if he's competent . . ." Noah couldn't finish the thought.

"Truthfully, Noah, you don't want to give up your railroads?"

"No."

"Even if it meant returning to real engineering—as you've always said you wanted to do?"

"No. The South may not win at all," he said, uttering the thought that most southerners found unutterable. "We may lose even if we have the railroads working well, but we will certainly lose if the railroads aren't working well. And I aim to make sure mine are working well."

" 'Mine'?" she said. "Since when did they become yours?"

"Since I started this job for Joe Johnston. And since somebody has come to try to take it away from me. I intend to save and preserve my railroads the way Joe Johnston intends to save and preserve his army. And it's not just me, Jane," he added. "Railroads are in my family. My father would never forgive me if I failed at that."

She laughed after he said that, and he caught her eyes, but she instantly glanced away from him. "In fact, even more important than saving and preserving the army or the railroads, we'd best be thinking of saving and protecting you," he said. "And soon."

"I do want to go with you," she said, continuing to avoid his attempt to catch her eye.

"I can't do that," he chuckled, though he was perfectly serious. "I have no idea where I'll be more than two or three days from now."

"Really?" she asked. "Then perhaps I should stay and wait for you here."

"Out of the question!" he said. "Sherman will come into Jackson the instant Johnston leaves."

"So? He'll leave, too." She was grinning, teasing him. "And then you'll come back."

"Absolutely out of the question. I'll make sure you are on one of the first trains out this morning."

"But Sherman *will* leave, won't he? And then you will return."

"Yes. I don't think the Yanks will occupy Jackson for long. They have bigger fish to fry. But I can't guarantee that they'll leave much for us after they depart."

"Then I'll just wait," she said.

"Jesus Christ, woman! Why do you want to invite danger? Do you want to get yourself hurt? You know what Yankee soldiers are capable of, don't you?"

"No," she said doubtfully.

Before she could explain herself, there was a loud noise on the stairs.

"In fact, you need protection in any case," he said quickly, for it had dawned on him that a single woman was scarcely more safe from her own countrymen than from the northerners. He remembered that he had provided her with protection in May, the first time Sherman came to Jackson. "You have that pistol I gave you?"

"The Colt?" she said. "It's under my pillow."

"Keep it there until I get you on that train. Then take it with you in your handbag."

"If you say so."

The noise on the stairs was followed by a loud pounding on the door.

"Noah! Noah! For God's sake, come quickly!" It was Gar Thomas.

"Run into the bedroom, Jane," Noah whispered. Then, "Coming, Gar."

Even as Noah spoke, Gar continued pounding and shouting his name. Jane, meanwhile, moved swiftly into the bedroom, picking up her dressing gown as she went.

"Gar! For God's sake!" Noah shouted. "I'm coming. You've managed to wake the dead." As he spoke, Noah slipped on a pair of trousers, then a shirt.

After that, he unlocked and opened the door.

"How in hell's name did you know where I was, Gar?" he said.

"Jesus, Noah," Gar said, breathless and panting, "there's

scarcely anyone in Jackson who doesn't know where you are when you're not working."

"What do you want?" Noah said, not pleased to learn that he hadn't managed to keep his relations with Jane secret.

"There's been a wreck!" Gar said as soon as he was able. "A big one—two trains head-on. About twenty miles west of Meridian." He stepped back. "It's bad! The train going to Meridian was full of women and children and old folks. There've been many injuries . . . many deaths."

Noah looked at him, uncomprehending. Jesus Christ! he thought. Of all the worst possible things! Then he stepped back inside, signaling Gar to follow him.

"How many dead?" he managed to say.

Gar just shrugged and shook his head.

"When?"

"Four or five hours ago," Gar said.

"That long?"

"The Yanks cut the telegraph."

"A grand time for that," Noah said. "The most perfect time imaginable." Then: "How in God's name did a train get on that track coming *toward* Jackson?"

At that moment Jane Featherstone appeared. She was wearing the dressing gown again.

"Hello, Mr. Thomas," she said. And then to Noah, "I couldn't help but hear what you two were saying. I'd like to help, if I may."

"Miss Featherstone," Gar said, acknowledging her entrance. But he quickly ignored her, for Noah had all his attention.

"How did the train get on that track coming back this way?" Noah repeated.

Gar looked perplexed and guilty, as though he were somehow responsible.

"We'll have to get out there fast," Noah went on. And then he started firing questions as fast as they entered his mind: "How much damage was there? Is the track usable? How long will it be out? Can we get word to Meridian? What equipment will we need to fix all this?"

"Wait, wait, Noah," Gar said as soon as he could make himself heard. "I left Captain Hottel in charge while I came looking for you."

"Is he doing all right?"

"I think so. He's..."

"We'll need cranes, big ones, winches, blasting powder," Noah said, ignoring him. "Doctors, bandages. Jesus! And two or three hundred men!"

"He's taking care of that."

"But we don't know how bad it is. We don't know how much damage there is to the track. I'm more worried about the track than the train."

"As I was about to say," Gar said, "the captain was sending some people out to the wreck in a locomotive to check out what happened. We'll have a report from them pretty soon—if we're lucky."

"You left him to manage that?"

"He was doing fine," Gar said. "And somebody had to find you."

"Who's told the general?" Noah asked, closing his eyes in pain at the thought.

"I sent someone."

"Jesus!" He looked at Gar. "Have you heard anything back from him yet?"

"No, thank God."

"Yeah." Noah didn't look forward to his next encounter with Johnston.

There goes all hope of getting Joe Johnston's army out of here for several days, Noah thought.

"All right," he said. "Let's move. Help me with my boots, will you?" And then he looked at Jane. "And I want you packed by the time I get back. Hear me? Pack!"

Jane Featherstone nodded to indicate that she heard and understood him. But she didn't give him an answer one way or another. She was thinking that the young Yankee captain, Sam Hawken, would probably enter Jackson along with the rest of General Sherman's army. With Sam Hawken on her mind, Jane Featherstone wasn't sure whether she wanted to obey Noah or not.

# ♦ THREE ♦

Shortly before dawn on Friday morning the fifteenth of July, Tom Stetson met Sam Hawken at a ford on the east bank of the Pearl River. The ford was crowded with refugees and deserters. All of them were dazed, quiescent, anxious. Before Vicksburg some measure of courage and confidence had quickened most of these people, but courage and confidence had long since abandoned them.

Stetson and Hawken reached the Union lines just before breakfast. During their journey back to their own lines, the captain was more than usually quiet and pensive. It was Hawken who had engineered the rail catastrophe of the previous evening, and he was now heartsick over the loss of innocent lives. Sam could steel himself to accept the carnage and mangled bodies of a battlefield; it was a function of his job to do that. But he had brought terrible suffering to a great many women and children, and he could not ignore that.

Stetson and Hawken found General William Tecumseh Sherman engaged in his morning ablutions. The general, trousered and shirtless, was outside his tent, leaning over a wide porcelain basin on a washstand set up in front of a tree. As the two men approached, he was splashing his face and sandy-red hair with water.

Though he and Tom had ridden hard and long to reach the general, Sam had decided not to waste time cleaning up and changing. His information, he knew, needed to reach the general immediately. So both he and Tom were still wearing the Confederate uniforms they'd had on the previous day.

A mirror was hanging from a peg hammered in the tree. And when the general glanced into it, he smiled wryly at the sight of two men who were apparently Rebel officers, armed and dangerous, standing not fifteen feet from his unprotected back. A few feet behind the two men in gray was Charles Fleming, a captain, who was another of the general's aides. Fleming had escorted Hawken and Stetson to the general from the guard post where they had initially been detained.

"Are you going to demand my surrender?" Sherman called out as he started to vigorously towel his face. "Or should I say my prayers?" He paused a moment, then continued, darkly, into the towel: "If it's to be prayers, I have a feeling that God will not listen to me."

"Captain Hawken and Lieutenant Stetson reporting, sir," Sam Hawken said.

When Sherman turned around, both of his officers were saluting and standing at something resembling attention. But they were both too filthy, trail worn, and exhausted to make any sort of military impression. The general was pleased. He would not have wanted his two spies otherwise.

He was so glad to have them back that he walked over to the two men and clasped them warmly, one after the other, on the shoulders. "It's good to see you, Sam, and you, too, Tom," he said familiarly, even though terms of endearment did not come easily to him. Then he looked solicitously at each one. "Let's get some food and strong coffee into you while you tell me your tale."

Sam nodded wearily and murmured, "Yes, sir."

"Grand," Sherman said. "Tell it to me at my table." Then he glanced up. "Orderly?"

A corporal moved out of the shadows. "Sir."

"Would you help me with my uniform, please?"

"Yes, sir."

Ten minutes later Sam Hawken and Tom Stetson were seated at the general's field table, sipping hot cups of the strong coffee the general had promised. Hawken sat opposite the general, and Stetson was on the general's left. In front of them were plates of ham and potatoes and eggs and bread.

Tom, as he took his seat, noticed yet again how closely Captain Hawken and General Sherman resembled one another. Each man was lean, wiry, and above average height (though of the two, only Sam could truly be called tall), with nearly the same shade of sandy-red hair. Both of them were also seemingly indifferent to the spit-and-polish look favored by parade-ground military men. Even when he was wearing a clean and newly pressed uniform, General Sherman looked unkempt. Each man tended his beard irregularly and impatiently, and each had hard, dark eyes that seemed to look right into a man.

There were some differences, too. Important ones. The general was older by fifteen years, and Sam was livelier and quicker to laugh while Sherman often had the terrible, implacable air of a hero in a Greek play. He acted like a man hounded by a hostile divinity.

Hawken's usual good spirits were not going to be much in evidence this morning, however. He was too burdened by the weight of the events of the past night.

"Go ahead," Sherman said to Stetson, noticing that the young lieutenant was hesitating, "start. Dig in." Then to Sam, granting him one of his few meager smiles, "Now for your report, Sam. Give me the heart of it first."

Hawken waited for a time, collecting his thoughts. "All right, then," he said at last, "the heart of the matter is that Joe Johnston's original plan was to hold his line only until noon today. At least until last night, he intended to evacuate his forces beginning this morning." Sam closed his eyes and shook his head sadly while Sherman watched closely with growing concentration. "I believe I have managed to delay his withdrawal at least for another day or two, though I'm neither pleased nor proud to have done what I did."

Sherman puckered his lips and pulled at his wispy, much-tugged-upon beard. After that, he leaned over the table and propped his chin up with his hand. "Go on," he said.

"I obtained passage east on a train leaving Jackson early yesterday afternoon," Sam said. "Before I left, I instructed Tom to take the horses and wait at a spot we chose on the other side of the river. Then I went to Meridian and commandeered a locomotive and tender and . . ."

"Just like that? Single-handed?" Sherman interrupted, smiling his cool half smile and shaking his head.

Sam nodded, raised his hands palm out a couple of inches above the tabletop, and sighed. "A major usually gets listened to with respect," he said, "even in the Confederacy. And by the time anyone realized that I wasn't the genuine article, I had a pistol leveled at the locomotive driver and his fireman."

Sherman nodded, still smiling.

"What I found out from General Dodge's spy, Miss Featherstone—a clever and unusual lady, by the way—was that the Rebs intended to run three trains out of Jackson early in the afternoon, including the one I took to Meridian, and then three more before evening. That meant that if I could ram the locomotive I'd commandeered into one of the later trains, I could . . ." He stopped and shrugged, leaving the general the task of completing his thought.

"I understand," Sherman said. "And you cut the telegraph?"

"Tom took care of that while I was on the way to Meridian."

"Good," the general said with an approving glance at Tom Stetson. "And I take it all went well after you left Meridian?"

Sam nodded. "A few miles west of the town," he said,

"I had the engine driver stop. I ordered the driver and his fireman off the cab and bound and gagged them out of sight of the right of way. They're probably loose by now. But I knew they'd be no danger to me before I'd finished with their machine.

"I drove it to a bit of a rise, where I could see what was coming, and waited, throwing wood into the firebox from time to time to keep steam up. When I caught sight of the eastbound train, I set my engine going, lashed the throttle full open, and jumped off.

"Not long after that, the crash came, and," he shrugged, "locomotives and cars were strewn everywhere, crushed and broken." He looked at Sherman, sad-eyed, grieving. "They were passenger cars, General. It was women and children who were being carried out on that train. There must have been two or three hundred of them packed on it. Packed," he repeated.

Tom glanced at Sam, expecting to find tears on the captain's face. But to his surprise, none were there.

"You know, General," Sam said when he resumed, "when I was with the spy, Jane Featherstone, I considered my choices. I knew that something had to be done to keep Joe Johnston in Jackson as long as possible. I knew that the best thing to do toward that end would be a raid by a detachment of cavalry to break the railroad to Meridian. But I also knew that in order to make that work, I'd have to come back here through the lines and ..." He looked up. "There simply wasn't enough time."

"It wouldn't have worked anyhow," Sherman said. "If I'd had a cavalry troop capable of cutting that line, don't you think I'd have done it already?"

"Yes, sir, I know that," Sam said. "And I knew it then.

"And I also considered," he went on, "trying to set fire to a bridge. But they're all guarded too well for one or two men to be of much use. So, I decided to try the crash."

"And, as you say," Sherman said quickly, "it worked."

"It did," Sam said. "But, sir, those were not soldiers fighting a war against us. They were civilians trying to get the hell out of the way. Women and children, two or three hundred of them . . . !''

"Stop!" Sherman said sharply—it was an order.

"Sir," Hawken said, pulling himself together.

The general waited for a long moment, watching Sam closely and with sympathy. Before he spoke to Sam, he gestured for his orderly to come over. "Corporal," he said quietly when the orderly was bent over beside him, "I understand that it's too early in the day for whiskey. But as far as I'm concerned, these two men are still into last night. I'd therefore greatly appreciate it if you'd bring the captain and the lieutenant a good stiff jolt of the best stuff you can find."

"Right away, sir," the corporal said.

"Good," Sherman said, and nodded.

"Thanks," Sam said, glancing at Tom to confirm that he, too, was more than ready for strong drink. "I could use it."

"I know," Sherman said. He tugged at his beard again. "I know too, son, what's going through your soul. You've got waves of remorse crashing around within you because you killed all those people, and you believe in your heart that none of them deserved to die."

"It was women and children," Sam repeated helplessly.

Sherman nodded. "That's right, women and children and old men and old women. None of them deserving what you did to them. Isn't that right?"

"Yes, sir."

"Right. And I think very highly of you, of both of you, for taking it so hard. You're not only courageous, you're caring. And both those things make me pleased to have you with me.

"The cold, hard truth is that you did just exactly what needed to be done. All of it—yesterday, last night. Even the babies lying dead in their mothers' arms on your account." He looked hard at Sam. "Do you understand that?"

"Yes, sir," Sam said. Then corrected himself, "No, sir."

"I didn't think you would. Let me tell you some more of the cold, hard truth."

At that moment the orderly arrived and placed two three-quarters-full glasses of whiskey in front of Sam and Tom.

"Was I right in pouring none for you, General?" the orderly said.

"That's correct, Corporal," Sherman said. "But do be so kind as to leave the bottle in case my friends go dry."

"Yes, sir."

Sherman looked at Tom, and then at Sam. "First of all, what happened was an accident. Not the crash itself—you intended that—but the results. You had no way to know in advance that the train was full of noncombatants. Am I correct in that?"

"You are, sir."

"But—and here's a chilling and maybe frightening thought for you, Sam—I will maintain that even if you knew in advance who was on that train, you did the right thing. And I would have commended you in your knowledge of that as much as I have already commended you in your ignorance."

"I don't see . . ."

Sherman waved him to silence.

"You do not have some people in a war and some people out of a war. It's not that simple. Just because you've taken a solemn oath and a commission from Congress that proclaims you a fighter, you believe that sets you apart from everyone else in this country? Do you believe that that puts you in the war and it leaves those women and children out?"

"Yes, sir, I do believe that," Sam said. "Women and children and old people are not at war with me. I believe that."

"You and too many others," Sherman said under his breath. And then, a little louder, "I wonder how many deaths that woman Featherstone is accountable for."

"But she *chose* what she's doing."

"That's just my point, son. You're right, she did choose. And if she gets shot for her choice, it's her own doing. But in a larger sense, no one chooses war, neither her nor you, nor me, nor Jeff Davis, nor Joe Johnston. It comes on you like weather. We're all caught up in this flood—the soldier who shoots at me as well as the woman in Jackson who, after we march into that town, spits in my face or throws a pail of shit down on my head.

"Every man, woman, and child in this country is caught up in this war just as much as you or I, Captain. They can't refuse it or turn it back or escape it any more than they can escape the rain or the tide."

He looked hard at Sam again. "Got that, Captain?"

"I hear what you're saying, General," Sam said and took a long sip of whiskey. It was clear to Tom, from the expression on Sam's face, that Sherman's words had made no impact on him. He still looked as though he carried full responsibility for the deaths of dozens of innocent people. "But, General," Sam said, putting the glass down, "you're wrong."

Sherman jerked his head back, surprised at being contradicted. But then he smiled his grim little smile. He liked this young Texan; he was tough—tough enough to tell Major General William Tecumseh Sherman that he was wrong.

"I'm not wrong, Captain," Sherman said, still smiling, "but I'm not going to debate you, either."

"I wasn't planning to debate you, General. I'd never win." And for the first time that day, Tom Stetson noticed a smile on Sam's face.

"Well, my friend," Sherman said, "it appears that you are capable of displaying some sense. So tell me how you managed to get back here from that wreck near Meridian in so little time. As we've been talking, I've been running the distances and the difficulties through my mind, and what I've come up with doesn't calculate. Not unless you've come up with a form of transportation only angels have heretofore been capable of."

"I'm no angel," Sam said with the hint of a twinkle in his eye.

"That's just as well," Sherman said. "I don't need

angels here in Mississippi. So how did you get here so fast?''

"The two trains behind the one I hit stopped when the engine drivers saw what had happened," Sam said. "And so I went up to the last one and ordered him to back up to a turnoff and run on back to Jackson to let them know what had happened. When he came close to the place where I'd told Tom to wait for me, I had him let me off. And here I am.''

"Nobody knew that you'd caused the crash?" Sherman said. "You were just a major who seemed to have his wits about him?''

"That's just about it," Sam said.

"Damn!" Sherman said. "That's lovely! You might have a tender conscience, but you are surely as bold a man as I've come across. And you move fast. I like a soldier who moves fast.''

"Thank you, sir.''

"I think I might have to keep you as my aide.''

"Were you thinking of letting me go?''

"No, of course not. Though I hate to think what will happen when Grenville Dodge gets word of this escapade of yours. He'll want you for his own purposes. I outrank him, but he never let that stand in his way.''

"I'd like to stay with you, sir.''

"By all means. Meanwhile, what are we going to do next?''

"Attack," Sam said simply. "Joe can't move for at least two days.''

"Pleasant thought," Sherman agreed. "Unhappily, it's not so easy.''

"Why not, sir?''

"It's like this, young Sam. I'm not going to batter myself senseless against the fortifications General Johnston has created between him and me. I tried that five days ago and found the experience less than exhilarating.

"What I need to do is cross that river and close his flanks—if Joe will wait for me long enough to do that. I don't expect him to do that, with or without his trains. But if I can do that, then I will attack. But in order to do it, I need a pontoon bridge, and Johnston's friend General Forrest has deprived me of the one that was being shipped here for that purpose.''

"But what about the fords?"

"No good," Sherman said. "They're fine for a few people at a time, but useless for my armies."

"And that's all we can do then, sir, wait?"

"There's another bridge reportedly on its way. It may arrive on time—and safely. And meanwhile I've sent patrols up and down the river to search for boats. They might find enough of them. . . ."

"You don't expect that they will."

"Joe is nothing if not thorough. If there are boats, he has them stored somewhere in Jackson, or somewhere else that will make them unavailable to me." Sherman glanced at Tom. "I've been leaving you out of this discussion," he said. "I don't mean to ignore you."

"I don't have anything to add, sir," Tom said.

"That puts you in the same boat with General Parke and General Ord," Sherman said. "Don't fret about not having any ideas. You're in good company."

The general pulled his watch out of its pocket, glanced at it, then rose abruptly. "I have to meet with the two generals in fifteen minutes. Then, after long and careful discussion, they will agree with me that there's nothing to do but wait. Perhaps that bridge *will* get here."

He started to leave, turned abruptly, and said to Sam, "I'm proud of you, young Captain Hawken. And I'm damned thankful that you work for me and not for those people across the way."

"Thank you, sir."

"You too, Lieutenant."

The general again started to march away, but it was as if he didn't want to leave, for he turned and addressed the younger officer.

"Sam," Sherman said, his face relaxing from its usual rocklike stiffness, "I have letters from Ellen and Willy." Ellen was Sherman's wife, and Willy was his nine-year-old boy, whom he adored. "She has agreed to bring Willy and the other children down from Ohio for a holiday as soon as this campaign is done. Willy asks after you especially."

"I'd like to see Willy," Sam said. "Very much." Sam and Willy had got along famously during previous visits the Sherman family had paid the general. Sam had become something like Willy's official military guardian. It was a job that he welcomed rather than resented, for Willy was lively and bright.

"I'll make sure that both of you spend time together after they arrive."

"I'd like that, sir."

Noah Ballard, in shirtsleeves rolled past his elbows, stared in dismay at the wreckage of the first of the passenger cars on the Meridian-bound train that the pirated locomotive had slammed into. It had been quickly determined that a Union spy had been responsible for the tragedy. The first passenger car had followed five freight cars, and had preceded four other passenger cars. It had broken cleanly in two, after which the front half had caught fire. The fire had also set the freight cars ahead of it ablaze, and all these leading cars had been crushed together into a sprawling pile like logs in a bonfire. Among the passengers who had managed to crawl away from the fire and carnage of the initial passenger car were a fourteen-year-old girl and a three-year-old boy. Both had lost their mothers.

The boy had been taken away somewhere to be tended to. They should have done the same for the girl, but she was left to search in the knee-deep wreckage for her mother and two younger sisters.

Those who'd been sitting in the rear half of the broken car had had better luck. All but eight of them had survived, though most of the survivors had suffered various injuries, mostly minor fractures and breaks.

Noah had arrived on the scene fifteen minutes earlier, but already he had a pretty good idea about the magnitude of the disaster.

The problems were so large he didn't want to think about them.

There were footsteps behind him.

"Noah?" It was Gar Thomas. Next to him was Captain Hottel, his immaculate gray uniform neither creased nor blemished by his descent into the hell of the wreckage. Gar Thomas had none of the captain's special gift for cleanliness. He was covered with grease and soil, and the bald spot on top of his head was sunburned an angry red.

"Yes, Gar," Noah answered absently.

"How much are you going to try to save?"

"How much of what?"

"Of the equipment and rolling stock."

Noah thought about that for a few seconds. "Probably none of it," he said quietly.

"What do you mean?" Gar said.

"I haven't completely decided yet, but my inclination is to yank everything off the tracks and just leave it. The important thing is to repair the track."

"All of it?" Gar said, incredulous. "You've got ten percent of our total locomotion not fifty feet from where you're standing."

"It ain't locomotion anymore," Noah said, his voice calmer than he felt. "Or at least that's my guess; I haven't gotten up there to see it yet. But my guess is that even if we could repair it, it would take weeks. I don't have weeks. I don't even really have tomorrow." He looked at Gar and then at Hottel. "Leave it."

"For Sherman?" Hottel said.

"I want to get this wreckage off the track so we can use what we have left."

Gar was shaking his head. Old railroad man that he was, he deplored waste. There was much that was beyond salvage in the wreckage, but there was much that could still be used.

"Do you remember what I told you yesterday in General Johnston's parlor?" Captain Hottel said. "About the dozens of locomotives and cars that may still be available in Mississippi?"

"What about them?" Noah snapped.

"Look around you," Hottel said with a sweeping gesture. "You need that equipment now more than ever."

"That's right, Captain," Noah said with growing impatience. "I need them desperately. And I can try to summon up spirits from the vasty deep," he went on, "but will they answer?" He shook his head grimly.

"Aye," Hottel said, "but what about me?"

"You?" Noah asked, raising his brows.

"You might recall that you made a suggestion that I look into the matter."

Noah looked at him. He vaguely remembered something of the kind.

"I have time for that, since you have this business as much under control as any mortal could. There's no need for me here, and no one will doubt that the South needs those engines."

Noah couldn't help but notice that Hottel had skirted the issue of whether he was supposed to be Noah's superior, or vice versa. That was an issue Noah wanted to thrash out no more than Hottel apparently did. In fact, as Noah thought about it, the captain seemed to be implicitly admitting that Noah himself was in charge of railroads in this part of the world, and Noah liked that.

"And you are proposing that you will find them and bring them in safely?" Noah said with a sharp glance at Gar Thomas. Gar shook his head almost invisibly, to indicate that this was the first he'd heard of Hottel's idea. With an almost equally invisible nod, he indicated that he thought the idea was a good one.

"I'm proposing that I do what I can to determine the location of the locomotives that are still in northern Mississippi. If and when I locate them, we'll work out together how best to deal with them."

Noah nodded, deep in thought. "How long will you take?" he asked finally.

Hottel shrugged. "Who knows?"

"And what if General Sherman gets to them first?"

"Then it will do us no good," Hottel said. "My own

estimate, however, is that after Sherman takes Jackson, he'll have his hands busy enough with destroying the locomotives and whatever else he can easily reach. My hunch is, further, that the wrecked equipment is scattered about here and there. His people might find some of it, but not all. So that leaves it for us to wait for the Yankees to leave and then bring all the equipment in.''

"You don't just leave locomotives under rugs and in cellar corners," Noah said. "I've never heard of anybody mislaying a locomotive, much less *fifty* of the damn things.''

"That's right," Hottel said without losing a beat. "That's exactly what I've been thinking. You don't just lose track of fifty locomotives—unless you want to hide them.''

"Huh?'' Noah asked, incredulous. "Who'd want to hide fifty locomotives? Why? They don't do anybody any good unless they're being used.''

"If you owned a railroad during wartime,'' Hottel said slowly, "how would you like your equipment disposed of?''

"For the good of my country,'' Noah said instantly.

"You're not thinking like an owner, Major. You're thinking like a soldier. An owner wants his equipment—his expensive and well-nigh irreplaceable equipment—safe and undamaged. *Hidden*, in other words.''

"Jesus Christ!'' Noah said.

Hottel stared at him.

"And you think you can locate all of this stuff in a few days?'' Noah asked.

"No more than a couple of weeks,'' Hottel said. "There are not many places where you can hide a locomotive.''

Noah thought on that for a time, then said, "All right, fine, let's say you do find the equipment. What do we do with it once we have it? It's going to do us no good at all in Mississippi.''

"We'll cross that bridge when we get to it,'' Captain Hottel said.

Noah turned to Gar Thomas. "Gar,'' he asked, "how come you haven't said anything about these locomotives, assuming that Captain Hottel is right about them?''

"You're talking about other railroads than the one I know," he said. "But what he says makes sense. I like it."

"I like it, too," Noah admitted. "Let's think about it a bit while we attend to matters here." He glanced up the track as he spoke, toward the place where the battered remains of the locomotives lay. "Come on with me," he said, "both of you. Let's see what these things look like after that crash."

"You go on," Gar said. "I've got to go take care of that girl. She'll kill herself in that wreckage."

Noah turned his head to look at the girl whom he had watched a few minutes earlier rummaging through the debris. She now seemed to be thigh deep in charred planks and was digging furiously with a more or less intact board. Her reddish-brown hair was in knots where once there had been curls, and her face was smeared with grime.

"Leave her," Noah said.

"But no girl should be doing what she's doing."

"Leave her. She'll be all right," Noah said, his voice hard and bitter. "There's nothing that girl would rather be doing right now. That kind of passion can only be satisfied by going through with it."

"All right," Gar said unhappily.

"Come on," Noah said, and the three men went to look at the locomotives. Noah knew, when he saw them, that his original guess had been right. There was no sense trying to save anything. The best thing would be to get all the wreckage out of the way, repair the tracks, and get on to something else.

And then, not far away, they heard a scream.

"It's that girl," Gar yelled, breaking into a run. "I knew I shouldn't have let her stay there."

Noah didn't answer him, but he, too, started running fast enough to keep up with Gar. William Hottel came up behind.

The girl was still screaming when the three men reached her. She was holding her hands out in front of her, waving them back and forth painfully. They were white and charred and blistered, because she had plunged them inadvertently into a still-smoldering pile of rubbish.

"Damn it to hell!" Noah said.

"You'll be all right," Gar said, rushing up to her and taking hold of her shoulders. But the girl refused to budge. She just kept screaming. Then the three men realized that she wasn't screaming because of her burned hands, but because she had uncovered the bodies of her mother and her two sisters. Most of their clothes, save for a few blackened scraps, and much of their flesh, had been scourged away by the flames. And indeed, the three bodies were only recognizable because of their number and their size and vaguely feminine shape, and because they were huddled so tightly together.

When he realized what these figures were, it was all Noah could take. He doubled over and retched.

When he was done, he went over to Gar and the girl. Gar had his arms around her, trying to pull her gently off the wreckage. But the girl would have none of that. She was crying out fiercely, "Go 'way! Go 'way! Let me be! I don't want you here!"

"Leave her," Noah said.

"What?" Gar said with an incredulous look.

"Do as she asks," Noah said. "Leave her. She'll calm down later. She doesn't want you or me with her in her pain."

"But did you see those hands? Those are dangerous burns."

"I know. But leave her. Let's get going. We've got five hundred men waiting down the way for directions, and I want them to have this mess off the tracks by nightfall."

"But the girl?"

"Send one of the men over in a while to look after her and her kin."

"He's right," Captain Hottel said.

"I . . ." Gar said, wanting to refuse to obey. The girl had managed to jerk out of his grasp, and Gar, realizing that she was not to be subdued, backed slowly away.

"I'll tell you something," Noah said as they walked toward the waiting soldiers. "When I catch the spy who did this, I'm going to personally tear his heart out."

"You'll have any help you need from me," Gar said.

"And from me," Captain Hottel said.


General Joseph Johnston withdrew from Jackson, Mississippi, on the night of July 16. As soon as he was aware of the Confederate movement, General Sherman, making no effort to pursue the retreating Rebels, ordered General Frederick Steele to move his Nineteenth Corps into the city.

General Sherman himself entered Jackson on the morning of the seventeenth. He came in on horseback with his aide, Sam Hawken.

The two men rode down State Street as far as the state capitol. They dismounted there, leaving their horses in the care of the commander of the company that had occupied that facility, and entered the building.

While they had been on horseback, the general had been deep in thought, and Sam knew better than to intrude upon him. But once they were inside the capitol, Sherman broke his silence. They were then walking slowly under the great, elaborately decorated dome. It was fifty feet high, and surmounted by a great lanternlike skylight that let in the sun. Their hard-soled boots echoed on the marble, making a hollow sound. Sam and the general were the only occupants of the vast and imposing space.

"This is where Mississippi enacted the Ordinance of Secession," Sherman said softly. He was the first Union general to stand under that dome since the secession ordinance was enacted.

"Here?" Sam said, indicating the space beneath the dome.

"Not here, no. But in the house chamber over there." He pointed. "Mississippi was the second state to join the Confederacy. And now I'm taking possession of it for the Union."

"It gives you a kind of thrill, doesn't it?" Sam said.

"Yes," Sherman said. "It's another corner turned. It makes the war that much closer to being over."

How much more will we have to fight? Sam wondered. And how many more women and children will die?

Sherman, who at times almost seemed to read his mind, spoke to Sam's questions, even though Sam hadn't uttered them out loud. "But my guess is that there are going to be many more dead women and children before this is done. It's not going to be easy on the ones who aren't soldiers. It'll be just as hard on them as on the soldiers themselves.

"And the war has at least two more years of life in it, as well. I wouldn't want to be a southern woman during these times, I can tell you."

"Two more years, sir? You really believe that?"

"At least," the general said, shaking his head slowly, grim-faced. "You've seen the new way they're fighting. After they tried to hold Vicksburg and lost it, and lost an entire army along with it, they're not going to try to hold anyplace any longer. They'll move out anytime we come close, just the way Joe did last night. And then if we finally do manage to corner Joe and beat him, they'll go on fighting with irregulars—guerrillas. They'll melt into the hills and woods, and then this goddamned war could last until 1900."

Before Sam could reply to that, the general led him to a stairway that went to the third floor. "Come on," he said. Suddenly energized, he accelerated to a brisk pace. "Let's go upstairs. I want to get a high up view of this city."

"Yes, sir," Sam said.

"Do you think I should have gone after Joe Johnston, Sam?" Sherman asked. As he spoke, he bounded up the stairs two at a time.

"I truly don't know," Sam answered quickly, breathlessly trying to keep up with his commander. This was not quite the truth. If he had been in command, he would have kept the pressure on his opponents. But he was not about to try to second-guess Cump Sherman right now, especially when Sherman was using him as nothing more than a sounding board.

"It would be a great pleasure to fight him, God knows. He's the best they've got, I think, except for Bob Lee. But

Joe is not quick to fight. He trades for time and territory. He'll move and stop, move and stop, the way the Russians did when Napoleon invaded. And when he finally does do battle with me, it'll be at a place where I won't want to fight him.

"Maybe I should have kept him bottled up here."

"We tried our best, sir."

"Yes, we did," Sherman said. "You did especially, putting the railroad east out of commission the way you did. That was good work."

"It wasn't good enough," Sam said. "They had the railroad operating again eighteen hours later. I was shocked that they fixed it so fast."

"So I guess they've found people who can do for them what Grenville Dodge has done for us," Sherman said philosophically. General Dodge had been in charge of a number of railroad repair projects in Tennessee, and he had completed them sooner than anyone imagined possible.

They were on the third floor of the capitol now. Sherman tried several doors, but they were locked. Finally he found one that was open, and they entered the office that was behind it. Across the room there was a wide, tall window. Sherman went up to it and threw it open.

"There, by God," he said. "Now we'll see what we've got."

"Yes, sir," Sam said.

Sherman leaned far out the window, breathing in the air deeply and smiling. He stayed that way for perhaps three minutes, then he pulled himself back inside and looked at Sam.

"Quite a view," he said.

"It is that, sir," Sam said.

"Do you think you've had a chance to take most of it in?"

"I think so, sir."

"Then tell me what you've seen."

"A fair-sized Mississippi town," Sam said cautiously, not sure what he was supposed to have noticed. "Some of it damaged by shelling."

"You know what I see, Sam?" Sherman said. "I see prosperity."

"Prosperity, sir?" Sam asked. That was the last thing he would have considered. Jackson may have been a prosperous town once, before the war, but now it was drained and beaten, just like most of the rest of Mississippi.

"That's right, Sam, prosperity. And I see military capability."

"Yes, sir." Sam didn't see much of that, either, but he was not about to contradict the general.

"That's right, Sam: prosperity and military capability. And I can't allow either one of those to exist here. I can't permit it."

"Yes, sir."

Sherman gave him a hard, cold stare. "You look doubtful."

"No, sir, I just don't understand. This place looks pretty well beaten to me."

"Not enough. Not enough." His voice, as he spoke, was quiet, cold, and even.

"Do you know why I didn't go after Joe?"

"No, sir, I don't."

"Because even if I caught him and beat him, that wouldn't have been enough."

"Enough?"

But Sherman didn't hear Sam. His face was intent, rapt. He was conscious only of his own thoughts. "The Russians let Napoleon drive all the way to Moscow. They let him have the city. You know about that, Sam? Of course you do."

"I studied that at the Academy."

"Of course you did. Anyhow, they gave him the city, but they left him nothing to eat. No supplies. He had the capital city of the largest country on earth, and he had no supplies. His army starved. The retreat from Moscow was what finally did Napoleon in."

"Yes, sir."

"I bet you anything that Joe is thinking that he's just like the Russians, and that he can lure us deep into the interior of the country and let us starve."

"Yes, sir."

"But there's a difference. Things are just the opposite."

"What do you mean, sir?"

"We'll never starve. Not so long as we've got the rivers and the railroads—which we have now—And the navy to control the oceans and seashores.

"What Joe Johnston doesn't realize is that *I* will be the Russians and *he* will be the French!"

"Sir?"

"He can move around all he .wants, but there'll be nothing for him to eat—no forage for his animals, no ammunition for his weapons, no clothes to keep his men warm, no tents to keep them dry.

"The Rebs are going to *have* to quit, because they won't have anything left to fight with.

"That's why, when I see prosperity and military capability here in Jackson, I get to thinking—I'm going to destroy it."

"The prosperity, sir?"

"No, Sam. I'm going to destroy the town and everything useful around it. I don't give a damn anymore whether I fight a battle or not. I only need to execute my plans in several more towns and cities, and the South will fall like a dead tree in an ice storm."

Jesus! Sam said to himself. He was torn between admiration and revulsion.


"Francoise! Francoise!" Jane Featherstone called out. She had been sleeping; her head was buried in a pile of pillows, and not much sound escaped.

There was no reply.

"Francoise! Francoise!" she called out again, raising her head to allow her voice to carry. "Where are you, Francoise, you lazy thing?"

There was still no reply.

"I don't want any of your games, Francoise, you beastly, lazy thing. I want you in here this instant!"

That didn't do any good, either, for Francoise was miles

away, sent off on the last train out of Jackson, the train that Jane herself had promised Noah Ballard she would be on. But she'd had no intention of going on that train. Her interest in Sam Hawken had become so great that departure was out of the question.

All this, for the moment, she had forgotten, so she called out to Francoise a fourth time.

Jane raised herself on her elbows and glanced at the clock on the bureau.

She stared at the clock face for a long time, until at last the time sank in and she jerked herself up to a sitting position. "Twelve-fifteen!" she cried. "Oh, my Lord! It's afternoon! Francoise, where *are* you?"

And then she remembered. "Oh, God, she's not here. She's off in Meridian or some damned place. Why did I let you go, Francoise?"

Jane shook out her hair, threw the light sheet that had covered her toward the foot of the bed, set her feet down onto the floor, and lurched unsteadily over to the bedroom window.

Jane's disorientation was not due to a bad night. On the contrary, she was confused *because* she had fared better than she'd done in weeks. Since there'd been no northern artillery to keep her awake, she'd slept like a child from the moment she'd said good-bye to Noah. She was unsure on her feet because she had slept so deeply and dreamed so peacefully.

In the street below several Union soldiers were milling about, full of swagger and exultation and mayhem. They had been breaking into businesses and private homes, performing a kind of preliminary looting in preparation for the more serious pillage that was to follow. At the moment a few of them had dragged a large piano out of the home of a doctor whose house was diagonally opposite the building where Jane maintained her rooms. Two soldiers were pounding at the keyboard while another haphazardly tore out the strings with a crowbar and another chopped at the wood with an ax.

Other soldiers had found trunks and boxes full of clothes. They were rummaging through these, flinging the contents every which way onto the street, paying little attention to the clothes themselves. Jane concluded that they must be searching for jewelry or other valuables, or else they were simply engaged in a orgy of destruction because there was so much that was available to be destroyed.

There were a few local inhabitants about, for not everyone had chosen to leave Jackson. In fact, the majority of the town's inhabitants still stayed on. The few remaining women suffered gibes and taunts, and even physical harassment.

They should have remained indoors, Jane thought, until the soldiers stopped marauding.

Jane had every expectation that the occupaton would be orderly and sane, and that the Union soldiers would respect the lives and property of those they had conquered. In this she was wrong.

As these thoughts went through her mind, she heard loud, lewd noises from just below her window. When she looked down, she saw three or four very young men in blue staring up at her and shouting gleefully.

She realized then that she was wearing only her sleeping gown, and she drew quickly back from the window. Then she was aware of what the young men were yelling: "Don't go away, darlin'. We'll be up there for you before you know it."

"Oh, Lord!" she sighed as a feeling of alarm hit her. Her apprehension grew when she heard boots and shouting on the stairway.

Jane Featherstone was not a woman who panicked easily. Danger excited and energized her. She would never become helplessly faint, or breathless, or fall prostrate with anxiety as so many other women contrived to do.

Moments later she'd bolted her bedroom door and was once again in her bed, propped against her pillows, with the sheet drawn up. The Colt revolver that Noah had given her was beneath the sheet, next to her hand. She had checked it the night before. It was loaded and ready to fire.

She heard doors in the hallway being opened. The shouts became more urgent. And they became more urgent still when the men broke into her parlor. Finally they came to her bedroom door.

"Is this yours, honey?" the ugly, oily voice outside said. She didn't answer. Her hand was tight on the pistol grip.

"It has to be," another voice said.

They tried the knob, but of course the door was bolted. That restrained the men for only a short while. There was a crash. Then the largest of the four burst into Jane's room.

He stood in the middle of the floor and stared at her. Soon he was flanked by the others. "Hoooeee!" he hollered, grinning like a boy with a filthy picture. "*That* is what I came to Jackson, Mississippi, for. Have you ever seen anything so pretty?"

"I haven't," the youngest of them said. He could not have been more than fifteen.

"Now, what I have to say," the third one said, giggling, "is that this here woman is right where a woman had best be, laying in a big, soft bed. The only thing is, this one is wearing too many clothes, and her legs ain't spread. My pap always told me that a woman's place was to make things easy for a man." He looked at Jane. "Come on, honey," he said, "spread those legs."

The fourth one, who looked more than a little dim, just grinned.

"I'd like you all to leave my room," Jane said softly, steely-voiced.

"Did you hear that?" the big one said. "What did the lady say?" He was already fumbling with the buttons of his trousers.

"I said," she warned, her voice even more steely, "that I don't welcome you here. I want you to get out."

"Not yet, honey," the big one said. "That ain't possible."

"I want you out of here, now."

"Hear her beg," said the boy who had been giggling. "I just love hearin' Rebels beg."

The big one's trousers by now had dropped below his knees, and he was hobbling toward the bed.

"I'm not begging," Jane said. "I'm ordering."

They laughed at that. Their laughter was at once boisterous and full of innuendo.

"You've got until I count to five."

The laughter kept up, louder. "Until five?" the big one snorted. "And then what are you goin' to do, pretty woman? Huh?"

She pulled the Colt out from under the sheet and pointed it at his middle.

"I'll put a hole through you where this is pointing," she said calmly. "Now go. Fast."

"Wait a minute," the big one said, waving his hand vaguely in her direction, as though the gesture might somehow deter her.

"One," she said. Then quickly, "Two. Three."

On three, the youngest one and the dim one began to back away in the direction of the door.

"You ain't gonna use that thing, are you, miss?" the big one said. "You don't know how."

"Four."

The older boy twisted indecisively toward the door, where the other two were exiting, then toward the big one. He was searching in his mind for some action to take, but what that action was eluded him.

"Five."

"You crazy or something, lady?" the big one screamed, for the muzzle of the revolver was leveled precisely at the spot where his stomach emptied into his intestines.

Hobbled by his trousers, he made a lunge at the bed. The gun made a sharp crack, and then the big man staggered backward. The noise was loud, and Jane had to shake her head to clear her ringing ears.

After a brief moment, she was alert again, and she looked at the man she'd shot, then at the others. The big man was now on his knees, swaying with pain. There were sobs and whimpers coming from his mouth, but Jane hardly noticed. The young one and the dim one were at the door. When they saw her looking at them, they turned white and fled down the hallway to the stairs. The older boy was staring open-mouthed at the big one. Blood was spreading over the front of his shirt. When he had launched himself toward Jane, he had lowered his body, and the bullet had punctured a lung.

"He's dyin'!" the boy managed to say.

"I know that," Jane said, calm and cold. "Now you move on out of here."

"Do you know what you've done? He's dyin'!" He was now squatting next to his friend, who had by this time crumpled down on the floor. Frothy blood was foaming out of the big man's mouth.

"Go." As she said this, she waved the gun slightly. It was heavy, and she had to use both hands.

"But he's dyin'!" The boy's hands had begun to paw at the big man's face. The pawing had no effect.

"Should I care about that?" she yelled. "Do you want me to care about him? Go!"

The boy had for the most part been in shock. But now the shock turned to rage, and he leapt up and spun toward Jane.

"You ain't goin' to . . ." he cried, but the firing revolver blotted out his voice.

He stared. The bullet had missed. "You . . . !" he whispered hoarsely.

"Out!" she said, and fired again. This time the bullet hit him in the fleshy part of his thigh. Despite the wound, he managed to drag himself out of the room and down the hall.

He was lying collapsed at the head of the stairs when a lieutenant and a sergeant who had heard the gunfire rushed up. Their own pistols were raised and at the ready when they burst into Jane Featherstone's bedroom.

But when they saw Jane sitting quietly in her bed, the pistol laid at her side, the big man, not dead yet, crumpled in a heap on the floor, all of their excitement and military training seemed to drain out of them.

"Oh, my God," the sergeant said.

Then the lieutenant raised his pistol before him, almost as though he were raising a cross as protection against a vampire. "What happened?" he managed to ask.

"What's it look like, Lieutenant?" Jane said. "Four men tried to violate me. I protected myself."

The eyes of both the lieutenant and the sergeant were locked on the dying man—on his wound and on the trousers that had fallen around his ankles.

"She's tellin' the truth," the sergeant said.

"I know she is," the lieutenant said. "But I don't know what the hell to do about this." Neither of them moved to help the man who was dying. Then they tore their eyes from him and turned their attention to Jane. "And I don't know what to do about her, either."

Jane was breathing hard and her hands had begun to tremble, but she managed to conceal her distress from the two soldiers.

She lay one hand on top of the other to calm them, then took a deep breath and spoke. "Lieutenant," she said, "I'd like to get dressed. And after that, I would appreciate it if you would escort me to Captain Hawken."

"Huh?" the lieutenant said.

"Captain Hawken is General Sherman's aide. He knows me. I'd appreciate it if you would take me to him."

"I can't do that," the lieutenant said. "You've just killed one of our men. We have to take you for charges."

She smiled sweetly. "Take me to the captain, please, Lieutenant, and I'm sure he will work out all the details."

"Even if the captain is an acquaintance," the lieutenant said, "I'm afraid I must go through the proper procedures before . . ."

"Um, Lieutenant Gregg," the sergeant interrupted, "maybe she has a good idea. If she is a friend of General Sherman's aide," he said pointedly, "then maybe he'd be the best one to iron out this mess." The sergeant was an old noncom in the regulars who knew the ropes. He knew when to drop a disaster into someone else's lap. The lady had given him the hint he needed about whose lap to drop this one into.

Jane gave the sergeant a radiant smile.

Happily, the lieutenant managed to catch on to the sergeant's drift. "I think you have a point, Sergeant," he said. "Let's do that." Then to Jane, "How soon do you think you can be dressed and ready to move?"

"I'll be no more than twenty minutes," she said. "Would you wait for me in the sitting room?"

"Of course, ma'am," he said.

"Thank you."

* * *

It took the lieutenant and the sergeant more than two hours to locate Captain Hawken, and another hour to arrange a meeting for Jane Featherstone with him. But, for Jane's purposes, the wait was worth it. By the time she was ushered into the captain's presence, the Union soldiers and officers who were dealing with her were treating her with deference. The confidence in her voice when she spoke of her connections with the captain and with General Dodge convinced her escorts that she was worth treating with care.

It was quite clear that no one was going to find the slightest fault with her or her action in shooting the boys who had assailed her.

And the initial meeting with Captain Hawken accomplished everything that she wished it would. When she finally was ushered in to him, he was setting himself up in the governor's mansion, where Sherman was placing his headquarters. Hawken listened to her account of the attempted rape, nodded curtly, and went into the general's rooms for a few moments. When he returned, he had papers for her that entitled her to special treatment by the Federal forces. And, he said, the body of the man she had shot would be removed from her rooms as soon as men could be found to do it. The other soldiers who had broken into her rooms would be appropriately punished, and he hoped she would be able to forget the incident. What the boys had tried to do to her was a criminal act, and it was unforgivable. But it had happened in the heat and madness of war, which might, he hoped, lessen the impact of it in her memory.

In fact, she had every intention of keeping the memory of this day alive forever—she had never felt so exhilarated.

The best part of her meeting with Hawken came at the end, when he agreed to call on her that evening. And, yes, he'd be delighted to dine with her.

Hawken, in accepting, had the foresight to offer her food, since there was scarcely anything to be had in Jackson. She accepted his offer with more than pleasure. She hadn't had a good meal in weeks.

Hawken had told her he'd arrive at eight. But he didn't appear until after nine. Earlier, a squad of soldiers had removed the body and even made some generally ineffective efforts to clean up the mess. She managed to conceal most of the remaining damage, however, by the artful placement of a few throws.

There was a dark bloodstain on the bedroom rug, though, that no amount of soap and water would remove. It did not displease her greatly that that was the case.

She wore a simple dress of blue linen with puffy sleeves. It wouldn't do, she decided, to wear anything finer. And besides, she had learned that simple styles were often more fetching—and becoming—than elegant and fashionable attire. She wanted the captain to pay attenton to her and not her clothes.

It was just as well that he was late, at least as far as her cooking was concerned. Jane missed having Francoise there to do the work. Nevertheless, in spite of her lack of confidence at the stove, the pork, black-eyed peas, sweet potatoes, and greens turned out perfectly edible.

Indeed, Sam seemed to hardly notice what he ate, and she flattered herself to think that that was so because he was noticing her.

Over the meal their conversation was spare, but easy and casual. He seemed to find peace in eating a quiet meal, and she enjoyed attending to him. It wasn't very often that Jane Featherstone played hostess, a lack that she regretted. So she relished keeping Sam's plate and glass filled, and she kept a demure smile on her face, and, with growing awareness, she knew that he found her silence attractive.

After supper he stood for a time before the piano, fingering the keys, making random sounds. As he did so, he contemplated her conservatory diploma.

"You must play well," he said finally, in his soft but firm voice.

"I'm competent," she said.

"You must play for me, then. Will you, later?"

"Yes," she said, "I'd be happy to."

Through the windows she could see that many of Jackson's

buildings were in flames. Sherman's men were relentlessly going about their business of destroying the town. But all this hardly impinged on her mind, even though the red and orange glow flickered through the room. She couldn't tell whether it impinged on his.

She placed herself at one end of the dark red, threadbare love seat. "Come," she said, "will you sit next to me?"

For a moment he considered it. Then, with a slight nod of assent, he said, "It would be a great pleasure to sit next to you."

"You said you are from Texas?" she asked after he was seated.

"That's right," he said. "When did I tell you that?"

"Three days ago," she said, "during your first visit."

"You have a good memory."

"Not actually. There are few Texans wearing your uniform."

He had no reply to that.

"Tell me," she said, inclining her head toward him, "why are you not fighting for the South?"

He smiled. "I don't like to be on the losing side," he said.

"That sounds like an answer you've rehearsed," she said.

"What do you mean?" he said.

"It's easy to say, and it's glib. But do you really mean it? Don't you have family in Texas? Attachments?" There was a flicker of distress on her face. "You are not married, are you? I'm right in assuming you have no wife?"

"No. Nothing like that. I have no family to speak of. My mother and father died some years ago from cholera. I was their only child."

"I'm sorry to hear that," she said automatically.

"So that has left me with no attachments—except to the army, I suppose."

"And so the army is your only family?"

"Something like that. The closest thing I have to brothers are some of the men who were with me at the Academy."

Somewhere in her mind Jane recalled that Noah Ballard had been at the Military Academy at about the same time that Sam was, but she thought it prudent not to mention that to Sam right now.

"Is that why you wear the uniform you wear?"

He shrugged. "When secession came, I was in the Second Cavalry in San Antonio under Lee. He was ordered back to Washington then. They had hoped to offer him a high command in the Union Army."

"I remember that."

"Right. He refused. He would only fight for Virginia. It happened I was ordered to acompany him, and on the ride from San Antonio to Corpus Christi, he and I had occasion for long talks."

"About who to fight for?"

"That's right. He told me he expected I would fight for Texas. He just assumed that."

"But you had other ideas?"

"It's not Texas that holds me, Miss Featherstone."

"Jane," she said.

"All right . . . Jane."

"It's not Texas that holds you?" she urged.

"No," he said.

"What holds you?" she asked.

"I was born in Texas, but I'm not a Texan. My home is the West. That's where the future is.

"Have you been to California, Jane?"

"No, of course not."

"But you will go there. It's part of your arrangement, I recall, with General Dodge."

"It's his idea to protect me, but I have no reason to do that. I like what I'm doing now."

"It's the future, Jane. California and all the territory between here and there. The railroads will make that land great. If secession fails, North and South, united, will become a great continental power. It will dwarf Britain and France and all the other little tin-pot nations in Europe.

"If the South can stay separate, then this continent will end up a couple of dozen countries, just like Europe."

She caught his eye, drew a long breath, then said, "You think a lot, don't you?"

"No. Not really. I don't have time to."

"Oh, no?" she said with a laugh. "Your words this evening say otherwise."

"I don't often get asked such probing questions."

She laughed again. "Now are you glad you made the choice you made?"

"Glad? What do you mean?"

"Did you expect to burn and pillage cities, make women and children homeless?"

"I don't like it," he said. "But the war is not my doing."

"Nor the orders to make sure that central Mississippi starves."

"What are you trying to say?"

"I'm asking whether you enjoy taking part in General Sherman's sacking of Jackson."

"No," he said. "But don't think that I disapprove of his actions just because I don't like them."

A fascinating idea flashed in her mind. I wonder if he is the one who caused the train wreck three nights ago, she thought. He is certainly a likely suspect.

She toyed with the idea for a time, and even thought of asking him outright, but decided against it. Too risky.

Later, perhaps.

"Enough of me," he said. "I'd like to hear about Miss Jane Featherstone—conservatory graduate, music instructor, beautiful woman, smart, unmarried spy. That's quite a pedigree. I want to hear more about you, Miss Jane Featherstone."

She managed a shy smile. "Oh, really. I don't know."

"You can do better than that."

Jane had in mind a story she had told before, a story of failed love, of marriage promised, then abandoned, followed by a life of loneliness and spinsterhood. But she decided that that story would not capture Sam Hawken's sympathy. It was too ordinary for him.

Unfortunately, she couldn't then imagine a biography better suited to his particular needs. Her aim had been to unsettle him, but she was aware that the longer they were together the more he was unsettling her.

"No, really," she said, "I'm not at all interesting. There's hardly any part of me you would want to hear about."

"You don't part with much of yourself, do you, Miss Featherstone?"

"But do let me play for you," she said, brightening. "And I can sing, too . . . or at least so I'm told."

Before he could reply, she was on her feet and offering him her hand. "Come," she said. "Sit next to me by the piano."

"The stool won't hold more than one," he said practically, letting her hand dangle untouched in front of him.

"Don't worry," she said. And then she skipped over to the piano. Beside it next to the wall was a straight-backed chair. She lifted that and moved it next to the piano stool. "There," she said after she was done. "Now come," she beckoned, flashing her most fetching smile.

"All right," he said.

When she was on the stool and he was seated beside her, she turned to him, letting her hand rest lightly on his forearm. "Do you know Chopin?" she asked.

"I've heard a little."

"Do you like it?"

He nodded.

"Then I'll play a nocturne. I love his nocturnes."

She placed her hands on the keys and began.

As Jane Featherstone played that evening, she knew that she had never played better, even at her graduation recital at the conservatory. She took him through three Chopin nocturnes with fluid charm, grace, and finesse, after which she sang some Foster songs. And then, noticing that he seemed to be taken with her performance, she switched to something stirring and passionate by Beethoven.

And when the piece forced her to lean over him to reach the keys of the upper register, her arm kept grazing his in a most pleasant way.

Toward the end of one especially ravishing climax, her

hands fell still and she lifted her face to his and found his lips. His hands moved to her shoulders, then drew her to him.

Jane sighed deep in her throat.

Sam Hawken drew his face away and laughed!

"Oh!" she blurted, shocked, wide-eyed. "What . . . ?"

"Up with you, girl," he said, rising abruptly and leaving her to take care of her dignity the best way she knew how.

He laughed again when she sprawled on the floor.

"What . . . ?" she cried again, in pain this time.

"You are quite the performer, Miss Jane Featherstone," he said.

"I . . . you . . ." she said, dazed.

"Do you need help?" he asked, bending down and dropping his hand hard upon her shoulder as he smiled infuriatingly.

"No!" she said furiously. "I don't need any help."

"Somehow I didn't think you would want my help. But still, on your feet, girl. You look damned silly on your ass." His grip on her shoulder was like a vise. He drew her to her feet by force.

"What's this all about?" she snapped, once she was standing. Then she added, "You bastard!"

"Hi ho!" he said with another of his infuriating laughs. "The maiden doth emit a word from the gutter."

"Bastard!" she yelled, eyes blazing.

His hand, she realized then, had not left her shoulder. Now the other hand was on the other shoulder and he was dragging her close to him. Before she could begin to consider what that meant, his lips were hard against hers. She softened, melted.

"I have a message for you, darling Jane," he said.

"What's that?" Her breathing was shallow and fast now. And it quickly became faster and shallower, for he was very close to her, so close that his body was just touching hers.

"You've tried to play me with all the skill you use on your piano. And I have to admit that you've been pretty good at it. But I want you to know that I'm not to be played with. I'm not one of the men you use as toys."

"I don't understand," Jane said, and as she said it a single tear welled at the corner of each eye and began its journey down each cheek.

"Of course you understand, my darling maiden, and perfectly."

"How could you," she said, starting to gather herself together now, "after we ate such a lovely meal together—and after I played for you and sang for you—how could you," she repeated plaintively, "turn on me so?"

"Well, that puts an interpretation on it now, doesn't it? It's strange, my sweet maiden, but all the time I had the distinct impression that all of those beautiful preparations were leading up to a seduction."

"I don't know where you got *that* idea," she huffed.

Laughing, he scratched his head with theatrical ostentation. "Oh," he sighed stagily. "Then I must have been totally mistaken about you. I had begun to suspect that you were leading me—delightfully—to your bed. But I couldn't have been right about that, my maiden, now could I. Good people would have us believe that no woman seduces a man—at least not since Eve. I was beginning to believe otherwise, but I must have been wrong." With that, he flourished an imaginary hat at her and bowed deeply. "At least about you, my dear maiden," he added at the perigee of his bow.

"Don't torment me, Sam," she said. Tears were flowing copiously by now.

"But you deserve it. You deserve worse."

"I . . . I . . ." she stammered.

"Shall I go now?" he said.

"No!" She didn't want him to leave; she needed him now more than ever.

He smiled. "Then I'll stay awhile longer," he said.

"Why do you need to hurt me?"

"I don't need to hurt you, Jane Featherstone. I need not to be played with and used. I told you that. I won't have you gaming with me the way you play with the men you seduce information from."

"What do you mean?"

"You know what I mean. It didn't take me long to realize what made you such a formidable spy."

"That's a lie," she whispered, turning away from him. "And it's cruel to suggest it."

He took her face in his hands and forced her to look at him. "Then shall I leave?" he asked.

"No," she admitted. She wanted him to stay, now more than ever. God, how she wanted him to stay!

"All right, then," he said, releasing her.

He turned to the threadbare love seat, and she approached him there, her face soft, her eyes wet and glistening.

"Now will you come into my bed?" she asked him, extending her hand.

"You still want that?" he asked.

"I want that very much," she said.

# ◆ FOUR ◆

*Kemble Island, Georgia*
*July 25, 1863*

"I see it! I see it now! There! There it is!" Miranda Kemble called out with a voice full of joy and anticipation. "Ariel! There! Lam, do you see?"

"Yes, yes, dear, I see it, too," Miranda's sister Ariel Edge said. As befitted her position as a wife and mother, Ariel was more sober voiced than her sister. But she was nonetheless every bit as excited as Miranda.

The two sisters were standing at the prow of a small sloop. Standing with them were their brother, Lam, and Ariel's five-year-old son, Robbie. The sloop had just rounded a bend of the Kemble River, which was a small estuarial offshoot of the Altamaha. Beyond the bend lay the reason why the younger Kembles were standing at the sloop's prow: Kemble Island.

The two young women were wearing light summer dresses. Miranda's was peach, while Ariel's was the palest green. Ariel had covered her head with a wide hat to protect her face from the sun, but Miranda was hatless, wearing instead a band of sherry-colored ribbon to keep her long bangs out of her eyes. In honor of the occasion, Robbie was dressed in a new white sailor suit made especially for him by his grandmother Edge.

Miranda, Ariel, and Lam's father, Pierce Kemble, sat on the deck a few feet behind this group. As had become his custom, he was by himself, sitting with his back propped against the mast. For most of the journey, he had kept his own company, and his dark expression made clear that he would not welcome an invitation to abandon his solitude and join the others even though they were at this moment so very near celebrating the much longed for goal of their little voyage.

Farther to the stern was Uncle Ashbel, who, contrary to his usual practice, had stationed himself near the stern, apart from the rest of the family. He lounged against the rail near the tiller, chatting with the pilot.

Aside from their mother, who was spending the war in London, and Ariel's husband, Ben, the entire family was on the sloop. For the first time since the start of the war, they were all together, and for the first time during the war they were all visiting the family plantation on Kemble Island.

And, oh, what a ravishing day for the journey! The sun was high and bright and not too hot. The air was clear and shimmering and smelled of the sea. The low, flat tidal islands they glided by were a green and golden paradise that war had seemingly left unstained.

When he heard his niece's cry of delight and saw her raise her arm to point, Ash Kemble jumped to his feet and let out a shout: "Hey-Ho!" And then he bounded quickly forward, pausing momentarily beside his brother in order to urge him to join the others at the prow. Pierce, however, was not to be moved from his private thoughts. He declined with a smile that might, in a pinch, have been called polite. And so Ash went on ahead, laughing and puffing away at the long black Cuban cigar that was clamped in his teeth and which jutted out of his face like a cannon. Cocked back on his head was a creamy, wide-brimmed Panama hat. His white linen shirt was loose, with the neck open wide and the sleeves rolled up to his elbows. His trousers were white,

too, and baggy. He was the resplendent image of a man at
his ease.

"Well, well, well," he said when he had joined the
others at the prow. "So there it is after all these long years.
And every bit as heavenly as when I last saw it."

As he spoke, Miranda was pointing ecstatically at the
main boat landing of the island. Above it and beyond the
dike, she could also make out the plantation mansion,
Kemble House. Standing at the landing, waiting patiently,
were a half-dozen slaves who had been warned of their
coming. When they saw the sloop, the slaves started to
wave and cheer.

Lam looked pleased to see that. "Ah," said Lam, "it's so
nice to see them again. And it's nice to see that they're glad
we're visiting." The cheer in Lam's voice, at least to
Miranda's ears, seemed a bit forced; it was more like relief
than joy.

But the relief was for a good reason. This part of the
coast had been under Federal control since close to the
beginning of the war. A powerful force of the Union South
Atlantic Squadron was based not five miles away on Saint
Simon's Island. And a settlement of over five hundred freed
Negroes, a consequence of Lincoln's Emancipation Procla-
mation earlier that year, had been set up on the same island.
The dwellers in the settlement sold labor and produce to the
base.

Like the Kemble plantation, most of the sea-island plantations had been abandoned by their white owners when the
navy arrived. So Lam was understandably apprehensive
about the loyalty of the servants.

"Of course they're glad to see us," Ariel said. "Why
shouldn't they be?"

"Oh, look!" Miranda cried. "There's Luna and Dorcas.
Wave, Robbie. We've told you all about Luna and Dorcas.
You must know them by now almost as though you'd
actually met them." Luna and Dorcas were both revered and
intractable slave women well into their seventies or eighties.

Obediently, Robbie waved.

"He's too small. He can't see," Ariel said, looking down

at her small son with concern. "Show Robbie, please, will you, Lam? Will you be a darling and lift him up?"

"I'd like nothing better," Lam said. "Up you go, my brave young man," he said, and swung the boy up over his head and set him down on his shoulders, straddling his neck. "There!" he said to Robbie. "There it is. Kemble Island, the finest and loveliest place in all the wide world!"

With a sharp crack, swiftly followed by rumbles and slaps of canvas against canvas, the mainsail was lowered. And soon after that, the sloop warped into the landing.

The inspiration for the voyage to Kemble Island had sprung from Miranda. It had been brewing in her imagination for many months, and that's where it would have doubtless remained were it not for the miraculous mixture of luck, persistence, and design that allowed her to pull it off. Somehow she convinced Ariel, Pierce, and Lam to come together even though their lives had been so profoundly separated by geography and circumstance.

After she sold her father, her brother, and her sister on the possibility of the reunion, she then had to sell them on its locale. When the subject was first broached, everyone but Miranda herself imagined the gathering would take place in Savannah, or maybe Charleston. No one save Miranda had dreamed they could go to the island, even though it was the one place in all the world they all wanted to visit. Since the area was occupied by the Yankees and by renegade Negroes, a visit to the island had seemed out of the question. Miranda, however, would have none of their fears. If they were all going to come together, then they would do so on Kemble Island. And though she was only twenty-two, she was strong-willed enough to wrestle her dreams into reality.

And yet, though she was courageous and determined enough to get her way about the visit to Kemble Island, Miranda knew in her heart that the trip was as risky and mad as it was dazzlingly wonderful. But she did not confess any of her private apprehensions to her father or her sister, who would have been frightened by them. Lam was no less aware of the dangers than Miranda, but he, too, kept silent.

And Ash was—well, Ash. No one had expected him to arrive in Georgia when he did, but somehow he had sensed he was needed at home.

Though Miranda hadn't seen him in years, he remained as infuriatingly savvy about her tricks and stratagems as ever. It wasn't long after their first embrace of greeting when he took her aside and told her that only madmen would sail into those islands. Every one of them, he told her sternly, was a nest of wild and raging free men—or else ferocious Union naval personnel. Then he laughed and kissed her and encouraged her not to lose heart. They would sail to Kemble Island, by God, and he would let no one and nothing stand in their way.

Miranda welcomed Ash's encouragement. His words and his warmth *did* strengthen her resolve. But still, there was never any danger of her losing heart, for the engine of her will was fueled out of sources that were deeper and more central than even her attachment to the island, or her love for her family. What most deeply burned in her and moved her to undertake the journey was her anxiety about her father.

Unlike the other Kembles, Miranda had not welcomed secession and war. As far as she was concerned, the continuation of slavery and all the other myths of the Great Cause were so much silliness.

And yet, when the war did come, she turned down a chance to leave Georgia and travel with her mother to London. Before she sailed for Europe, Fanny used all her considerable powers of persuasion to encourage Miranda to sail with her. But Miranda refused her—not because she *wanted* to stay, but because someone had to take care of her father.

That argument, understandably, carried little weight with Fanny Shaw. Fanny leaned on Miranda harder than she'd ever leaned on her daughter before, but Miranda, in spite of her youth, was every bit as forceful as her mother. She wouldn't budge. Pierce needed her.

Pierce himself was a man with little talent for enduring hard times. He was thus not equipped for dealing with all the crises the war brought down on him. His chief talent, in fact, was the pursuit and capture of beautiful women. His greatest skill was for extravagance and the squandering of wealth. His profession was speculation.

Knowing this, Miranda understood that he couldn't be left to his own devices.

At the beginning of the war, Miranda lured Pierce to Kemble Island, where she hoped to keep him peacefully out of trouble. But as soon as their position there became untenable, he lured her to Charleston, where he managed to lose $50,000 on failed blockade runners—very nearly all that he had left from the proceeds of his great slave sale in 1856. He then speculated in land in Georgia just as land values began to plummet, and factories in Tennessee just before the Yankees overran them. He traveled to New York after that in order to arrange for the smuggling of weapons to the South. He was arrested there and placed in confinement for a year at Fort Lafayette. He was released when he gave his parole not to work again for the South.

Miranda, meanwhile, had settled near Atlanta on one of the Kemble properties, Raven's Wing, a cotton plantation. The property, happily, had been willed to her and not to her father. As a result of her grandfather's foresight, the skill of his lawyers, and the resolve of the trustees of the estate, Pierce was unable to obtain title to it.

After his release from prison, Pierce made his way south. After a struggle, Miranda persuaded him to join her at Raven's Wing. "I can't live like a child or a refugee on the property of my own daughter, Miranda," he wrote her. "If I am to live with you, it must be as your *father*," by which she knew he meant "master." She refused his demands, and he refused to live with her until it became clear that he had nowhere else to go. By the time he arrived at her home, he managed to forget—or else ignore—the galling fact that he had to live on property that was his daughter's and not his own.

Running a cotton operation the size of Raven's Wing was no easy task for a woman, especially a woman as young as Miranda, but she handled it and was even able to make the property turn a small profit.

Pierce was harder to handle. The limits placed on his life by the war and his personal failures left him angry and frustrated. Since he was powerless to maintain his customary extravagance, he could not busy himself with his usual speculations. To make things worse, few of the women he customarily pursued were available to his charms. His speculations were limited to wagers upon the fall of playing cards, and his conquests of women came only with those whom he could purchase for a night.

None of the activities necessitated by his reduced circumstances could satisfy Pierce. And soon this lack of satisfaction made him despondent. As her father's spirits sank, Miranda's fears for him grew.

Nothing that she had tried to do for him had had any effect—until she engineered the trip to the island. She hoped that the reunion would be the medicine he needed to snap him out of his melancholy.

Pierce Kemble was a silly, extravagant, and not particularly well-meaning man who had done his best to treat Miranda badly and he'd failed at that, too; Pierce couldn't even succeed in cheating his daughter out of her inheritance. Miranda was well aware of his failings, but Pierce was her father and she loved him. She was nothing if not loyal, and her loyalty waxed ever greater as his string of failures grew.

Ariel had fared better than her sister during the war. Her marriage to Ben Edge had been a happy one that had been blessed with a beautiful, vivacious child. She didn't see Ben himself, of course, as often as she would have liked, but under the circumstances, she could hardly complain. In fact, she saw him more often than most southern wives saw their husbands. Ben was serving with the Army of Virginia, so it wasn't hard for him to obtain leave now and again to see his wife and child.

While Ben was away, Ariel and Robbie lived with his parents, a warm and caring couple who adored her and their grandchild. Since the Edges were Lynchburg people, they lived relatively far from the war and its dangers. Even after the defeat at Gettysburg, everyone trusted that Robert E. Lee would keep the war distant.

Miranda's brother, Lam, had for the past several months served with Nathan Bedford Forrest's cavalry in western Tennessee and northern Mississippi. As a result of a daring action during the time of the siege of Vicksburg (he had led a raid into Memphis and burned considerable quantities of Union stores and ammunition), he had been promoted to colonel and given a squadron of his own. His current leave was another part of the reward for the raid he had led on Memphis.

All the Kembles—with the possible exception of Pierce—had more or less successfully endured the war. But only Ashbel had prospered from it. His shipping business was more successful than ever. Most of the ships his companies controlled he'd kept traveling between South America, Asia, and Europe. As a consequence, he hadn't suffered when the war disrupted the North American business.

At the same time, he recognized that enormous profits were still to be made trading with the South as well as the North, in spite of all the disruptions of the war.

Ash had no more faith in the Great Cause than Miranda, but he had welcomed the war when it came. He recognized early that for the right person, the blockade was not a barrier to profits—it would nourish and expand them. He was well aware that shortages would make many goods dear: luxury fashions from Paris and London, drugs and medical supplies, percussion caps, and much more. And he knew he could provide them.

He set up joint ventures with British partners to handle shipping to northern ports. And he set up another joint venture to run the blockade. Even though he'd lost two of the six sleek, low-slung, fast blockade runners that had been built for him on the Clyde, that operation still turned a profit of four times his initial investment.

Though Ashbel had been spending most of his time in London, he'd decided to come home for a time to take a firsthand look at how things were going in the South. He wanted to find out what the Confederacy most needed so that he might provide it. As it happened, his arrival coincided with the journey of the other Kembles to Kemble Island.

* * *

All the slaves on the landing wharf proved to be ancient. The younger Negroes, the ones who had not been sold at Pierce Kemble's great auction seven years before, had disappeared to God only knew where. Every one of those who remained to care for the plantation had been alive at the turn of the century.

Age did not diminish the warmth and joyousness of their greeting, however, when the Kembles stepped ashore. Their love for their masters remained, even in these harsh and trying times.

Miranda was the first off the boat, the first to embrace each of the slaves, and the first again to climb the stairs to the top of the dike. There she beheld the tabby buildings— the plantation house and the kitchen and the outbuildings, and beyond these the slave quarters and the rice mill. Everywhere were the old, dark, moss-shrouded trees, the oyster-shell roads, the blaze of flowers.

"Oh, how lovely!" she exclaimed, ignoring for the moment the state of considerable disrepair it all was in. Neglect blossomed into decrepitude all too quickly in this overbenign climate.

She glanced below. The male slaves were wrestling with the luggage and the crates of food and drink. The work was heavier, probably, than their strength was capable of. The two men who crewed the sloop were helping them, though, and so was Ash. Miranda had to smile to see that, for the oldest of the slaves, Pompey, was trying to argue Ash out of performing the labor but Ash ignored him.

Ariel and Robbie were already ascending the stairs to join Miranda, while Pierce and Lam had moved off into a corner of the dock, where they were quietly talking.

When they saw Ariel and Robbie climb the stairs, Dorcas and her sister Lettia heaved themselves after them. They weren't about to let them loose by themselves.

When she reached the landing, Ariel looked around for Miranda. When she saw her, she caught Miranda's attention and drew her aside.

"I didn't realize that Father was so . . ." Ariel said,

searching unsuccessfully for the most telling word. She took Miranda's hands in her own, then found the words she was searching for. "He's unreachable!" she said. "He's impossible to touch. Your letters never indicated that . . ."

"I know, darling," Miranda said, breaking in and clutching Ariel's hands tight. "I didn't tell you, and I'm sorry for that. But I couldn't."

"I understand, Miranda, dear. Truly I do. But how can we change him? What can we do?"

"I don't know, Ariel. Truly I don't. Only," she paused, "I thought to bring him—and all of you—here in the hope that the island will work its magic."

"Let's hope then," Ariel said with a glance in Robbie's direction. Robbie was at the moment racing toward the main house with Dorcas, hopelessly outdistanced, trying to catch him.

"Robbie! Robbie!" Ariel yelled. "You stop! You stop this second! Hear?"

"No, Mama," Robbie called, "I don't hear." And he continued on his romp.

Ariel caught Miranda's eye, and they both grinned, gave a nod, and together dashed after Robbie up the path to the house. They were followed, panting and wheezing, by Lettia and Dorcas.

The house itself leaned a bit, and the roof sagged, and the exterior badly needed paint, and all too many windows were missing panes. But as far as Miranda was concerned, Kemble House had never looked more inviting.

Inside, the air was dank and musty, even though Dorcas and Lettia had opened all the windows and aired it out and cleaned everything top to bottom not three days ago.

"It's fine," Miranda said. "Don't either of you worry. It's just fine."

While Ariel took Robbie outside to play, Miranda explored the house. Lastly, she went to her old room. She sprawled out on her bed for a few moments just as she had as a little girl. And then she sat in the rocking chair by the window where she used to read or just stare out at the green rice shoots and the canals and the workers bent over their labor.

"So where would you like me to drop this load?"

"What?" she said, jerking up, startled. Uncle Ash was standing in the doorway, holding bags.

"These àre yours, I take it?" he said.

"Oh, yes," she said. "I'm sorry. I was sitting and dreaming. I didn't expect anyone." Then she made a shrug and an offhand gesture. "Just drop them, Uncle Ash. Anywhere will be fine."

Ash walked into the room and placed the two bags against one of the walls.

"You travel light," he said. She smiled. "At least compared with your sister."

"We will only be here for two days. We'll have spent more time traveling than relaxing. And she has to pack for two," she added in Ariel's defense.

"Are you glad you've made the trip, then?"

"That's what I was sitting here dreaming about," she said. "This is the best place in the world. The place that is most . . . well, magical."

He gave a slow, meditative nod. She wasn't sure whether the nod was in agreement or simply in acknowledgment. "I like it here, too," he said, moving over to the window and staring out. He stood there silently for a time, then looked at her. "May I sit down, Miranda?" She hadn't realized it, but he wanted to talk with her.

"Oh, Ash, I'm sorry. I've been rude. Do please sit down there on the bed, if that's all right?"

"That's just fine," he said. He walked over to the bed and sank down on it, placing himself just opposite where she was sitting. "There's a reason why I carried your bags myself," he said. "I haven't had time to be alone with you.'"

"You look like a man with something serious on his mind."

"That's right, my young girl, I do."

She folded her hands in her lap, waiting.

"First of all, I've brought a letter for you from your

mother," he said. "From London." As he spoke, he withdrew an envelope from a pocket of his trousers.

Miranda brightened. "Oh, my, how lovely!" she said. "There've been so few letters because of the war. I so want to learn all about what she is doing." She took the envelope from Ash and tore it open. It contained a single brief sheet. Miranda's face fell—she'd wanted pages and pages.

"I'm afraid I gave her little time to compose her words," Ash said, seeing his niece's disappointment. "I left London rather suddenly, on a whim."

"Yes, I see," Miranda said, frowning. She didn't believe Ash's excuses. It was just like Fanny not to take the time or the effort to write.

"Read it," Ash said.

Miranda nodded, then unfolded the page and looked down at her mother's well-remembered large, open scrawl, undivided by separate paragraphs:

> My Dearest Darling Miranda,
> It has been so long and lonely here in London without you. I miss you SO VERY MUCH. Even though I am extraordinarily busy of late— had your uncle Ashbel told you what I'm doing? LADY MACBETH! —you are constantly in my thoughts and feelings. I scarcely go an hour without recalling my dearest darling daughter. The city is at its loveliest at this time of year. But without you it is a domain of gloom. And then Ashbel paid me a visit and told me he planned to voyage to America and to visit YOU! And that he was leaving the following day! Oh how I envied him! So I fetched my pen—on the INSTANT!—and began to write this, knowing how little time I had to tell you all I *MUST* tell you. And as I composed my thoughts, I came to realize that I *MUST* tell you the thought that is *most* pressing on my mind of late: I *MUST* have you here with me. I can't have you there— suffering, deprived, famished—while I languish

here in the lap of luxury. Come to me! Leave
with Ashbel! He will carry you with him on his
ship! Join me! And meanwhile send my deepest
love to Ariel and your brother when you write
to them. Your most loving and lonely Mother,
                                      Frances Shaw


Miranda glanced up at her uncle when she'd finished
reading. "You've read this?" she asked, her face showing
clearly the pain her mother's words had caused.

"Yes," Ash said. "Fanny showed it to me before she
sealed it."

"Should I go?" she asked.

"You'd surely be happier with your mother than you are
here," Ash said.

"You know how much I want to do as she likes, don't
you?"

"I can see that in your eyes."

"But you know that I can't go."

"Yes," he said softly. "I can see that in your eyes, too."

"I love her, and I miss her, and I want to be with her. I
have no love for the South, and I could run away from the
place in an instant, but I love my property too. Raven's
Wing would collapse without me. And of course there's
Father. At the moment, he has first call on my love."

"The war has not treated your father well," he said after
a time, "has it?"

"No," she said, taking a deep, long breath, "it hasn't."

"And you're worried about him, aren't you?"

She nodded.

"Well, so am I," he said. "He has always tended to
melancholy. That's why I've accepted the way he's lived his
life—the spending, the women, the gambling. All of them
are ways to make the darkness bearable."

She looked down at her hands. "Yes, I know," she said.

"I haven't seen Pierce since the start of the war," Ash
said. "But I've never seen him so despondent." He looked
up sharply. "What do you make of that?"

"I don't know," she said helplessly. "I've simply watched

his mood grow darker, ever since he was released from prison." She looked puzzled. "You know, Ash, he'd never admit it, but he liked prison. He bloomed there. He could be indignant and angry, righteous and brave. It gave him something to hold on to. But after he was let go, he just crumbled." She looked up at him. "Does all that make sense?"

"It makes very much sense, my dear."

"You know how he loves this place."

"Yes," he slowly drawled, "that he does."

"So I had the idea that as long as we could all be together for a brief time, then we should all come together here."

"Something like taking a cure?"

"Much more than that," she said. "A home place where his heart could breathe and heal."

"Let's hope that it helps," Ash said, starting to rise. And then he added, "I want someone with him all the time."

"Are you that worried about him?" Miranda said, more than a little alarmed. "You don't think he would . . . do himself damage?" She blurted out the last words in a rush.

"I think that I will feel better if someone is with him all the time," Ash said, avoiding a direct answer to her question. "I have invited Lam and your father to play cards for the rest of the afternoon. After that, we'll see. . . ."

"And what would you like me to do for him?"

"Give him all your love, Miranda. It's what he feels he is most lacking."

"I'll do my best," she sighed. She was more worried about her father than ever now. Ash's confirmation of her own fears had increased her anxieties about Pierce rather than alleviating them.

There was a sharp rap on the door sill, for Ash had left the door itself open when he'd entered the room. When Miranda looked up to see who was there, she saw Lettia standing in the doorway. "What you two lookin' so glum for?" Lettia said.

Miranda brightened automatically. "Uncle Ash and I haven't seen one another in ever so long," she said, covering up. She didn't want the servants aware of her worries. "It's sad to be so long apart, don't you think?"

"You been long away from us heah, too. Are you sad 'bout that?"

"Very sad, Lettia," she said. "And I'm delighted to be here."

"That's good, miss, 'cause I missed you, too."

"Well, I have a game of cards ahead of me," Ash said. "I'd best be seeing to it."

"I'll see you at supper, Ash."

"Until then," he said, and left the room.

While Ash was making his exit, Lettia bent over into the hallway behind the door and picked up a pail of water. "I've brung you some warm water to bathe with," she said. "I speck you pretty hot and tired and sweaty after yo' travlin.' "

"Oh, I am, Lettia. Thank you."

"Let me po' it in the basin over there, and I'll leave you with some nice dry towels, and den you can sponge yo'self off."

"That will be divine."

A few minutes later, after Lettia had poured the water, departed and shut the door behind her, Miranda stripped off her traveling clothes and underthings and gave herself a leisurely and cooling sponge bath. She dried herself in front of the long mirror next to the dressing table, and then brushed out her hair.

She hardly ever paid attention to the scar on her breast, but it caught her eye now. It was the one she'd received on the train ride up the Hudson on the day before Lam graduated from the Military Academy—a most memorable day.

The scar began just beyond where the pink corona around her nipple shaded into white. It was three inches long and an inch and a half across at its broadest, and diamond shaped—wide at the top, flat at the top and bottom. But to Miranda, the scar was not a diamond; it was the wide bulbous smokestack of a railway locomotive.

Miranda let her fingers idly graze the scar, and while she

did, she thought back over the trip up the Hudson and the golden afternoon with Lam and his two friends.

Would they still be friends, she wondered, if they were here now? They'd seemed so close and inseparable then. But now? They'd all moved down such different paths: Lam into the cavalry, Noah into the engineers . . . and Sam Hawken had remained in their enemy's army. He was, she'd heard, an aide to General Sherman.

Sam was the one Miranda recalled most vividly, the one who'd left her with the greatest emotional charge, and the one she'd most like to meet again. But he was the one least likely to ever step into her life.

"Where is he?" she asked herself as she recalled their mad and wonderful tumble down the hillside together. "Where are you now, Sam?"

She turned away from the mirror, slipped on a light shift, and threw herself onto the bed. She planned to nap until Dorcas came around and told her to dress for supper.

But her nap was interrupted when she heard loud and violent shouting downstairs. She jerked her head up and listened, straining to make out words. The clearest, loudest voice she recognized belonged to her father, and she could make out Lam's, too. But she couldn't hear Ash. And she couldn't tell what the shouting was all about.

What time is it? she wondered, glancing out the window. Outside, the sun was still bright. She couldn't have slept for more than an hour or so, she guessed.

And then, mobilizing herself, she rose from her bed, splashed some water on her face, and put on the clothes she'd planned to wear for the evening.

Five minutes after the angry shouting woke her, she was in the study, where the men had set up their card game.

Her father was no longer there. He'd stormed outside while she was dressing. Ash was standing by a window when she entered the room, and Lam was pouring himself a stiff glass of whiskey from a decanter on a sideboard. The card table was overturned, and cards were strewn across the floor.

"What happened?" she asked. "Where is Father?"

Ash looked up and shook his head.

"Ash, tell me," she demanded. Then she looked at her brother. "Lam?" But her brother didn't return her look. "Ash?" she repeated.

"What do you think?" Ash sighed, indicating with an inclination of his head the wreckage of the card game.

"Stupid, suspicious, vindictive bastard," Lam said.

"Father?" Miranda asked.

"Who else?" Lam said, drinking deeply from the glass. "Could there be anyone else around here who is stupid and suspicious?"

"Tell me what happened," she said.

"That doesn't matter," Ash said before Lam could speak up.

"But I want to know," she said.

"No, you don't," Lam said, realizing that his uncle was right in trying to keep a lid on the affair. "It's best to forget it."

She glanced from one to the other, and seeing that they were both resolute, she gave in to them for the moment. "And where are Ariel and Robbie?"

"Napping still, I imagine," Lam said, taking another long, deep sip.

"Then I'll go look for Father," she said.

"You'd do better leaving him alone," Lam said.

"No," she insisted. "Somebody has to take care of him."

"The vindictive bastard can't—or won't—take care of himself."

"Why all this rage," she asked, looking at Ash, "about a game of cards?"

When he did not answer, she turned and left the room. She walked through the parlor to the front hall and went out onto the front lawn, where she scanned for signs of her father. He was nowhere to be seen.

"Miz Miranda!" It was Dorcas calling. She had undoubtedly been hovering near the study. "Miz Miranda! You shouldn't be out theah in the heat of the day widout a parasol or a hat. You come in right now an' git somethin for yo hair an' yo face, you heah?''

"I'll be all right, Dorcas," Miranda said. "Don't you worry."

"Wid you pale skin, you gonna burn," Dorcas went on, shaking her head with exasperation. But Miranda, ignoring her, set out to find her father.

At which task she had no success. She searched for an hour and a half by which time the sun was sinking, and then gave up. He could not have failed to hear her calls. If he'd wanted to respond to them, he could have.

As she walked through the plantation settlement and then along the paths through the marshes where the rice would normally have been growing at this time of year, she couldn't help but notice how run-down everything was. The deterioration depressed her at least as much as the disappearance of her father.

She returned to the house, where she found Ash and Lam still in the study. Ash had by this time poured himself a whiskey, and Lam was clearly working on his second—or fifth.

"I couldn't find him," she said when Ash looked at her.

"Best to leave him alone," Ash said, "to cool off."

"I thought you told me earlier this afternoon," she snapped, bitter and frustrated at her inability to locate Pierce, "that you thought somebody ought to stay with him all the time."

Ash nodded. "That's right," he said. "I did say that. And I tried to go with him when he rushed out screaming at the top of his voice. But he would have none of it, he told me. 'I don't want you or your concern,' he said." Ash shrugged. "So I let him go."

"I hope he falls in a canal and drowns," Lam said.

"Lam!" Miranda barked. "Don't you say such things!" And then she looked at Ash. "What *did* happen at that card game? It's beginning to feel to me like there was a battle here bigger than Gettysburg."

Ash's lips widened into a grim smile. "One might take it that way," he said. "But, truly, Miranda, it's best to think

nothing of it. We played cards, and Pierce lost and there
were accusations.''

"You weren't placing wagers, were you?" she broke in.

"No," Ash said, "not at all."

"And all of a sudden," Lam said, "out of nowhere, it
seemed to me, Father raised himself up and struck me in the
face and screamed louder than ever."

"I don't see a mark," Miranda said.

"I was across the table from him," Lam said. "Too far
to do me any damage. And then he flipped the card table
over and screamed some more."

"And you didn't provoke him?" Miranda asked.

"No," Ash said. "He didn't."

"And that's when he stormed out?" Miranda asked.

"Not quite," Lam said. "There was more yelling, and he
tried to reach me again with his fists, but Uncle Ash held
him back. Next he stormed out."

Miranda's shoulders sagged, and tears started forming in
the corners of her eyes.

"Why?" she asked Ash. "Why do you think he did it—if
neither of you provoked him?"

"I would have guessed because he was losing," Ash
said, "and it bothered him. He is *such* a child most of the
time. But I don't know, Miranda. There was something else,
and I don't know what it is." Ash turned to Lam, seeking
his agreement.

"I've never seen him this way," Lam said. "And I don't
like it."

Miranda looked first at Lam and then at Ash. "All right,"
she said, "the instant Father returns, tell me about it, unless
I see him first."

She was beginning to fear that the trip to Kemble Island
was a bad idea after all.

Pierce reappeared after sundown. There was still plenty of
light then, however, more than enough for Miranda to see
clearly how destroyed he looked: He had fallen into a marsh
that had once been a rice paddy, his clothes were caked with

dirt and slime, and his face was florid and unhealthily flushed. A film of bright sweat covered his flesh.

When Miranda approached to give him help, he waved her off irritably, the way he must have done when Ash had earlier tried to go with him after he'd broken up the card game. When she persisted, he screamed, "Get away from me. I don't want your help, you hear? I don't want you messin' with me."

"Daddy!" she said with pain in her voice. "What's wrong with you?"

"Let me alone, I said."

"But you've fallen into a ditch and you need help."

"No, I do not need help," he snapped. "I had a short dizzy spell from too much sun and heat, and I got dunked a little, but I'll deal with it." He pivoted around to leave her, but then he stopped, twisted his face toward her, and added, "I'll deal with it my way."

"Daddy!" she repeated more insistently.

"I said, you nosy little bitch, that I don't want you fussin' with me." As he spoke, he approached her, balling his fist and cocking his arm, evidently intending to strike her.

As he pushed nearer, Miranda backed away. "Father!" she cried out, alarmed.

He staggered a little. Then he pulled to a halt and gazed out of misted eyes—not really seeing her, she realized. It was as though he were in a trance.

Has he gone crazy? she asked herself.

"I'll see you at dinner," he managed to say.

Miranda's father put himself in order by dinnertime, as he promised, which lifted Miranda's spirits a little. And she was greatly relieved that all through the meal he didn't break into another blind rage, though he was silent and sullen the entire time.

The servants laid supper out half an hour after dark. They spread it on tables they'd carried outside onto the lawn, and it was quite a glorious spread—a dozen of the freshest channel cats fried and buttery crisp, a haunch of pork roasted on a spit, steamed shrimp and crabs, rice from their plantation, spinach, peas, string beans, and tomatoes from the garden, and wine that Ashbel had carried all the way from France.

After supper the men retired to the study for cigars and brandy, and the two sisters chatted with one another and played with Robbie on the veranda. At nine Ariel rose to put Robbie to bed. She would retire with him, she told Miranda. "I have to be up when he gets up," she said by way of explanation, "even though you must think I'm going to sleep terribly early. And I'm just exhausted after all that traveling."

Miranda came to her feet then, too, so as to give her sister and Robbie good-night kisses. She kissed Robbie first, and lifted him up and gave him a big hug. After she put him down, she approached Ariel. "Before you go," she said with a worried look, "there's something I want to ask you."

"I know what it is," Ariel said with a tight grimace. "You want to ask me about Father, don't you?"

"That's right. I don't know what to do about him."

"Does anyone?" Ariel said hopelessly. "He has been so baffling! Is he going insane, or is he ill or what?"

"That's right," Miranda shrugged. "Or what?"

Ariel gave Robbie a sidelong glance. She didn't want him listening to this kind of talk. But Robbie, happily, seemed disinterested. He had found a clan of june bugs that he could torment.

"Ash brought me a note from Mother," Miranda said. "She sent you her love."

Ariel smiled. "How is she?" she asked.

"From what little she said, she seems quite well. She's playing Lady Macbeth. She adores that role."

"Lady Macbeth, really?" Ariel said. "How very perfect for her, yet how far from her real-life role. It's a shame she could not put some of the steel in Father that Lady Macbeth put in the man she married."

Miranda shrugged again. "It would have done little good. Father could not have been a king, even a criminal king like Macbeth. Perhaps an ambassador or an envoy or even a chief minister—but never a king. I sometimes think that that was the chief difference between Mother and Father. She is a leading player, and he is not and can never be."

"I suppose you're right," Ariel said.

"She asked me again to come to London," Miranda said.

"And?"

"I'd go eagerly and instantly if it weren't for my property. And for Father."

"I know," Ariel agreed. "But do stay with him. You will, won't you? I can't. I have my child and my husband. But Father needs someone, and he has no one save you."

"I know that."

"Then I'm much relieved."

"I wish I could say the same,' Miranda said.

"Good night, darling. I simply must take the little beast to bed before he dismembers all the june bugs on Kemble Island."

"That's no great loss if he does, the ugly, sticky things. Aagghh," she gagged and wrung her hands.

"Kiss me good night," Ariel said.

The two sisters kissed tenderly, and then Ariel gathered up her son and carried him off to bed. He was kicking and crying out as they went, but only feebly.

Once Ariel and Robbie were safely indoors, Miranda returned to her seat, planning to sit quietly in the dark and meditate until the stinging insects drove her inside.

But when she reached her seat, she found her father sitting in the chair that Ariel had left.

"Oh!" Miranda said, startled. "How did you come out so quietly, Father? I didn't hear you."

"I decided to take a walk," he said, his voice drained and weary. A half-smoked unlit cigar dangled from his mouth. "I left from the back door. You and your sister were so busy with one another you didn't pay attention to anything around you."

"I guess not," Miranda said, sinking into her chair. She looked at her father expectantly. She wanted to ask him how he felt after the ordeal of the afternoon, but she decided she should not be the one to bring that up. So she waited, trying to look concerned and receptive.

"I heard you and your sister talking," he said finally, after a long silence.

"You did?" Miranda said in a neutral voice.

"So you've received a communication from your mother?"

"Yes." '

"I hear that she wants you with her."

"Yes, Father, she asked me to come to England."

"Why don't you go?"

"I can't," she said. "I have my land to take care of, and . . . " She stopped.

"And me? Was that what you were about to say?"

"Yes."

"I want you to go. I don't need you, and I don't want you."

"Father," Miranda sighed.

"It's an illusion of yours, perpetrated by your all too fervent imagination, that you can do me the slightest bit of good. I know you'd rather be in London with your mother," he nearly snarled, "than enduring the sufferings of the nation that begat you."

"It's not the sufferings of the nation that upset me. I'm worried about my father."

He waved off her explanation with a flick of his hand. "I've been thinking." He paused. "I have new plans." He paused again. "This place is underused, and it could be productive again. I could make it so."

"Father, what a lovely idea. I couldn't think of a more perfect task for you to perform." She tried to catch his eye, but had no luck. "But I wonder if you realize, dear, all the difficulties that would present. There's no one to work the land, for instance. And the Union squadron is based hardly five miles from here. They would never allow you to return."

"You silly bitch," he said with hard, cruel laughter in his voice, "do you know what you are saying beneath your kindness and concern? You're telling me you want me all to yourself. You want to own me the way your mother tried. I escaped her. I'll escape you.

"Go to your mother," he went on. "I don't want you

with me any longer. It's that simple." His face was toward her now, and his expression was painful to see, full of what Miranda took to be longing. In contrast with his harsh words, his eyes seemed to tell her: *I need you!*

Meanwhile, his bitter speech continued, "You're a weight on my life," he was saying. "Around my neck. You choke me, Miranda. Go to your mother."

Miranda was stung. He'd hurt her, and she was reeling. She so wanted to help him and care for him, and protect him. He couldn't really mean what he was saying! "I don't understand," she said. And truly she didn't understand. His words said one thing, but she read on his face a message that was completely different.

"How can I tell you more simply and directly that I want you out of my life, Miranda. What more is there to say?"

"But," she said, then stopped herself, thinking it would be better not to object anymore for now. She lifted herself out of her chair. "Good night, Father. I do love you, and I don't want to leave you."

"But you will," he said, "if I have anything to say about it."

"Let's talk again some more tomorrow, shall we? I'm tired."

"Good night, Miranda," he said without looking at her.

Miranda went up to her room, but it was a long time before she found sleep.

The Kembles were subdued and quiet at breakfast the next morning. It was Sunday, but the hush was not on account of the day of the Lord.

Miranda scarcely touched her food, even though what the slaves had set before them was better, fresher, and more abundant than what she could obtain in Atlanta. There was crisp bacon, corn bread with butter and honey, eggs scrambled in the bacon fat, and even tea. She couldn't recall the last time she'd tasted real China tea.

The cause of their haunted mood had not appeared yet, but that did not diminish the sense of darkness and anxiety that had descended on the family.

Robbie finished early and wandered off to play. He was a lusty eater; he didn't dally over his food like other five-year-olds.

He'd brought from home a carved wooden horse on wheels that he adored—a model of a Trojan horse, though Robbie was too young to recognize that provenance. It was more than a foot and a half high, and it had a trapdoor on hinges in its belly—the inside of the horse was hollow. Robbie kept buttons and dead bugs in the space, and a feather from a gull and another feather, black and glistening, from a crow.

He liked playing with his horse in the front entrance hall more than anywhere else in the house, for the room was empty of furniture and the floor was bare of rugs. Thus he could send the horse racing for long distances without hindrance.

The Kembles, who were still at table, could hear the horse rumble across the floor and then bang into a wall.

Ariel volunteered to put a stop to the ruckus, but Uncle Ash told her not to worry about it. And when neither Lam nor Miranda contradicted him, Ariel decided to leave well enough alone.

The noise continued for a time, but inexplicably it stopped. The moment the sounds ceased, Ariel raised her head from her cup. It could have been no more than a second after that when they heard a great, heavy thud. Someone had fallen down the front stairs.

A sudden chill gripped Miranda. She had no doubt who it was.

All four of the Kembles jumped up at once to see what was the matter. Lam leapt to his feet so quickly that he upended his chair behind him. Miranda, though, paused long enough to set it right.

By the time she reached the hallway not more than a couple of seconds behind the three others, Robbie was shouting, *"Grampa! Grampa! Grampa fall down!"*

Kemble House was large and sprawling, but by no means elegant or well designed. And the staircase, in keeping with everything else, was not at all grand. It was steep and straight and utilitarian. A third of the way up the stairs Pierce Kemble lay in a sprawl of arms and legs, head downward, unconscious. Saliva trickled from his half-open mouth, and blood had started to seep down onto the wood. It was impossible to see, though, where on his body or head the wound was.

All feeling seemed to desert Miranda when she saw Pierce lying there. The shock of the sight was too great for her to bear, but somehow, on instinct, she continued to move.

"Father!" she screamed, racing toward him.

Ariel was screaming the same thing, but Miranda didn't hear her.

All of them save Robbie were making a dash for Pierce. They created a hopeless jam at the bottom of the stairs.

"Each of you!" Ash shouted, taking charge. "Back up! Ariel! Miranda! Lam! Move back!"

After several attempts at catching their attention, they obeyed him. And then he alone ascended the stairs to have a look at his brother. He first felt for a pulse at Pierce's neck. Finding it, he looked at the three waiting below and gave a quick nod to show that their father was still alive.

"Thank God!" Miranda said to herself silently.

After feeling the pulse, Ash lifted an eyelid with his thumb and peered. When he finished, his look was grimmer.

*"Grampa! Grampa fall down!"* Robbie was shouting. He'd been shouting all along, but Miranda had not until this moment heard him. Now, however, his screams bored into her mind like a drill. It was hard to tell whether he was becoming hysterical or whether he was simply excited and curious.

"Would you take him out of here, please, Ariel?" Lam said, surprisingly gentle.

"Yes, surely," Ariel mumbled. Then in a single movement, she turned and swept Robbie into her arms.

"My horse!" he shouted, his voice charged with distress.

"Here," Miranda said, reaching down and passing it to Ariel. "Can you handle the horse and Robbie both?" she asked.

"I do all the time," Ariel said. Then she caught her sister's eye. "Let me know..." she whispered.

"Yes. The instant I do I'll come to you."

Miranda returned to the foot of the stairs. While she and Ariel were tending to Robbie, Ash had lifted his brother up so that his head was no longer dangling over a stair tread.

"What is the matter with him?" she asked Ash.

He took a long, deep breath before replying, "If I had a guess, I'd say apoplexy. And," he paused, "it looks to be serious. There's a pulse, but it's fluttery, and his breathing is shallow and weak."

"Is he dying?" Lam asked, going directly to the point.

"Damned if I know," Ash said in a voice that indicated he was convinced that his brother was close to death. "Come, help me move him back to his bed."

"Should we do that?" Lam asked. "Do you think it's safe to move him?"

"We can't leave him here on the stairs," Ash said practically, "pretty near upside down. Come on. We can at least give him the benefit of what comfort we can offer."

Lam moved up the stairs, and Miranda followed him. For the first time she realized that her father had not changed out of his sleeping clothes. He was still wearing his long linen nightshirt.

"Miranda," Ash said, "you get back down the stairs. We won't need you yet, not until after we've put him into his bed. You, Lam, grab his shoulders. I'll take his legs."

Miranda backed away, complying.

"What do you think, Miz Miranda?" It was Dorcas speaking. She was flanked, as usual, by Lettia. Both of them had been standing out of the way for some time, but Miranda hadn't realized they were there. "You think he's gonna be all right?"

"I don't know, Dorcas," Miranda said. "I sure wish I did."

Struggling—more because of the confined space than because of the weight—Ash and Lam carried Pierce up to the landing, and then, shifting him around so that he'd be easier to manage, they took him to his room.

When Ash let Miranda in to see her father, she saw that he was still unconscious and that he didn't look at all good. His hands were pale and clammy, but his cheeks, neck, and forehead were flushed. His color was unhealthy. His face looked overheated and angry.

Miranda looked at Lam, then at Ash, then back to Lam. "I'll sit with him," she said.

"All right," Ash said.

"Shall I stay, too?" Lam asked.

"No. One of us is enough."

"All right," Lam said, much relieved.

"But you can bring me some warm water in a basin. And some towels. He ought to be washed off."

"All right. Anything else?"

"No. Just that."

"Damned shame there's no doctor," Lam said.

Ash shook his head. "It doesn't matter," he said. "A doctor won't help him any—though it might give some comfort to you or your sister to have a doctor here."

"You think he's dying?"

Ash let his eyes drop, but didn't answer.

"There have to be doctors over on Saint Simon's, where the naval ships are," Miranda said, trying to work up some measure of hope. "We could at least send somebody over there to see, and maybe fetch one."

No one responded, and she didn't follow up on her suggestion.

Miranda spent the morning by her father's bedside. She sat almost as unmoving as he, for she was filled with a foreboding, pain, and guilt that paralyzed her. In her mind she believed she was the one person who was closest to Pierce Kemble, the one person who understood him best, and so the one person who was most responsible for him.

And in her deepest heart she knew that he was near death.

Because of that, she replayed over and over the scene that had happened the night before on the porch. She was convinced that it was the event that had triggered Pierce's collapse. She blamed herself for not being more sensitive and gentle to him. And she magnified her conflict with her father into a battle that was larger and that left more permanent scars than the one between her father and Lam the previous afternoon.

How could I have allowed it to happen? she asked herself again and again. Why was I so unfeeling? How could I have let him feel so alone and rejected?

She was determined now in his last moments not to reject him as she felt she had done the night before.

Sometime in the afternoon her father opened his eyes. He might have been that way for a while, for Miranda herself had been dozing off. When she opened her eyes and saw her father staring at her, her body shook spasmodically, as though she'd had an encounter with a spirit from another world. "Oh!" she cried. It was a strangled cry; her throat was so tightly clutched that she had very little voice.

After a time, though, her control returned. She rose from the armchair she'd placed next to his bed and bent down over her father.

"Father?" she said, kissing him lightly.

He lay there unmoving, staring up at her with eyes that might or might not have seen her.

"Father, how do you feel? Can I bring you anything? How can I make you more comfortable?"

There was the slightest stir of tension in his throat muscles, but Pierce was not able to make a sound.

"He's paralyzed," she said to herself. "And I don't know what to do."

She stayed that way for a few minutes, wondering whether she should ring for somebody to come help her. While she watched him, she saw movement. He managed a long, slow dropping of his lids. Then the lids opened again.

"Is that on purpose?" she asked, partly to him and partly to herself. And then to him: "Can you do that again?"

No response.

There was a hand bell on a table next to Pierce's bed. She reached over and shook it hard and long. As she rang the bell, she kept her eyes focused on her father's face.

"There!" she said. "There it is again!" Her father's lids

had once again drooped shut, and there was a barely perceptible tremor of his lips.

Moments later Ariel rushed in.

"What happened?" Ariel asked, breathless.

Miranda told her, even though she had hoped it would be Ash who responded to her rings. He would know what to make of her father's condition.

"Do you think he has regained consciousness?" Ariel asked after Miranda finished telling her what she had seen.

"I can't think of any other explanation for it," Miranda said.

Ariel stared, and Pierce obliged her by shutting and opening his eyes once more.

"Oh," Ariel said with a shudder. To her, Pierce's action was not hopeful; it was creepy.

And then his face almost seemed to animate, and his mouth moved as though he was trying to shape words.

"Father!" both women said simultaneously.

There was a sound in his throat.

"He wants to speak," Ariel said.

"Where's Ash?" Miranda said. "He'll know what to do."

"I don't know," Ariel said. "He vanished outside this morning, and he didn't return for lunch."

"Why did he have to go off," Miranda said, annoyed, "and leave us alone?" She then wiped her father's face with a dry cloth. "What are you trying to tell us?" she said to him.

Pierce made no response. He had faded once more into unawareness.

Ariel and Miranda watched him silently for a time, and then Ariel said, "I'll go find Ash, or Lam, or somebody."

Miranda nodded absently. "Yes. Good idea," she said.

Ariel made as though to leave.

But then, "No wait. Please!" Miranda cried. A wave of anguish had passed through her heart; the fear made her shudder.

"What, Miranda?"

"I have to tell you something," Miranda said. Ariel looked at her. "I brought this on him."

"You?" Ariel asked, staring without comprehension. "Not you, Miranda."

"No, I *did*," Miranda said. "It had to be me. Last night," she went on, "after you left for bed, he and I talked . . . and we fought. A horrible fight." Tears began forming in Miranda's eyes.

"A fight?" Ariel asked in wonderment. "What about?"

Miranda explained, and Ariel, with ever-growing disbelief, listened.

"And that's all?" Ariel asked when Miranda was finished.

"Well, yes," Miranda said.

"Don't blame yourself, darling. He fought *everyone* yesterday. It wasn't just you. It's not your fault—especially for this." She pointed at the inert form on the bed.

"Don't you see? His words to me were so . . . *final*. It wasn't just a fight. He wanted me out of his life. He wanted me with Mother."

"Isn't that exactly where you'd really like to be? With Mother?"

Miranda didn't answer that.

"Maybe he was just trying to be kind to you."

"But if you could have only seen his face," Miranda said. "His face said that he wanted to stay with me. His face said that he needs me!"

Ariel looked away for a moment; she stared out the window. "He's a hard one to figure out, darling. He always was, and if he lives, he always will be. Don't try to understand him. And don't blame yourself."

"He's my father," Miranda said. "He needs my love, and I failed him last night, when he most needed me. And now look at him!"

They both switched their gaze toward Pierce.

His eyes were open and alive with awareness. He focused first on Ariel, then on Miranda.

"Oh, my Lord!" Ariel said.

He was trying to speak, but words still could not come.

"He heard us!" Miranda said. "He was listening! He heard me tell you about last night."

"Do you know something, darling," Ariel said, more than a little exasperated with her sister's persistent harping, "I doubt that he's able to hear anything."

"But he wants to tell me something," Miranda went on, racing full speed down the track she'd set herself on. "Look at him," she cried. "See? Look at his face. He wants to explain!"

She was right about at least one thing. There was motion again in his face. his features were more animated than they had been since she had begun her vigil that morning.

"What is there to explain, darling?" Ariel asked.

"Whether I should go to Mother or stay here," Miranda said. "I have to know what he wants me to do. I have to know his last wish for me!" She stopped, then resumed. "I have to know that, because he is . . ." She did not finish the thought, for in her heart she felt he could hear her every word.

"What difference does that make?" Ariel, always the practical one, asked. "If he survives this, you must stay with him. If the worst happens, do as you will."

But Miranda who was not far from hysteria now, ignored her. Her father was dying, and she had unfinished business with him. The decision she wanted from him touched her like fire. She felt this was as important a decision as she would ever make in her life.

"Father," she said, turning away from Ariel and back to Pierce, "you were listening, weren't you?" She stared at him hard and long, searching for a sign.

At last one came. His lids moved. When that happened, she drew in her breath slowly, brought her face down within inches of his, and spoke into his ear.

"You heard, didn't you, Father? And you will tell me what you want me to do, won't you?" she said. "And you can give me an indication of that with your eyes?"

She waited. In time the lids moved.

She looked at her sister. "There!" Miranda said triumphantly.

"You're making too much of this," Ariel warned.

"No!" Miranda insisted. "I'm not at all. Don't you see? I've *reached* him!"

But Ariel, fearing that further denial would only provoke Miranda more, turned and left the room, hoping to find the men.

"Shall I leave and got to Mother?" Miranda whispered in her father's ear after Ariel had departed.

She waited, watched.

There was no movement on her father's face.

"Shall I stay here, then? In Georgia?"

She watched.

Slowly the dying man's lids flickered, dropped, opened.

Miranda trembled. The next words she spoke ever so slowly and with greatly exaggerated clarity. "You are telling me to disregard your words last night?" she said in his ear. "You didn't mean them, did you?"

Another wait. Another watch. Finally there was another movement of his lids, the barest flutter. Then Pierce stared into her face with eyes full of emptiness and pain.

He had given her the sign that she'd wanted.

Then, in blessing and farewell, Miranda lifted his head in her arms and cradled him, showering his face with kisses. After that, she pulled away from him, satisfied. She returned to her chair and collapsed into it, waiting for the others to arrive.

Pierce Kemble died that night, without, in his brother Ash's opinion, ever having regained consciousness after his fall down the stairs. In this, Ariel and Lamar concurred.

But Miranda maintained otherwise. She was convinced that she and her father had reached one another during that long and harrowing last afternoon of his life. And long after she had returned to Atlanta, she continued to believe that Pierce had communicated with her.

Pierce Kemble was buried in the family plot on Kemble Island on Monday, July 27, 1863.

# ◆ FIVE ◆

Okolona, Mississippi lay approximately a hundred miles north of Meridian as the crow flies, and about ten miles more than that on the Mobile & Ohio Railroad. That made Okolona almost an eight-hour journey by train from Meridian at an average speed of fifteen miles an hour.

The train that was carrying Major Noah Ballard and Captain William Hottel to Okolona consisted of a locomotive, a tender, a flatcar with a barricade of cotton bales along its sides, and a single passenger car. In the best of worlds, it would have made better time, but the condition of the tracks and roadbeds dictated otherwise. Much of the Mobile & Ohio track north of Meridian had been wrecked by raids from General Grenville Dodge's cavalry. The tracks had been repaired, but not nearly up to peacetime standards. To do that was impossible. Not a single piece of track had been manufactured in the states of the Southern Confederacy since 1861.

Under those conditions, fifteen miles an hour was excellent time.

The train left Meridian at five in the morning. In addition to its two passengers, it carried a platoon of

153

riflemen (a squad on the flat car and another squad in the passenger car). They were there for protection against the threat of General Dodge's cavalry. Federal horse soldiers were ranging unhindered ever closer to Meridian, attacking and destroying any target that pleased their fancy.

The presence of the squad of guards put Noah Ballard in a cold fury as he sat on his seat and watched the farms and countryside roll by. He didn't regret having them— he was not a fool—he regretted the need. The Confederacy was contracting. What was theirs last week belonged to the northerners now. And a simple journey like the one he was on today had to be conducted timidly, almost apologetically.

All things considered, the prudent thing would have been to undertake the journey under cover of night, but Noah had vetoed that idea. The prudent thing, he reasoned, would be pretty much the same as admitting defeat. As far as Noah was concerned, the territory from Meridian north to Tupelo was still contested.

Noah Ballard's cold rage had started on the morning of the savage train wreck between Jackson and Meridian, a wreck that had been engineered by a Union spy. His rage had been building with ever more alarming reports of rape and pillage by the troops of General Sherman. The Yankees were systematically laying waste to Jackson and all the lands around it. That they were winning the battles Noah could accept. But the harm the Union armies were doing to the land, the towns, the productive capacity of the nation, and to the women and children and old people—*that* was unforgivable.

This wasting of the South was not a consequence of fair and honorable defeat in armed combat—it was a crushing humiliation. And that Major Noah Ballard could only take as a personal insult. It was an assault upon his own dignity. It was an assault against the right order of things—tantamount to saying that anything is permitted in war because civilized limits and boundaries don't hold any longer. The result was dead mothers, mutilated children, and starving old people.

It was said that the Union brass believed the devastation would shorten the war, but to Noah Ballard, the opposite was the case. With word of each additional outrage, his resolve grew. He would fight on until he had nothing left to fight with. And he was sure everyone else in the South would act likewise.

If the war turned out to last a hundred years, so be it.

When Noah was not nourishing his fury at the destruction of Mississippi and the humiliation of the South, he worried about Jane Featherstone. Noah had secured a place for her on the last train out of Jackson on the sixteenth of July, and she had given him her word she would use the space reserved for her. But Jane was not on the train when it arrived in Meridian, and she had not made an appearance in the days following Joe Johnston's exodus. Jane was resourceful, Noah knew, but she was nevertheless a woman, attractive and vulnerable, and Sherman's savage hordes were not famous for observing the sanctity of womanhood. Noah cared about Jane, and he missed her.

Captain Hottel sat a few rows up from Noah, chatting with the sergeant of the squad of guards. His face was animated, and the sergeant was listening with rapt attention. The captain was quite a charmer.

Noah had not seen much of the captain during the days following the retreat from Jackson, and that had suited Noah just fine. It wasn't because he disliked Hottel; rather, he didn't want to have to deal with the possibility that Hottel might invade the territory Noah had come to call his own—the railroads that remained available to Joe Johnston in eastern Mississippi. But it turned out that Noah had nothing to fear on that account. William Hottel had devoted his entire energies to finding the missing railroad equipment.

The expedition they were on now was a demonstration of the success of his efforts.

When Hottel had returned to General Johnston's headquarters, his report had played down his success. He had told Noah and the general that, yes, he'd had some luck. Yes, there were locomotives hidden here and there both north of Meridian and north of Jackson. But perhaps, he'd gone on to say, there ought to be a report independent of his, a report based on another personal examination of a small but representative number of the locomotives. More than one head was needed, he claimed, to judge how to dispose of them.

The obvious choice for this second personal examination was, of course, Noah. And so here he was.

In fact, Noah was powerfully curious to find out what Will Hottel had discovered. But it was more than just curiosity that fired him. He was beginning to see these locomotives as his personal contribution to the Confederacy. They were needed, he knew, just as much as cannon and horses and regiments of soldiers. Fifty trains pulled by the fifty previously lost engines could support an army of seventy-five thousand men.

Case in point: Lee's army in Virginia was dangerously underfed—not because there was not enough in the South for those men, but because the food could not be transported fast enough to make up for the near absence in the South of ordinary salt. Without salt as a preservative, food spoiled. Fifty new trains would not only provide food enough for Lee's army to survive, they would provide other sorely needed materials that would allow him to rebuild it. If Lee had had those fifty trains at his disposal, he would not have been forced to take his army north in June on the foraging expedition that was cut short near the town of Gettysburg in Pennsylvania.

Noah Ballard couldn't do anything about cannon or horses or regiments, but he could do something about locomotives. If, that is, they could be transported to a part of the Confederacy where they could do some good.

But that was not a problem Noah hoped to solve this day. First he wanted to see what Captain Hottel had come up with.

The train arrived at its destination, a spur of track just south of Okolona, at 12:15 in the afternoon. The engine crew had done well to make such good time, and the major and the captain both congratulated them before they set off on the final leg of their journey, which was to take them up the spur.

The spur itself was not serviceable to trains. It was overgrown with grass, bushes, and shrubs, and sections of track had been ripped up for use elsewhere, or looted by Yankees.

"How far are we going to have to go like this?" Noah asked Hottel after they'd hiked perhaps a half mile.

"Another mile, as I recollect," Hottel said.

"What you're going to show me better be worth the trip," Noah said.

"You won't be disappointed," Hottel said. "I guarantee it. It'll seem like the best party you've been to in months."

"Let's hope," Noah said doubtfully.

Noah and Hottel pushed their way through the thick, lush Mississippi summer growth for another forty minutes. At last, sweating and beating off mosquitoes, they arrived at a large, tumbledown, weather-beaten shed.

"Is that it?" Noah asked, wondering how the thing was still able to stand.

"That's it."

Though they were hard to see in all the growth, the tracks entered the shed beneath wide, tall doors. These were chained shut. Off to the side was a smaller door that Captain Hottel pointed out. The two men walked over to it, and Hottel did something with the lock and chain at the door and pushed it open.

Inside it was dim and musty; the only illumination came from chinks and holes in the roof and walls. There was enough light, though, for Noah to see what he'd traveled all day to look at: three grand, powerful black Baldwin locomotives and their tenders. One of them stood just behind the wide double doors, and the other two were side by side behind the first one.

"Well, I'll be damned!" Noah exclaimed. "Will you look at those? I've never seen anything so beautiful! Three of them! How do you like that? Just sitting there like panting virgins!" Though he wasn't exactly surprised to find what Will Hottel had led him to, he hadn't expected three of them, nor had he expected the three to be in such pristine condition.

"I thought you'd find this place interesting," Hottel said, with exaggerated understatement.

"It's paradise," Noah said.

"No," Hottel said. "For that you need real virgins."

Noah laughed, then took a quick turn around each of the locomotives. The name painted on the side of the cab of the one in front was "Dart." The other two were "Javelin" and "Perseverance."

After making one circuit of the engines, he climbed aboard Dart and examined the cab. Hottel remained below.

"It's in perfect shape," Noah called down after a moment. "I don't see much wear at all. The paint isn't even baked off the firebox door."

"There shouldn't be much wear on these," Hottel said. "From what I could find out, that one was in service for not much over a year. The others slightly longer."

"And then they got hid?" Noah asked as he climbed down from the cab.

"Yeah," Hottel said. "Walter Goodman kept only his old and tired locomotives in operation." Walter Goodman was president of the Mobile & Ohio. He was currently in Meridian working as a civilian adviser on General Johnston's staff. "He ordered his best and newest to be put out of harm's way."

"How'd you find these?" Noah asked.

"I asked around for a few days," Hottel answered. "But that didn't do much good. Anyone who knew anything about this kept pretty quiet about it.

"When that didn't work, I took a train out and drove slow up the track and explored every spur and siding." He looked at Noah. "These aren't the only three. I've found twenty-three others hidden between Meridian and Tupelo; a lot of them were brought down from Tennessee when the Yanks overran it." Tupelo was about twenty-five miles north of

Okolona. And Tupelo was, in turn, about seventy-five miles from the Tennessee line.

Noah was having a hard time encompassing all that Hottel was telling him. Walter Goodman was a leader among the people of Mississippi. No one had given more outstanding service in these trying times than he had. Thus Noah had a hard time coming to grips with any reason why a southern patriot like Walter Goodman would withhold from his country the most valuable things he was capable of giving to it.

"This is real hard to believe," Noah said, articulating what was on his mind. "I can't imagine somebody like Walter Goodman keeping twenty-six prime locomotives from us."

"The Ordinance of Secession did not repeal original sin," Hottel said patiently.

"I guess not," Noah said.

"Anyhow," Hottel said, brightening, "I promised you a celebration, my young friend, and I'm prepared to deliver."

Hottel had carried with him a leather satchel which he had slung across his shoulder. He slipped it off and set it on the ground, then removed a jug of sour mash whiskey. "This is good stuff," he said. "I know the man who makes it." He handed the jug to Noah. "You don't mind if I didn't bring glasses?"

"It makes no difference to me at all," Noah said just before he lifted the jug to his lips. After he'd taken a long pull, he handed it back to Hottel. "You're right," he said. "It's good stuff."

"I've got some bread and cheese and corned beef, too," Hottel said. "You want to eat it in here, or outside under a tree?"

Hottel's glance at the open door showed where he'd rather go, but Noah was perfectly satisfied to be where he was. Having just gone through two hellish weeks trying to move an army with a handful of antiquated locomotives, he wanted to let his soul feast on the sight of the three nearly new machines that Hottel had uncovered.

"Here's fine," Noah said, "if that's all right with you."

"If that's what you'd like," Captain Hottel said, a little grudgingly. He searched around the shed for a few minutes and returned with a canvas tarp. "Let's spread this out, and . . ." At that he paused, for another idea had come to him. He was looking at the big doors in front of Dart. "Let's open the doors and let some light in," he said.

Soon they had the doors open, and bright midafternoon sunlight streamed in on them, as well as on Dart's imposing, outthrusting pilot and its high, bulbous smokestack. The two men sat comfortably on the tarp, eating their lunch and drinking William Hottel's good sour mash whiskey.

"Walter Goodman couldn't have managed it if it hadn't been for the confusion," Noah said after they had finished with most of the food. "Jesus, twenty-six locomotives are harder to conceal than twenty-six elephants."

"It wasn't easy," Hottel agreed.

"It burns my ass that he tried it. It's just the same as treason. If I had my way, I'd shoot him."

"I take your point," Hottel said carefully. "But you've got to look at it his way, too. He's looking after his property. If he doesn't protect his investment, then chances are it's lost forever."

"I'd still shoot him," Noah said.

"I'd probably treat him more gently than that," Hottel said. "And, my young warrior, bear this in mind, too, as you go thirsting for blood. Walter Goodman has plenty of influence among those who wield the scepter in our part of the world. You'd best treat him with a measure of diplomacy, while never once forgetting that these locomotives, and the twenty-three others he's concealed, still belong to him. We'd be much better advised to court his favor and not his enmity."

Noah thought on that. "I take your point," he said after a time.

"The thing is," Hottel said, "we've got to find some way to pry these and the others out of him. And be aware, too, that his aren't the only engines that have been hidden. There are more north of Jackson."

"More? Where? On the Mississippi Central and the Mississippi & Tennessee?" Noah asked. "Are you telling me that Walter Goodman wasn't the only railroad man to hide his rolling stock?"

"You're getting the idea pretty good," Hottel said, then took another swallow from the jug. "There are forty-one more engines up there."

"Jesus! Forty-one?"

"It kind of takes your breath away, doesn't it?"

"It's more like a dream," Noah said, "when you're falling down in pitch dark and you don't know what you're going to hit. Or when."

"Maybe so," Hottel agreed with a sharp nod. "Maybe so. The way I see it," he continued, "most of the railroad owners in Mississippi got together when the writing got writ on the wall and decided on a plan of action. And when cars and locomotives came down from Tennessee, they hid that windfall, too. They concealed the best of their stuff and the stuff from Tennessee, and they left the rest for you, who couldn't know any better. Like you said, they took advantage of the confusion and the magnitude of the disaster that was going on all around."

"I'd have them hanged, drawn, and quartered," Noah said bitterly.

"You may be right, my friend. But like I said, we've got to play the diplomat."

"Why?"

"If we work it all the right way," he said, giving Noah a meaningful look, "and if you can contain your appetite for vengeance, then we can maybe get hold of that equipment and put it to good use for the South."

"That's just dandy," Noah said. His face was skeptical, but his soul longed for the outcome Will Hottel was hinting at. "I'm glad we've begun to find this stuff, and I'm glad we've got the goods on Walter Goodman and the others like him, but I don't see how any of this is going to do us the slightest bit of good—not here in Mississippi. We need the stuff in Georgia and Virginia and the Carolinas, and there's no way to get it there.''

"Don't be so sure," Hottel said.

"Huh?" Noah said, reaching for the jug. He took a jolt, then set it down between himself and the captain. "What do you know that I don't? There's no rail line that we can use that goes east—not unless General Johnston can make a miracle and retake the Memphis and Charleston.''

"Not likely," Hottel agreed.

"Well then?"

There was a pause while Hottel put his thoughts together. "You know, young Major Firebrand Ballard," he said finally, "you're a pretty good man. I've seen you at work, and I like what I've looked at.''

"Thanks," Noah said, screwing up his forehead. What's he leading up to? Noah wondered.

"Do you know why I'm here now?" Hottel asked. "The real reason?''

"I know what your orders said," Noah said.

"That's right," Hottel said. "But you could not have missed the fact that I didn't spend a great deal of time attending to the business detailed in my orders.''

"I did wonder about that," Noah admitted.

"That's because Colonel Sims gave me other orders, secret ones at the direction of the President himself." Colonel Sims was the head of the Railroad Bureau. "My secret orders have to do with the investigation that I've done, and will continue doing, into the whereabouts of hidden railroad equipment in northern Mississippi.''

"Go on," Noah said. "That does explain a few things I've been wondering about.''

"I expect it does.''

"And then?"

"That was the first part of the orders," Hottel said. "Discovering the equipment. The second part concerns bringing the equipment back east and the disposition of it there.''

"What happens to it there?"

"The Railroad Bureau gets to do with it as it sees fit. If

we can bring those engines back east, they will all go to the Bureau.'' He looked significantly at Noah. 'You know what that means?'' he said.

Noah did know what that meant, and it sounded good to him. The Confederacy would have its own railroad instead of, as now, having to beg equipment and rolling stock from what seemed like ten thousand petty railroad lords. The situation with railroads was crazy and irrational. A nation of the midnineteenth century could not fight a modern war with a feudal system of railroads.

"And how do you propose to move it there?'' he asked.

"What we'll have to do is ferry it across Mobile Bay.''

"That can't be done,'' Noah said instantly. "We don't have anything down there that can handle something as large as a locomotive.''

"Then we'll make barges, or whatever it takes.''

"And then, even if you could get the stuff across the bay, the tracks between there and Georgia are all narrower gauge than the five feet they use in Mississippi.''

"We'll work something out,'' Hottel said. "We'll adapt.'' He looked hard at Noah. "The point is, we need that equipment badly, so I'm determined to get it there, no matter what it takes to do it.

"And you're going to help me because I realized almost as soon as I first met you that you were the only man in Mississippi with the fire and the drive to do it.''

Noah just looked at him. He was flattered, of course, but he was also eager to do the very thing the captain had in mind.

"You want to help me, don't you, Major?'' Will Hottel said, his face glowing with heartfelt sincerity.

"You know I do,'' Noah said.

"Good,'' Hottel replied with a brisk nod.

"Is the general aware of your secret orders?'' Noah asked.

"Not yet,'' Hottel said. "I was instructed by Jeff Davis himself not to tell anyone, not even Johnston.'' He paused. "And you know what Davis thinks about Johnston.''

"Yeah, I know,'' Noah said. The enmity between Davis

and Johnston was famous. "But you will tell him, won't you? You'll have to."

"When it proves necessary," Hottel said. "I'll deal with it."

"Right," Noah said.


When the Union cavalry attacked them, Noah Ballard and Will Hottel's train was about eighteen miles south of Okolona on its return trip to Meridian, and Noah Ballard was sound asleep. He had looked forward to a peaceful and restful journey back to General Johnston's headquarters—a peacefulness that was considerably enhanced for Noah by the rocking of the train coach and by William Hottel's sour mash. By his reckoning, he hadn't had a good, sound, uninterrupted sleep since 1862.

After they reached Meridian, he knew, he could look forward to anything but rest and peace.

What would he—and Captain Hottel and General Johnston—do now that Will Hottel had come up with sixty-seven locomotives? And what about Walter Goodman? Would he and the other railroadmen willingly give up their equipment? That seemed hardly likely in the light of their record so far.

And these weren't the only problems Noah would face. There was also General Joseph Johnston himself. He would have a lot to say about the disposition of the engines, and what he had to say might well be different from what Noah Ballard wanted to hear.

Rather than worry about all of that, however, Noah curled up in a seat and nodded off. Eight hours of sleep was a thousand times more inviting than eight hours of worry.

The train was chugging around a curve when the engine driver blew the whistle hard and threw on his brakes. The whistle was a signal to the corporal standing at the rear of the passenger car. When he heard it, he swung the brake wheel at the rear of the platform around and around, and the train heaved to a stop.

As soon as the car ceased moving, the corporal leaned

over the side in order to get a view ahead. What he saw was a great pile of cut wood and brush piled onto the track.

Above the track was a rocky, partially wooded hillside. The hillside, he thought, would make a splendid place to set up an ambush.

The corporal had no more thoughts after that one. A carbine cracked, the first shot of a volley that slammed into the locomotive, the tender, and the two cars. The slug from the first shot crushed the corporal's cheekbone and tumbled into his brain.

Inside the passenger car, men were starting to pick themselves up and grab their weapons. Noah, who had pitched forward when the train made its sudden stop, was sprawled on the floor, struggling to raise himself up to something resembling consciousness—his mind was fogged with both lack of sleep and good sour mash. Even so, his hand had reached for his revolver, and, somehow in his fog of slumber, he was checking the load in the chamber.

William Hottel had crawled up the aisle and was now next to Noah.

He was trying to say something, but the noise of the firing drowned out his words. Noah shook his head and made a cut-off motion with his hand to tell the captain to quit trying to make himself heard.

By this time, Noah was awake enough to put together a set of purposeful actions. He lifted himself up and looked around, and he didn't like what he saw: the troops were firing out of both sides of the car. They were bracketed.

"Shit!" he yelled at the top of his voice.

"You bet!" William Hottel yelled in answer; Noah's obscenity was loud enough for him to hear.

Noah slowly and carefully peered just above the level of the windowsill in order to get some idea of the size of the forces arrayed against them.

He had about two seconds of clear viewing before he dove down for cover.

"*Shit!*" he screamed again. "There must be at least fifty of the bastards on this side alone!"

*"How many!"* Hottel yelled.

*"Fifty!"*

"Son of a bitch!"

Why doesn't the driver set us in reverse and get us out of here? he asked himself.

Then he answered his question with the obvious answer: because he couldn't.

He quickly raised himself up above the window ledge and fired a pair of shots. Then he sank down out of sight again.

"They're wavin' a white flag!" somebody yelled before he could set himself in action.

For a time nobody paid attention, but then somebody else yelled, "Cease firing!" It was the lieutenant who commanded the platoon, Noah realized after a moment. The lieutenant kept yelling until all the shooting stopped. There was no noise of firing from the flatcar either as they, too, saw the white flag.

Two minutes later the man with the white flag made his way to a grassy knoll sixty feet from the train cars.

"Colonel Tyler would like a word with your commander," he shouted. "With your permission, he'll come aboard your train."

The lieutenant, whose name was Downer, glanced over to Noah for instructions.

"Tell him, Lieutenant, that Colonel Tyler can speak to us just fine from that knoll. I don't want him here in our train."

"As you like, sir," Lieutenant Downer said, and shouted that message out the window.

"Colonel Tyler ain't goin' to be pleased," the man with the flag replied.

"Tell him," Noah instructed the lieutenant, "that it isn't our business to attend to Colonel Tyler's pleasure."

The lieutenant repeated the message.

Colonel Tyler turned out to be a little banty of a man, shorter even than Joe Johnston.

While Tyler walked up to the knoll, Noah made his way to the rear platform of the car. He decided he would do the talking and not the lieutenant.

"So what's on your mind, Colonel?" he shouted once the colonel was within hearing distance.

"Do you have a name, sir?" Colonel Tyler asked. He had a cool, mocking voice. It was the voice of a man who was enjoying himself; he was obviously delighted with the predicament he had caused Noah and his men.

"Ballard," Noah answered. "Major."

"Glad to make your acquaintance, Major," Colonel Tyler said. "Now may I come aboard?"

"No."

"You're not real hospitable."

"No," Noah answered, "I'm not. Now tell me what's on your mind."

The colonel gave Noah a good hard look. "Very well, Major Ballard," he said, grinning broadly. "First of all, we've got you beat."

"I wouldn't say that," Noah said.

"Notwithstanding that, you are beaten," he replied. "Second of all, you'll be glad to know you've been beaten by fellow southerners who have chosen not to pursue the errors of our brethren. We're the First Tennessee Cavalry." The First Tennessee Cavalry had been recruited by Grenville Dodge from eastern Tennessee, where many of the people had remained loyal to the Union. Southerners in blue were not much loved by their brothers in gray—understandably.

"Third of all," Tyler went on, "we want your surrender. But fourth of all, once you've given yourselves up, we'll let you free. We don't want you; you can go home." He stopped and looked pointedly at Noah. "How's that for a deal? You can't do any better than that."

"I don't like it," Noah answered automatically.

"What's the matter with you, Major Ballard, you crazy?" Tyler yelled, exasperated.

"What he says sounds fine to me," Will Hottel said. The captain had come out onto the platform and placed himself near Noah's elbow while Noah was talking to Colonel Tyler.

Noah looked at Hottel and then at Tyler. "I'll need some time," Noah said, giving the colonel an uncertain look.

"You have five minutes," Tyler said.

"All right."

"And, Major?" Tyler added.

"Huh?"

"If you have any women on your train, consider them. If you surrender now, I can promise they'll be safe. If we have to come and get you—some of my troops are pretty hungry for loving."

"Go hang yourself," Noah muttered under his breath. He had had no intention of surrendering, but especially not now. There were no women aboard the train, but that mattered not at all to him. He would never give himself up to pirate southerners.

Once they were inside the car, Will Hottel grabbed Noah's shoulder. "If I were you," he said uneasily, "I'd go along with Tyler."

"Not damn likely," Noah said.

"So we surrender," Hottel said more insistently, "and then we go free. I don't see anything bad about that."

"I don't know whether it's bad or not," Noah said. "I'm just not going to do it."

"Look here, Noah," Hottel said, "put some sense into yourself." The big man was shaking Noah hard by the shoulder. "Why get killed when there are better alternatives? And," he added with renewed emphasis, "they'll let us free. Goddamn, be sensible."

Noah shrugged Hottel off and stepped away from him. "Will," he asked softly, "do you actually believe a word out of that man's mouth?" Before Hottel could reply, Noah turned to Lieutenant Downer. "We don't have much time left, Lieutenant, maybe three or four minutes. So Captain Hottel and I are going to see what we can do to get us out of this mess."

"What do you mean?" Hottel asked, not at all liking what he was hearing.

"Just do what I tell you, Will," Noah answered.

"Wait a goddamned minute, Noah," Hottel said, choking the words out. "If they see you doing anything at all, the truce is off."

"That's right," Noah said. "All the more reason to move fast."

"I don't like this," Hottel said.

Noah moved over to Hottel and yelled in his ear: "Come on!"

"You're mad, Noah Ballard!" Hottel said. But he mobilized himself to follow.

When they reached the front of the car, Noah opened the door and extended his head cautiously, turtle fashion. There were two men collapsed on the wood plank floor of the platform, and there was also a good deal of blood. From the quantity of blood on the platform, he had little doubt about their fates.

Noah opened the door wider and made a summoning motion to the sergeant who was in command of the squad up ahead on the flatcar. When the sergeant was close enough to communicate in whispers, Noah, without opening the door wide enough to show himself to any watchers on the hillside, explained what he wanted if the firing started again.

Once that was clear, Noah drew his head back inside the car and turned to Hottel.

"Do what I do, and do it fast!" he said. "Don't hesitate! Don't pause!"

"What are you going to do?"

But Noah didn't answer. By the time the words were out of Hottel's mouth, Noah was out of the door and scrambling down the steps in as low a crouch as possible. When he reached the gravel of the roadbed, he ducked under the car platform and flattened himself.

Seconds later, Hottel joined him.

"Jesus Christ!" Hottel said. "What did you do that for?"

"We're going up to the cab, you and I," Noah answered.

"What for?"

"To drive the train."

"How are you going to do that?"

Noah looked at him. "The easy way," he said, without trying to hide his sarcasm.

He set off on his stomach underneath the axles of the flatcar and, moments later, the tender.

The two men had been noticed by the troops on the hillside. Soon there were shouts for them to come out and show themselves and surrender. Then cavalry carbines were firing at them. As soon as that happened, the two squads on the train started to return fire again, and the fighting resumed.

When Noah, much bruised and scraped, reached the coupler that joined the locomotive to the tender, he paused to catch his breath, then rose to a squat, hoisted his foot up to the coupler, and sprang into the cab.

The engine driver and the firemen were both dead—which was as Noah had expected. The driver had pitched out of the cab onto the side of the roadbed, and the fireman, once he was wounded, had tried to hide in the tender.

Noah gave Hottel his hand and pulled the big man up into the cab. Both men then huddled below the level of the window ledge and took long breaths until they calmed a little.

"You move pretty fast for a big man," Noah said to Hottel after a moment.

"That's what they said to the bear when his tail was on fire," Hottel said.

"Yeah," Noah agreed, "I guess so!"

"Speaking of fires," Hottel said, his attention now turned to the locomotive's firebox, "this one ain't going real hot."

"We'll need to add wood," Noah agreed. "I'll get it," he added when the other man gave him a look that said that a trip to the tender was the very last thing he was willing to undertake.

There was a narrow passage down the center of the tender, and the cut wood was stacked on either side. Noah gathered himself and leaped across to the tender and into the aisle. Then, in the relative safety of the stacked wood, he raised himself up, picked up a load of pine logs, and heaved them over to the cab. Hottel had the fire door open by then, and he stuffed the logs into the firebox.

It took a few minutes for the steam pressure to rise again,

and Hottel spent that time trying to make himself small, for bullets were snapping and ricocheting all around him. It was not just an impossible task, it was ludicrous, because William Hottel was too big to hide in such a tiny cab.

Noah, who was enjoying the relative security of his barricade, did not gloat over the big man's predicament. Will had lost his nerve earlier, but he was doing himself proud now.

When Noah judged the steam pressure had built up enough, he hurled himself back across the gap between the locomotive and the tender and, before the Union soldiers on the hillside above and below the train could bring fire against him, he wrenched the lever that controlled the reverse gear hard backward. Then he opened up the throttle as hard as it would go and plunged down to the floor of the cab.

The locomotive puffed hard, lurched back a little way, shoved against the tender and the two cars, and shuddered to a grinding halt.

The brakes of the passenger car were still closed down.

"Jesus fucking Christ!" Noah muttered. Then he yelled. "*Shit!*" Still screaming his anger and frustration, he pushed the throttle back to neutral. After that, he reached up and pulled the whistle cord, and huge shrill blasts filled the air.

"What's that for?" Hottel asked after Noah had let go of the cord and was back down on the floor of the cab beside him.

"I want some soldier back there with half a brain to open up the car brakes."

"How will you know they've done it?"

"Trial and error, I guess," he said. "In about half a minute I'm going to open up the throttle again."

Hottel gave him an approving look. "You've pretty well got this situation under control, haven't you?"

"Not yet," Noah said.

When he tried the throttle again, the locomotive and tender again jerked back into the cars—but this time the cars moved!

"That's it!" Noah cried. "That did it!"

The train lurched again, shuddered, staggered backward, slowly building up to walking speed, then crawled a little faster.

The Federal cavalry kept firing at them, but there was nothing they could do to halt the train. And they couldn't pursue them either—their horses were tied for safety's sake on the far slope of the hill.

This setback didn't seem to upset the First Tennessee Cavalry. On the contrary; just before the train chugged around the bend and out of sight of their attackers, Noah glanced out of the cab window. There on the hillside in full view stood several score men in blue, led by Colonel Tyler, and they were all laughing.

Noah pulled the train to a stop a few miles north of the spot of the ambush and waited for an hour. Then they resumed their journey toward Meridian, edging cautiously forward. When they reached the barricade again, they discovered with relief that Colonel Tyler and his men had gone to commit mayhem elsewhere. Fifteen minutes after they reached it, they had the barricade pushed off the track.

Nine men from the train had been lost in the encounter with the First Tennessee Cavalry.

"That was a damned fool thing to do," Hottel said, once they were under way once again. There was as much admiration as anger and frustration in his voice. "I hope you realize that. It was brave, and all that, but all we accomplished was just to let off spite. We didn't do any damned good at all. If you'd surrendered, they would of let us just as free as we are now."

Noah rode on awhile without speaking. "You're probably right," he admitted finally. "But it seemed the best thing to do at the time."

"I thought you were a cooler man than that. You're an engineer, for God's sake. Somebody who doesn't act on impulse. Somebody who doesn't act until after long, careful consideration."

"What makes you think an engineer has to always act the way people expect him to act?" Noah said with a rueful smile. "But the truth is," he continued seriously, "I did have to make a move this time, even if it was jut to lash out. I'm glad I did it. I'm thrilled that I caused them as much consternation as we did. We did ourselves some good."

"To tell *you* the truth," Hottel agreed, to Noah's surprise, "I'm glad, too."

"It was worth it to risk your life that way, you mean?" Noah said.

"In times to come, I'll remember this afternoon with approval, if not pleasure."

"I'm surprised to hear that," Noah said. "I had you pegged for a different kind of man."

"People like me don't always act the way people expect us to, either," Hottel said.

"I'm pleased to learn that," Noah said.

"So tell me," Hottel asked, "what did get into you?"

"I had to pay them back," he said with a bitter edge to his voice.

"Pay them back for what?"

The image of the screaming girl with her blackened and blistered hands raged in his mind, along with the image of men in blue standing on a hillside laughing at him.

"I can't tell you now. I'm sorry. Someday, maybe."

From now on, he realized, I'm not going to let myself be drawn into tilting windmills the way I just did. There has to be a better way to get back at them than that.

A few hours later, they were in Meridian.

## Big Black River, Mississippi
## July 30, 1863

"Bong! Bong!" young Willy Sherman shouted at the top of his voice. As he shouted, he dragged a wooden railroad train through the red-brown sand along a beach by the side of the Big Black River. Two days earlier, Willy, his mother, and three of his brothers and sisters had arrived at the campgrounds along the river where the army under General Sherman had bivouaced for the summer. Willy was nine years old, and he was currently accompanied by General Sherman's aide, Sam Hawken.

Ten feet above Willy on the bank and ten yards downstream, Sam kept himself lazily busy with indolent target practice. He sleepily fired his revolver at floating leaves and wood chips that passed by in the sluggish current. He hit most of what he fired at, even though his mind wasn't completely focused on the task.

Among the matters that occupied his attention was the presence of a new arrival in camp. Miss Jane Featherstone had appeared the previous afternoon. At that time she had practically thrown herself at Sam's feet, begging that Sam put her up and take care of her. As General Grenville Dodge's top agent, she told him, she deserved nothing less.

After checking with General Sherman, who agreed that something had to be done with her, suitable quarters were found until arrangements could be made to ship her to a safe place—somewhere out of their hair.

The suggestion was again made that Jane avail herself of General Dodge's offer to send her to San Francisco. She refused. She liked it where she was, and she liked espionage. She'd be overjoyed, she informed Sam, to engage in more espionage, if Generals Dodge and Sherman so desired.

Sam told Jane that he would take her request under advisement.

Now and again, when the spirit moved him, Willy would veer off from playing with the train and slide into the water, for which reason he was at the moment wearing no clothes.

"Bong! Bong! Bong!" he kept shouting happily. "The Okolona Express!"

Sam, observing him from above, wondered where he got that name. Had the boy heard about the attack on the train near that town the other day?

Meanwhile the wooden train lurched along under the guidance of Willy's hand. Though he had smoothed out a kind of roadbed in the sand, the track didn't work as well as Willy intended. His wheels kept digging in and bogging down. That didn't faze Willy, however. He kept moving the train ahead with flinty purpose toward the ambush that he had planned up ahead. Just around a bend, twelve soldiers in blue, on horseback, waited.

Seconds later the soldiers fell on the defenseless train and wrecked it so thoroughly that Willy was able to veer off into the water yet one more time.

"Take off your clothes and come on in!" he yelled, splashing like a porpoise.

"Not now, Will," Sam said, holstering his revolver. He'd had enough target shooting for the day. "Can't."

"You're just yellow," Willy said.

"There are uses for cowardice," Sam said.

"That's a lie," Willy said, and put his head under the water.

The boy frolicked in the water for some time before returning to his toys. The day was growing hotter, and the water was inviting. Sam took in with pleasure the sight of the boy splashing and bobbing with such joy and exhilaration. It was as peaceful and unthreatening here as in Ohio, where Willy and his mother and his other brothers and sisters made their home.

Sam Hawken could relax now, maybe. The summer campaign had pretty well wound down. The Mississippi River was secure from its headwaters to the Gulf, and it looked as if Sherman's army would be resting and recovering here on the Big Black for at least a couple of months. And Sam himself had nothing more important to do than baby-sit Willy Sherman. And that, as far as Sam was concerned, was neither an obligation nor a burden—it was a delight. Willy was a splendid little man whom Sam adored almost as much as Willy's father did.

Sam should have felt good—or anyway, he should have felt relieved. But he didn't. He felt empty and out of his element. He liked watching the boy splashing in the river. Yet he knew in his deepest soul that Willy was out of place here in the heart of the war. Just beyond the bank were not homes and families, quiet streets and shade trees and picket fences, but rank upon rank of tents and dusty, rutted roads and tens of thousands of hardened soldiers resting from their work of killing and destroying.

And outside of camp there were miles and miles of horrors, a ravaged, pillaged land.

And the thing was, it was in that land and not here with the boy where Sam felt most at home. It was as much his element as the sea was to dolphins. He was grateful for the rest and the comfort of the camp, but he knew where his real place was. It was time for Sam to make a journey to some other Jackson. Though he did not see it the same way Jane did, Sam was as avid for espionage as she was.

The boy had paused for a moment in his play and was now standing still in a shaft of sunlight, thigh deep in water, face upturned, eyes closed, drinking in the rich, bright heat.

He himself must have looked very much like Willy Sherman at that age—tanned, carrot-topped, freckled, and with irrepressible energy.

A rustle farther up the bank shattered his recollection. When he looked over his shoulder to see what the rustle was, he saw Willy's father.

"General," Sam said, rising to his feet.

"How are you surviving your encounter with the enemy, Sam?" Sherman said.

"Wounded but still undaunted," Sam said. Then added, "He's always a delight, sir."

Just then Willy's head emerged from the stream, and he shook the water off to see who had arrived. "Daddy!" he screamed.

"Hi there, Sergeant," Sherman said, using the nickname he'd recently acquired. The general's troops had taken to calling Willy that after Willy kept constantly turning up at his father's side. The boy was as much the favorite of the soldiers as he was of his father. "Get yourself dry and put some clothes on, and I'll take you for a ride out of the camp. Would you like that?"

"Oh, yes!" Willy shouted. He rushed up the bank and started to stuff his feet into his trouser legs.

The general gave him a stern look. "Dry first, I said. Your mother will have my head if you catch a chill."

"Here," Sam said, and threw the boy a towel that he'd kept handy. "Catch."

"Sam?" Sherman said, turning to his aide as soon as he was sure that Willy was obeying.

"Yes, sir."

"It's actually you that I've been looking for," he said, catching his eye. "General Dodge has come into camp as of this morning. I thought it would be useful if you participated in a meeting I'm setting up with him after lunch."

"Yes, sir," Sam said.

"Well, Sam," Sherman continued with a sigh, "the general, as I feared he would, has heard about your exploits in Jackson, and he has some ideas about another job for you on similar lines. Much as I need you with me, I think he probably has a point."

Sam felt a stirring within him. Grenville Dodge had many superior talents, but the most surprising of these was that he was the spymaster for General Grant.

"I'll tell you, General," Sam said, cocking his brow with amusement. "I can't guess what sort of thing General Dodge wants me to do, but if it means leaving Willy in the lurch, I just can't do it. The boy would be lost without me."

"That boy," General Sherman said with a snort of laughter, "would miss you mightily for maybe thirty minutes or so. Then he'd find some other gull to charm. Don't you worry about young Willy. It'll do him good to be a little lonesome for a change."

"You're being over hard on that poor boy," Sam said, smiling. "And I would miss him if I had to go off someplace, I truly would. But"—he caught Sherman's eye—"I am more than a little curious about the job General Dodge has in mind for me."

"Rein in your curiosity until after lunch, Captain," Sherman said, pleased to see his eagerness. "The word had best come from General Dodge."

"Yes, sir," Sam said. "Where would you like me to meet you?"

Sherman glanced wistfully at the shade under the cottonwoods by the bank. Then he looked purposefully at Sam. "I've scheduled us at my quarters at two, Sam. But after further reflection and consideration—in light of the strategic and tactical necessities of our situation—I've come to the conclusion that here on the bank might do very nicely."

"It would be considerably cooler," Sam allowed.

"Exactly," Sherman said. "Or at least marginally so."

"I'll see you then, sir," Sam said.

"Sergeant!" Sherman bellowed in his best command voice, "why the devil does it take so long to put your clothes on? If that river was Rebels, you'd be flat on your back with lead in your skull by now. Move it!"

Willy looked up at his father, and then he speeded up his dressing.

Grenville Dodge was a slight, clerkish-looking man with a high-pitched voice, nervous eyes, and long, thin hands that he kept folded most of the time. The only part of him that seemed to move when he talked was his face. Dodge was only a few years older than Sam, but his land speculations in Iowa and his exploits as a railway engineer had given him a national prominence that resulted in a general's commission. Even though it was gained politically, the commission was deserved.

Dodge, Sherman, and Sam Hawken were spread out in the grass under the shade of a cottonwood tree at the top of the riverbank. They were not far from the beach where Willy had been playing earlier that morning. Each of the men had carefully laid his wide-brimmed hat and his service revolver beside him, and on account of the heat and the humidity, Sherman had unbuttoned the top buttons of his uniform blouse, and he was lying semireclined with his back propped against the tree.

Sam followed Sherman's lead and loosened his own buttons, even though he saw that General Dodge had kept his collar tightly fastened. Sam decided that a little bit of comfort wouldn't offend General Dodge. And even if it did, the general's disapproval was easier to endure than the steam-bath heat of Mississippi.

"All right, Sam," Sherman was saying, "you've doubtless figured out a lot of what I'm about to tell you. But anyway, in order to keep things proper, let me deal a few of the cards, and then I'll leave the rest to General Dodge.''

"All right, sir," Sam said with a polite nod. He kept his face calm now, even though he was anything but calm. He was in fact eager to hear what the generals had to say, and more than eager to carry out their plans.

"Is that all right with you, General?" Sherman asked General Dodge.

"Be my guest, General," Dodge said.

These two don't like each other an awful lot, Sam thought to himself, but they do treat each other with respect.

"Anyhow," Sherman said, "General Grant and *his* superiors, meaning the President and God, are of two minds about what our next campaign should be. One mind is to go south from here and take Mobile and then swing east. The other is to turn down from eastern Tennessee and march on Atlanta." Sherman looked at Dodge. "Over to you, General," he said.

General Dodge blinked a few times before taking up the line of conversation. "Thus," he said to Sam without expression, "I've a job for you, Captain. Something that you'd be more than well suited for, if the past is any indication."

"Yes, sir?" Sam said, waiting. So they want me either to go to Atlanta or to Mobile, he thought. Either was fine with him.

"After your excellent undercover work assessing the situation in Jackson for General Sherman, the idea inescapably presented itself that you might be useful in a similar role. I want you to go to Atlanta for me, Captain. I need to have an accurate report I can present to General Grant about the city's present condition. You're the best person we know to do that."

Sam nodded. "Yes, sir," he said to General Dodge. Then to both men, "I appreciate your confidence."

"You don't sound especially eager to go," Sherman said, noting hesitation in Sam's voice. Sam thought it would not be appropriate or seemly for him to appear to leap at another opportunity to become a spy. "You sounded more eager before lunch," Sherman went on. "What has changed your mind?"

"Nothing has changed my mind, sir."

"You are aware, aren't you, Sam," Sherman said, "that this is a voluntary mission. You don't have to go if you don't choose to."

"You are also aware of the risks you will face," General Dodge added. "But," he continued in the same breath, "I'm sure you are also aware of how vitally important it is to us to know exactly what is going on in that place right now. It's the railroad hub of the Confederacy. It's their Chicago. There are ordnance factories there, iron mills, rolling mills, cotton mills, military hospitals. They could lose Richmond and still function, but they can't lose Atlanta. That city," he said, raising his voice, "is the heart of the South."

"You'd make an impressive preacher, General," Sherman said to General Dodge. "I think I'd buy me a ticket to any heaven that you set yourself to describing." Then to Sam, "You will do it, Sam, won't you?"

Dodge was about to say something, but Sherman waved him off.

Sam thought for a time. "Yes, of course I will, sir."

"Good, Sam," Sherman said.

"Thank you, Captain," General Dodge said.

"This is the way it is, Sam," Sherman said, still waving Dodge off. "The practical problem we've got to face is Joe Johnston. That is, as long as Joe is in command in the west."

"The thing about Joe, as recent events have demonstrated, is that he's not a brawler. He picks away at you with a thousand cuts. He saves his army and takes a slice at us here and a slice at us there, wherever the advantage lies with him.

"That's fine as far as it goes," Sherman continued. "If he wants to play the game that way, we'll go along with him for a while. I'll let him march all over the Confederacy if he so chooses. But I'll burn everything I pass by. So after I leave, he'll have nothing to come back to. In other words, Joe Johnston won't make my rules."

"So, Sam, if we can pin Joe Johnston someplace where he has to stay, and if we can fight him and beat him there, then we will have done ourselves considerable service."

"And you think he can't afford to lose Atlanta."

"I think that Jeff Davis can't afford to lose Atlanta. And that means that Atlanta will be the anvil we'll crush Joe Johnston on. It's also the greatest strategic prize in the South right now.

"That's why we need up-to-date information about what's going on there. We especially need to know the condition of the railroads: How useful will they be to the defenders of Atlanta. How much material are they capable of handling? How worn down are they? Do they have enough transport available to support an army north of the city?"

"You must understand, Captain Hawken," General Dodge said, "that all the above considerations will operate only if the President and General Grant decide that our next objective should be Atlanta. There is a large body of thought that maintains that we would be better off making for Mobile. Or," he shrugged, "other places."

"Which may be," Sherman said with a dismissive hand. "But the reason we want Sam Hawken to go to Atlanta is the strong likelihood that the rest of our western armies will follow you, Sam."

"I understand, sir."

"I estimate," General Dodge said, getting down to particulars, "that your mission will take no more than a month or so. We will arrange for you to play a part that will allow you to make safe entry and exit anywhere in the South—and you will play a part very much like the one you played in Jackson."

"When would you like me to go?" Sam asked.

"I'd like to see you rest awhile longer," Sherman said. Then he laughed wickedly. "How about three days from now?"

"I'll be ready, sir," Sam said.

Atlanta! he thought as the two generals rose to leave. He would plunge into Atlanta the way Willy Sherman plunged into the Big Black River.

And then he recalled that there were Kemble lands near Atlanta, a fact that he might find use for.

Whatever happened to Miranda Kemble? he wondered.

## *Meridian, Mississippi*
## *July 31, 1863*

Meridian, Mississippi, was one of the many new towns the railroads had created. Incorporated in 1860, it lay at the junction of the Mobile & Ohio Railroad, which ran north and south along the Mississippi side of the Mississippi–Alabama border, and the Vicksburg and Montgomery. When the Civil War began, Meridian had a population of about one hundred. But because of its strategic location at the crossing of these two major railroads, it was made into a Confederate military camp and division headquarters. Troops were stationed here and arsenals and cantonments were built. And after he evacuated Jackson, General Joe Johnston made it one of his temporary headquarters.

To the west, the land had been purged and pillaged. Much of Jackson was now a charred ruin. Its business section was wasted, as were the majority of its private homes. And, so far as the soldiers of General Sherman could determine, they'd left standing no gins, mills, factories, warehouses, tanneries, blacksmith shops, office buildings, railway tracks, machine shops, depots, or roundhouses for thirty miles around Jackson. Whatever trestles or bridges they found, they put to the torch. Miles of rails were burned and bent so out of shape that they could never be used again. Many more miles of rail were torn up.

Sherman's foragers, meanwhile, had stripped the countryside of corn, hogs, sheep, poultry, cattle, horses, mules. They'd taken every buggy, carriage, and wagon that they could seize, as well as all the stores they could find: flour, grains, salt, sugar, candles, boots, shoes, bacon.

What they didn't take, they put to the torch—corn cribs, immense stores of wheat, furniture, books, clothing.

The wreckage and devastation were so severe that the

citizens who remained in and near Jackson were in danger of starving. Even producing a subsistence crop seemed hopeless.

When Sherman withdrew his army from Jackson at the end of July to take up summer quarters on the Big Black River, he left behind a wasteland, a town of dead, swollen horses, and a smell of brick dust and rotten, stagnant water in ditches.

His men called Jackson "Chimneyville" now.

General Johnston's new headquarters in eastern Mississippi represented something of a military innovation: a rolling command post improvised in a hastily transformed railroad passenger car. The bench seats were ripped out and replaced by a long conference table and, for the officers, light upholstered chairs and settees. For everyone else, there were hard-backed chairs. At one end he'd placed a heavy mahogany bed for himself. This could be screened from the rest of the car by means of heavy, deep scarlet brocade curtains.

The rolling command post turned out to be something more than a general's whim. Johnston was able to use it to move around his command with greater facility and comfort than horses provided. The general was so thrilled with his innovation that he spent very little time in Meridian.

Though Noah Ballard had many important matters to discuss with the general, Noah did not meet with him until Friday, the thirty-first of July, and in this meeting Noah was only one of several participants.

It was midmorning, and Johnston was sitting at the head of the long headquarters conference table. Seated at his left were Walter Goodman, the president of the Mobile & Ohio, Griffin Butterworth, the president of the Mississippi Central, and Anson Floyd, the superintendent of the Mississippi & Tennessee. All three men appeared decidedly ill at ease. Although there was no immediate legal significance to this meeting, Johnston was in a prosecutorial mood, and the railroad men had much to answer for.

On Johnston's right were Noah Ballard and William Hottel. Off to the side a clerk took minutes.

In front of the general was a copy of the report that Noah

Ballard and William Hottel had jointly penned, detailing the whereabouts of various pieces of railway equipment that had been, as the report diplomatically stated, mislaid here and there in northern Mississippi.

Johnston had had more than a day to digest the report. Even amid the overwhelming crush of his many concerns, it had startled him.

After the greetings and introductions were made and the several military and civilian gentlemen were seated, General Johnston picked up his copy of the paper and held it out in front of him the way Hamlet might have held Yorick's skull.

"I trust," he said with a thin smile, "that all of you good gentlemen have had the opportunity to read this paper that Major Ballard and Captain Hottel have presented to me." There were nods and bows of assent from the men at Johnston's left.

"I wonder what you gentlemen make of it," the general continued. "I must admit that I myself was left with something more than curiosity after I had finished reading it." With a theatrical gesture, he let the report drop to the table.

"It appears to have been a well-researched and thorough-going piece of work," Walter Goodman said, all innocence. He was a short, roundish man in his early fifties, and he, it was soon evident, had taken upon himself the responsibility of speaking for all the railroad men. "I think we should all congratulate the major and the captain for their fine and careful work."

"You don't find yourselves," Johnston went on slowly and precisely, "with any quarrels as to the accuracy of the ... ah ... allegations? The locomotives and other equipment, Walter, Griffin, Anson"—he stared at each man in turn, using their Christian names, for Johnston and the railroad men were well acquainted—"are as represented? The numbers and condition and so on?"

"I would presume so," Walter Goodman said with a resigned shrug, "insofar as their information is certainly more up to date than ours."

Johnston's face suddenly turned hard. "Then how the hell do you explain it, Walter?"

"Explain it?" Goodman said, still innocent.

"Yes, sir, exactly so," Johnston said through drum-tight lips. He paged through the report until he found the list of numbers he wanted. "Here it says that Captain Hottel has uncovered twenty-six locomotives that he indicates were somehow 'lost' somewhere along your line." He glared at Goodman. "*Lost*, Walter?"

Goodman shrugged again, more impressively than before. "It's wartime, General. You know how it is. Confusion. Mayhem. The right hand doesn't know what the left hand is doing. The report states things pretty much the way I know them. Certain pieces of equipment were mislaid. They, as it were, fell through the cracks."

*"Twenty-six locomotives?"*

"I don't find that impossible to conceive, General," Goodman said evenly.

"And neither do you other gentlemen, I take it, find it impossible to believe that forty-one other locomotives have fallen through the cracks in your jurisdictions?"

"No, General, not at all," said the chorus to the left of Johnston.

Goodman was growing increasingly animated, to lend greater force, Noah was convinced, to his attempts to explain away acts that were hard to justify. Floyd and Butterworth had poker faces. They would leave the hard work to Goodman.

"So I would be wrong," Johnston said, "in drawing the inference that the twenty-six locomotives were secreted away at your orders, Walter, in order to preserve them from the ravages of war?"

"Absolutely," Goodman said without blinking.

"And similarly with you, Griffin? I'd be wrong in drawing the same conclusion with you, that" —he glanced at the paper in front of him— "you ordered the concealment of twenty-one locomotives?"

"I gave no such order," Butterworth said.

"And you, Anson," the general said softly, glancing at

the paper, "in your case the number of locomotives is twenty?"

"No, I did not order these locomotives hidden. Indeed, I'm delighted that your officers were able to locate· them. Now perhaps we can save them from that bastard Sherman."

Johnston turned his attention to the clerk who was taking minutes. "You got all that, Corporal? For the record,"—he gave the railroad men a sidelong glance to make sure that none of them missed a word he was saying—"please make sure that it is clearly written in these minutes that Misters Goodman, Butterworth, and Floyd deny any knowledge of or complicity in any effort to conceal the existence of a total"—he paused to add up the sum—"of sixty-seven locomotives, so as to prevent their risk in wartime operations." His tight smile turned wicked. "These gentlemen will sign as true these minutes after they are presented to me." He looked at the railroad men. "Does that satisfy you gentlemen?"

"Yes, surely," Walter Goodman said.

"And," he turned to Noah and Will Hottel, "I trust that you officers have no evidence to the contrary?"

"None, sir," Noah said, straightfaced. None that would satisfy a court of law. He had no doubt, of course, that the three men were lying. But as Will Hottel had pointed out, what good would it do to catch them in their lies? Should we put them up against the wall and shoot them? That was not a viable choice. It would not save the locomotives, which had become Noah's prime objective right now. Hottel had convinced Noah that they'd have to protect the railroad men if they were going to save the locomotives.

"From what we could learn, and from what we observed," Hottel said with a glance at Noah, "we have judged that the locations of the locomotives are consistent with the explanation that these gentlemen have given. It appears that they were simply lost in the confusion."

"All right, then," Johnston said, "I'll go along with that. You will be relieved to know, gentlemen, that none of you has done anything that could be called reprehensible. It is my conviction, and I trust our courts would so decide, that the withholding for personal gain of material that is of strategic importance to the nation is treason. It appears that none of you is guilty of such an act, and I'm pleased.''

The railroad men, Noah could see, were breathing easier. And well they might; they'd gotten off the hook. Joe Johnston did not like to be betrayed by men whom he looked upon as his own kind. If there were actual proof that they had betrayed him, he would have had their hides.

''Now for the question of what to do about all of this expensive—and more or less unusable—equipment,'' Johnston said, sinking back in his chair and trying to relax.

Walter Goodman and the others looked apprehensive—an apprehension that Noah shared. Noah turned to the general, and the sight shook him. He hadn't before realized how haggard and worn Johnston had become since the fall of Jackson. His complexion was grayish, his eyes were flat and lusterless, his body sagged.

''Excuse me, sir,'' Will Hottel said, ''but I don't believe that I would agree with your characterization of the locomotives as 'unusable.' ''

Johnston raised his hand to stop Hottel from continuing. ''You'll get your chance to make your case, but not today. I'm not disposed to listen to opposing arguments today.'' As he said that, he glanced significantly at the railroad men.

''As you all know, or can at least guess,'' he continued, ''there is no longer much point in our trying to maintain a military presence in Mississippi.'' Walter Goodman looked more than a little alarmed, but he didn't say anything. ''I realize that some of you might take issue with that judgment, but there it is. Our resources are limited, and we need to consolidate our limited resources as best we may. This is something of a euphemism, gentlemen, for retreat. But whatever it's called, there's no help for it. We're moving east because that's where we are right now capable of defending.

''Now, given that, what do we take with us?'' He paused and then shifted into the mode of a military-academy lecturer. ''Answer: anything we need that we can carry or move there. Locomotives require tracks. We have no tracks now to the east: ergo we leave the locomotives behind. Question two: if we leave them, who gets them? Answer: General Ulysses Simpson Grant. That is not acceptable to me, ergo we will destroy the locomotives.''

"No!" the railroad men cried in a single chorus.

Walter Goodman rose to his feet, evidently believing that that might better make his point.

But the general would have none of that.

"I told you all," he said, rising to his feet and staring Goodman back down into his seat, "that I am not of a mind today to entertain opposing views."

He remained standing. "That, I believe, will be all. Anyone holding opinions on the matters under discussion today will please put them in writing, and I will deal with them at the appropriate time.

"Meanwhile I'd appreciate it if Major Ballard would remain behind after the other gentlemen depart. He and I will discuss the implementation of the conclusion of my second corollary.

"That will be all, gentlemen."

The railroad men seemed staggered by the general's abrupt decision and his indifference to any arguments to the contrary. But none of them seemed willing to test the general's resolve. They stood shakily and uttered polite parting words.

Everyone but Noah began to file out. As they were leaving, Noah examined Will Hottel's face, trying to make out why the captain seemed to be taking the general's decision to destroy the locomotives so quietly and passively. But Noah found no clue. He seemed, if anything, distracted, as though he were unconcerned about this morning's calamity. That intrigued Noah, and it made him realize that he wanted the captain by his side when he had his coming encounter with Joe Johnston.

"Do you think it would be useful," he asked Johnston, "for Captain Hottel to remain behind with me?"

"No, Major," Johnston said, shaking his head, "you'll do splendidly on your own."

"Yes, sir," Noah said, trying hard to stifle his annoyance.

After the others had all left through the door at the rear of the car, Johnston asked Noah to take a seat at the conference table again, and Johnston himself resumed his place at the head of it. His mouth was twisted into a bitter smirk.

"Well, well," he said. "I guess I've fried those bastards' bacon. What do you think, Major?"

"Sir, I don't know what to think."

"I'll tell you what I *know*, Major. I know that those fine gentlemen were lying. I can read between the lines of that report you wrote as well as the next man. You don't just *mislay* machinery worth thousands of dollars. Would Walter Goodman or Griffin Butterworth or Anson Floyd mislay a five-hundred-dollar slave? Hardly. Those fine gentlemen have done a very evil thing, and I'm going to make sure they are punished for it, punished where they hurt most— where they hoard their money. And the way I'm going to do that is to have those locomotives destroyed. Walter and Anson and Griffin will never again see the money they put into those splendid pieces of iron."

Then his gaze snapped hard toward Noah. "So tell me, Major, why did you cover for them?"

Noah looked away for a moment, retreating from the general's attack. The wrong answer here could make an already bad situation much worse.

He decided, for lack of a better choice, to tell the truth.

"The way I see it, General," he said, "is this. First, I saw no proof that they hid anything, though you're right, I'm pretty sure they did. Second, I didn't think it would do any good to try to punish them. Third, after I cooled off, I figured they'd be hurt enough if we took the locomotives out of Mississippi and brought them to Georgia or the Carolinas or Virginia. The thing is, General, this country needs those locomotives. We don't need them as scrap metal lying all over northern Mississippi; we need them hauling loads back east."

"How are you going to get them back there?" Johnston said almost casually, but Noah could hear the steel hardness in the back of the general's throat.

"We'll take them down to Mobile and barge them over to the other side of Mobile Bay. It should be easy after that."

"Can't be done." His voice was like a crack of lightning.

"I have to respectfully disagree, General. I'm pretty sure that I can do it."

But Johnston only shook his head. He would not budge.

Noah then considered telling Johnston what he knew about the real mission that Will Hottel was on, but he decided against it. Hottel had told him specifically that knowledge of his secret orders was to be kept from General Johnston. And though Noah disagreed, he decided it wasn't his business to say anything different. If Hottel wanted to tell Johnston what he was up to, then he could do it himself.

"No, son, no," Johnston said, mellowing, "it won't work. Even if you could, as you claim, get those machines to Georgia, it would cost too much time and too many people. We don't have anything left that we can spend, son. Nothing."

"That's what I'm saying, sir. We don't have anything we can spend anymore. We can't build locomotives anymore, and here in our pockets are sixty-seven splendid locomotives, many of them almost as new as when they came out of the factory."

"And do you know what would happen once you got them to Georgia or wherever, provided you could somehow bring them there?"

"What do you mean, sir?"

"I'll tell you what would happen. You think they will be put into the service of the Confederate States of America. That won't happen. Vultures like Walter Goodman or Griffin Butterworth will grab them for their own uses. Every tinhorn railroad president is going to demand he get some of those locomotives. He'll find some pressing, overriding, unbeatable reason why he needs the damn things more than his country. And you know what, Major Ballard? He'll get them."

"They'll go to the Railroad Bureau," Noah said. "They have to!"

"Why do they have to?"

Because, Noah thought, that is what Will Hottel told me was in his orders. but I can't say anything about that.

"It's only reasonable, sir," Noah said lamely.

"Reason never made even the beginnings of an explanation for any actions of the good and fine gentlemen of the South," Joe Johnston said.

"That's a very gloomy view, sir, of . . ."

"People like Walter Goodman?" the general interrupted. "Anyhow, you go and figure out how you are going to wreck all that equipment—what you need, how many people—and then come back and tell me what you want, and I'll give it to you."

Noah, believing that the general was done with him, rose to leave.

"Sir, thank you for your time."

"I didn't tell you to leave yet," Johnston snapped. "Sit down, Major."

"Yes, sir," Noah said, and took his seat again.

"You know, Major, when it comes down to it, I can understand pretty well what motivates people like Walter Goodman. There's probably a more refined and gentle word for it, but 'greed' will do until I can think of the kinder word. What I can't for the life of me understand is this." He gave Noah another steel-hard look. "I thought you were a very smart man, Major. Probably one of the two or three smartest men who've ever served under me."

"Thank you, sir," Noah ventured.

"Don't thank me yet," Johnston snapped. "What I can't understand," he continued, "is why a smart man like you would do just about the most dumb-ass, damn-fool useless stunt I've ever heard of."

Noah knew what was coming, but since there was nothing he could do about it, he just waited for the ax to fall.

"So, Major, enlighten this poor old man. Tell him why a smart man would take on just about singlehanded an entire troop of Yankee horse soldiers."

Noah took a breath, as though getting ready to speak.

"Not yet, Major," Johnston said, raising his hand. "I'm not through with my say yet." And at that he gave Noah a withering look. "I have always believed, Major, that our southern officers were the boldest, dashingest, most courageous warriors ever to walk the earth. And the most foolish, because to them, war isn't a contest that you have to win—it's a spectacle where you have a chance to show off. They're not after victory; they're after glory.

"Now I can understand that, just like I can understand Walter Goodman. But you, sir, confound me. What you did, Noah Ballard, makes no sense either as an attempt at glory or a try for victory. What the hell were you up to, boy? Why did you have to risk your life, and a good many other lives, too, when the Yankees told you they were going to let you go anyway?"

Noah took another breath, a long one. Then, even though he was sitting ramrod straight in his chair, he straightened himself up even more. He stared at a point about three feet behind General Johnston's head.

"Sir," he said, "I know it was a damn-fool stunt. And I deeply regret it."

"Well, boy," Johnston said, "at least your smarts haven't totally deserted you. But I still don't know why you did it."

"I lost my head, sir," Noah said after a pause. "I was angry, and I saw what seemed to be an opportunity to strike back."

"And how exactly did you think you could strike back?"

"I know that Colonel Tyler of the First Tennessee claimed that he would have released us after we surrendered to him. And he probably would have, I admit. But I didn't *want* to surrender. I thought that if I could reach the engine cab, I might get the train to back up and then we wouldn't *have* to surrender. And Colonel Tyler and his folks would have egg on their face."

"And what likelihood of success did you believe you had?"

"I thought there was a pretty fair chance of success at the time." He paused. "And events proved I was correct. We got away from them."

And they laughed at us as we left, Noah said to himself.

Johnston just sat there and stared at Noah with an expression that wasn't so much disgust as regret, which was worse. "Well, son," he said finally, "that does put some light on your actions. You were pissed over recent setbacks, so you determined to tweak the Yankees' noses. You've comported yourself in a fashion suitable, I'd venture to say, to a fifteen-year-old.

"Yes, sir," was all Noah could manage.

"You, Major, are worth more to me than a troop of cavalry, because some of the time you use your head. So don't go off half-cocked again, ever. Hear me?"

"Yes, sir," Noah whispered.

"Now get the hell out of here," the general said. "And let me know by tomorrow morning what you plan to do about wrecking the locomotives."

When Noah Ballard emerged from General Johnston's headquarters, Will Hottel was waiting for him, smiling like the cat who just swallowed the canary.

"Who died?" Hottel asked when he saw Noah's expression.

"What?" Noah asked, dazed at what he'd just undergone.

"Was it your mother or your sweetheart?"

"Oh," Noah said. He wasn't amused. Why is he so full of joy? Noah wondered.

"So," Hottel said, "tell me what went on in there."

"More painful than purgatory, but not so long as hell."

"That bad?"

Noah shrugged. "I got chewed out for the business I led you into the other day."

"He didn't appreciate what you did?"

"Hardly."

"Nor your reasons for doing it?"

"Even less."

"Well, that's too bad," Hottel said with a sympathetic sigh. "Did you bring up the locomotives?"

"He won't budge on that," Noah said.

"Well, come on, then," Hottel said. "We're going to Butler's." Butler owned and ran what passed locally for a hotel. Much more important than its accommodations for travelers was its saloon.

"What for?" Noah said. "I don't need to drink right now; I need to get away by myself."

"No, you don't. You need to come with me to Butler's. Goodman and the other two are there now."

"What do I need to see them for?"

"Just come."

Goodman, Butterworth, and Floyd had taken a round table in a corner of Butler's Saloon. It wasn't an especially large table, but by dint of considerable squeezing, both Noah and Hottel were able to fit in.

"Drinks, gentlemen?" Goodman asked as soon as the maneuvering was successfully completed.

"Nothing for me," Noah said.

" I'll have what you men are having," Hottel said. They were drinking rum. Goodman motioned to Butler, and Will Hottel's rum arrived shortly.

"That was pretty damned rough in there," Butterworth said.

"It sure as hell was," Floyd agreed. "I'd always heard that Joe Johnston was stubborn, but I never realized how stubborn. He just about takes the prize for bullheadedness."

"I guess he probably does," Goodman said. Then he turned to Will Hottel, but his gaze included Noah, too. "Despite the way things went in there, I want to thank you two gentlemen for standing by us."

For covering up for you, you mean, Noah thought bitterly. He didn't like these men, and he wasn't proud of what he'd done to save their asses.

"And for holding steadfast to the truth, as you saw it," Goodman continued. "I expect that we'd have been in considerable hot water if you both had decided to speak and write other than the way you did."

"We do our duty," Hottel said somewhat sanctimoniously, Noah thought. Noah just nodded.

"Yes, thank you both." Floyd and Butterworth raised their glasses, and Goodman joined them.

"Now if you gentlemen could only save those locomotives as successfully as you've located them," Goodman said after he'd lowered his glass. "For that, of course, I would be eternally grateful."

Floyd and Butterworth gave him a look, but he ignored them. "It would have been a great shame if the equipment had remained . . . lost to the end of the war."

"With respect to the preservation of those locomotives," Will Hottel said carefully, "we may not be totally without resources, even in the face of the very stubborn General Joseph Johnston."

"Do please elaborate on that, Captain," Goodman said, keeping his anticipation and curiosity closely reined. "Is it because of your awareness of those resources," he asked, looking pointedly at Hottel, "that you saw fit to bring us all together now?"

So it's Hottel who called this gathering, Noah said to himself. Why? And why has he been in such a good humor after the general's decree?

"Yes, of course," Hottel said easily, spreading his arms welcomingly. "I didn't want to see anyone plunged into despair," he smiled, "over a situation that might prove transient."

"Yes?" Goodman said. "What do you know that we don't?"

"That Colonel Sims, the chief of the Railroad Bureau, currently has the ear of Secretary Seddon." James Seddon was the Confederate Secretary of War. "And that I have been in communication with Colonel Sims by telegraph ever since I began to make my, ah, fortuitous discoveries of locomotives in northern Mississippi. This knowledge Colonel Sims has transmitted to the Secretary. And, I take it, the Secretary has expressed considerable interest in the equipment."

"What does that mean practically?" Walter Goodman asked cautiously.

"I think it means practically that the Secretary might be persuaded to order General Johnston to change his mind about destroying the locomotives *if* you gentlemen would be prepared to give them to the Railroad Bureau." His eyes flashed at their sudden consternation. "As a loan," he added with a smile, "until the completion of the war."

"But that's impossible," Anson Floyd said. "Those are our locomotives. We require them here."

"I agree," Butterworth said. "What you have proposed is tantamount to their destruction."

"Perhaps you gentlemen have forgotten," Hottel pointed out, "that many of those machines originated in Tennessee and were brought south, presumably for safe keeping. Perhaps half of them, in other words, are not legally yours to start with. What I am suggesting is that we attempt to take these locomotives where they will be most useful."

Noah now began to realize why Hottel had been so pleased with himself all morning. He probably stood to get the locomotives for the Railroad Bureau. And he stood to get the cooperation of these men in doing it—something that Noah had never believed possible.

"What I think you're telling us," Walter Goodman said, "is that if we donate the equipment to you, then we might get it back at some later date."

"Exactly," Hottel said with a smile.

"And that if we don't donate it to you, then you will stand aside and let Joe Johnston have it destroyed."

"Exactly."

"That doesn't leave us much choice, does it? Either way, we don't have much to run our railroads with."

Hottel frowned in mock sympathy. "I'm sorry to hear that," he said. "But I trust you energetic and resourceful gentlemen will manage somehow. Meanwhile I do need your backing on this—so Colonel Sims assures me—if we are to win Secretary Seddon's approval. He doesn't want to act unless he has the assurance that you men are willing to go along with the idea."

Goodman pondered that for a time. Then he bowed his head with all the enthusiasm of a condemned man lowering his neck to the block. He looked at the other railroad men. "Well?" he asked, and they both gave resigned assents.

"Then I can assume that all of us are together in this endeavor?" Hottel said.

"Yes, we'll do it," Goodman said, and the others nodded.

"How about you, Noah?" Hottel asked. "I haven't heard from you since you came into Butler's. I had every expectation that you'd be delighted at the outcome of this gathering."

"Let's do it," Noah said, feeling considerably less pleased than Will Hottel had believed he would. This whole meeting was leaving Noah Ballard very uneasy. And yet he knew that he was obtaining his greatest wish—he was getting the locomotives.


Three days later a telegram arrived from the Secretary of War in Richmond. The gist of it was that every effort was to be made to preserve the sixty-seven locomotives in northern Mississippi and to transport them to Atlanta by whatever means proved feasible.

# ♦ SIX ♦

*London, England*
*August 14, 1863*

Fanny Shaw fidgeted in her Drury Lane dressing room while her attendant removed her costume. Fanny had just completed a performance as Lady Macbeth, and she was thrilled with herself. The role was one of her favorites, with its mixture of fire and ice, passion and treachery. It was a role for which she was well suited. Fanny shared with the wife of the Scottish king a kind of ambition and force of will that most men found unbecoming in the fair sex. She was not, however, as willing as Lady Macbeth to sacrifice the lives of others to her ambitions.

Fanny's performance this evening, she was convinced, had been electrifying, and the audience—a full house—had responded with gratifying enthusiasm. There was absolutely nothing in the world so exhilarating as wave upon wave of applause from a theater full of people. Adulation was a much more potent drug than laudanum or alcohol.

Once she was out of the flowing, heavily draped gown, Fanny slipped into a light robe, sat down before her dressing table, and stared into the mirror. She'd observe herself in this way just twice more before the run of *Macbeth* would be finished.

She regretted that, but she was also looking forward to the freedom the end of the run would yield. Friends in Dorset had begged her to visit them for a week. She would grant them their wish gladly, for they had fine horses, and Fanny loved riding. She rode like a man, in trousers, astride her horse rather than sidesaddle. And she sat her horse better than most men did, better even than most longtime cavalry officers. Her penchant for taking solitary rides had been one of the thousand causes of friction between herself and her former husband, Pierce Kemble.

Fanny had not yet learned of Pierce's death.

There was a sharp, loud rapping on her door.

"Tell them to go away, will you please, Becky?" Fanny asked her attendant, Becky Grantham. "I don't want admirers this evening."

"Yes, ma'am," Becky said.

While Becky went to the door, Fanny worked at her greasepaint with a cotton cloth.

There were words at the door between Becky and the visitor, but Fanny was much too involved with the task at hand to pay attention to what was said. Nor did she notice Becky approaching with an armful of long-stemmed white roses.

"Look, ma'am," Becky said excitedly.

"Not yet," Fanny said. She was wiping away the makeup on her eyelids.

"You'll want to hurry, ma'am," Becky said.

But Fanny took her time.

"There," she said when she was satisfied. "Now what have we to look at?" She turned to Becky and cried out in amazement. The girl held more than three dozen white roses, and she was beaming like a new bride.

"Oh, my," Fanny said softly. Then louder, "Oh, my! Who could have possibly done this for me?"

"There was no card, ma'am."

"No card?" Fanny said, perplexed.

For the first time, Fanny noticed a figure standing in the shadow between Becky and the still open doorway. He was a cripple, bent and gnarled of body, shabbily dressed, with a slouch hat and a muffler obscuring most of his face.

"Who are you?" she called out. "How did you get in?"

Becky turned to him. "I thought I told you to stand outside," she said to the man, annoyed that he would disobey her. "I didn't tell you to enter."

"I'm sorry, mum," the man croaked, "but I wuz s'posed to bring the flowers to the lidy personal, and so I done it like I promised."

"That didn't mean barging into a lady's dressing room, you ugly mongrel," Becky said.

The man's body seemed to sag even more, if such a thing were possible. "Sorry, mum. I wuz only doin' me dooty, if yer gets me meanin'."

"Come on," Becky said. "Out with you." And, roses and all, she moved to drive him out the door. The man shuffled to obey her, moving awkwardly sideways like a crab.

"Wait," Fanny said.

Both Becky and the man came to a stop. The man inclined his face a little toward Fanny, but not enough to reveal any of his features.

"Who sent you?" she asked.

"A gen'lmun. 'E woul'n't give 'is nime," the man said in his croaking voice. "But 'e wuz a forrin'r, I'd judge from the wiy 'e spoke. Tall, wealthy, 'andsome, dashin', powerful, alluz gits 'z wiy—if yer gets me meanin'." Fanny gave him a hard, penetrating look. " 'E ast if yer wuz free ter dine wif 'im. An' 'e sez I'm not ter tike no fer an answer."

There was something about the man's voice beneath the croak that Fanny recognized, and something about the man, beneath the bent, gnarled body and the crabwise shuffle, that was familiar. The man's voice was a pretty fair imitation of an East End guttural, but his vowels and consonants were actually disguised southern American.

"How am I to meet this . . . gentleman," Fanny said, perceiving in a flash who the man really was, "if I do indeed choose to dine with him?" Fanny asked.

I'll give him back as good as he's giving me, she thought, laughing to herself.

"I'm ter tike yer to 'im," the man said.

"I couldn't possibly be seen with the likes of you," Fanny said firmly.

"Yer'd be much 'vised to do't, mum. The gen'lmun don't tike no fer an answer, like I said. An' 'e's a mean one. I'd hite ter tike the cons'quence uv refusin' 'im, if yer tikes me meanin'."

"After such a recommendation," Fanny said in her best and most outraged Duchess of Malfi tones, "how can I dare to take this man's offer. I'll *never* do such a thing." Then she turned to Becky. "Deposit the roses with their original bearer. I do not choose to accept them." Then to the man: "But before you retrace your steps to your master, do me the kindness of showing me your face."

"No-o!" the man cried out with horror, flinching backward and raising his arm to shield the small patch of flesh that was visible. "Yer don't want ter see me fice. You'd die ter see it, mum."

"I won't hear that," she said, laughing, to Becky's astonishment. And before either the man or Becky could grasp what she was doing, Fanny was out of her chair and striding to him. He tried to scuttle away, but she was too quick for him. She ripped off his hat and muffler and grasped his chin, lifting it up so that she could take a hard look at his face.

When she had revealed who it really was, she roared with laughter.

"Ash Kemble!" she cried between peels of delight. "Ash! You mountebank! What did you do this for? Why don't you approach me as any normal man does?"

"Because I'm not a normal man," he said, laughing with her and straightening himself up to his normal height. "And you, my love, are no normal woman."

"And these are *your* roses, of course," she squealed, grabbing the entire bunch from her shocked attendant and twirling herself around with the roses in her arms.

"They're yours now," Ash Kemble said.

"Becky!" Fanny said, still whirling ravishingly. "This gentleman is my dear friend, Ash Kemble, an American and the uncle of my children."

"Pleased to meet you, sir," Becky said, still much taken aback.

"Stop," Ash said to Fanny, laying a restraining hand on her shoulder. "You'll have yourself intoxicated even before we start on the champagne." And then he held his other hand out to Becky. "I'm delighted to make your acquaintance," he said. And she curtsied.

"But Ash," Fanny asked, for it had at that moment dawned on her that he had just returned from Georgia, "you haven't brought my Miranda back." If Miranda had returned with her uncle, Fanny realized, she would have accompanied him now.

"She chose to stay at Raven's Wing," he said quietly.

"But why?" she asked, upset. "There's no reason for that—unless *he* influenced her decision."

"No, Fanny, I don't think he did. But," he paused, grim-faced, "I have some serious news, and this is not the most pleasant place to tell it."

"Bad news?" Fanny asked, alarmed.

"Ariel, Miranda, and Lam are well," Ash said, calming her.

"Then tell me," she demanded. "Don't leave me hanging."

"At dinner," he said.

The restaurant he chose for her was a small, elegant place in Mayfair owned by an exiled Polish revolutionary named Tadeusz Kopicki. It was for all intents and purposes a private club; no sign or nameplate announced it to the vulgar public, and no one who was not well-known to Count Kopicki was admitted.

Ashbel Kemble was admitted instantly and with the obsequious deference usually accorded by the count to a member of the British Royal Family. The count effusively escorted Ash and Fanny to a private dining room, left briefly, and returned with a magnum of Dom Pérignon, a bucket of ice, long-stemmed, fluted crystal glasses, and a multitude of extravagant fluorishes.

Once Fanny and Ash were comfortably seated and their glasses were shimmering with champagne, the count announced that he would return shortly with their meal.

"I took the liberty of ordering in advance," Ash said after the count had departed.

"Thank you," she said. "That takes a considerable load off of me," she added with a sly, coquettish smirk. "But," she went on in a rush, "tell me your news. I want to hear about my girls and about Lam. Is the South losing? Are the reports accurate? I hope so! I truly hope the Confederacy is defeated soon and solidly."

"In time. In time," he said, raising his glass to her. "I have much news for you, but you'll hear all of it, I promise. First, however, a toast to you."

"Yes, my dear," she said reluctantly, still impatient to learn what he was holding back from her, "I'm delighted to see you safely again, too." And she touched his glass with hers. They both sipped once. Then he got down to the business of telling her the tale of his trip to Kemble Island.

The story of the events leading up to the death of her former husband fascinated her. Even after so many years of separation, she still hated him, yet she was saddened to learn of the attack of apoplexy that killed him.

On the other hand, she was delighted to learn that Ariel's boy was turning into such a beautiful, happy, and mischievous child. She had seen the boy just after he was born, shortly before the start of the war, and Ariel had managed to send a photograph of the two-year-old to her in London. But now that he was a real person, and therefore interesting in his own right, Fanny wanted to know as much about him as she could.

Her great disappointment, predictably, was that Miranda had chosen not to escape from the terrible war-torn land when she had the chance and when she no longer had her father's needs to consider!

"What could possibly have gotten into the girl?" she asked Ash. "Why does she stay in that dismal hell, when she could be with me here in the comforts of London?"

"I don't know, Fanny," Ash said. "I'm as baffled by her choice as you are."

"It's not baffling; it's mad! Why didn't you abduct her? You have ten times the sense that she does. Knock her on the head and tie her up and carry her off."

Ash laughed at that. "It's not my practice to force my will on women."

"Fiddlesticks!" Fanny said, shaking her head in frustration.

"As you may have noticed, Fanny, your younger daughter has a will of her own. In this she rather takes after her mother. It seems to me possible that the very reason you adore her so—id est, you are both as alike as peas in a pod—is the reason why she has chosen to remain behind rather than come here. There she is on her own. Here she is your daughter."

"She's helpless and without protection there."

"I wouldn't say that," he said honestly. "She has managed to run Raven's Wing with some success, in spite of the war. I even think she likes it."

"What's a young girl like her doing running a plantation?"

"Fanny," he laughed, "you of all people are not the woman to find fault with her for her independence."

"It's not the same as it is with me," Fanny muttered weakly.

"Oh?" he said, tilting his face toward the ceiling and raising his eyebrows dramatically. "I don't see very much difference. I truly don't." He faced her again. "But," he said more seriously, "I plan to make another trip to Georgia almost immediately. I'll be going to Atlanta, among other places. If you like, I'll keep track of her." He laughed again. "And I don't mind that chore. I adore the child myself—perhaps nearly as much as you do."

"You are going back so soon?" Fanny asked, drawing in her breath. A thought had suddenly formed in her mind.

"I arrived in Liverpool night before last on my own *Miranda*," he said. He had named two of his fleet blockade runners after Fanny's daughters. "I'm leaving as quickly as she can be restocked and loaded with cargo."

"Why?" Fanny asked. "Why must you risk that perilous

voyage so soon after you've returned? Don't you have other responsibilities?" She was referring to his other varied business interests. The bulk of his shipping business had no connection with running the blockade to southern ports.

"Because of the nature of this cargo, or of a portion of it, at least," he amended. "The bulk of *Miranda*'s cargo will be brass shell casings. But I'll also keep in my own cabin eight chests of even more valuable goods."

Her eyes widened. "What?"

"Morphine, chloroform, quinine. The South is almost bereft of these drugs, and casualties are mounting. An ounce of morphine or chloroform will fetch a hundred gold dollars in Atlanta."

"How large are the chests?"

"Fifty pounds apiece."

"And you want to take personal charge of them?"

"Exactly," he said. "Those chests should bring me over half a million dollars in Atlanta."

"You *are* a sly one, Ash Kemble," she said, her voice brimming with admiration. But then suddenly she shuddered with alarm. "What if . . . ?" She left the thought unfinished.

"What if I'm attacked by pirates? Highwaymen? Federal gunboats? Dragons of the deep?" He smiled.

"Don't joke about it. At least two of those are very real possibilities."

"That's why I must take personal charge of the chests."

"Yes, I see," she said a little absently. The thought that had been forming in her mind had taken much firmer shape. She leaned toward him and extended her hands, grasping his. "I will go with you," she whispered, her soft voice thrilling with audacity.

"Fanny!"

"I must!"

"Why, Fanny?" he managed, much taken aback, shaking his hands free of hers. "Whatever for? Surely not to help me guard my cargo!"

She laughed at the absurdity of that. "No, no. I don't care about your cargo. I must have passage to Georgia, and that's where you are going. I must go to Miranda so long as Miranda refuses to come to me.''

''I think that such a voyage would be ill-advised,'' Ash said carefully. He knew better than to refuse her outright. ''It *is* dangerous, and you are not exactly well loved in Georgia.'' Fanny had published three volumes of her journals, written during her stay in Georgia with Pierce. The journals, on the one hand, were a vivid personal account of life in a southern plantation, and on the other they were a fierce phillipic against slavery. They had an impact only slightly less than *Uncle Tom's Cabin* itself.

Fanny raised one of her shoulders, and shifted her eyes down toward that shoulder. ''I don't want to hear any of your logic, Ash Kemble.'' She snapped her eyes back to him. ''I've made up my mind. I'm joining you!''

''No, Fanny,'' he said. ''It's impossible.''

''Ash, I'm going with you to Georgia—I must. The risk is mine. Don't speak to me of impossibility. Tell me when your *Miranda* sails.''

''Fanny! *No!*''

''Now that that's settled,'' she smiled brightly, drawing away from him and relaxing in her seat, ''and you are resigned to my presence on your ship, pour me another glass of champagne, please my darling.''

''Fanny, no,'' he repeated, more weakly this time. All along, she had seen, correctly, that he really wanted her company and was only going through the motions of standing in her way.

''Champagne, darling,'' she repeated, extending her glass.

''Yes, Fanny,'' he said.

## Meridian, Mississippi

A telegram from Secretary of War Seddon arrived in Meridian, Mississippi, on the first of August. The telegram ordered General Joseph Johnston to authorize the ''salvage of locomotives said to be stored in the northern portions of the State of Mississippi and the transport of said locomotives by the fastest and most feasible means to Atlanta, Georgia, for further disposition.''

General Johnston sent a return telegram to the Secretary indicating that he would comply with the Secretary's orders. Then Johnston did nothing at all to implement Seddon's commands. Or rather, to give Johnston his precise due, he did very little.

First, Johnston determined that Noah Ballard and Noah Ballard alone would be responsible for bringing the locomotives to Atlanta. And then, having so determined, Johnston found that he was unable to spare Noah Ballard from more important work, disregarding the fact that Noah had nothing at all to do. The Yankees in Mississippi were camped for the summer. The military action in the western Confederacy had shifted to the area around Chattanooga, which General Bragg was trying, and failing, to hold with his Army of Tennessee against General Rosecrans's Army of the Cumberland.

Under these circumstances, there was not a great deal for the army in eastern Mississippi under Johnston to do, except to lick their wounds, regroup, and see about getting resupplied, insofar as that was possible.

When Johnston tired of Noah Ballard's respectful submissions that he would be more profitably employed following the wishes of Secretary Seddon and salvaging the locomotives, Johnston ordered Noah to proceed to Jackson, which the Union forces had evacuated before the beginning of August, in order to make an inventory of the railroad equipment and facilities there. "I need to know what's left there after Sherman's wreckers did their worst," he said.

"But, sir," Noah asked with courtesy, "what about the sixty-seven locomotives we should be fetching now?" He hoped the general would catch his implication. The longer they delayed retrieving the machines, the greater the likelihood that the Yanks would discover at least some of them.

"You're talking about a substantial expedition," Johnston said, "when you go up there and get those damned things. I can't just send a few men to work them; I've got to send men to keep Grenville Dodge's people off the operation.

You've had a bit of experience with what I'm talking about, and I just can't spare any troops for that purpose.

"You go on over to Jackson and find out for me what I need to know. And perhaps we can talk about those sixty-seven locomotives after you get back."

There's no stopping Joe Johnston, Noah thought afterward, when he's intent on putting something off. He is the most brilliant master of delay in the history of warfare. Fabius Maximus is a novice compared with him.

Fabius Maximus was the legendary Roman general who harassed Hannibal without risking a pitched battle. He won the war by delaying rather than fighting.

Will Hottel, who was a man of vast resources, claimed that he could overcome Johnston's persistent disinclination to do anything about the sixty-seven locomotives, but even Hottel had limits to his resources. It would take time to make things work, he said.

And so Noah Ballard went to Jackson.

As the train slowly clanked and sputtered its way west, Noah's mind kept returning to Jane Featherstone. He'd still had no word of or from her.

Why? he wondered. Where can she possibly be? Dead?

Somehow he doubted that. Jane was too elusive and quick for the Grim Reaper.

But if she was alive, he had many questions to ask her.


On Wednesday, August 19, a company of Union troops broke into the shed south of Okolona that contained Dart, Javelin, and Perseverance. The troops belonged to General Grenville Dodge's Second Division of the Army of Tennessee, and they were accompanied by a dozen and a half railroad engineers, mechanics, and trainmen. Once inside they started on the task of putting the three locomotives in working order.

It was not easy, for the engines had been in storage for many months. Rust had blossomed insidiously in all the hardest to reach places. Whatever had to be tight had worked itself loose. Whatever had to be loose had become solid. Oil had to be soaked into every joint, bearing, and coupling.

Meanwhile, as the engineers and mechanics worked over the locomotives, a track crew put down the spur that led to getting the main line back in shape.

The locomotives and the track were ready for operation by Monday, the twenty-fourth. On that day Dart, Javelin, and Perseverance were driven about twenty-five miles north of Okolona and placed on a spur on the Tennessee side of Tupelo.

By Thursday, the twenty-seventh, eleven other locomotives that had been concealed at the orders of Walter Goodman had been refurbished enough to allow them to be driven up to the spur along with Dart, Perseverance, and Javelin. The Union officers who had done the sleuthing that had discovered the locomotives had not found the remaining twelve in the area.

The orders that had resulted in this operation had their origins in a conversation on the night of August 17 between Brigadier General Grenville Dodge and Captain George E. Spencer.

George E. Spencer was Dodge's adjutant. Though an adjutant functions for a general much as in civilian life a secretary functions for an executive, Spencer was not a mere adjutant. He was an extremely useful man outside as well as within the army, with close and deep associations with any number of powerful and influential people. In time he would become a United States senator who numbered among his friends men like Thomas A. Scott, Jay Gould, Andrew Carnegie, and other tycoons. At the moment, in addition to handling General Dodge's correspondence, he watched over many of Dodge's more complex, sensitive, and personal requirements. Spencer was in charge, for instance, of the lobbying efforts to obtain for the general his second star. But he was also "a genius," in Dodge's words, in "getting inside of the enemy's lines."

It was quite late on the night of August 17, but Dodge was still up working, dealing with the twin mountains of paperwork created from his dual role as division commander and spy master.

He normally worked late; he liked the quiet and the absence of the unpredictable and pressing jumble of demands that running an army division put on him during the day. But this night he was especially busy. Earlier that day Dodge had received a message from Dr. Thomas C. Durant (a Doctor of Medicine, though he rarely practised that profession). Durant had requested Dodge's presence in New York a few days hence. It was an invitation Grenville Dodge could not take lightly. Thomas C. Durant was the leader of the group of men who were promoting and organizing the transcontinental line that would become the Union Pacific Railroad Company. Construction was scheduled to start in the spring of next year, and Durant wanted very much to induce Dodge to leave the army and take charge of the project.

Though no specific offer had been made, General Dodge was sorely tempted to accept it if it were to come.

"Captain Spencer to see you, sir," an aide said to General Dodge. The aide and the captain both stood framed in the wide double doorway of the room in the Corinth, Mississippi, town hall that Dodge used as his office.

"Come in, George," Dodge said without looking up from his paperwork. "Come on in. Sit down."

The aide moved aside, and Spencer walked past him.

George Spencer was a stout man with a round face and curly, corn-colored hair and chin whiskers. Normally he kept his hair and whiskers carefully groomed, but that was not now the case. He had been on the move for over thirty-six hours, and all other things being equal, he would as soon have been in bed as calling on his superior.

"Don't bother with that saluting business," Dodge said, still intent on his papers. "Not among friends. Just sit yourself down and make yourself comfortable."

"I didn't plan to chat, General," Spencer said hesitantly, remaining on his feet. "It's late, and I don't want to take your time, but I've just learned information that I was sure you'd want to hear."

At that, Dodge lifted his face from his papers for the first time. "Go ahead, George, sit down. It's late enough now anyway that another half hour or so won't make much difference. Take a load off your feet; you look like you need it. You can tell me what you've got to say, and then I want some advice from you."

"All right, then," Spencer said gratefully. A chair wasn't as inviting as a bed, but it would do.

The room was dark except for the lamp on Dodge's desk. After Spencer had pulled up a chair close to it, he sighed. "You're right, General, I've had a rough one."

"So tell me about what you've found."

Spencer began, "Do you remember that two-car train the First Tennessee ambushed a couple of weeks ago? The one that was full of military and carrying a pair of officers on some kind of errand?"

"I recall it."

"Well, that gnawed at me in the back of my mind for a while. Nothing specific, but I just kept wondering what the Rebs were doing up at Okolona. And the more I wondered, the more I got curious about the errand those two officers were on.

"One of them is a major, but I don't know his name. The other one's name is Will Hottel, and he's a captain. More interesting, he's the man the Railroad Bureau in Richmond has put in charge of the railroads in these parts. He's been seen here and there at other times by friendly civilians that I talk to now and then. They've seen him poking around and about the railroad lines north of Meridian and Jackson—the Mobile & Ohio, the Mississippi Central, and the Mississippi & Tennessee. So after I learned he was poking around, I started to get interested in why he was poking around.

"There's a spur off the main line south of Okolona. It looks abandoned." He leaned a little closer. "It's been *made* to look that way. Up the spur about a mile there's a shed. That also looks like nothing much. That's what those two officers were out to see."

"The shed?" Dodge asked.

"Yeah. What's in it."

"Well, then?"

"They've hid three locomotives in there. Pretty ones. Baldwins. In lovely, nearly pristine shape."

"They hid them?" Dodge asked. "Why'd they go and do that?" It was hard for Grenville Dodge to understand why anyone would want to take a locomotive out of use. The purpose of locomotives was to pull loads, not to sit rusting in sheds. Putting up a locomotive in a shed was as senseless as sleeping in the snow when you have a house with a stove and wood to burn in it.

"Right," Spencer said. "They hid them . . . but not just these three. There are at least eleven more hid away, eleven more that I've found out about, anyhow. And every one of them," he added, "is a fine machine, not the worn-out, disrepaired hulks that the Rebs have been forced to use lately."

"That's the craziest thing I've ever heard!" Dodge said, his eyes blazing.

"I'm not testifying to the sanity of all this, only to the fact."

"And somebody clearly thought he was doing the reasonable thing," Dodge said, trying to imagine what that might be.

"That's it," Spencer said. "After I found the engines, I began to wonder why anyone would want to keep them out of action. What I concluded—and it's clear as day once you think about it—is that the owners of those machines would rather keep them for themselves, rather than waste them in the war."

"It's shortsighted," Dodge said with a sharp, contemptuous snap to his words.

"Maybe so, but that's what they've done. And then somehow or other this man Hottel got wind of them, and I would suspect that in a short time he's going to send out people who'll bring them down to where Joe Johnston can use them."

"So what do we do with them before that happens?" Dodge asked. His question was addressed to himself more than to his adjutant.

"Do you want to know what I think?" Spencer said.

"By all means," Dodge said.

"Confiscate them. We can use them."

Dodge shook his head. "Our orders are to wreck all that's useful. And it would be the easy thing to do," Dodge said. "Easier than bringing them here, or wherever. Less time and effort, fewer men. And," he continued, still considering, "it would be interesting to see the look on Joe Johnston's face when he learns we've destroyed those locomotives."

"Possibly," Spencer said. "But also realize that those are mint-condition locomotives that we can use as well as they. And think of the look on Joe Johnston's face when he learns that we are pulling troops and ammunition and supplies with *his* engines."

"I like the way you're thinking," Dodge said. "But I've still got orders to consider." Then he brightened. "I'll tell you what, let me tell you my news, and then we'll worry about those locomotives."

"Fine," Spencer said, drawing his chair even closer. He could tell that Dodge, a normally cool and taciturn man, was excited, and he was curious to discover what the excitement was about.

"I received a letter from Dr. Durant today," he said. "He wants me to come to New York to meet with him about the transcontinental railroad. He didn't say so outright, but if you read between the lines, it seems as if he wants me for the chief engineer's position."

"And will you go there?"

Dodge smiled. "Of course, wouldn't you? I'll take a month off. I can claim some kind of sick leave."

"And will you take the chief engineer's position, should it be offered?"

"I don't know. That's why I wanted to talk to you."

Spencer gave a grave nod. It was a hard decision, he acknowledged. "It would mean resigning from the army," he said, "at a time when things seem to be coming closer and closer to a head. And at a time," he went on with more feeling, "when all the efforts to earn you a second star and

the command of a corps are coming to a head, too." He
looked hard at Dodge. "You've made a pretty fair general,
sir. You should have a larger command." He breathed a
deep sigh. "On the other hand, you may never have another
opportunity like the one Tom Durant is hinting at." He
shook his head. "It's a hard choice."

"That it is," Dodge agreed.

The two men sat in silence for a time, considering the
implications of what had been presented.

Finally Spencer spoke. "I wonder what the chances are of
delaying a decision."

"What do you mean?"

"Can you ask the doctor to let you hold out until the war
is over?"

"I don't think he will buy that. They're starting construction next spring, as he won't let me forget. He must have
mentioned that four times in his letter."

Spencer nodded. "Well, there's nothing to do but go see
him and listen to what he says. Wait, find out the facts, and
see what you must do."

"You're probably right," Dodge said, not totally convinced. He didn't like uncertainty.

"In fact," Spencer went on, "I'd like to act the same
way with regard to those locomotives."

"How do you mean?"

"I'll bring them up the line while you're gone—somewhere
safe and easily protected. And then after you return you can
decide how to dispose of them."

Dodge thought a moment, then gave a nod of assent.
"Yes. All right. Do that," he said.

Spencer rose. "It's time I took leave of you, General,"
he said.

"Good night, George," Grenville Dodge said.

After Spencer's departure, Dodge began his last chore for
the night. He pulled out a half-dozen blank pages for a letter
to Anne, his wife.

Anne was a fearful woman who had never been pleased
that her husband had joined the army. She hated that he had
to risk himself, but she hated it even more that he had to be

away from her. Thus he was sure she would not welcome it if he responded favorably to Dr. Durant's overtures.

He stared at the blank pages, wondering how he would fill them when he had nothing to say to her that would give her comfort.

Her last letter to him was somewhere on the desk. Where? He groped around until he found it in a pigeonhole. He slipped it out and opened it to the last page.

> I am so afraid [he read] Oh, God, this war! What shall we not be called upon to sacrifice if it lasts much longer? If anything happens to you, I shall want to die! Yes ! I feel as though I could not live! When you are with me, I can endure anything and do anything, but alone—oh, to be left in this world alone! What would become of me?

He shook his head and laid the pages down and then stared once more at his own blank pages. He took up his pen and began to write,

> My dearest Anne,
> How I've missed you during the last week. I've thought of you hourly . . . or even more often.
> The war, you'll be happy to learn, is quiet in these parts. It's almost as though we are at peace. The crops are growing ripe. My troops might as well travel unarmed.

He stopped. Now what do I say? he thought, again at a loss for words. Damn! Why can't I ever tell you anything close to the truth, the way any soldier writes his wife?

"Oh, Anne, Anne," he said aloud, "you are so dear—and so tiresome."

Sometimes I wish you had a heart more like the one God gave Jane Featherstone, he thought. To have your sweetness joined with her boldness. Now *that* would be a woman!

* * *

Jackson, Mississippi, had been left so desolate by William Tecumseh Sherman's troops that there was little in the town for Noah Ballard to inventory.

And yet, though the devastation continued to anger and sadden him, it did not prove to be a complete curse to Noah. Because the inventory took so little of his time, he was free to pursue activities other than those specified by General Johnston. He journeyed up to Canton, for instance, which was about twenty miles north of Jackson, and discovered there a nearly intact railroad machine shop that was somehow overlooked by Sherman's marauding soldiers. This machine shop was likely to prove indispensable when it came time to refurbish the locomotives north of Jackson.

He also had time to make inquiries about Jane Featherstone.

Nothing he learned about her was nearly as satisfying as his uncovering of the Canton machine shop. As far as he could determine, Jane had simply vanished, along with the building that had housed her. The entire block on which she had lived was now charred rubble.

From interviews with survivors, he found out about the rape attempt on the morning Sherman's troops moved into Jackson. Some Union soldiers had broken into Jane's rooms, but Jane had a revolver which she did not fear using. She had shot and killed one or two of the criminals. The others had fled from her rooms, but they were soon captured. After that she was not seen again.

Or at least she was not reliably seen. An old man Noah talked to claimed he had seen Jane in the company of a Union captain. But the old man, who took most of his nourishment from rum and whiskey, could not be trusted.

Late on Saturday afternoon of August 29, Will Hottel arrived in Jackson. He came accompanied by a colonel of cavalry with whom Noah Ballard was familiar, though the two men had not talked for ages.

While he was in Jackson, Noah's fury grew along with his sense of paralysis. He was as powerless as a prisoner in

a castle keep to attack the causes of his many disappoint-
ments. And Jane Featherstone's baffling absence only served
to magnify his fury. Her disappearance dripped like acid in
his heart.

In order to keep himself occupied while waiting for Joe
Johnston to move himself, Noah had taken on the job of
supervising the rebuilding of the Jackson railroad yards.

As Hottel, his new companion, and a third man drew near
him, Noah was occupied with the erection of a large water
tank. A crew had constructed a scaffolding beside one of the
tracks, and now they were setting up the framework for the
tank itself on a platform they'd laid at the top of the scaffolding. When it was finished, it would be a huge, straight-sided
barrel. A long tin spout, close to a foot in diameter, would
deliver water to the tanks in locomotive tenders.

Noah was standing on top of the scaffolding at the center
of the platform, while workmen installed the framework of
the huge barrel. It was close to sundown, and not nearly
enough work had been completed that day to satisfy him.
He was weary, impatient, and testy.

"Noah!" a voice called. "Noah Ballard!"

"Hello!" Noah answered vaguely, turning around, searching for the source of the voice. He saw three men striding
toward where he was working. He could not see their faces,
for they were silhouetted by the declining sun, but he knew
two of them from their shapes. One was Will Hottel, and
the other was Gar Thomas, who had been working all day at
the ruins of the depot. The voice, however, came from the
other man. It was a voice he recognized, and recognizing it,
his weariness, impatience, and testiness started to fade. "I
know you!" he called out louder.

"Noah Ballard, you old bastard, come down from that
tower this instant!" the other man answered. "That's a
command from a superior officer."

Noah finally saw the man's face, and as he started to
scramble down the scaffold he called out to him, "Lam
Kemble! Why, son of a bitch, it's *you*! I never imagined!"

When Noah reached the ground, he dashed across the
rails and ties to his friend and, disregarding his own grease

and filth, embraced the impeccably attired colonel—complete to pearl-gray, wide-brimmed felt hat with plume.

"Lam! Jesus Christ it's good to see you!" he hollered, though Lam Kemble was right next to him, and as he hollered, he pounded his fists hard against Lam's back.

Lam endured the pummeling with amused toleration but when Noah stepped away from him to drink him in with his eyes, he could not resist a tease. "I believe, Major," he said frostily, "that striking a superior officer is punishable by hanging, drawing, and quartering. In your case you will be hanged by your drawers and quartered with poxed whores."

Noah answered that by giving him another blow—a light, playful one—on his shoulder. Then he stepped back again so that he could decide how his friend had changed.

Hardly at all, he concluded. Lam was every bit as boyish and eager as he'd been on graduation day at the Academy. From the testimony of his appearance anyhow, Lam had had a superb war—promotions, decorations, bravery, dash and glory. Lam had made himself the perfect image of the man every boy lusts to grow up to be.

He's enjoyed his war more than I have mine, Noah thought to himself sadly and bitterly. But he allowed himself the sadness and the bitterness for only a moment.

"Ah, you look simply splendid, Lam!" he said, beaming. "A colonel no less! My Lord, a colonel! I'm pleased for you, sir!" There was only the slightest tinge of mockery in the "sir."

"And you, Major," Lam said in his most arch tones, wrinkling his nose as fastidious matrons do when they detect unpleasant odors, "appear purposefully employed." Then he broke into a brilliant smile and clasped his arms around his friend. "But I am absolutely delighted to see you, Noah. It's grand to see your face. And," he said, stepping back, "I have even better news." Noah cocked his head. "We are to be working together."

"Not a dashing cavalry officer with a poor, plodding, misbegotten engineer," Noah said with a greatly exaggerated southern drawl, showing his friend that he could still dish it out. "Why, poor Lamar, that must be a horrendous comedown for you.

"But," he added in his normal voice, "tell me about it. And about all your news. Tell me everything you've been up to for the—oh, thousand years since I've seen you. And tell me what your family is up to. And," he added, his mind flashing on a golden afternoon years in the past, "I *must* learn all about your delicious sisters!"

"My sisters?" Lam said with mock incredulity. "Whatever do you want to hear about them for?"

"Yes, do that, Colonel," Will Hottel interrupted. He and Gar Thomas had hung back while the two friends had made their greetings, but now, wearing a grave and businesslike expression, he moved in. "But not here. It's not the place for serious discussion. Let's go somewhere quiet."

"Absolutely," Gar Thomas said. "We've done just about everything we can do here for today."

Noah looked for a moment at the uncompleted tank, and then nodded his acquiescence. The men at work there had already begun to wrap it up for the night.

"Where in this waste," Lam asked, looking about, "is there someplace quiet?"

"Would my home do?" Gar asked with a shy, tentative look. "In fact, it's suppertime soon. My wife, I expect, could even put together some kind of meal for you—not a feast, mind, as there's damned little available, but enough to take the edge off. Anyhow," he added quickly, embarrassed by the near starvation that he and his family, like nearly everyone else in and around Jackson, were forced to endure, "I can offer you a nice, quiet, cool place to sit and talk."

"We'll take you up on the location," Noah said, "but we'll decline with regrets the offer of a meal." He said that because he was only too aware of how strapped the Thomas family was for food.

Gar turned to Lam. "Colonel," he said, "I insist on feeding you. It will be a great honor. Really, I do insist."

Lam glanced at Noah, who gave him a warning look and a practically invisible negative shake of his hand. "Thank you, Mr. Thomas, but I must also decline."

Gar started to try to persuade Will Hottel then, for his pride and his sense of honor required it, but seeing the look on Hottel's face, he decided against it with a sigh of relief.

"Mr. Thomas," Hottel said, "I think your home is a fine place for us to gather, and there we will all gather and bring ourselves up to date, for there is indeed much to catch up on, after which there is much to transact. Nevertheless, I must delay my arrival there. I have other business to transact before I can let myself relax." He turned to Lam. "I'd appreciate it if you would hold off discussing the matter we've come here to discuss until I return."

"But I'm dying of curiosity," Noah said.

"Oh, no," Hottel said. "You're not dying of curiosity, Major Ballard. Hardly. Without your curiosity, Noah, you'd surely die."

"What's all this bullshit about?" Noah asked Lam. "If he can't tell me, you surely can."

"I think," Lam said after a quick confirming glance at Hottel, "that I better not."

"Goddamn," Noah said.

"You're a patient man, Noah, as recent days have abundantly proved," Hottel said. "You can wait." Then he turned to Gar Thomas. "Would you do me the kindness of pointing out the way to your home?"

Gar Thomas gave Hottel instructions; then he, Noah, and Lam proceeded to Gar's house while Will Hottel went off on his own.

By the time Will arrived some two hours later, Lam Kemble had recounted for Noah the high points of the wartime parts of the Kemble family chronicle, and Noah had told Lam his own news—much more briefly. Noah had litle appetite to dwell on his own story, and besides, he was more interested in the doings of the Kembles, especially the doings of the delicious Kemble girls. Pierce's death touched him; he had liked Lam's father. But Miranda and Ariel . . . !

Brief mention was also made of Sam Hawken, but the subject of Sam was not one that either friend found much to his taste.

When Hottel hammered on the front door Noah, Lam,

and Gar were seated in the parlor while Mrs. Thomas, a furtive little woman with hesitant, uncertain eyes, kept herself out of the way in the kitchen.

"Halloo!" Hottel called. "Halloo inside! I need help. Will someone give me a hand?"

Gar moved instantly toward the door, but Noah and Lam quickly joined him. When they reached the entrance hall, Gar had already let Hottel inside.

In his arms was a load of food in so many different packages that it threatened to spill catastrophically—a pair of chickens, eggs, vegetables, rice, potatoes, flour for baking, sugar, salt and a jug from Will's apparently limitless supply of sour mash.

"How in the name of hell did you find that!" Noah cried.

Gar stared, his face white.

Lam moved in to lend Hottel a hand.

And Mrs. Thomas, hearing the commotion, darted in to see what was the matter. When she saw the food, she swayed precariously. Then after steadying herself against the wall, she moved in to take charge of the astonishing bounty that Hottel had brought.

She might have been pretty, it occurred to Noah, under different circumstances. It also occurred to him that she was at least fifteen years younger than her husband and that her eyes kept flicking in Lam's direction when she thought she was not being observed.

"Thank you, Captain," she said, as she relieved Hottel of some of his packages. "I . . . I . . . we don't know how to thank you enough, my husband and I and our sons."

"It's thanks enough," Hottel said smoothly, "for me to witness your joy."

"Yes, thank you so very much," Gar Thomas said, coming out of his stupor, "I can't tell you how grateful we are."

Hottel bowed his acknowledgment.

"How did you find all of this?" Noah asked.

But the captain just smiled enigmatically and lifted his shoulders in a slight but expressive shrug.

By now Mrs. Thomas was scuttling off to the kitchen

with her load of food, with Lam closely behind her. "But you can repay me for this," Hottel said to her as she was leaving the room. "I'm not letting you off scot-free."

"What is it you wish?" she said, looking back over her shoulder at him.

"A meal," he said with an imperious clap of his hands. "No, not a meal, a banquet!"

She looked at her husband, who gave her a nod. "Yes, of course, Captain. I'll do my very best."

"I'm sure that will be superb," Hottel said. "She's a lovely woman," he continued, for Gar Thomas's benefit, once she had left the room.

"I'm pleased you think so," Gar said.

"What are we doing standing here?" Noah asked. "Why don't we sit in the parlor. And perhaps at long last you can bring me up to date about the business you've come to discuss."

"Yes, splendid idea," Hottel said "except for the discussion. We'd best put that off until after supper—though I know how anxious you are, Noah, to hear our news."

"It's not anxiousness, Will," Noah said, "it's torture."

The meal that Mrs. Thomas prepared was no banquet, but though plain, it was good. At mealtime the two Thomas boys, twelve and fourteen, appeared. They ate as though this were the only meal of a lifetime.

"There are folks in Jackson who've eaten dogs and cats," Gar explained after dinner, when the men had retired again to the parlor and lit the cigars that Hottel had produced from one of his pockets.

"It's a fact," Noah agreed. "A meal of dog meat is a luxury for many here. And things can't improve soon."

"There's a rumor that Grant has ordered Sherman to send relief," Lam said.

"If Sherman sends anything," Noah said, "it'll be sand and cinders."

"He'll send food," Lam said, "if Grant tells him to. Cump Sherman may be a wild and crazy son of a bitch, but he does what U. S. Grant tells him to do."

Noah just shook his head. He didn't believe rumors about help from anybody wearing a blue uniform.

"So what have you got," he said to Will Hottel, "that you've been holding back from me for the best part of a day?"

Hottel broke into a wicked grin. "I've got you on pins and needles, have I? You're sitting on the edge of your seat, are you?"

"You know I am, you bastard," Noah said.

"All right, then," Hottel said, taking a long draw on his cigar. "The main thing you'll probably want to know is that we can move on those locomotives now."

"Well, son of a bitch," Noah said with relief. A great load had just been taken off him. "How did you light a fire under General Johnston?"

"I didn't," Hottel said. "James Seddon did."

"Well, I'm grateful to whoever did it."

"But I don't have all good news," Hottel said gravely. "One of Grenville Dodge's officers, or else one of his spies, got wind of the engines hidden north of Meridian on the Mobile & Ohio."

"Shit," Noah said under his breath. He looked at Lam, who was shaking his head. Then he turned back to Hottel. "So what did they do?"

"They searched for and found about ten or fifteen of them. You remember those three we looked at south of Oko-lona? They found those, and they moved them north of Tupelo."

"Shit," Noah repeated. "When did this all happen?"

"Within the past week or so."

Noah was silent for a time, his rage building. Then he let out a blast of white fury, *"Goddamn Joe Johnston!"* he said slowly, distinctly, the words measured, the volume scarcely louder than his normal one. No one had any doubts, though, about the magnitude of his anger. "While I've been here in Jackson sitting on my ass, the goddamn Yanks have gone off and taken my engines. Goddamn it all to hell!"

"You see why I waited to tell you this news?" Will Hottel said.

"You mean that they've got Dart and Perseverance and the other one?" Noah said.

Hottel gave him a nod.

"Goddamn!" Noah said, then rose abruptly and began to pace swiftly back and forth across the room, muttering to himself as he pounded the floor.

Lam and Gar both started to say something to him, but Will Hottel shook his head no before either man could begin. "Let him walk it off," he said softly.

"And how well are they guarded?" Noah asked moments later. "Doubtless by a division," he said, answering his own question. "Goddamn the Yanks for their population. They could spare a corps to guard my locomotives!"

"So they've become *your* locomotives?" Will Hottel asked innocently.

"You know what I mean, Will," Noah said.

"I don't mind your getting a little proprietary," Will said with a twinkle in his eye, "but I don't know how Walter Goodman would feel about that."

"He can choke on it," Noah said.

"Who's Walter Goodman?" Lam asked

Hottel explained. Then he went on, "Are you serious about wanting an answer to your question about how well the engines are guarded?"

"Absolutely," Noah said. "I want to get them back."

"Splendid!" Hottel said with a meaningful glance at Lam. "They've stationed a regiment as guards."

"An entire regiment?"

"As you said, they have men to spare."

"Shit."

"But," Hottel said, "we're not entirely defenseless. That's where our Colonel Kemble comes in."

"Lord, Lam," Noah said, "I forgot that you told me we are going to work together. Which means, naturally, that I forgot to ask you how."

"That's all right, my friend," Lam said. "No one ever gave you high marks for memory.

"What I've got for you and Captain Hottel is a squadron of cavalry, three troops of approximately thirty-five men that Nathan Forrest was prevailed upon to give up. You've got us for the three weeks it is estimated it will take to transport the locomotives to Mobile."

"It's not a lot to work with," Noah said.

"But my squadron," Lam said, "is the best in the world." His look said he wasn't completely joking. "General Forrest was fit to be tied, even though we'll only be gone from his command for three weeks."

"I'm eternally grateful to the general for making the sacrifice," Noah said, "but it's still not a lot to work with." As he said this, however, a notion was beginning to percolate through his mind.

"We could," Hottel said coolly, his eyes locked on Noah's, "leave the locomotives alone and grab the ones we know they don't have and run."

"There is no goddamned way that I will allow them to keep my locomotives." Noah turned to Lam. "There's no goddamned way I'm going to do that!"

"I'm with you, Noah," Lam replied.

"How do you propose to go about it?" Hottel asked.

Noah thought for a while. "I will," he said, "consider what we have to work with, and I'll let you know tomorrow." The notion had begun to take clearer shape, but he didn't feel ready yet to bring it into the open.

"All right, then," Will Hottel said. "We've made a beginning, haven't we?"

*Atlanta, Georgia*
*September 6, 1863*

"You like me, don't you, Sam?" Jane Featherstone said. "I want very much for you to like me."

It was past midnight. Rain beat on the window of the fourth-floor hotel room where Jane and Sam Hawken had made their home for the past two weeks.

Thunder growled far away. Then for a brief instant it was

like daylight, and then a brief instant after that came a long, tearing crack—as though the whole fabric of the world were ripping apart—followed by deep rolling booms.

The room was only a small single, but it had been all that was available in the Trout House. Indeed, it was the only available room in any hotel in the city. The room they had obtained had been made available only because of the nature of Sam's profession; he was thought to be a minister of the Gospel, newly called to leave his former ministry in Nacogdoches, Texas, in order to render aid to the poor, sick souls in the heart of the South.

Or something like that.

"What makes you think that I don't like you, Jane?" Sam Hawken asked without looking up at her. He was busy making notations in the journal he was keeping, recording the results of his daily—and nightly—observations.

"If you liked me, you'd stay with me tonight," she said with a smile she meant to be fetching, but which Sam took to be hungry and needy.

"My liking you has nothing to do with the reason I'm going out tonight."

"On such a night, Sam? With all the rain and the mud? Really, Sam, darling, I could think of a thousand reasons not to go out on such a night—a thousand and one, if you add the risk."

"That's smart thinking, Jane," he said. "The very reason why I must do it now. I'm counting on the weather to keep inside some of the squads of soldiers who patrol the streets. They're watching for people like me and you, Jane."

"Do you ever listen to me, Sam?" she asked with a punishing look. "I've said to you more than once that there are whispers in the hospitals." Jane had volunteered her services as a nurse, because Grenville Dodge had believed that hospitals would be good sources for intelligence. His assumption was turning out to be as correct as most of his ideas; her information would add much to the report that both of them were preparing. "There are suspicions that a spy is on the loose in Atlanta. You've been lucky; you've managed to handle night watchmen and street patrols. Your luck can't hold. They are sure to step up their vigilance, even in this weather.

"And besides," she brightened, "why go out into certain danger when there's me here instead?"

"I'm not sure which danger is worse, you or the Rebels," he said to her with a grin. It was a cool grin; he was half serious. "No, Jane," he continued, all business. "I've got to go now. If suspicions are growing, it's best to get the work out of the way fast."

"You're impossible," she said petulantly.

Sam was seated at the small table he was using as a writing desk, and, save for the hat and the old Mexican poncho he'd use to fend off the rain, he was dressed to go out in dark boots and clerical blacks. Jane, dressed in a sheer cotton nightdress, had sprawled out on her stomach. She lay diagonally across the bed, with her feet touching the headboard and her head propped in her hands. She was lying that way so as to bring her face close to him. But when he showed no inclination to give her what she wanted, she gathered herself up and moved across the bed, sitting up and placing her back against the headboard. In making the move, she managed to show large areas of flesh—interesting areas, it seemed to her—but he failed to pay attention. And so she sat scowling.

This is what he had written during this evening's session:

Atlanta is abundantly endowed with railroads and the facilities to handle vast quantities of heavy freight and to service every sort of equipment. Even so, the burden the war has placed on these facilities has proven too great for them to bear. This is especially true of the single-track Western and Atlantic line running north from Atlanta to Chattanooga. The line and the Atlanta yards are so choked with traffic that there is often what amounts to a continuous line of locomotives and cars from Marietta, twenty miles away, to the city.

The scarcity of mechanics and spare parts has

resulted in a serious increase in breakdowns and
unusable equipment. And this means that tons of
urgent freight such as food, ammunition, weapons,
and medicines lie rotting in the rail yards.

Lubricants are also scarce, although some operators have resorted to rendering pig fat. And there is
no whale oil to be had for headlamps.

Most tellingly, thermal efficiency of locomotives
operating out of Atlanta has severely declined. In
1861 the lines could expect to achieve as much as
eighty miles per cord of pine. Now they are lucky
to get sixty.

Conclusion:

Atlanta was created as a railroad town. It has
become the center of distribution and transport of
the entire lower South. Most of the food grown in
the lower South passes through here, as well as all
the munitions and finished iron from Alabama and
Georgia factories and works, leather goods, cloth,
axles for railroad cars, et cetera, et cetera. It has
also become the largest hospital in the lower South
for those wounded in battle. The transport of the
wounded to the clinics here places an even larger
burden on the already much overburdened facilities.

The entire system is dangerously close to grinding to a halt.

For instance, there are sufficient accommodations in the town for perhaps twelve to fifteen
thousand people, at most. The current population is
estimated at double that. Many of the overflow are
living in abandoned railroad cars.

The streets and roads are so badly holed, rutted,
and pitted that there are times when traffic cannot
proceed.

And it costs more money to live here than most
people possess. Here is a sample that I have recorded
of prices of common items:

Flour ...............@$35 per hundredweight
Eggs................@$1 per dozen

Coffee...............@$4 per pound
Bacon...............@$1.50 per pound
Potatoes............@$12 per bushel

Sam laid his pen down. "Enough for now," he said.

"What did you say?" Jane asked.

"Enough," he said, louder.

"Enough?" she repeated hopefully.

"Yes, Jane," he said, "I've done all I can here for now."

"Then you've given up the mad idea of venturing out into the storm?"

"You are persistent, Jane," he said with a wry shake of his head. "Where did you learn your pertinacity?"

She smiled. This time her expression was truly fetching and captivating. "It's inborn," she said.

"There are times when it's wiser to surrender," he said.

"Well then, my darling, do that now. Surrender. Come here and stay with me," she said with a gesture that could mean only one thing.

He rose to his feet, still shaking his head—regretfully now, for lovemaking with Jane offered real, though temporary comforts. He gathered up his journal and carried it to his bag. It was old, a much battered and worn leather valise held together by a pair of leather belts. It was very obviously a piece of luggage a minister of the Gospel would have toted around for many years, and thus it was for all intents and purposes invisible. That was the intent, for one of Grenville Dodge's clever craftsmen had constructed a false bottom for it.

Sam removed the clothes that he was keeping in the bag, unlatched eight catches that you would miss unless you were aware of them, lifted the false bottom out, placed the journal in the space the bottom covered, then replaced it and the clothes.

"I don't know when I'll be back," he said to Jane. As he spoke, he moved before the mirror. What he saw was a tall, very gaunt, hollow-cheeked man with a high forehead, salt-and-pepper hair, and hard-looking hazel eyes. The man

in the mirror could have been fifty. His appearance was
another creation of one of Grenville Dodge's clever craftsmen.

"Stay," she drawled.

He shook his head. Then he picked up the Mexican
poncho and slipped it over his head. It had seen more
service than the valise. Among the many signs of hard use
were a dozen holes. These could have come from moths,
from wear, from gunshots, or from some misfortune only
God knew. But, like the valise, the poncho did the job.

Next came a revolver, which Sam stuffed into his trousers
at the small of his back, and then a knife, which he
concealed in the upper part of his boot. Then a three-inch
length of candle and a small box of lucifers; these went in a
side pocket of his black frock coat. Last came his black,
wide-brimmed porkpie hat, which he fitted onto his head,
and a Bible, an old beat-up New Testament, which he
placed in a breast pocket. Already in that pocket was a
pencil he would use later to make notes in the Bible.

"Go to sleep, Jane," he said, as he made his way to the
door.

"I can't sleep until you come back to me," she said in a
voice heavy with melodrama.

"Oh, Jane!" he laughed, and left the room.

He moved quickly and quietly down the backstairs, and
he was soon outside in the driving rain. Jane was right about
one thing, he thought. Anyone who went out in this dismal
stuff was crazy.

Braxton Bragg had declared martial law in the city and
suspended habeas corpus a year ago, in September 1862,
when Atlanta's strategic importance to the South became
evident. As the city grew to be increasingly fortified, the
number and frequency of the patrols watching the streets
and the comings and goings at the railroad station grew
concurrently.

Sam had a believable explanation for being out on a dark
and stormy night such as this one; but he preferred not to
have to explain himself at all. Though he was "a minister of
the Gospel," he was also a stranger in Atlanta, and for that
reason some would find him suspicious—especially if the

hospital rumors Jane had been hearing turned out to be accurate.

Though he didn't intend to stop there, his first goal was "the car shed," as the rail depot was called, between Pryor and Loyd streets, near State Square. It was his practice to check the rail yards every evening for anything that seemed new or interesting before proceeding on to his other goals.

For the first days of their stay in Atlanta, Sam and Jane had engaged in no espionage activities. They had devoted themselves with steadfast devotion to the work of establishing their credibility, he as a man of God and she as a nurse. After they'd done that in a manner that seemed satisfactory, they'd set themselves to more serious—and risky—tasks.

On previous nights during the past week, Sam had paid surreptitious visits on three of the major Atlanta factories: the Atlanta Rolling Mill, which produced plates for Rebel gunboats, among these the ironclad *Merrimack*; the Atlanta machine works, where ammunition was made; and Winship's Foundry, where freight cars and other railroad equipment were manufactured. He'd seen, additionally, a pistol factory, a sword factory, several rifle factories, and a machine shop where cannon were rifled.

Tonight his goal was the Confederate arsenal, which produced shells.

During his postmortem tours of Mississippi battlefields, General Sherman had picked up and examined a number of spent shell casings. Every one of these was stamped: MADE IN ATLANTA. He picked up so many MADE IN ATLANTA shells that he began to think the South would not be defeated until the factory that made them was destroyed.

As Sherman pondered this, the realization grew that it was not just the arsenal but the entire city of Atlanta that had to be destroyed. For the arsenal was only one of many Atlanta factories producing the materials of war.

Because of Sherman's interest in the Confederate arsenal, Sam had been ordered to make that facility one of his first stops. But once he was on the scene, Sam had found other, more pressing priorities.

The visit could be put off no longer.

Sam breasted his way through the driving rain along slat-planked sidewalks and across the swamps that had once been intersections. As he struggled through the murk and the mess, his head drawn deep into the poncho, turtle-fashion, he pondered how to handle Jane Featherstone.

Dear Jane. She is quite a handful. And so damnably attractive.

And yet, the more she gives herself to you and the more she puts herself in your hands, the more you feel responsible for her. And then the siren song of her helplessness plays in your heart. Soon pity binds you to her.

He did like Jane. He didn't lie to her about that. There was much about her that was delightful. She had a brightness and an effervescence and a vibrancy that few women of his acquaintance possessed.

And how readily . . . eagerly . . . hungrily . . . she took him to her bed. She liked the act of love, and she liked it without condition. She flowed into it the way a fine horse flows into an all-out run. She left out nothing of herself.

He recalled her first impression on him. How plain she had appeared then.

She was in no way plain. . . .

But he wondered how a woman so vivid, capable, and brave, who had turned the tables on four would-be rapists, could be so clinging and desperate.

And he wondered even more why he was not really deeply curious about her. He did not wish to understand her. He wanted to be rid of her.

As soon as their assignment was done and they were both safely back behind Union lines, he would have to find some way to do that.

Sam was near the car shed now. As he passed by, gray shadows in the rough forms of men swam in front of him, looming in the dark rain like dead souls.

"Halt," came a muffled, watery voice. "Who're you? What's your name and business?"

As they came closer, Sam was able to make out five very wet gray-clad soldiers. All of them carried rifles with wicked-looking bayonets, and one carried a bull's-eye lantern. It was lit, but the light scarcely extended beyond the limits of the glass port in front of it.

"Simon Jeffes is my name," Sam said, coming to a halt. He did his best not to appear in any way suspicious. "Reverend Simon Jeffes," he amended. "I'm a minister of the Lord."

"What the hell are you doing out on a night like this, Rev'rend?" said the corporal who was in charge of the little patrol. He looked to be around seventeen years old, if that, and he was not very sure of himself. It was good that he was so young, and a corporal, because he would be easy to win over. But Sam didn't want him getting nervous.

"I'm on an errand of mercy, sir," Sam answered. The boy corporal ought to like that "sir," he thought. Anything to increase respect. "I was called upon by a young lady who asked me to give succor and prayer for her grandmother, who appears to be near death. Her family lives in one of the boxcars abandoned off to the other side of the yard. When the girl asked me, I instantly granted her request. How could I refuse, sir, without ignoring the lesson of the Good Samaritan?"

"Where's the young lady now, Rev'rend?" the corporal asked suspiciously. He was a country boy who obviously put great store in being shrewd; he'd rather die than be caught in a trick.

"She's only a girl, really, sir, to tell the truth," Sam said, trying to fill his voice with the proper amount of unction. "Her name is Sally Witherspoon, and she could hardly be more than fifteen. A sweet girl, she is, too. And pretty enough to turn a young soldier's head."

"Why ain't Sally Witherspoon with you, leadin' the way, Rev'rend?" the corporal pressed.

"Why, I left her with my dear wife," Sam said with his blandest face, "to get herself dry and to find some rest and solace. I know these Witherspoons, sir; I've been to see them before. I know the way there just as well as I know the streets of Jerusalem where Jesus walked. With the Lord's help, sir, I'll find the Witherspoons again without a hindrance— even in this infernal weather."

"You can fergit the 'sir,' Rev'rend," the corporal said with a scowl. "It's jest Corporal."

"Very well, Corporal," Sam said. "Please forgive me if I've given offense."

"The thang is, Rev'rend," the corporal said, "you ain't s'posed to be out here in the train yards at night. Nobody's s'posed to be out here now 'cept us that is keepin' watch."

"But an old lady is dying, sir—excuse me, Corporal."

"I git that, Rev'rend. An' I unnerstan that. But you still ain't s'posed to be in here. An' that means you ain't s'posed to go visit them folks that live in them boxcars."

"Are you suggesting, Corporal," Sam said with the beginnings of righteous annoyance, "that I return to the poor girl and tell her that the Army of the South has refused me permission to proceed on my work of mercy? Are you telling me that you are denying an old woman her last comforts?"

"Well, I warn't sayin' that exactly," the boy said, retreating into uncertainty.

"Whyn't you let him go, Corporal?" one of the troopers said. "He's jest a preacher goin' about his business."

"You stay out of this," the corporal said. "I know how to deal with the preacher."

"Well," Sam went on huffily, "then you do that. I can't stand here all night. And neither can you. So what do you propose I do?"

For a minute or two the boy stood there with the rain running down his face, deciding on his options. For some reason—probably innate country suspiciousness—he didn't want to believe Sam's story.

"I'll tell you what I'm gonna hafta do, preacher. I cain't let you run loose in the yards, so I'm gonna hafta take you to the place where those Witherspoon people are holin' up."

"That's awful kind of you, Corporal," Sam said.

Shit! he thought.

"So you jest lead the way, an' we'll follow you."

"I'm much obliged to you," Sam said, furious but successfully hiding it, "for your most kind help."

The corporal turned to his men, "Form up," he ordered.

As the five soldiers started to slowly gather themselves to trudge across the train yard, Sam resolved his own uncertainties about what he had to do.

"Come on, then!" he said to the corporal. "Quickly! Old Mrs. Witherspoon will be a week in the ground by the time I get there to minister to her." Before the corporal could pull together his tiny force, Sam set off at his briskest walk. He had to lose the boy and his squad. Tomorrow he'd worry about making that act plausible to anybody who asked him about it.

"Hold up, preacher," the corporal shouted. "Wait a minute."

"You come on now, Corporal," Sam shouted back, speeding up to a trot, "I can't wait any longer. I've got a lady dying who needs attending to."

There were more than two dozen trains in the yards in various stages of being made up. They made a very satisfactory maze—especially in the intense dark of the storm.

"You stop now, y'hear?" the corporal yelled. By the time the sounds of his voice reached him, Sam could hardly make out his words. But he was pretty sure he could also hear the boy ordering his men to spread out and search for him.

"You're under arrest, preacher, y'hear?" the corporal called. "You show yourself now. That's an order!"

Heading in the opposite direction from the side of the yard where the boxcars had been abandoned, Sam ducked behind a locomotive, loped alongside the cars behind it, and, coming around the last car of that train, he sprinted across the twenty yards that separated that train from a string of flatcars. He lowered himself to a half crouch and scuttled along by the side of the flats.

As he did this, he heard a commotion three or four tracks away. He paused to try to catch what was going on.

"I've got him!" somebody was calling. "He's over here!" The shouting and other noise all converged on the commotion.

And then the corporal's voice called, "Goddamn! That ain't him. It's jest an old drunk sleepin' it off in the rain.

Y'all git off your asses an' ketch that bastard. Go on, move!''

Sam sprinted again. Moments later he was out of the yard.

And soon after that, he was on the corner of Peachtree Street and Walton. The Confederate arsenal was located near that corner.

He looked up and down. The streets were empty. He stepped back under an overhang, and once he was out of the rain, he removed his hat and poncho and then his black preacher's coat. The coat was reversible. One side was black; the other side was gray—the uniform of a Confederate captain. This uniform had proved invaluable the one time he had run into a night watchman in one of the factories he was investigating. He'd told the man he was on an unannounced inspection. Sam so frightened the watchman that he actually conducted Sam on a guided tour of the facility.

Sam slipped into his newly gray coat and poncho; then he replaced his hat. He did not do the last well, for when he was back in the street, the first gust of strong wind sent it sailing into the darkness. He chased after it, but his search proved fruitless.

If there's time after I'm done, he thought, I'll see what I can do to retrieve it. There probably aren't many people who can connect the hat to me, even if it's found.

Still, he knew it was best to retrieve it. He didn't like loose ends hanging.

The doors of the arsenal, of course, were locked and bolted. There were windows, but because he didn't want to risk breaking into them where he was visible, Sam moved around the Walton Street side of the arsenal to an alley and walked far enough down it to take stock.

There was a delivery bay with a loading platform, but that offered no way inside. About seven feet above the platform were two small windows, the only windows on the alley side of the arsenal.

He could reach the sills of the windows; that was easy enough; but even if he could have raised himself up there, he didn't have hands and arms enough to hold himself and break through the window at the same time.

A four-wheeled loading cart was placed against one wall of the loading bay. He pushed it over beneath one of the windows, and standing on it, he could see over the windowsill and into the dark building beyond. Next he slipped out of his poncho, wrapped it around his hand and arm, and pushed in the window. Glass fell and shattered inside. He hoped that he'd be able to open the window from inside once he had broken through, but that proved impossible, as the window frame was painted shut. So Sam had to remove the pieces of glass that would cut him when he slid through.

Once the glass was out of the way, he shook out the poncho and dropped it back over his head. Then he pushed himself up over the sill and went inside, lowering himself down to the floor.

Sam stood there for a considerable time, waiting, listening, taking in the feel of the place. It was a large, open, barnlike area, perhaps four times as long as it was wide.

When he was sure there was no one else moving about, he fetched the candle and matches out of the pocket where he had placed them. He made himself a light, and then he started to make his examination of the interior of the building.

He wasn't searching for anything in particular. The arsenal contained no great or precious secrets. Rather, he was after an overall sense of what the Confederates were capable of producing here. His job was to put together for Dodge, Sherman, and Grant the kind of report that would give them an overview of the city, based, insofar as possible, on Sam's own direct observations.

Sam moved among the ghostly machines, the lathes and forges, the drills and presses. He followed the whole process of manufacture from the raw materials to the finished shells. After that, he proceeded to the offices and checked the production and delivery records—input, output, rate of production. And then he made notes, in a code of his devising, in the margins of his Bible. In his code, words, signs, and symbols seemed to have a religious significance, but he had assigned to them other meanings. Thus "angels" were cannon. "Holy angels" were rifled cannon. Numbers that seemed to refer to chapters and verses referred to production data.

All the myriad marginal scrawls that proclaimed Preacher Jeffes's faith and piety actually recorded the facts of Captain Hawken's espionage.

The arsenal offices were located above the main plant floor, in a windowed gallery. In order to return to the loading platform window, Sam had to descend the wooden staircase back to the plant floor, then cross the floor itself.

He snuffed out his candle, opened the glass-paned door, and stepped out onto the stair landing, pausing to take a final look at the space below. From the landing the shop floor appeared gray and dim, but it was possible to make out shapes and masses. When he was once again down on the floor itself, he knew he would be in near total darkness.

Sam froze. He didn't like what he saw—a pair of shadows near the window he'd used to break in. A pair of shadows that moved like men.

Their movements came to a halt, and one of the two made a gesture that could have been an arm, or a pistol, pointing. The arm was pointing at Sam.

The windowed office gallery was no place to be now. It was a trap with glass walls, and he was silhouetted against them.

He dropped to a crouch below the window level, at the same time drawing the revolver that he'd stored at the small of his back. Then, keeping a low profile, he slipped down the stairs as swiftly and as silently as he could. At the bottom he veered to his right, into a dark forest of lathes and drill presses. Once he was there, he stopped and waited.

He heard scuttling and scraping, like large rats. The noises appeared to come from some distance to his left, but it was hard to judge how far because the large, empty space echoed.

Sam continued to wait and listen, peering into the shadows. He made no sounds; he scarcely even breathed.

There was a small light now visible across the floor,

swaying as its bearer moved. The light came from a bull's-eye lantern, and the man who bore it was making a careful, systematic search.

It didn't take much of a mental leap for Sam to recognize what he was searching for.

For an instant he wondered what had set the searcher after him; there had been no watchman here when he entered. Had someone noticed the broken window? That didn't seem likely.

He remembered that he had seen two searchers from the gallery landing. Where was the second one?

The man with the lamp was near the stairway to the gallery.

It was the moment to move.

He considered returning to the window where he had made his entry, but he decided against it. The second man might have stationed himself there. Sam threaded his way noiselessly through the machinery toward the Peachtree Street side of the building. He'd exit through one of those windows.

Once he was as far as he could get from the window he had originally come through, he wrapped the poncho around his head and arms, arranging it so he could see through the head hole. Then he gathered himself up to leap through the window.

"Where yo goin', Rev'rend?" a voice behind him said.

The voice belonged to the young, nervous corporal he'd run into at the train yard! Goddamn!

Sam trembled, poised to spring away.

"Don't do that," the corporal ordered. "Don't even thaink of doin' that. I've got a pistol aimed on you, an' I've kept it dry enough to do what it was made for."

Sam let his body relax, but only the slightest bit.

"You've prob'ly got you a pistol yerself somewhere's in that tent you've put over yerself. So whyn't you jest drop it slow, an' then, keepin' slow, raise up yer hands."

Sam complied. Shit! The revolver clattered on the floor. The corporal had come upon him from behind, and Sam was still turned away from him. He started to turn to face the man who'd captured him.

"Don't do that, Rev'rend," the corporal ordered. "You can jest stay on there with yer back to me."

"As you like," Sam said. Then he added, "Sir."

"Don't git smart, Rev'rend. It's Corporal, like I told you already, Rev'rend—though I don't guess it's really Rev'rend, is it?" The boy couldn't see his gray uniform coat in the dark. Which was just as well, Sam thought.

"You've never seen a man of God in the Confederate arsenal, Corporal?"

"Don't git smart, I told you." Then he called out, "Barney! You! Barney! I've got him! You can come on over to where I am, down by the Peachtree Street end."

The man with the lantern was soon standing alongside the corporal.

"Shine yer light on him, Barney," the corporal said. "On his head." Barney did as he was ordered. "Now you can turn yerself around, Rev'rend." Sam did as he was told, and the corporal's and Barney's eyes both grew wide.

"Good Lord!" the corporal said. "First yer a rev'rend, and now yer a captain. What you goin' to be next, man—a angel?"

Sam shrugged.

"Now you can tell me what you was doin' here," the corporal said.

"That's between me and God, Corporal."

"Don't git smart!" Sam was starting to annoy him.

"Do you have a name, Corporal?"

"It ain't gonna be Corporal long, not after I take you in."

"Congratulations, Sergeant. What's your name?"

"What's yers?"

"Simon Jeffes," Sam answered.

"I'm Davis," the corporal said, "Jeff Davis."

Barney snorted.

"How do you do, Jeff," Sam said with a straight face.

"Actually, I'm not Jeff," the corporal said. "But my last name's Davis."

"How do you do, Corporal Davis."

"Yer gittin' smart agin."

Sam gave him an impassive, bland look.

"We'll need to tie his hands," Corporal Davis said to Barney. "You go fetch some cord to tie him with, all right?"

Barney went off.

"How did you know·to come in here, Corporal Davis?" Sam asked.

"You lost this," Davis said, proudly producing Sam's hat from a pocket where he had stuffed it. "I didn't trust you from the beginning, and I was right not to. Word's gone out to be on the partic'lar lookout fer a Yankee spy. An' so when you shows up in the train yards an' then runs off, I knew it had to be you. We chased after you—three of my men off to the cars where people are livin' an' Barney an' me off t'other side.

"We thought we'd lost you fer sure, but then I finds this hat an' knew you'd gotta be close. An' then after that we sees the window broke in the loadin' bay.

"So . . ."

"You'll be a good sergeant, Corporal Davis."

"What d'you mean by that?"

"It was a compliment. I guess you're not used to praise."

"Don't git smart," was all he could manage.

Barney returned with cord.

He made a move to tie Sam, but Davis held him up. "You better check him fer other stuff besides that revolver that's on the floor. Here, give me the lantern."

Barney passed over the lamp, then went to Sam. "Hold yer hands up higher," he said.

"Anything you say, Barney," he said, but pointedly failed to move his hands or arms.

"Hit him, Barney," Davis said. "Make him want to keep his mouth shut."

Barney struck Sam hard with his open hand on the side of the mouth. Sam's head snapped back; blood flowed down his chin. Barney was a big boy—Sam estimated that he was even younger than Davis—and he hurt when he hit, even when he hit flat-handed.

"Now raise your hands higher," Barney ordered again. "Straight up." Sam didn't quite do that. He was able to bring his hands nearly together without the other two paying attention, for Barney was starting to search him. As Barney began, Davis realized that the soldier would be in the way if he had to shoot Sam.

"Move him over a bit," Davis ordered, "so I have a clear shot." Sam did as he was told this time without any sarcasm. He wanted them to think the blow had done its work.

Barney flipped the poncho over Sam's head and let it fall down onto the floor. Then his hands were in Sam's pockets. Pretty soon he had come up with the Bible.

"Let me see that," Davis said.

Barney tossed it over, and Davis caught it. It was a near miss, because Davis's hands were occupied with the lantern and the pistol, but he had quick, young reflexes, and he was able to stop the Bible before it fluttered to the floor.

It was the next act that undid him.

Barney's eyes were lowered; he was occupied with the pocket that held the candle and the matches.

Sam closed his hands into a double fist and brought them down onto Barney's head, at the same time jerking his knee up so that Barney's face was caught in a vise.

Then he whipped the head up and lashed it down into the knee again, grinding.

Barney screamed, a high-pitched infant's wail of pain.

Barney's head was now in a vise grip, and Sam was propelling him toward the corporal like a battering ram.

Davis, who by now was not thinking clearly, fired his revolver. He didn't hit Sam; the slug struck Barney in a buttock.

Barney howled louder, and then Sam drove Barney, wound and all, into Davis.

"You goddamned bastard!" Davis yelled as he lost his balance. The Bible dropped, and so did the lantern. It crashed and broke when it hit the floor. The pistol went off again, but this time the bullet sailed away into the vast spaces of the shed.

Before he could fire another time, Sam was on top of him, wrenching the pistol away. Davis managed another shot in the struggle. This one slammed into one of the windows of the gallery offices.

And then Sam had the pistol, and he was using it on Davis's head like a bludgeon.

"Stop! Stop!" Davis screamed. But Sam did not stop until Davis was staring at him in a defenseless daze.

In crashing down, the lamp had spilled kerosene onto the floor. The lamp flame had ignited it, and now tongues of flame had begun to reach out for other fuel. Sam stamped it out before it could spread. He didn't want a fire, or at least he didn't want one yet. But the flames gave him an idea.

"You, Barney," Sam said. Barney, whimpering, looked up. "Use that cord you brought for me and tie up the corporal's hands and feet." Barney moved slowly. "Faster, goddamn it!" Sam said, making a kicking motion in the direction of Barney's wounded buttock.

By the time Barney had finished and Sam had bound Barney's hands and feet, Corporal Davis had regained consciousness.

"What you gonna do now, Rev'rend?" he asked. There was the chill of fear in his voice.

Sam was starting to gather straw used for packing. He was going to build a pile of it over the kerosene spill.

"You've come around, I see," Sam said. He didn't especially want to answer the corporal's question. He didn't want to tell them that he was not safe unless they were dead.

"Yer gonna make a fire, aren't you? Yer gonna set this place on fire."

Sam didn't answer. He dropped a load of straw on top of the kerosene. Then he went to find some paper.

"Yer gonna kill us, aren't you?" the corporal asked when Sam returned.

"It looks like that," Sam said, not liking to admit it.

Barney was crying again, and he had pissed his pants.

"So why'd you bother tyin' us up? Why didn't you jest shoot us an' be done with it?"

Sam looked at the straw and the paper and saw that it would do the job. He went and retrieved his Bible, his hat, his revolver, and his poncho.

"Why didn't you just shoot us an' be done with it?" the corporal said one more time.

Because, Sam thought to himself, dying in the fire is not the same as my shooting you in cold blood.

He couldn't bring himself to say that, however.

He took out his matches and set the pile alight.

"I'd rather die from your bullet," the corporal said. "Don't let me burn alive."

"I'm sorry," Sam said. The flames were spreading. He had to get out.

"I've never seen such a cold-fish bastard," the corporal said.

Sam closed his eyes for a moment and took a long breath. Then he lifted his revolver from his belt and shot both men in the head—first Barney and then Corporal Davis.

It was not his proudest act.

# ◆ SEVEN ◆

<u>Atlanta, Georgia
September 7, 1863</u>

By morning the rain had stopped, but the sky was still gray and threatening. The sun did not start to break through until after noon.

Shortly before two that afternoon, a long, mule-drawn farm wagon crept snail slow up Peachtree Street, much to the driver's distaste. It was Monday, which made for considerable traffic. The mules were old, the wagon's load heavy, and the mud that still clogged the roadway didn't help speed up things, either. But none of these realities lessened the impatience of the driver, a good-looking sixteen-year-old slave whose name was Horace. Horace wanted to *move*. But he couldn't move, at least not very much, and there was nothing he could do about it. So Horace seethed.

Seated on Horace's right was Miranda Kemble. Miranda did not share Horace's impatience. She liked Atlanta, and she liked taking in the bustle and energy of the town this Monday afternoon. Though Miranda and Horace were on their way back to Raven's Wing after a three-day stay in Atlanta, as far as she was concerned, she could have stayed longer. Her friend Sally Mayfield had invited her into town as a break from the labors of running Raven's Wing. It was

245

a welcome break, for Sally was bubbly, engaging, and warm, with a delightful pair of seven-year-old twin daughters, and it was a chance to do some business, for Sally's husband, Thomas, owned a hardware and dry-goods store, and Miranda had fresh vegetables she could barter with. Though Thomas hadn't had much that was useful in stock, Miranda still came out with a few needed tools and a few yards of denim and calico that could be made into clothes for the field hands.

"You hear about the fire las' night, ma'am?" Horace asked. As he spoke, he threaded his way impatiently between a wagon unloading beer barrels and another packed full of cotton bales that was stalled in the mud. "Burned down the arsenal."

"It was all Sally could talk about, Horace," Miranda said. "It must have been the biggest thing to hit Atlanta this year, the way the news spread so fast. All through lunch Sally went on and on about it."

"It's all the whole town's talkin' about," Horace said. "And it must of been sumthin', fire an' 'splosions. Ain't been 'citement like that in a long time in this town."

"We don't need excitement like that in this town," Miranda said with a slow shake of her head.

"I'd a liked to see it, all the same. Found a couple of bodies in there, too," Horace said. "Don't know how they got there or who they wuz. Maybe they started the fire. What do you think, ma'am?"

"I couldn't say," Miranda said vaguely. She was distracted. A man and woman were walking along the sidewalk a few feet ahead of her wagon. The man was wearing the uniform of a Confederate captain; he carried an old and well-worn leather bag held together by belts; he was tall and hatless, with gunmetal-gray hair. The woman wore a striped dress and a sunbonnet, and she carried a small carpetbag in her left hand.

Since she was behind the pair, Miranda could not make out either of their faces. But she knew the man's walk.

"What ev'ybody thinks, though, is that it wuz Yankees

that set fire to the arsenal. What d'you think 'bout that, Miz Miranda?''

"If I were a Yankee, I'd certainly do my best to burn the arsenal down to the ground," Miranda said.

"Ain't that the truth?" Horace said.

"Horace," she said, "do you think you could speed us up a little so that I could get a look at that man's face?" She pointed out the man she meant.

"I've been tryin' to speed up all afternoon," Horace said, making no effort to hide his exasperation.

"I know, Horace," she said, smiling. Horace was a high-stepper, and that appealed to her. "But you might try finding a way to go even faster now that you know I want you to."

"Yes, Miz Miranda," he said, then asked, "That man there?"

"That's right," she said, "the captain."

"Let's git goin', then!" he cried with an impressive flick of the reins. "Come on there, Mandy. Git movin'. You an' Lassis git goin'!"

The two mules lurched a bit, but the movement was more side to side than forward. When it was absolutely clear that the mules had no intention of proceeding any faster, Horace looked helplessly at Miranda. He flicked harder on the reins, but to little avail. He didn't expect much from the mules, and they didn't give him anything he didn't expect. "These two mules got two speeds, Miz Miranda. An' one uv 'em's stop."

"I'm getting out, then," she said, "Stay here. I'll only be a second." She just had to find out who that man was.

"Yes, ma'am," Horace said.

In a flash Miranda had gathered her skirts, swung down off the wagon, and raced to catch up with the couple.

"Excuse me," she said, tapping the captain on the shoulder.

The couple stopped and turned to her.

Miranda drew in a short, choked breath. The man staring at her was Sam Hawken! He was gray-haired and beardless, and much older looking than the cadet she'd met at West Point, but she had no doubt who it was!

"Sam!" she gasped.

The man stepped back, shaken.

But the woman with him had more presence. "I'm afraid you've made a mistake," she said coolly. "My *husband* does not answer to that name."

The words passed by Miranda without lodging in her mind—all of them except "my husband." What she saw, though, was recognition in Sam Hawken's eyes.

And then he managed to pull himself together somewhat. "My wife has it right," he said with apology in his voice. "My name's Harris. James Harris."

Miranda looked at him hard and long. Then she glanced at the woman. Then back to the man. She was sure of what she saw.

"The last time I saw you, Sam," she said firmly and without the slightest hesitation, "was over seven years ago."

"Seven years!" the woman exclaimed, throwing her hands up. The span of time itself, she seemed to be saying, was proof that Miranda had to be mistaken.

"I'm Miranda Kemble," she said breathlessly. "We met at the Military Academy. We fell down a ravine together, and we danced at your graduation ball."

"Seven years?" the woman asked. There was annoyance in her voice now. "Aren't you being a little presumptuous to assume that . . . ?"

Miranda paid no attention to the rest of the woman's words. She was too preoccupied by a powerful urge to reach out and touch Sam's face. At the same time she felt a slight but perceptible tension across her breast. The flesh of her railway locomotive scar, it seemed to her, was tightening.

"I have never been near the Military Academy," the captain said. "I was never north of Virginia."

"You're lying, Sam," Miranda said quietly.

"We cannot listen to this kind of thing," the woman said indignantly. "May we leave now, James, before we have to endure more of this mad girl's presumption?"

"Young lady," the captain said, more gently than his companion, "I'm sure your attention is well meant. But believe me, I'm not the person you take me to be."

His eyes were drinking her in, Miranda could see, no matter what words came from his mouth.

She knew what she had to do.

"Captain," she said, making her voice cold and businesslike, "you do look very much like a man I met some years ago at West Point in New York. The resemblance is quite close—save for the hair color. The man I knew had reddish hair."

"Well, then?" the other woman said, as though that settled it. She made another move to leave. The captain turned to follow her.

"No, wait," Miranda said. "Listen to me before you run off."

"All right," the captain said, turning to face Miranda again. As he turned, the woman's hand snaked out and lit on his sleeve, dragging at him.

He doesn't want to run away from me, Miranda thought. At least not yet.

"The man I knew," she continued, "was a Texan. Even so, he remained in the Union Army after secession."

"As you see," the man said, indicating his Confederate uniform.

"Come on, James," the woman demanded.

"He's still a Union soldier," Miranda said. "I would have heard if he had subsequently changed his mind. He and my brother were close friends. My brother has never forgiven him for what he did."

"What's that have to do with me?" the captain asked.

"Just this," Miranda said. "You know the rumors that a Yankee spy's loose in Atlanta, and the rumors today that the spy set fire to the arsenal."

"What are you saying?" the woman asked.

"I'm about to suggest that the Atlanta authorities would be fascinated to learn of the astonishing resemblance between 'Captain Harris' and the man I know for a fact is in the Union Army."

"That's utterly ridiculous!" the woman snapped. "You'd turn us in on the basis of"—she looked Miranda up and down coldly—"an encounter seven years ago between a child and a young officer whom you haven't seen since? You're mad, girl."

But the man held his hand up. "Wait a minute," he said, and then he added to the woman, "dear."

"The answer," Miranda said with an iron edge in her voice, "is yes, I would. And not only that, I'd be absolutely correct." She gave the captain a wicked glance, "Wouldn't I, Sam?"

He held his hand up for her, too. "Wait a minute, young lady."

"It's Miranda, as you know perfectly well," she interrupted.

"All right, Miranda," he said cautiously, "if that's what you'd like to be called. But I'd like to call you by your surname. What did you say it was?"

"Kemble, as you know."

"All right," he said slowly, "Miss Kemble. Tell me, did I see you riding in a wagon just before you approached me?"

"Yes," she said. "Why?"

He's been watching me all the time out of the corner of his eye! she thought.

"I've been hearing you threatening to turn me in, Miss Kemble, on account of some suspicions you have that I'm a spy. As you've been telling me this, I've been hearing— underneath the words—another message. Miss Kemble, your threat sounds like a bargaining chip. Are you trying to make a deal?"

Miranda tried to catch his eyes, but he avoided her.

"I wouldn't put it that way," she said.

"How would you put it, then, Miss Kemble?"

"Well," she said slowly, "what I had in mind was to give you a choice. Either I turn you in, or you put yourself in my hands."

"I won't stay here another second," the woman said.

"Wait," he said. And to Miranda, "What precisely does putting ourselves in your hands mean?"

"I don't live far from the city," she said. "You would come stay with me for a few days. You would come and enjoy my hospitality—and the safety and seclusion I can offer."

"Why?" the woman asked, as perplexed as she was angry.

"You'd take us there," the captain asked, "to your home? In your wagon?"

"Yes," Miranda said.

"I wouldn't mind having a safe port in a storm right now," he said under his breath.

Miranda came close to him, stood on her toes, and whispered in his ear, "They are after you, aren't they, Sam?"

She backed away, and as she did so, he switched his attention to the woman who accompanied him. "Travel by railroad train has its disadvantages," he said pointedly to her, "doesn't it, my dear?"

The woman slowly shook her head.

"Then you *will* come with me?" Miranda asked.

"Done!" he said.

"What?" the woman asked.

"Get yourself aboard that wagon over there. We're going to take a trip."

"What's got into you, James?" she said.

"Move, Jane," he ordered. "Here, hand me your bag." She grumbled, but she did as she was ordered. He walked out to where Horace was waiting and swung his leather satchel and her carpetbag back behind the seat. Once that was done, he helped Jane aboard, and after her Miranda.

"We're going to have guests, Horace," Miranda said as the straining mules finally heaved the overloaded wagon into motion.

"Yes, ma'am," Horace said, his eyes wide with curiosity.

"Well, then, Miranda," the captain said with a warm, wide smile, "here we are!"

"Yes, Sam," she said, beaming.

This time, he did not contradict her.

*Egypt, Mississippi*
*September 9, 1863*

For ten days crews of soldiers and mechanics had worked under Noah Ballard north of Meridian along the part of the Mobile & Ohio still under Confederate control. They'd been repairing and refurbishing the locomotives that George Spencer and his bands of "privateers"—Will Hottel's words for them—had missed.

The way Noah chose to carry out this operation surprised many of the men under him. Because Dodge's forces ranged so near and operated so freely, the expectation was that Noah's action would be conducted quickly and in secret. The working locomotives would haul the nonworking ones to safety behind Confederate lines. While the nonworking ones were repaired in the shops at Meridian or Canton, the working ones would be sent to Mobile, which was the next stage of their journey to Atlanta. They would be followed by the others, as soon as repairs were completed.

If other more pressing considerations had not intervened, Noah would have adopted that course. And in fact, it was the plan that was under way under Will Hottel's direction north of Jackson, on the Mississippi & Tennessee and the Mississippi Central. But it was Noah Ballard's choice— confirmed by Will Hottel and Lam Kemble, and even by General Joseph Johnston—that the activities on the Mobile & Ohio be made abundantly visible.

While Will Hottel quietly gathered the forty-one engines north of Jackson and sent them south, Noah set about lighting for Grenville Dodge a brilliant beacon on the Mobile & Ohio.

As it happened, Noah and the others were not yet aware that General Dodge was a thousand miles away in New York City. But that fact did not negate the value of the beacon they were putting themselves to such trouble to build.

According to the plan they agreed to, the working locomotives would be made ready to move, and the ones that required repairs would be fixed on the spot, if possible.

Three locomotives requiring serious repairs were dragged out of the sheds where they'd been stored, and placed on sidings in plain sight of the main line. If this provoked questions—and it was intended to—the questioner was told that the mechanics had insisted on working where they could see what they were doing. If the questioner turned out to be a Federal spy, all the better. Noah wanted these engines to be noticed.

Once the operation had actually been set in motion, General Joe Johnston surprisingly turned cooperative. Among other things, Johnston made his own personal locomotive and railroad car available to Noah Ballard so that Noah could closely monitor the work of the mechanics and train crews.

More importantly, to Noah's surprise Johnston had approved the most crucial elements of the scheme Noah had devised to recapture the fourteen locomotives the northern privateers had stolen. The plan involved the erection of six exact scale-model locomotives near Shannon, a town halfway between Okolona and Tupelo. These locomotives were constructed out of canvas, papier-mâché, wood, and paint. Once the six were in place, a crew very ostentatiously set about "putting them in working order." The plan additionally involved moving a brigade of infantry up to Shannon. They prepared concealed positions in the vicinity of the six model engines. These positions were not set up to protect the counterfeit locomotives, but to trap any enemy force that ventured near them. After digging and then concealing their trenches and breastworks, the brigade made camp in a wood not far from the six phony engines. It was impressed upon the troops in the brigade that they must not advertise their presence there.

When the telegram he was expecting from Lam Kemble reached him, Noah was not far from the town of Egypt, which was ten miles south of Okolona and twenty miles south of Shannon. Noah had come there to inspect the work being done on one of the locomotives they'd placed in the open—one of the genuine locomotives parked on sidings beside the main lines. While Noah looked over the work on the engine, his own train was backed up onto the same siding, and a line from the car had been attached to the telegraph wire that ran alongside the track.

None of the locomotives that Noah had seen was in worse repair than this particular engine.

Noah, accompanied by the chief mechanic and a lieutenant who was in command of the infantry company guarding the trainmen, stood at the front of the engine. The engine's piston assembly was spread out in pieces on a canvas sheet.

"It looks to me like you've got yourself more than a little work," Noah said.

"I'll say," the mechanic sighed. "Much more. This one's worse than it looks. The slide valve's cracked and the valve rod's broke, and if I had my way, I'd like to do some work on the cylinder and the piston, too. But I think we could make do enough to get this thing moving under its own steam, except for one thing: the pipes and the fire tubes are all rotten."

"It won't hold steam, then?" Noah asked.

"Not enough to get it moving."

Noah thought for a moment. "What do you think we should do, then? Abandon it and go on to one that can be made to work? Or is it worth hauling down to Meridian?"

"Oh, it can be made to run again," the mechanic said. "But it needs a complete overhaul in a genuine shop."

"All right, then," Noah decided, "pack all this up and we'll move it with the others."

"Right," the mechanic said.

"I'm going to Okolona today," Noah said, turning to the lieutenant, "and maybe to Shannon, if there's still time. If you run into any problems, send me a message on the telegraph."

"Yes, sir," the lieutenant said.

"And, Lieutenant," Noah added, "there's a chance, as always, that you'll come under attack. I don't expect it here, so far south, but there's a chance." The lieutenant had already been briefed about this possibility, of course, but Noah felt he should repeat it even so. "If that happens,

Lieutenant, your orders about protecting the locomotives are canceled. Withdraw. This one ain't worth saving."

The lieutenant smiled. "That's an order I'll be glad to obey."

"I hope it doesn't come up. If anything happens, it's likely to be at Shannon or Okolona."

I wonder why they haven't done anything yet, he thought. We've been at it for ten days, and there hasn't been a peep out of the Yankees in Corinth.

On his way back to the train, he ran into a sergeant who was looking for him. The sergeant had a telegram in his hand.

"You'll want to read this, Major," the sergeant said. "It's from Colonel Kemble. It looks like the one you've been waiting for."

"Let's hope," Noah said, taking the flimsy and unfolding it.

Noah read:

THE FISH ARE BITING STOP IT LOOKS LIKE A WHOLE SCHOOL STOP WE HAVE CAUGHT SOME STOP COME ON AND CATCH SOME FOR YOURSELF STOP LAM

As soon as he'd read it, Noah let out a wild whoop. And then, not satisfied with that, he started pounding the sergeant on the back. "That's it! That's the one!" he said to the sergeant when he was coherent again.

"Then you're going to want to move out right away?" the sergeant asked.

"Instantly!"

The four parts of the message told Noah the following. First, Union forces had descended upon the decoys near Shannon. Second, the brigade of infantry hiding in the wood had come out, sprung Noah's trap, and pinned down the attackers in positions near the counterfeit locomotives. Third, the attackers were, as Noah had expected and hoped, the Third Tennessee Cavalry. And fourth, Lam was ready to move on the next part of the plan as soon as Noah arrived.

"Let's get on up to Shannon, Sergeant," he said.

## Raven's Wing, Georgia
### September 9, 1863

Miranda Kemble ran for all she was worth up a briar-and-bramble-covered hill that bordered the east side of her property. Because of the undergrowth, it was hard going, but she knew her way well, having climbed up to the ridge crest many times before. Behind her—far away, she hoped—she could hear her pursuer crashing after her.

She stopped to listen for him more carefully, and to catch her breath and survey the damage the thorns had done to her skirts. She'd get hell from Alabama, the Negro woman who took care of Miranda's clothes and other such things, but the momentary scratch of conscience that thought produced didn't at all swerve Miranda from her purpose. She was as happy and excited as a hound that's treed a coon.

Sam was still far behind her, as she knew he would be. She could hear him crashing and blundering and shouting useless curses.

She let out a long, mocking laugh, even though the noise would betray her. But, damn it all, she had no intention of letting the quarry elude the pursuer. She only wanted to delay the capture for dramatic purposes.

Her chest heaved and pounded, her heart raced like mad, her face was slick with sweat, and her skirt and petticoats were in shreds.

He was shouting from far away, "You better damn well have a cast-iron bottom, you little cub, because when I catch you you'll feel my hand harder than you've ever felt a hand in your sweet, young life."

"Oh, don't do that!" she yelped pitifully. "Please don't! I'll be good, I promise." And then she gave another loud, mocking laugh and dashed off up toward the crest of the ridge.

Once she'd reached the top, she turned right and loped a hundred yards to a huge, old elm tree of long acquaintance. When she reached its base, she slipped out of her shoes and stockings and hid them under dense shrubs nearby. She flung up her arms and made a leap for the lowest of the tree's branches.

Winded from her mad dash up the hill, Miranda missed on her first try. She tried again, and again missed. Sam was dangerously close to the crest of the ridge.

Miranda put all her soul into her next jump, and this time her hands felt the reassuring roughness of the hard elm bark. She hung down for ten or fifteen seconds, her bare feet dangling, her chest pounding powerfully.

After another few seconds, her strength returned and she swung her legs up, scissored them over the branch, and heaved the rest of her body across it.

"Where have you vanished to, girl?" Sam was calling.

Too close. There was no time to rest.

She scrambled quickly up into the obscurity of limbs and leaves, laughing joyfully to herself as she climbed.

Miranda's private sanctuary was twenty feet from the base of the tree. Two fat branches forked near the trunk, making a safe and comfortable resting place where Miranda had spent many a lazy summer afternoon.

She settled in and took stock of herself. She inspected the scratches from twigs and branches, and decided these would disappear fast, except for one ribbon line of blood along her neck. She plucked up the hem of her skirt and wiped at it, then toweled her cheeks and forehead. Then, bending her head down and lifting her hair, she dabbed at the damp back part of her neck. She arranged her dress across her knees but left her ankles and a little bit of leg showing.

Through a wide opening in the leaves and branches, Miranda was able to see her house and most of her land. As always, she liked very much what she saw.

"Where are you hiding, you little cub?" Sam shouted. He was standing practically underneath the spot where she sat.

She giggled.

"Do that again," he said, twisting about uncertainly, his ears cocked.

She obliged him, only louder this time.

"Have you turned into a bird?" he said, looking up, but she was well hidden in her nest of leaves.

She whistled like a bird, then giggled once again.

He still was unable to locate the source of the sound. "How did you get up in the air?"

"Wings," came a whisper from above.

"You know what I think we've done?" Sam said as though to himself, but he said it loud enough for her to hear. "I think we've got us treed a moo-bird. It's damned rare, but damned good tasting. You've never eaten until you've tasted moo-bird fried over an open fire."

"Who're you talking to?" she said.

"To Tiger," he said after a slight pause. "He's my hound." Sam made panting, eager barking sounds. "That's right, Tige, you know we've got a moo-bird treed, don't you?"

Tiger howled up the tree trunk, *"Aaahhooo!"*

"What do you think, Tige?" Sam said. "Shall we shoot her down or climb up there and grab her by the neck?"

"Oh, don't do that," Miranda called down plaintively. "Please don't come up here. Please!"

"That settles it, Tige. We've got to track her into her lair. It's risky and dangerous, but I'm sure you're up to it."

*"Aaahhhoooo!"* Tige answered.

Miranda laughed.

With a bound, Sam caught hold of the low limb Miranda had used, and then he swung himself up into the tree. Moments later, he was sitting beside her, taking in the loveliness revealed through the opening in the leaves, as well as the loveliness that was curled up next to him.

"Well," he said, "you've led me a merry chase. For more than two days you've led me a merry chase . . . The truth is," he went on reflectively, "you've led me a chase for seven years—ever since you dragged me off that cliff."

"I'm not speaking to you," she said.

"Oh?" he said, looking down his arched nose at her. "What do you say to that, Tige?" Then he played Tige's part: *"Aahhoo."*

"I'm still not speaking to you."

"Why not?"

"You have to give the password."

"The password?"

"That's right," she said. "This is a magic place—my magic, special place." She caught and held his eyes. "Mine. No one besides me has ever been up here."

"I'm honored," he said.

"But its magic won't be released without the password."

"All right. But will you give me a hint?"

"No. No hints." She looked away from him, waiting.

"Password, password, password," he said. "What do you think it is, Tige?" Tige growled.

She laughed, but she still waited, implacable.

"You're impossible," Sam said.

"Now it's my turn to be honored," she said.

He laughed then, and his face brightened. "I've got it!" he cried.

"The password?"

He nodded slowly, letting the suspense build.

"Well, then, tell me," she demanded.

"Two days ago," he began in his most formal and high-toned manner, "I met you in Atlanta, where I was accompanied by a lady whose acquaintance you made at that time. Her name, as you know, my dear little cub, is Jane Featherstone."

"I'm waiting for the password," Miranda said.

"You'll get it," he said. "Be patient."

"All right," she said huffily, but her eyes flashed most fetchingly.

"Previous to our encounter with you, Miss Featherstone and I were engaged in a sensitive matter on behalf of the national government."

"Yankee spies," she said, wrinkling her nose. Espionage was an occupation that Miranda found distasteful, yet exciting.

He shrugged his acknowledgment. "That matter having been completed, we found it necessary to take our leave of Atlanta quickly and discreetly."

"What's the password?" she demanded.

"Wait."

"All right," she said with a grudging shake of her head.

"You're quite stunning when you shake your head that way," he said.

"That's not the password," she said, "but you're sailing on the right course."

"Our intention at the time was to board a train," he resumed in his formal manner, "even though we both recognized that such a move might entail some measure of risk. We had reason to believe that our activities on behalf of the national government might have aroused suspicions among the inhabitants of the city of Atlanta.

"And then," he said in a great burst, "glory be to God, *there you were, in a graceful, resplendent golden chariot*!"

"I have a somewhat different recollection," she said. "But never mind."

"Be that as it may," he said, "you offered Miss Featherstone and me hospitality and the safety of your lodgings in spite of the compromising position you placed yourself in by doing so." He caught her eyes. "For this I am eternally grateful."

"You're welcome," she said. "What about my *password*!"

"Be patient, my dear."

"I'm not speaking another word until I hear it, even if you keep talking for hours."

"I was saying," he sailed on, ignoring her ultimatum, "that you welcomed me and my companion. And you did that sincerely and unquestioningly.

"I'm positive you had a lot of questions, just as I'm equally positive that there was much that you did not approve of.

"I propose now to answer some of those questions."

Miranda cocked her head. It was a gesture that Sam remembered from the first time they had met, a gesture that she shared with Jane—one of the few qualities that the two women had in common.

"How do you know what my questions are if I haven't asked them?" she inquired with an innocent look.

"I thought you weren't uttering another word," he said.

"I lied," she said. "Answer me."

He laughed. "Hundreds of questions have been written across your face, Miranda. You have a most expressive face."

"All right," she said, liking that.

"As to your most pressing question," he said, and she cocked her head again, "you didn't fail to observe the close proximity of Miss Featherstone and myself."

"Proximity is putting a rather nice turn on what you were doing, don't you think," she said acidly, "my darling *Mis*-ter Harris? Or is it Reverend Jeffes, or somebody else?"

"'Proximity' seems appropriate to me," he said.

"Oh, my," she said, and then laughed. "That was Adam's excuse." Her voice deepened like a man's. "You must understand, Lord, that little Eve was so very *proximate*, and in such a state of . . . *dresslessness* . . . that I was completely beside myself and could do nothing save to fall."

With that, Miranda stretched out and gave Sam a shove on the shoulder. He was so surprised by the move that it was all he could do to avoid tumbling to the ground.

"Jesus Christ, Miranda!" he said, once he had recovered himself. "Whenever I spend time with you, I'm driven into swift, sudden descents. No man of flesh and bones can stand up to a lifetime with you."

"You were saying something about Jane Featherstone," she said sweetly, "were you not?"

"What I was going to say, goddamn it," he snapped, "is that I like you better than I like her. That you don't have to fear her."

As Sam spoke, Miranda began to feel giddy. Her mind was spinning, and her balance on the fork of the tree was becoming dangerously precarious. Her hand found his, and that steadied her.

The last thing he said was very near to being the magic password.

"You don't think I'd have ever had anything to fear from her, do you?" Miranda said. "She's nothing. A snit."

"Actually, Miranda, she's better than that. And you have been afraid of her—don't try lying about that. You've been jealous of her from the instant you eyed us on the street."

"No, I haven't," Miranda whispered.

"But the primary reason you have nothing to fear from her is that it's you I love."

"I don't believe you."

"Yes, you do," he said.

When Miranda looked at him, tears were in her eyes. And then she smiled through her tears. "I didn't fall," she said.

"What?" he asked, not understanding her.

"I didn't fall off the branch," she said, "when you told me that you loved me. And I didn't take you with me," she brightened, "when I didn't fall."

"Oh, yes," he said. "I should be grateful for that small favor."

"It's not a favor, Sam. It's a reward. A reward for loving me—or at least saying that you do." And then her face blazed with her most enchanting, most magical expression. "Oh, and by the way, you've successfully uttered the secret password."

"It's lovely here, isn't it?" Sam said to Miranda. "I can see the magic in it." When Miranda led Sam up to her treetop refuge, it was midafternoon—a hot and humid Georgia afternoon. Now, several hours later, the afternoon had faded into a balmy and pleasant evening. But neither of them showed any desire to descend to the common world below them.

"I adore it here," Miranda agreed. "And," she added, "it's mine."

He looked at her, not quite understanding. "That's important to you, is it, that it's yours?" To Sam, pride of ownership seemed to belong properly to the male of the species. But then he had never actually owned much more than the clothes on his back.

"It's the reason that I'm here in Georgia, Sam, and not in England," she said soberly, "if that's what you mean. Finally, in all my life, for the first time I possess and control something important to me." She glanced momentarily through the window of leaves. Then continued.

"When I was a girl, it was always a pull from my mother

or my father. With her pulling for her own way, and him pulling for his, there was very little left over for me. Now I have some things that are mine, and I refuse to give them up."

"I guess, in a way, it is what I mean," he said, "though you have the words for it and I don't." He stopped and drew in his breath. "It's just that you are a surprising young woman."

"Surprising?"

"I'm taken aback by the choices you've made."

"Choices?"

"The thing is, Miranda," he went on, "I'm just a little astonished that you've taken on a large plantation in wartime."

"First of all, Sam," she said with a light, playful laugh, "it's not a large plantation. It's a rather small one. And secondly, I take it that your astonishment stems from the fact that I am running it at all. A woman is not supposed to be capable of such competence, isn't that so?"

He smiled and then blushed—thereby admitting the truth of her charge.

"How many farms, plantations, and other enterprises in the South do you think women are managing?" she asked more seriously. "Now that the men are all off fighting and dying," she went on, "who do you think is taking care of all that's left behind?" She caught his eye. "What they do they've had to do. It's what is necessary. What I do I've done from choice. I like it."

"And you've given up the safety and the comforts and the pleasures of London—and your mother—in order to do it?"

"Yes, of course. It's what my father wanted me to do on his deathbed, but it's what I would have done anyway, even if he hadn't made the choice for me."

"Amazing," Sam said, liking Miranda all the more for her courage and integrity.

If Miranda Kemble had entertained any secret dreams of falling in love with Sam Hawken when she invited him to Raven's Wing, Sam's first hours there had dashed them. As soon as Sam and Jane Featherstone arrived, Miranda began to have doubts about the wisdom of her impulse.

From their initial encounter, Jane despised Miranda, but that was understandable. Jane was jealous. The virulence of her jealousy was increased when Jane realized that she had never managed in the least bit to bind Sam to her. But when she realized that Sam cared more for a girl whom he had briefly met years ago than he would ever care for Jane herself, she went into a silent frenzy.

Yet Jane, for all her hostility, proved to be nothing but a bother for Miranda, a momentary irritation. Most of the time Jane simply sulked alone in her room. She slept apart from Sam, of course. During those moments when Jane deigned to join the others, she either complained or else begged Sam to stop wasting time. They had obligations; they ought to be on their way.

But Sam was another thing. He was not an irritation; he was a problem.

On the long wagon ride from Atlanta to Raven's Wing, he had been silent or he dozed. After his initial flash of pleasure and excitement when he finally admitted knowing Miranda, he'd lapsed into intense and almost frightening solitude. He was fiercely untouchable. And he remained that way for the first part of his stay in Miranda's home.

Sam resisted all her efforts, for instance, to charm him into talking about himself. He refused to discuss the seven lost years, even though she made it clear she wouldn't press him on the issues that most troubled her—his espionage and his connection with the Featherstone woman. At other times he listened patiently but distractedly to her tales of the Kemble family.

The only time he showed a passing interest in Miranda's ramblings came when she explained how her attachment to Raven's Wing was purely personal. It had nothing to do with the South, with the Great Cause, with the plantation aristocracy, or with slavery.

He even showed a tremor of astonishment when she told him that she had placed a document on file with her lawyer in Atlanta. The document stated that those slaves she owned would become free upon her death or the termination of the war, whichever came first. The Negroes she owned would be free today, she told Sam, if that had been a practical choice. But releasing her slaves into freedom in the Georgia of 1863 would condemn them to much worse than anything they would possibly suffer at her hands on her land. And they knew it.

And he showed even greater astonishment when he learned that she wished and hoped that the South would lose the war.

"You can't mean that, Miranda," Sam told her on the porch of the main house late on his second evening at Raven's Wing. "How can you be indifferent to the land of your birth? How can you wish it to be defeated?"

Miranda considered answering his question by asking the same one of him, but she had the good sense and the sensitivity to drop that thought.

"I'm not indifferent," she said. "I'm not at all indifferent. Just the reverse. I care so much for the South that I want my people to shake off the soiled and evil garments we've clothed ourselves with. We can then grow and change and take the greatness we have reached for and fought for. But, Sam, we must be stripped and naked first."

The look he gave her was hard and appraising. And troubled.

"Meanwhile my primary attachment is to Raven's Wing, and only Raven's Wing."

Sam's face froze. Seconds later he abruptly leapt to his feet and, without explanation, strolled out into the night.

When he returned over an hour later, she was still seated in her rocking chair on the porch.

"You haven't gone to bed yet?" he asked.

"It's too hot to sleep," she said, "And besides, I was waiting for you."

"Waiting for me? Why?" His face showed genuine surprise. "I shouldn't think I've been acting like someone you'd wish to wait for."

"I've waited seven years to see you again," she blurted,

without realizing as she said it that he could and would take a different meaning from what she intended.

"I should be flattered, I guess," he said with a chill in his voice that disturbed her. "But I'm not much moved by melodrama. I can't believe you, girl. Are you telling me, Miranda Kemble, that you actually *pined*"—the word curled sarcastically off his lips—"for me for seven years? I'm nothing but a passing encounter when you were, what was it, fifteen? I don't deserve so much romantic attention, dear girl."

"You're wrong!" she cried, hurt and angry. "Absolutely! Sam Hawken, I haven't pined for you for seven years. I would never *pine*"—her sarcasm matched his—"for anyone for seven years. What I meant to say is that I liked you when we met seven years ago, and I'm glad to see you again."

In that, she was speaking the literal truth. But she was at the same time more than merely glad to see him. She knew, even if he didn't care to admit it, that a spark had been lit between them at West Point, and that it was growing now.

She could not for the life of her understand why he was so cold and distant.

"You knew what we were, Jane and I," he said, "when you picked us up off the street in Atlanta?"

"Yes," she said. "You are Union spies."

"And that doesn't bother you?" he asked softly, patiently, as though he were addressing a child.

That softness stung her into fury. "Of course it bothers me!" she screamed, bursting into tears. "It bothers me that you lie and steal and kill and betray, all for the sake of *what*? For the sake of the Union? For the sake of victory in a war? Is that the kind of price that makes victory worthwhile, Sam? And it bothers me that you have been living with Jane Featherstone! As though *she* is your wife! It bothers me that she has had"—Miranda searched for the words—"carnal intercourse with you!"

"What business is that of yours, little girl?" He tossed that off casually, but his face, as she read it, was rigid with torment.

She didn't spend a long time trying to read it, though, because she was out of her chair and pounding that face with half-closed fists almost as the "little girl" taunt came out of his mouth.

Of course he didn't spend a long time waiting to restrain her, and it didn't take her long after that to put herself under control and apologize for her outburst. But then when she was back in her chair, she saw that the torment was still in his face and his eyes were moist with unshed tears.

They were both silent, neither knowing what to think or do next. Finally Sam spoke. "I don't know what's happening to me."

"You don't?" she asked, breathing the words in as she spoke them.

"Do you know you sound as though you think you do."

"I don't," she admitted. But she liked much better this vulnerable side of him than the cold and solitary face he was attempting to maintain.

"I'm ashamed to tell you this," he said, "but all the time I've been here accepting your hospitality and safety, I've purposely ignored you. And I've purposely paid no attention to all you've been telling me about yourself. I didn't want this meeting, and I didn't want our reunion." As he said this, he looked painfully at her. "I didn't want our reunion to prosper. I didn't want you to touch me the way you have."

"But I *have* ... touched you?" she asked, not daring to show her hope.

He gave her no answer to that question. "I think I may have succeeded in keeping myself detached from you," he said, pressing on with his own agenda, "until earlier this evening, when you told me of your feelings about the war and the South and your property. I'm ashamed to tell you this, too, maybe more than I'm ashamed of the other things. But when you talked then, I saw instantly how you could be used for my purposes."

"How do you mean?"

"For espionage," he shrugged. "That's when I left you and took a walk."

"And now you have returned," she said. "And . . . ?"

"And I decided I won't do that."

"How would you have used me?" she asked.

"You have property. You have slaves. You have friends. You are respected. You have influence. And you have a secure place from which to operate. Believe me, Miranda, you would be most useful to me."

"What changed your mind?"

"You did. I couldn't do it to you."

"I've changed you?" she asked, smiling and grateful, liking him more than ever.

"No," he said. "You haven't changed me. I haven't changed. People don't change other people, and certainly not after a few hours."

"Yes, they do," she said.

"I have to sleep," he said. "I have to go to bed."

The next morning Sam Hawken was actually smiling. For two days he had scarcely smiled at all. But now, though he didn't lose his reserve, he almost seemed cheerful.

The smiles disturbed Jane Featherstone, and in consequence she redoubled her demands that Sam immediately take her back to Mississippi. She even began to threaten to leave by herself and take her own chances. "I'll have to do that," she said to Sam in Miranda's hearing, "as long as you persist in lazing away your life here in Lotus Land."

Sam only laughed. Then he asked Miranda to join him for a stroll about her property. She accepted, of course, adding the suggestion that they pack a lunch.

One thing led to another, and by midafternoon they were playing games with each other—children's games like hide and seek. But the hide and seek Sam and Miranda played was not quite the same sport that younger boys and girls enjoy.

"You *have* changed, Sam," she announced as night fell and they finished their descent from her tree. "You aren't a different man from the one who came here the other day, but you've let parts of yourself out of hiding."

"Do you really think so?" he asked.

"Yes, my love, I do."

"Like what?"

"Kiss me."

"All right."

They kissed.

"There's one part of you that's been set free," she said, smiling brilliantly.

"Wag your tail, Tige," he said.

*'Aahooo!'* Tige said.

## Shannon, Mississippi
## September 9, 1863

"You're wasting time, Noah," Lam Kemble said with quickening impatience. It was almost dark, and Lam was eager to move. An entire squadron of cavalry and a substantial contingent of mechanics and train crews were set to take to the road with him—and with Noah, if he could be made to budge. They all had to be twenty miles north before daybreak tomorrow.

"I know I'm wasting your time," Noah said. "But I'm enjoying myself, and it's a long time since I've done that."

"That's all very well and good," Lam answered, exasperated, "but let's get going. The better part of the regiment that's guarding your locomotives has moved out—presumably to march down here to rescue these people. We've got a long all-night ride ahead of us. And we've got to get to where we're going before dawn, or else all this effort will be wasted."

"I won't be long, Lam," Noah promised.

Noah Ballard stood in a shallow trench, peering over a breastwork. Lam was at his right, fidgeting. On Lam's right was Luther Jarvis, a colonel. Jarvis was in command of the infantry brigade here in Shannon. And on his right were a sergeant and a couple of troopers.

Beyond the breastwork, open meadowland spread out for a quarter of a mile. Down in the meadow, fifty yards from the breastwork, the First Tennessee Cavalry had dug in as best they could around the counterfeit locomotives. It was a damned poor place to make a stand—which was the reason why Noah chose it. Except for the main-line railway embankment, there was no cover at all between the breastwork from which Noah watched and its brother 120 yards away.

No shots were currently being fired. The Tennessee Yankees had no desire to expend what little reserves of ammunition they had left, and the southerners had no desire to destroy them. Neither did they desire to force the Yankees' surrender. The First Tennessee Cavalry were just fine where they were—they were bait.

The Yankees were lying low, and they were very quiet.

"Noah!" Lam said, trying again, exasperated. "Would it please you to move?"

"Just a minute, Lam," Noah said. Noah had every intention of doing what Lam asked, but first he had some pressing business to settle.

"I'd order you to move," Lam said, "me being a colonel and you a major. But I have a strange feeling that in all this insane and jumbled up business you might actually be the man in charge."

"Colonel?" Noah said, addressing Luther Jarvis, "Would you favor me with something?"

"I don't see why not," Colonel Jarvis said.

"What I'd like to do right now is talk to the commander of the First Tennessee Cavalry. He's a man named Walt Tyler, and he's a colonel. Could you send somebody out under a white flag to set that up for me?"

"You don't need to do that, Noah," Lam said.

"You go on and I'll catch up with you," Noah said.

"Don't be silly. This is a military operation, not a Sunday ride in the country."

"I can be through with what I need to do in five minutes. Is that all right, Colonel?" he said to Jarvis. Then added, "Would you go and send someone to contact Colonel Tyler, please?"

Fifteen minutes later, Noah and Walt Tyler were squared off opposite one another halfway between the southern and the northern lines.

"What do you have in mind to talk about, Major?" Tyler

asked, very proper and correct, after the two men had made their introductions.

"Nothing that's real earthshakingly significant, Colonel. Don't get your hopes up. I'm not going to let you surrender."

"Well, then," Tyler said, looking more curious than put out, "I'll ask you what I have in mind." He made a sweeping gesture that took in his own positions around the counterfeit locomotives and the Confederate positions before him. "I haven't the slightest idea what's going on, Major. Canvas and papier-mâché locomotives? You've got us trapped well and good, but what for?"

Noah laughed at him. "Don't you remember me?" he asked suddenly.

"No," Tyler said slowly, "I can't say that I do." He paused awhile, then said, "Should I?"

"We met briefly some weeks ago a few miles south of here. I was on an armed train you and your men ambushed. A locomotive and a couple of cars south of Okolona."

Tyler looked at Noah quizzically. "Yeah, sure, I remember that. What about it? We let you go, didn't we?"

"That's right. You sent us running, and I guess I ought to be grateful for that. But before you did that, you toyed with us, enjoying yourself at our expense, and I want you to know that it burned my ass."

Tyler shrugged. "So?" he said. Then he smiled grimly. "You know, Major, I'm kind of glad I made an impression on you. I intended to do that."

"Fine. I understand," Noah said slowly, almost casually, but with acid in his voice. "And I know that fighting men like to have their good times and all. But I want you to know that I've put you in a worse position now than you had me in then. And I want you to know that I'm thinking about you all the time, and that pretty damn soon I'm going to make you endure a lot more powerful hell than you made me feel."

"What do you have in mind?" Tyler asked, stone-faced.

"Consider the possibilities," Noah said. He wanted the man to feel he was dangling helplessly on Noah's hook. "You have some time. Imagine to yourself what you'd be doing to me if our places were switched. Then tremble a little, because what I have in mind is a lot worse.''

Tyler stepped back and swept his eyes up and down Noah, as though taking his measure. ''You know something, Major Ballard? I think you must be a madman.''

''Good evening, Colonel,'' Noah said. ''Just consider the possibilities.'' With that, Noah turned on his heel and rejoined Lam behind the breastworks.

''You ready to go now, Noah?'' Lam asked.

''Yeah. Let's go.''

''Magnificent!'' Lam said. And in the same breath he turned to Colonel Jarvis, ''Luther, we're off. Good luck.''

''Good luck to you,'' Colonel Jarvis said.

Lam and Noah set off from the field positions to the place where their horses were waiting.

# ◆ EIGHT ◆

September 10, 1863

Ashbel Kemble's blockade runner *Miranda* was as sleek, fast, and elegant as a leaping dolphin. She was 252 feet long, with a beam of 31 feet, and a depth of 11 feet. To make the barest of silhouettes against the sky, she was low to the water and painted dull gray, and save for her two lower masts and her funnels, everything aloft had been taken down. She carried a crew of forty-nine hands, and her maximum speed was seventeen knots, unusually fast for those days. *Miranda* was bound from Liverpool to Charleston, South Carolina, with a load of percussion caps, cartridge bags, shellac, and saltpeter, as well as eight chests of medicines kept separately in the owner's cabin.

On the night of September 9 and 10, *Miranda* was forty-five nautical miles due south of Savannah, Georgia, which put her just over a hundred nautical miles from Charleston, South Carolina, her intended destination. She would make neither port, and both her captain, whose name was Anthony Meyer, and her owner, who was a passenger on that voyage, knew it.

It was past midnight on the tenth as *Miranda* labored slowly and painfully south. She was sorely wounded.

The previous day she had had a run-in with the nemesis

of blockade runners, the United States cruiser *Niphon*. Though *Miranda* was faster than *Niphon* by two or three knots, she had not been able to take advantage of her greater speed. When she encountered *Niphon*, *Miranda* had been south and east of Charleston, proceeding in a blanketing fog at a cautious six knots. The fog lifted, and there stood *Niphon* at two cable lengths, as astonished as *Miranda* but eager to pounce. *Miranda* was a long-sought prize. *Niphon*'s crew and officers relished the chance to grab their personal splits from the sale of her cargo.

*Miranda* poured on steam and ran south, racing for the shore. With her shallow draft, she could hug much closer to land than *Niphon*. Yet it wasn't her shallow draft that saved her; it was a sudden squall. The sheets of rain made her invisible to her pursuer. During her flight, *Miranda* took a terrible beating. Her hull was damaged and she was shipping water. One of her two boilers was useless, and her port paddle wheel was no better than halfway up to par.

The squall had long since passed, and *Miranda* was now laboring slowly along at four knots. Shipping water as she was, Captain Meyer estimated that she was safe for perhaps another twelve hours. And that meant that Charleston was out of the question—even if the Federal naval patrols had not been out in such force. Savannah, which was nearer, was also out of the question, but for other reasons. In April 1862 Federal forces had captured Fort Pulaski, whose guns commanded the long, narrow channel of the Savannah River. After that, few Confederate blockade runners attempted to reach Savannah.

Captain Meyer and *Miranda*'s owner, Ashbel Kemble, had few options. And these few choices were complicated by the fear that they would run into the *U.S.S. Florida*, which patrolled these parts.

Captain Meyer, First Officer Muller, Ashbel Kemble, and Fanny Shaw, who was a nonparticipating observer, discussed this situation in the wardroom.

Meyer and Muller believed their best chance was to make a dash up Ossabaw Sound, below Savannah, and then land the ship. Most of the land around there was under Confederate control, and this was not the case with the sea islands from Saint Catherines on south. These were occupied either by Yankee garrisons or renegade slaves. Even if the ship could be safely landed on one of those islands, her valuable cargo would surely be lost.

Ashbel Kemble remained silent during most of Meyer and Muller's deliberations. Though he offered occasional observations and suggestions, his policy was to leave the practical running of his ships to the officers he had entrusted with the job—even in grave circumstances such as they were in.

The captain, for his part, was glad to have his owner's confidence, but he also wanted to make completely certain that the owner approved of the next move he intended. That move was going to be the last act of *Miranda*'s final voyage, and Meyer did not want any blame for it to fall on himself.

"I take it by your silence, Mr. Kemble," he said, "that you approve our new course?"

"Yes, Captain," Ash said. "*Qui tacet consentire*. Go ahead with you." And then a smile flickered across his face. "But you *are* aware, are you not, how close we are to Kemble lands?"

"Yes, sir," Meyer said. "I've not forgotten that." The mouth of the Altamaha River was twenty-five miles to the southwest. Several of the small islands along that waterway belonged to the Kemble family. "I'm also aware, sir, that there's a Federal naval squadron based at Saint Simon's Island."

"I haven't forgotten that either, Mr. Meyer," Ash said, lifting his hand in acknowledgment. "Go ahead with you," he repeated. "And let's see if we can reach shore before we all get very wet."

"Mr. Muller?" Captain Meyer said, turning to his first officer. "Would you see to our new bearings?"

"Right away, sir," Muller said.

The mate bowed, then left the room.

After he had departed, Ash looked at Fanny. "Any regrets, my dear?" There was an amused twinkle in his eye. The man was irrepressible, Fanny thought. Neither the danger they were in nor the imminent loss of his ship, and possibly of his cargo, seemed to disturb him. He'd laugh on his deathbed, then slap Satan on his back and offer him a Havana cigar when he reached his likely final destination.

"Regrets, Ash?" she asked. "About this voyage and its dangers? No. No regrets. I've been far too long apart from my children. It's time I see them again, even if it's risky to do so."

"Actually," Ash said, grinning, "I was wondering how much you've missed Kemble Island. We're close to it now, and you spent pretty close to ten years of your life there. *Miranda* can't make the island—she draws too deep for that—but we could certainly reach Little Saint Simon's. That's only a short pull to the big house."

"I hate that place, Ash Kemble. I never want to see it again. You know that. You know I don't even want to talk about it."

"The years haven't dulled your anger?"

"Not at all," she said. "Those were the nine worst years of my life, and I'm distressed to be even this close. I can feel its noxious presence. Evil rays emanate from it."

"As you can see, Captain," Ash said by way of explanation, "Mrs. Shaw has strong opinions about the Kemble plantations."

Captain Meyer nodded coolly. The wise thing for him to do was to stay well out of the game these two were playing.

"All the more reason to head north," Ash continued. "We can't let the good lady be overcome by noxious rays."

"You *are* a devil, Ash Kemble," she said, teasing him back. "If I didn't know better, I'd have guessed you arranged our recent misfortunes simply to bring me this close to Kemble Island. The last time I was there, I left it in the dead of night, alone, on a boat which I myself rowed to Darien. That escape will forever be for me the final chapter in my life at Kemble Island—at least," she added, "if I have any say in the matter."

Captain Meyer, after these words, gave a questioning look. He was curious to fill in this piece in the scandalous tale of Fanny Shaw and her former husband, the late Pierce

Kemble. Much of the tale was public knowledge, but the juiciest parts had eluded the press.

However, the captain's curiosity was not fated to be satisfied that night.

A sailor pounded on the wardroom door.

"Mr. Muller's compliments, sir," he said once he was inside. "He'd like you to know that we've spotted a ship's light north of us. His estimate, from the ship's course and speed, is that it's a Federal cruiser, probably the *Florida*."

"Does he think we've been spotted?" the captain asked.

"He didn't say, sir."

"Did he say where their course will intersect ours?"

"He didn't say that either, sir."

"Right," the captain said. "Return my compliments to Mr. Muller, if you please, and tell him to turn us a hundred and ten degrees to port for the time being. And tell him I'll join him above directly."

"Yes, sir," the sailor said and left.

Captain Meyer didn't waste any time. He left the wardroom hot on the sailor's heels.

"I'll come as well," Ash said, following the captain through the door.

Fanny, seeing no reason to stay where she was, brought up the rear.

Soon they were all in the wheelhouse trying to accustom their eyes to the darkness. There was no moon, and not a light was showing on the *Miranda*, not even a cigar. Smoking was forbidden on deck. The engine room hatchways were screened with tarpaulins, and the heat down there, normally fearsome, was now murderous. But the men there kept their complaints to themselves. The ship was quiet as a breeze, except for the steady beat of the engine and the splash of the paddle floats.

In the anxious silence, these sounded distressingly loud.

"Has she altered course at all?" the captain was saying to the mate when Fanny grew close enough to hear them. The pilot, Mr. McGowan, stood on the mate's right.

"No, not that we can tell. Not that it much matters. She appears to be headed for Saint Simon's, and whether she sees us yet or not, she's going to pass within a couple of miles of us.''

"Damn," Captain Meyer said. "When?"

"At the four knots we're making now, probably by dawn."

"Damn," the captain repeated.

"Maybe we could get close to shore and lay low until they are past," McGowan offered.

"That's what I would do in an instant," Meyer said, "if the holds weren't already filling faster than our pumps can work. We don't have time for that luxury."

"What's happening?" Fanny whispered to Ash Kemble.

"It looks as if we've run into the *Florida*," Ash said, "on its way back to Saint Simon's, which is her home port. The captain has already changed our course to bring us away from her and closer to shore. But that takes us away from where he wanted us to go."

"It means we're headed in the general direction of the Altamaha," Fanny said, "doesn't it?"

"Something like that," Ash said evenly.

"Dear God!" she sighed. "So we're going there after all?"

"It's a strong possibility, Fanny."

"I feel like King Macbeth when he sees the woods moving," she said.

He smiled. "It must be upsetting for you, seeing all the anguish you've invested in that place. But," he said, pausing to find her hand, "it is better to be alive there than drowned in a sinking ship. And you must also realize that no one is a slave there any longer. And, after all, Pierce is dead."

"I know all that," she said. "And thank you, sweet Ash, for trying to comfort me."

"But it doesn't do any good?" he said.

"No, it doesn't, my dear. I'm afraid that where Kemble Island is concerned, I'm unconsolable."

"Where is Mr. Sutherland?" the captain was asking. Sutherland was the chief engineer.

"In the engine room, sir," Muller said.

"Ask him up, would you please?"

"Yes, sir."

"Mr. McGowan," the captain said, "how acquainted are you with the waters near these shores?"

"Passably," McGowan said.

"Mr. Meyer," Ash said with an affirmative nod.

The captain glanced at him, and then he caught on.

"Oh, I'm sorry, sir," he said. "I lost track of the obvious."

Ash smiled. "I've sailed these waters from before the time I could tell a tiller from a spar."

Sutherland appeared then. "How much more can you get out of the engine you have left, Mr. Sutherland," the captain asked.

"We might push two or three more knots out of her."

"Do it."

"We'll take on more water, sir," Muller warned. "I don't know how long she can take the stress."

"I know. I know. But do it." He glanced at Ash Kemble for support, and Ash gave him a slight nod. "Would you like to give us a course, sir?" the captain asked Ash.

"No, Mr. Meyer, not yet. Make for the Altamaha and let me kip out for a couple of hours. Wake me if anything dire is about to befall us." He looked at Fanny. "I'd advise you to sleep for a while, too. You'll need to be rested up. You're going to get wet soon, and you'll want all your energy."

"How can you sleep at a time like this?" she asked.

"How can you stand in front of a thousand people and show yourself off?"

"Those things aren't comparable."

"Yes, they are," he said. "Some things I'm good at. Some things you're good at. Now go below and lie down. That's an order."

Fanny decided not to protest.

She awoke to the sound of booming kettledrums.

What play is this? she thought, panicked. What are my lines? There's a cue and I've missed it! Kettledrums? It has to be *Hamlet*. Am I the queen or Ophelia? But I can't be. At the drums they are both dead. At the drums the play is nearly ending. . . .

Her eyes were shut tight, and then the room shook. And then someone was shaking her.

"Fanny!" a voice said. "Wake up!"

She opened her eyes. The face that was bending over her belonged to Ash Kemble.

"Ash!" she said.

"I must run, Fanny," he said. "Dress quickly. We're being shelled."

She shivered and sat up abruptly.

"Shelled?" she asked.

"We're running for the beach," he said, striding quickly for the door. "Hurry."

Fanny was dressed and on the deck five minutes later. A few cable lengths off *Miranda*'s port side was the Federal cruiser they'd been worried about last night. As they'd guessed, she was the *Florida*, and she was shooting solid shot and shells at *Miranda*. Many of them were finding their target.

Off *Miranda*'s starboard prow, about a mile and a half ahead, was a line of low dark green, and below that the white cotton of surf.

*Miranda*, Fanny noticed, was two feet or so lower in the water than normal.

"Get below, Fanny," Ash said when he saw her. "I didn't tell you to come up here. You'll be safer in your cabin, or else in the wardroom."

"Why?" Fanny answered firmly but, she hoped, reasonably. "If we're to sink, aren't my chances better up here?"

"But you're more protected below from shot and shells."

"I'll take my chances," she said.

He looked at her, shaking his head with exasperation, but he didn't press her further.

"How long until we make the beach?" she asked.

"The question," he said, "is how long until it's too shallow for the *Florida*?"

"Consider it asked," she said.

"I don't know," he said.

*Miranda* drove on, shuddering heavily as she went, settling ever deeper. It was only a matter of a short while until the water in her holds would douse the fire in her one remaining engine. But Mr. Sutherland was nevertheless wrenching every last bit of steam pressure out of the boilers. He knew his machines; he knew his boiler wouldn't burst, even though he had the needles far past the rated red line.

Still, even with the absolute best that he forced from his machinery, *Miranda* could only creep along at six and a half knots. *Florida* was inching ever closer, flinging broadside after broadside as she came.

"Will we do it?" Fanny asked Ash during a moment when he paused to catch his breath. He had been roving everywhere up and down the deck, lending a hand where a hand was needed, shouting, exhorting the men to put out their best. And she had not left his side.

"Aye," he said. "I think so. Maybe."

At that moment, *Florida* switched to grape and canister and raked *Miranda*'s deck.

"Down!" Ash screamed, and threw Fanny to the deck by main force, then flung himself down on top of her.

Other men were screaming from pain and fright. Many of the sailors on deck were severely wounded. Some were dead or dying.

Broadsides of grape and canister continued for ten minutes, then ceased.

"Are you all right?" Ash asked Fanny when he was sure the lull was not imaginary.

"Yes, Ash," she said. "Please get off me."

"Of course," he said, complying. He stood up and looked around. *Florida* had fallen back. They were in water too shallow for her.

Fanny worked herself to her feet and cast a glance first at the approaching shore, then at *Florida*, which was in the process of pulling off and heaving to, and finally at Ash himself. She recalled as she glanced about that Ash had committed himself to acting as pilot. "Shouldn't you be in the wheelhouse?" she asked.

"It was the plan, wasn't it, for me to pilot us home?" he answered. "But that plan became moot when *Florida* came up on top of us. We're simply driving in at our best speed for the beach."

She nodded.

He pointed to the particular piece of shore they were headed for. "However," he said, "it just so happens that I know that place. It's Little Saint Simon's Island. We own it."

"You mean to tell me that in all the vast coastline of North America, I'm to be shipwrecked and stranded on Pierce Kemble's plantation?"

He flashed a smile. "And I think we should consider ourselves surpassingly lucky to be landing here."

"I still . . ." she said. But he broke in, his face swept with fierce intention.

"Come, Fanny. We haven't much time. We have to save the eight chests in my cabin. They are the one portion of my cargo that I *must* save. You'll help me carry them up on deck."

She nodded. "All right," she said.

Twenty-five minutes later, *Miranda* lunged headlong into the beach of Little Saint Simon's.

The crash, when it happened, proved to be considerably less catastrophic than Fanny had expected. But *Miranda*, after all, was moving at a rate only slightly greater than walking pace. And as an additional precaution, Ash Kemble had lashed Fanny loosely to the foremast—after he and she had lashed his eight chests to deck rings.

As *Miranda* plowed into the beach, *Florida* was lowering a pair of longboats. Her captain was not prepared to allow the Rebels time to salvage any of *Miranda*'s rich cargo—a cargo that belonged by rights to himself and his crew and the Federal republic. Or at least, so the captain believed.

### Baldwyn, Mississippi
### September 10, 1863

As *Miranda* was suffering her final moments on the shore of Little Saint Simon's, Fanny Shaw's son, Lam

Kemble, was receiving the report of a mounted scout. Lam was then seated on his horse, Horatio, a few miles north and east of Tupelo, Mississippi, not far from the town of Baldwyn. Noah Ballard, also on horseback, received the report along with him. A hundred yards behind them was Lam's 120-man squadron of cavalry. These were dismounted and resting. But they remained near their horses, expecting action shortly.

"Colonel, they've got down there pretty much what you told me to expect," the scout was saying. He had just returned from a quick study of the fourteen locomotives that were Lam and Noah's objective. "There's evidence of a fair herd of troops there recently. But they've gone south, by the looks of things, to lend help to the First Tennessee Cavalry. What they've got guarding the engines, sir, is a couple of companies—green by the looks of their shiny new uniforms. They've set up some pickets around the engines, but they ain't dug in. There ain't much in the way of defenses. When I was watching them, you understand, most of the men down there was asleep. But the ones that weren't was just mostly lolling about."

"And the officers?" Lam asked.

"Still in the tents."

"It sounds like they don't expect to be bothered," Lam said. He looked at Noah. "What do you say?"

"What about the locomotives?" Noah asked the scout. "How are they set up?"

"There's a spur, like this," he motioned with his hands, "that angles off the main line. All fourteen are in a line on the spur."

"How are they facing?" Noah asked.

The scout thought a second, then said, "They're facing the main line. They must of backed 'em in."

"Right!" Noah said. "Let's go while the sun's still at our backs."

Lam gave a sharp nod. "Mount!" he called out softly. The word was passed quickly down the line of troops, and moments later the squadron was on the move.

Lam's squadron made a massed cavalry charge.

And they were splendid—men side by side cantering and

then galloping out of the sun like a great, living scythe.

First the pickets, and then two entire Federal companies broke and ran.

Their retreat was unfortunate, for the plan was to capture and hold these men until the operation was finished. They were not in themselves dangerous, but they could send word of the presence of the Rebels to people who were dangerous. Grenville Dodge's forces in northeast Mississippi numbered in the thousands, and the cavalry under his command could move out on short notice.

Lam took the normal precautions to insure against surprise. The telegraph wires had been cut, and teams of scouts patrolled in a great arc around the northern perimeters.

But the escape of the Yankees was still a misfortune. It diminished their margin of time, and Noah's schedule was already tight.

After the fourteen locomotives were secured and inspected, they were passed over to two-man crews, who were to make them ready for travel.

It was no surprise to Noah, when he made his inspection, that the Yankees had left the engines without either fuel or water. That's what he would have done in their place, especially if he was using green troops to guard them, as they had done.

Having foreseen that eventuality, Noah had prepared for it. A train carrying wood, water, and two armed companies on flatcars fortified with cotton bales was due to arrive at seven A.M.

When his supply train didn't arrive on schedule, Noah was not immediately apprehensive, but he asked Lam to order the troops to scout around and gather what wood they could. Anything at all that was more or less loose and would burn would do: fences, sheds, corn cribs, telegraph poles.

At eight o'clock Lam sent a dozen men riding south to see about the cause of the supply train's delay.

By nine, the wood gatherers had collected enough of a fuel pile to work with, once the pieces were chopped and divided among the fourteen locomotives. But that left the water problem. All fourteen tanks in the locomotive tenders were dry.

Within half a mile of the spur there were small springs, and a farmhouse had a working well. But there was no way the water from either the springs or the well could be transported to the tenders in sufficient quantities to be useful.

"We could all drink ourselves full," Lam offered to Noah, "and then piss in the tanks. A hundred men ought to be able to piss enough to make steam for fourteen locomotives."

Noah was not amused.

"How about using a hundred horses and a hundred men to haul the locomotives," he countered.

Lam was no more amused by that idea than Noah had been by Lam's.

One of the wood-gathering parties, exploring farther afield than any of Lam's men had done previously, rode to the end of the spur, which was about a mile and a half from its junction with the main line. What they found was a gravel quarry. The gravel was used as ballast for the roadbed of the rail line, but it was not currently being worked, and so the pit was half filled with water. This information was passed on to Lam and Noah, but neither paid much attention to it. The water there was no more accessible than the water from the springs.

Just after ten, the twelve men who'd been sent down the track returned. The supply train had broken down just north of Tupelo, and the locomotive would have to be taken to the shop in Meridian for repairs. Meanwhile another engine had been called up to replace it. It ought to arrive, it was reported, sometime that evening.

The day was turning hot, and the latest scouting reports indicated that Federal forces were not yet active nearby. So Lam released a third of his troops for a swim in the quarry pit. In an hour another third would have their turn.

As these men started out for the quarry, Noah decided to join them—not because he much felt like swimming, but because he wanted to have a look at all that water. Perhaps

when he got there, he'd come up with some ingenious way
to bring it the mile and a half to his tenders.

What he found when he reached the pit was a small,
muddy lake and a long, low weather-beaten shed. The shed
contained rusted picks and shovels, wheelbarrows, three
broken water pumps, and a few fifty-foot sections of ragged
canvas hose. The pumps and hose had been used to drain
the pit when it was being worked.

On further inspection, Noah determined that a good
mechanic might salvage a working pump from the three bad
ones. And temporary patches might allow the hoses to carry
water, though they would never again be watertight. He
went to find a mechanic and a seamstress.

I have three good mechanics here, he said to himself as
he made his way back down the spur to the locomotives.
But where in hell am I going to find a seamstress?

"You're going to think I'm mad," he said to Lam, who
was munching on a peach. The three mechanics were
already on their way to the quarry. "But if we had a
seamstress, I think I could water the tenders."

"A seamstress?" Lam asked incredulously.

Noah explained why he needed someone who could sew.

"Right," Lam said, and smiled.

Noah took that smile—mistakenly—as a sign of regret.
"What I think I could do," Noah said, "is walk over to that
farmhouse and see if the woman there could do the job for
us."

"Well, you're right," Lam said. "I can't get you a
seamstress."

"Then I'll go over to the house."

"Wait," Lam said. "I said I can't find a seamstress.
That's because we're all men here, and a seamstress is a
woman, by definition."

"I'm not up for jokes, Lam. It's getting on to noon, and
we've got fourteen deathly idle engines here."

"You ever heard of sergeants, Noah?"

"Sure I've heard of sergeants."

"I thought you might have heard of sergeants, you

coming out of West Point and all. But the way you're acting, I thought maybe you forgot.''

"What do you mean?'' he asked, although he already realized what Lam was leading up to.

"A lot of things in the cavalry need sewing. That's what sergeants are for. They all have needle and thread in their saddlebags. Career sergeants—not the other kind that need their daddies to show them where to aim when they piss. What kind of career sergeant would leave home without needle and thread?''

The first sergeant Lam grabbed, whose name was O'Rourke, proved Lam right, and Noah led him back to the quarry.

While O'Rourke and the mechanics were busy, Noah had the last tender in the line uncoupled. A team of horses then hauled it back to the end of the spur.

By two-thirty they had a single pump working, along with enough hose to connect the pit with the tender.

An hour and a half later, they had filled the tender's tanks, which held two thousand gallons, and they'd pulled the tender back up to its locomotive.

They steamed up the locomotive successfully, and after that it was a matter of shuttling it back and forth between the quarry and the other locomotives. They'd fill up the tanks, load up the pump and hose onto the tender, pull up to the line of engines, and transfer 150 to 200 gallons into each one, enough water for the journey to Tupelo, where the tanks could be filled completely.

The night before, when they had cut the telegraph between the fourteen locomotives and General Dodge's headquarters in Corinth, Lam Kemble's scouts had left intact twelve miles of line north of where they were. And then they'd set up a telegraph post at the far end of the line—in order to give Lam and Noah early warning of Yankee activity. The free-ranging teams of scouts would report in to the telegraph post every hour or so, or whenever there was a sign of enemy movement south.

At 6:27 Lam's telegrapher brought him the first bad news all day. A Yankee cavalry force, two hundred strong, was moving swiftly down the road toward Baldwyn. They'd reach the spur before dark.

At 6:34 the telegrapher brought another message. A twelve-car train loaded with soldiers and light field pieces had passed the telegraph post. The train looked to be moving at about fifteen miles an hour, which meant that Lam and Noah could expect it in less than an hour.

"It looks to me like General Dodge's people have finally got wind of us and have gotten off their asses in a big way," Lam said.

"We've been lucky we've had so much time," Noah said. "We originally planned to be steaming out of here by ten this morning, if you recall."

"How much time before you can move the engines?" Lam asked.

"Another hour, hour and a half to finish filling enough to move. And we have to build up steam, too."

"You can be doing that at the same time?"

"Of course. I plan to."

"Then I'll see what I can do about delaying that train. We don't have to worry about the cavalry that's coming—not yet."

"When did you tear up the tracks north of here?" Noah asked.

"What do you mean, tear up the tracks?"

"A section of track," Noah said reasonably, "thereby preventing rail passage south—which is where *we* are. When did your people do that?"

"They didn't do that. How was I to know that they should have torn up tracks?"

"Because you're a colonel in the Confederate cavalry, you horse's ass, with a good command and a West Point education. And I always thought you were smart."

"You should have told me."

"Shit," Noah said. "Any virgin in Mississippi could tell you about tearing up tracks."

"There aren't any more virgins in Mississippi."

"Go on, get out of here. Get busy. Make yourself useful. Do something destructive."

*Kemble Island, Georgia*
*6:30 P.M., September 10, 1863*

"I've *never* had such a mad, harum-scarum day in all my life!" Fanny Shaw whispered. Her whisper was due to the proximity of a twenty-foot Federal longboat two boat lengths away out on one of the numberless channels of the Darien River. The Darien was itself one of the estuarial arms of the Altamaha.

"Hush, Fanny!" Ash mouthed, holding up a restraining hand. He was covered with mud and slime and sweat. Leeches clung here and there on his arms and legs and neck. He was too exhausted to deal with them now. Even with all his seemingly boundless energy, he looked near to collapsing with weariness.

Fanny was about to say something else, but thought better of it. She also thought about slapping at the mosquitoes that were lighting on her unprotected face and neck, but she thought better of that, too. She was acting with admirable restraint, she thought to herself as she suffered.

Fanny, Ash, and First Officer Muller were in a twelve-foot boat, hidden a few feet up a tiny branch of the Darien. The growth that covered them was thick enough to make them invisible to the Yankees gliding a few yards away. It was also thick enough to muffle any conversation the three on the smaller boat might have ventured. But it was safer to keep silent.

The Federal longboat passed safely out of sight and earshot.

"Now can we leave this place, Ash?" Fanny asked.

Ash shook his head. "We'll stay here until dark. Then we'll row up beyond Darien. They'll be watching the town for us." He glanced at Muller. "What do you think about that, Mr. Muller?"

"Whatever you say, Mr. Kemble," Muller said.

"I'll be eaten alive by bugs, Ash!" Fanny groaned.

"If I'd had my choice, Fanny, I'd have ordered up a different course of events for you. But here we are."

Ash's intimate familiarity with the maze of waterways around the Kemble plantations had come in handy, after all.

Once *Miranda* was on the beach of Little Saint Simon's, they had very little time to abandon her and escape. The captain of the *Florida* had pursuing boats in the water even as *Miranda* drove to shore. Another boat was dispatched to squadron headquarters ten miles away on Saint Simon's Island; reinforcements would not be long in coming.

Meyer and those of the crew who could be moved took to two longboats, while Ash, Fanny, and Muller—and the eight chests of drugs—went in a smaller boat.

Before taking care of his own business, Ash led the captain and his longboats to the town of Darien. Darien was long deserted because of the war, but it was on the mainland, and it was in the opposite direction from the Federal base. The captain and his men could make their way to safety with relative ease.

The captain and crew having been disposed of, Ash and Muller rowed Fanny and the chests along the snaking back channels to Kemble Island itself. They stowed the boat up one of the canals behind a floodgate, and while Muller stood watch over the boat and its cargo, Fanny and Ash made their way to the main house, where they gathered digging tools.

There was a patch of woodland suitable for concealing eight fifty-pound chests on the north side of General's Island. This island, also Kemble land, lay east of the main island between Kemble and Darien. Fanny had passed by it many years before on the famous night when she had rowed away from the Kemble plantations.

The way they had to take to the woodland on General's Island was tortuous. They had to go carefully; the Federals were out in surprising force, searching for survivors from the *Miranda*. They must have somehow sensed that they had significant prey in their sights.

There was another reason, too, for the tortuous course Ash took. He wanted to make certain that First Officer Muller would never again find his way to the spot Ash had chosen for burial of his chests. Ash had no reason to mistrust Muller, but the light of honor and responsibility dims in the presence of goods that can be turned into half a million dollars in gold.

A squad of Yankees was working through the north woods of General's Island even as Ash and Muller placed the chests into the ground. A mere squad was not enough to find Ash Kemble on any Kemble island. Ash could have eluded a division of Federal troops on General's Island.

They finished burying the chests late in the afternoon, and then started back toward Darien. But when they approached the town, they were surprised by a Federal picket boat that had been lying hidden in one of the branches of the Darien, just as Ash was to do a couple of hours later.

The Federals fired, and there was a chase. And the chase grew complicated when the Federals were joined by another boat, which had been positioned to head Ash's boat off.

As the Yankees closed in, Ash turned into a channel invisible to all who had not grown up in these parts. After the first hundred feet, it was as much semisolid mud as water, and the two men had to climb out and drag the boat across it. But the discomfort did not displease the two men at all. The Yankee longboats could never follow them through any muck they had to drag their smaller, shallower draft boat through.

Night fell, but still they were forced to stay hidden in their cave of branches and undergrowth and mosquitoes. Federal longboats with lanterns at fore and aft kept cruising by late into the night.

"What can they possibly want with us?" Fanny asked at one point.

"I don't know," Ash said. "Chances are, I suppose, that they caught somebody in the crew, and they talked."

"But still," Fanny persisted, "why us?"

"I don't know."

"They'd."

"They'd very much like to get hold of Mr. Kemble, ma'am," Muller said quietly. He was not much of a talker at the best of times, and during the chase and the burial of the chests, he hardly spoke at all. This statement was the most that Fanny had ever heard from him. "Chances are they know he's in the swamps. He's as famous a blockade runner as they're ever likely to get hold of.''

"You should be flattered, then," Fanny said after she had taken that in. "Honored."

"I could do without such honors," Ash said, his voice grim. "I've lost one of my best ships, a good part of one of my best crews, I'm muddy and stinking and covered with leeches, and I'm skulking in a marsh like a hunted animal. If this is an honor, maybe I'd like a little more ignominy.''

Fanny tried to make out his face in the wet, pressing gloom, but he was only a blur. She was looking for Ash's usual self-mocking grin, his devil-may-care flash of eyes. But somehow she didn't expect to find that now. Ash's loses had finally broken through his seemingly impenetrable defenses.

Even Ash Kemble has a soft and vulnerable core, she thought to herself.

She almost said something more about that, but stopped herself. Anything she said to Ash now was likely to hurt.

She crossed over the boat and slid next to him on the wide seat.

"What are you doing, Fanny?" he asked absently.

"Hold still," she said.

He turned and faced her. His eyes—she could see them now—were blank. She could also see leeches on his neck and arms, many of them already fattened on his blood.

She reached out, and with a deep grimace of fright and revulsion, working more by feel than by sight, she started to pluck them off his flesh.

"What are you doing, Fanny?" he asked.

"I can't take care of the Yankees, Ash, but I can take care of the leeches."

*Baldwyn Mississippi*
*Nightfall, September 10, 1863*

The estimates of Lam Kemble's scouts turned out to be incorrect. The Federal cavalry reached Noah Ballard's fourteen locomotives ahead of the troop train. That was because the train had slowed to five miles an hour due to their concern about the possibility that the tracks had been ripped up.

But it was the cavalry that attacked—not as Lam had done at dawn, in a massed charge, but dismounted, in skirmish lines. And not all the Federal cavalry sighted by Lam's advance scouts attacked the engines. Half of them rode on ahead to take up positions along the track in case the Rebels succeeded in breaking free of the initial efforts to capture them.

Lam's troops had been placed in position not far from the locomotives when word of the approach of the Federal forces came. They were not heavily dug in, for they did not expect to stay for long. The locomotives should be ready to move any time. But the delays kept coming—bearings in one froze, a control rod broke free of a crosshead in another. Neither was a major problem, and both were being repaired with considerable dispatch, considering the situation. But both engines were near the front of the line; none of those behind could move without those moving first.

Meanwhile the Federal cavalry were already pinning people down with their gunfire. Luckily nobody was really in much danger. It was too dark to aim at anything smaller than the bulk of the locomotives themselves. And indeed, they didn't succeed in hitting even these very often. But their plan seemed to be to keep the Rebels busy until the troop train arrived. With these reinforcements they would smother anything the Rebels could put in their way.

It looked as if they might succeed in their plan.

The skirmishing had been going on for half an hour before Lam Kemble came to brief Noah about what was going on. Noah had enough on his mind, Lam reasoned, without having to deal with the combat situation, too.

When Lam did finally go to Noah, it was because the military situation they were in threatened to turn very bad very shortly. The troop train had halted a mile away, and the troops had disembarked and were already marching down the track.

"What's going on, Lam?" Noah said without looking up

from the control rod he and two mechanics were working on with desperate intensity.

"Things are not real good, Noah," Lam said. "We've got to get out of here."

"Give me fifteen minutes, Lam," Noah said.

"Sooner than that," Lam said. "We're in for a lot of trouble."

"Give me ten minutes, then," Noah said without looking up. "What's the problem—the *new* problem."

"The immediate trouble," Lam said, "is the gunfire that's going on right now—but that we can handle. There can't be many more of them out there now than there are of us. At least half of the cavalry rode on up ahead. But the bad news is that the troop train has finally got here, and it's carrying artillery. They're arriving any minute, and when they start using their cannon, we might as well slip away quiet and fast, because there's no way we can sustain cannon fire."

"I understand."

"What I'm telling you is this, Noah. I'm a colonel and you're a major. This operation is your deal, and it's been yours to run. But when it comes down to the survival of my own men, I'm in charge. I'm not going to wait around for your lame engines to get fixed when they start firing their cannon. We're going to ride like hell out of here."

"I understand, Lam," Noah said through tight lips. He seemed emotionless, though he was anything but: he was ready to explode. "Give us five minutes. We'll move in five minutes or else you all leave. We don't have much else to do here, and the trains are steamed up and ready."

"I'm sorry, Noah."

"Go take care of your people, Lam. I'll take care of my lame engines."

Lam walked away without another word. He couldn't think of anything to say.

By the time he reached the place where he had set up his command position, the volume of fire from the Union lines had doubled. The first of their infantry reinforcements had arrived, and they were starting to press forward. Bugles cried, and weapons flared, but it was impossible to see in the darkness what exactly was going on. Would they attack all along the lines, or would they feint and probe and try to punch ahead to a breakthrough?

Lam's line was 150 yards from the locomotives. He ordered his people to pull back, but slowly. He also had the horses made ready for instant departure.

The Union troops had their cannon in place and ready to fire only moments after the bulk of the troops from the train arrived. The cannon flashed for the first time the same instant fourteen locomotive whistles screamed as one, a single mad orgy of noise so loud it drowned the terrifying roar of the cannon.

There were one, then two, then three cannon flashes. Grenville Dodge had his men well trained; they'd moved with great speed to bring up the artillery. But their effect was much diminished by the majestic elephantine thunder of fourteen locomotives, not quite in unison, but close, lumbering forward off the spur and onto the main line of the Mobile & Ohio.

*"Let's get the hell out of here!"* Lam hollered above the roar. His horse soldiers lost no time obeying him.

Two of the three cannon were firing canisters into the positions recently vacated by the Confederate cavalry, while the third hurled shells in the direction of the locomotives. Some of the shells found their marks, and did damage. But none of the damage was sufficient to impede the momentum of the engines as they pounded ahead, groaning forward.

Noah Ballard set himself up in the lead locomotive, Perseverance. The other thirteen followed at hundred-yard intervals, all accelerating to a speed that just matched a comfortable canter for a horse.

After he had made sure that the members of his squadron were all accounted for, mounted, and heading south in good order, Lam Kemble rode his own horse, Horatio, up beside the cab of Perseverance.

Noah leaned far out of the cab window, reached out, and grasped Lam's hand. For a long moment the two men rode together joined that way, until Lam had to swerve aside to miss an obstacle.

When he was again riding beneath the cab window, he called out, "What do you think?"

"I think, by God, that we did it!" Noah yelled.

"We did!" Lam answered. "And it was whisker close!"

"Thanks, Lam," Noah added, growing more serious, "for standing by us until we could make our move."

"For you," Lam said, with a hint of his old grin of bravado, "anything. But only for you."

"Did you lose many?"

"Surprisingly few," Lam said. "Ten or fifteen casualties— they're on some of your tenders, or should be—and three or four deaths. For that we owe the darkness."

"So the long wait had its small payoff."

"Appears so," Lam said. And then, "I have to go. We'll keep to your flanks, the way we talked about this afternoon."

"Much obliged, Lam," Noah said with a wide flourish of his hat. "Much, much obliged."

There was a section of track a dozen miles north of Tupelo that for nearly four miles went straight and flat as a line on an engineer's drawing. At other times and in other circumstances, the Mobil & Ohio engine drivers would have opened their throttles wide and let their engines go flat out. Noah went into the flat section so elated that he was tempted to do that tonight, even if it meant leaving his cavalry escort behind. But the temptation died as soon as Perseverance entered the section. For Noah could see a gleam on the tracks maybe two miles ahead, a gleam that quickly grew to a smudge of flames. The second unit of Union cavalry, the ones who had gone on ahead, had staked out a position up ahead, and they had signaled their intentions by means of a flaming barricade.

The engine driver of Perseverance went into action as soon as he saw what the gleam was. He blew his whistle three long blasts—the signal for the other thirteen engines to stop. And then he started letting off steam.

Noah thought about that move for a time, not liking it.

But he didn't contradict his driver. At least not yet. He glanced to his right and left. Lam Kemble was already spreading his troops out in a wide, curving fan shape.

He drew up next to Noah's cab. "We're going to attack," he yelled.

"Splendid," Noah yelled back.

"You're going to want to wait until the issue is decided, aren't you?"

Noah thought for three or four heartbeats, then made up his mind. "No," he yelled. "I've decided to push through."

"Through the bonfire?"

"That's right."

"Jesus!" Lam said. Then, "But maybe that's the best way."

"It *is* the best way. You won't have to stop. You'll just sweep on through the Yankees. It means minimal risk and minimal casualties for everybody."

"Will your machines make it?"

"They should," Noah said, glancing to the engine driver for support. "What do you think?" he asked.

"The engines should be fine," the driver said. "I don't worry about them." He paused. "But I am worried about the track. If that fire has been burning for long, it'll have burned through a lot of ties and maybe warped some of the track."

"What's he say?" Lam asked, unable to hear the driver.

"He said that the flames may have ruined the track."

"So what do you want to do?"

Noah turned again to the engine driver. "Short blasts!" he yelled, meaning short blasts on the whistle, the signal for full speed ahead.

As Lam veered off to lead his charge, the fireman of the Perseverance poured wood into the firebox, and the machine surged ahead.

"*Sabers!*" Lam called out to his horse soldiers. Noah couldn't hear the call, but he saw through the dark dozens of flashes of silver illumined by the headlamps of the engines following behind his own.

Perseverance was pulling far ahead of the cavalry now,

bearing down on the bonfire, making a noise like the bursting seams of hell.

The engine's pilot struck the burning mass. The locomotive shuddered, slowed, shuddered again. Then the pilot scooped the logs and brush on the track up and away. Flaming embers, balls, and faggots hurtled into the air. Fiery missiles streaked up and out and over and behind Perseverance, and for a long, incredible moment, the engine was surrounded by a terrible spreading, arcing bloom of flames.

And then they were on the other side of the fire. And they were undamaged.

The tracks, Noah thought almost in afterthought, had held.

He craned out of the cab window to see what was going on behind him. As he did so, he remembered that the Federal troops would probably be firing at him. But when he saw what was actually going on, any fear of that left him. Lam's squadron had swept down on the Federals, and through them.

"Slow down again," Noah ordered, and the engine driver obeyed.

Once they had passed well beyond the Federal positions, Lam's horsemen closed in around the fourteen locomotives.

They'd all be in Tupelo in a short while, and in Meridian by morning.

## Raven's Wing, Georgia
## Night, September 10, 1863

Sam Hawken's fingers traced lightly the tip of Miranda Kemble's nipple. He moved his finger pads tenderly across it, feathery but firm, as delicate and confident of his touch as a master musician, and then trilled down onto the rose-tan flesh that encircled it. There was a long moment when his fingers stopped their moving, resting in the slow, steady rise and fall of her breathing. When his motion resumed, he inscribed with the nail edge of his index finger the borders of her railroad-funnel scar.

Miranda lay unclothed on her bed, and her nakedness was in itself pleasant, conjoined as it was with his. As he played his fingers around and about Miranda's breast, Sam gazed at her, resting with his chin propped up by his other arm, his legs and body curled languidly over her, semi-encircling her. Both man and woman were sheened with a light film of sweat, which in the soft illumination of the lamp next to the bed, made their bodies glow and set her hair alight, ginger-golden, fanning recklessly across her pillow. Sam's fingers occasionally strayed lovingly into it.

Her smile, whenever he thought about it, took his breath away.

"I love these curves," Sam said quietly, almost inaudibly, running his hand over her breasts and flanks. "Woman curves."

She looked at him. "It's not often that I think of myself as a woman."

"How do you think of yourself, then?" he asked. "I can't think of you as anything but a woman."

"I still see myself as a young girl most of the time. Do you believe that?"

"I can begin to understand it," he said.

"A little girl," she continued, "my mother's pretty daughter, or my father's—curly-haired, sweet, smiling, and agreeable. I don't like the little-girl part of me. But then, at other times I see myself as a businessman, maybe, or a plantation operator, and I like that part of me more. But I scarcely ever see myself as a woman."

"Until tonight," he said, and caught her eye, "my stunningly beautiful young woman. We'll have to make certain that you have more opportunities to entertain that thought," he said.

"More nights like tonight?" she said with a sly smile.

"Ten thousand more nights like tonight." As he said that, he stretched so that his lips could reach hers. She parted her lips to receive him.

A little later his fingers returned to the scar, exploring it, skimming gently over every part of it.

"You must have questions about that," she said.

"Yes, you're right," he said. "I do." He kissed it.

"It happened on the day I met you."

"At West Point?" he asked wonderingly.

"No, on the journey up. On the train."

"How?" he asked, screwing up his face. He had a dim recollection of an accident the morning they met.

"A flaming ember from the engine flew through the car window and landed on me."

He looked at her. "I remember something about that. A burn?"

"A burn," she agreed. "A bad one. It was quite painful. It was so severe that it very nearly prevented me from getting to know you. Mother wanted me to rest all that afternoon for the ball, but Uncle Ash insisted that I go for a walk with Lam and his friends. You were one of Lam's friends."

"I *was* one of Lam's friends," Sam sighed sadly.

She looked at him. "You miss him, don't you?"

"Yes, I do. He was a good friend. And so was Noah Ballard." He turned his face from hers.

"You haven't asked about Lam all the time you've been here," she said. "Do you want to know about him?"

His lips formed a wry smile. "All right."

She told him about how the war had treated her brother.

"What do you know about Noah Ballard?" he asked. "Lam must have kept you more or less up to date on him."

"You'd think that," she said. "But I haven't heard much news of him. He's in Mississippi under Johnston. I think Lam mentioned the last time I saw him that Noah had something to do with the fortifications at Jackson."

Sam shook his head, maintaining his sad, wry amusement. "We may have been in Jackson together, then," he said. "Imagine that."

She lifted herself up and took his face in her hands and forced him to look at her. "You'll see them again after the war, and you can be friends again then."

"It hardly seems possible," he said, thinking of the heavy obstacles to their friendship that existed. It was hard to imagine any way that the end of the war could remove those obstacles.

"Just wait," she said, kissing him. "You'll see."

Sam shrugged. "Maybe...." his voice trailed off, helplessly.

"I wish you would never leave," Miranda said to him later. They were still lying on her bed, but now they were deeply relaxed, spent and calm.

"I wish I would never leave," he answered, with a sad smile. "What I'm giving up has infinite attractions, and what I'm going to I'd just as soon leave behind for good. But," he said, sliding his fingers across her forehead, "you'll still be here for me—when we can make this night more permanent."

"I'll always be here for you," she said, "wherever you are. And if you can't come back to me, then I'll go to you, or with you. Consider this night permanent. Will you?"

"Yes, Miranda," he said. "I will."

She gave him a radiant, fetching smile. "But you will stay another day or two, won't you? What difference will another day or two make to them? And besides"—the smile altered from fetching to bawdy—"it will make such a difference to me!"

"Truly, I have to go. My obligations are real, and I don't think I can hold Jane back any longer."

"Jane!" she sneered contemptuously.

"Contempt comes easy to the winner."

"Sam!" she yelped, digging her knuckle deep into his side. "I hope there wasn't a contest."

"No," he acknowledged, "there wasn't. When you appeared, there wasn't a chance of a contest."

"Well, then," she smirked triumphantly.

"But I still have to leave you. You know that."

"Yes," she said. Then she looked at him earnestly. "But, Sam?"

"What is it?" he smiled. "You're perfectly lovely when you put on your serious face."

"I know," she said with the trace of a smile. "But we must be serious for a moment."

"All right," he nodded.

"You will be careful, won't you, around the Featherstone woman?"

"Jane? Naturally," he said vaguely. "I'll watch out for her."

"You have to do better than that, Sam. She's a dangerous person. She dreams vendettas and daggers. And she hates me. She'll hate you, too, now for loving me. Watch out for her. Watch what you eat and drink, and cover your back."

He laughed at her—uncomfortably. "Jane Featherstone is no pussycat, Miranda," Sam said. "But she's not what you fear she is, either."

"Listen to me, Sam. Do it." She cocked her head then in the gesture that Sam remembered well. "In fact, would you be willing to guess where she is now?"

"In her room, asleep," Sam answered.

"I'll bet she has been outside my door for the entire evening."

"Jane? Why?" Sam said, "Jane knows she's lost to you. She'll just sleep and go on to something else."

"It's because she has lost that she will want to know everything that happens between us," Miranda said, making a move to leave the bed. "Shall I go open the door and prove which of us is right?"

"No, Miranda. Stay where you are."

Miranda smiled, snuggling against him. "All right, Sam. If you say so. I'll do what you say. I'll always obey you. You *know* that I will."

"That's the one thing about you," Sam said, "that I will never count on."

Miranda was wrong. Jane Featherstone was not at that moment listening outside her door. She was sitting on the ground outside Miranda's window. Miranda's bedroom was on the first floor of the house.

## Meridian, Mississippi
### September 12, 1863

Noah Ballard and Will Hottel strolled through the rail yards of Meridian, admiring the results of their labors of the last weeks—over five dozen working locomotives and tenders ready to be transported to where they could be put to best use.

"So this is all of them," Will said to Noah. Hottel, as always, was impeccably uniformed and smoothly shaved. Noah was in shirtsleeves.

"All we could save, anyhow," Noah said, always cautious and precise. "Sixty-one locomotives, more or less in working order."

"You should be proud, Noah," Hottel said. "If it hadn't been for you . . ."

"There's pride and honor enough to go around, Will," Noah said. "We did good work. All of us."

Hottel took in a long, pleased breath. "Still," he said, "I stand by that statement. If it hadn't been for you, these engines would still be scattered all over north Mississippi."

"All right, Will," Noah said, "I won't keep arguing with you." Noah was aware, beneath his good breeding and his modesty, that there was truth in what Hottel said. The engines would not be sitting here in Meridian if Noah had not put his shoulder to the job and come up with the plan that got the Yankees so excited and distracted up along the Mobile & Ohio that they missed completely the more important, secret goings-on north of Jackson on the Mississippi Central and the Mississippi & Tennessee.

Will Hottel had done his part superbly. He'd moved the machines quietly and efficiently. When trouble and obstacles came, he maneuvered around them, using whatever it took to make things work.

Bridges had been destroyed by Sherman's men on the Tallahatchie and the Yalobusha rivers between Grenada and Sardis, but Hottel improvised ferries, and the locomotives beyond the Yalobusha were moved south. Whole five-mile sections of rails were ripped up, but he scrounged and begged and stole replacement rails, and he found crews to lay them. Many of the forty-one engines he was gathering turned out to be in much worse shape than the ones Noah had to work with. But Hottel managed to salvage all but four of them.

"So when will we start moving them down to Mobile?" Hottel asked.

"I'll start Wednesday or Thursday," Noah said, "I want the mechanics to check them all over and fix whatever is fixable. The big stuff we'll leave for Atlanta. My father's shops can handle all kinds of problems that we can't handle here."

"Speaking of him," Hottel asked casually. "have you heard from your father lately?"

"He writes sometimes, and I write sometimes. Not often. He's probably as busy with the war as we are."

"I can believe that," Hottel said.

"Though actually, now that we're speaking of it, I've gotten three good, long letters from him over the past couple of weeks. He's showed considerable interest in the progress of our locomotives."

"Well, *there's* no surprise," Hottel said with a merry laugh. "I don't know of a railroad man who'd fail to be fascinated about the fate of those sixty-odd engines. I'll bet your father breathed a little harder and his heart beat a little faster whenever he got a letter from you over the past few days."

Noah laughed. "Well, I guess you're probably right," he said. "John Ballard is more loving and solicitous of his locomotives than most grooms are of their brides on wedding night."

"So what have you told him?" Hottel asked.

"Just that we're coming," Noah said. "As soon as we can get the machines over Mobile Bay. There's not much else to tell him."

"Good," Hottel said. Then he said slowly and carefully, but still casually. "By the way, Noah, you didn't mention my orders from James Seddon, did you? They've got to be secret, even from your father."

"Of course not," Noah said. "Why would I do that?"

"I'm sorry I asked. Forget about it."

"And, Will?" Noah said. There was a new, imperative note in his voice. He had switched from his friendly to his command aspect, and Hottel instantly picked up on the change.

"Yes, Major," Hottel said.

"What I'd like is for you to go on down to Mobile tomorrow. I'd like you to start working on how to move the locomotives across the bay."

"Yes, sir. I'd be glad to do that. It's what I was going to suggest."

"If this were a well-run operation," Noah said, "I'd have already had somebody working on that weeks ago."

Hottel laughed. "You've done what you've had to do," he said. "And we've all made out all right that way."

"You're such a diplomat, Captain Hottel." Noah laughed.

"I try to be obliging," Hottel said.

## Lynchburg, Virginia
### September 13, 1863

After services that Sunday morning at the Episcopal Church of All Saints, the Edge family, everyone save Ben, who was on duty, lingered outside the front steps of the meeting hall and socialized with the old and dear friends of James and Mary Edge.

Somewhere near one in the afternoon, the Edges embarked in their carriage and returned home for their regular Sunday afternoon supper, the lavishness of which the war had scarcely dimmed. After supper, James played some hard-fought games of checkers with young Robbie, games that James contrived to lose. Then he took the boy and himself upstairs for naps.

While the men napped, the two women sat quietly in the parlor. Mary read in her Bible from the Book of Psalms, finding texts suitable to times of sorrow and travail. And Ariel sewed on the new and very fine uniform coat she was preparing as a Christmas gift for Ben.

Sometime after five in the afternoon, while Mary and Ariel were dozing lightly in their chairs, they received two unexpected visitors.

Or rather, more precisely, the visitors had come to see Ariel.

Elizabeth, the housekeeper, shook Ariel gently awake. "Miz Ariel," she whispered, "They's two gentlemens to see you, honey. One of 'ems a preacher, and t'other's a colonel."

"Show them in, Elizabeth," Ariel said. But a glance at Mary, who was sound asleep and snoring with her head slumped onto the seat back made her think better of that. "No, Elizabeth, don't do that," she said, rubbing her eyes and stretching. "I'll see them outside on the porch."

"Yes, ma'am," Elizabeth said.

Ariel stood, straightened her skirt and blouse, and composed her hair and face. Then she went to greet the colonel and the preacher. A pinprick of dread lodged in her mind as she took a last look at Mary Edge on her way out of the parlor. And as she passed through the house to the front porch, the dread swelled stronger. Before she even saw the colonel or the preacher, she had the conviction that their visit was official. And terrible.

The colonel introduced himself. He was hard and leathery, clearly a field officer and not some flabby-waist who spent his time far behind the lines. His name was Hightower, and he was here, he said, because General Early was unable to make the journey himself. General Early sent his regrets, he said.

The preacher's name was Eastwood. He was dressed in clerical blacks now, but it turned out that he, too, was one of Early's officers. He had the rank of captain.

Both men held their hats uncomfortably over their midsections.

Ariel waited. Finally Colonel Hightower brought himself to speak the words she knew were coming, the words her dread had predicted he would say to her.

"Mrs. Edge, it's my sad duty to inform you that your husband, Colonel Benjamin Edge, died two nights ago. He was a fine officer and a fine man, and we will all miss him, ma'am."

"Colonel Edge?" she asked—choked by her confusion and rising grief. "He was a colonel?" Ben had been promoted only a week earlier, but Ariel had not heard about it.

"How did he die, Colonel?"

"There was a typhoid outbreak, Mrs. Edge," he said sadly. "Our regiment lost more to the disease this September than we have to enemy action."

"Typhoid?" she choked. He got sick and died? she thought bitterly. Just like anybody else? Couldn't God have spared a bullet for him? He had plenty of bullets to go around. At least He could have let him die bravely.

"I'm sorry, ma'am."

"Typhoid!" she looked at him. "Couldn't someone have told me? I would have gone to him."

"I'm sorry, ma'am. That was impossible." He spread his arms wide, helplessly.

"I can't . . ." she said, sobbing, "I can't . . ." She swayed dizzily, and Reverend Eastwood put a hand out to offer support, but she shook him off.

"Perhaps you'd like to sit down?" he said. "Or go inside?"

"No," she said. "I'll stay here, and I'll stand."

James Edge appeared at the doorway. He was in shirtsleeves, and his braces hung down around his knees. "What's happening, Ariel?" he asked.

"It's Ben, Pa."

"He's dead, isn't he?"

She nodded.

"I'm sorry, sir," Colonel Hightower said, quickly echoed by Reverend Eastwood.

James Edge stepped out onto the porch and looked far up the street, as though he expected that his son would somehow appear there, a speck in the distance that would grow into a real person. Then he slipped his arms through his braces and swept his hair, which was still uncombed after his sleep, back across the top of his head.

"Won't you come inside, gentlemen?" he said.

"I'm afraid we can't, Mr. Edge."

"You have other visits to make, I imagine," James Edge said with a trace of resentment in his voice.

"I'm afraid so, sir."

"Well, then, thank you for coming."

"I'm sorry, sir," Hightower said.

Ariel didn't say anything. Her face was stony and help-less, impervious to the others around her.

"We would like to offer a prayer for the soul of Ben Edge," Reverend Eastwood said.

"Well, all right," he allowed. Prayer was the last thing he wanted right now.

Ariel didn't wait, though. She swept off at high speed into the house.

"Where are you off to?" James Edge asked. She paused momentarily in her flight.

"I'm going to tell Robbie."

"Let him sleep, Ariel. That can wait."

"No, it can't. I've got to tell him."

"At least see these gentlemen off, please, dear."

"You can do that, Pa. Robbie has a right to know. The house he's going to wake up into is going to be a madhouse with crying and grief. And he has a right to be warned."

"All right, then, get on with it."

She turned briefly to Hightower and Eastwood. "Thank you for coming," she said.

"We're both sorry we had to do it." She inclined her head slightly to them, then went upstairs to Robbie—and the hardest thing she had ever done.

# ♦ NINE ♦

*Raven's Wing*
*September 15, 1863*

My Very Dearest Sister,

My heart *flew* out to you, my dearest darling, the instant I read your telegram yesterday. I was absolutely shattered at your tragedy. Ben was *so* fine, and *so* good, and *so* loving. We *all* loved him. And we will all miss him so very much! It was never as though we had lost you when you became an Edge. He became one of us, too. A Kemble. And so losing him is like losing one of us—like losing Lam—or even you, my darling.

I want you to be sure, in your time of tragedy, that you know my love is with you. And my grief is with you. And my mourning is with you. And my prayers.

You're never, never far from my thoughts. But now I think of no one else.

You'll be reading this, my dearest, after Ben's funeral, so I would like to venture a suggestion to you. Would you consider coming down to Raven's Wing, you and Robbie, to spend some time with me? I would love to have you. And more important—more on this in a moment—I'm not alone here now. I'm sure that James and Mary Edge need you, and I wouldn't dare to take you away from them in their time of need. But still, if they can find a way to do without you and Rob, then I will adore welcoming you both here with all my love and warmth.

What I have delayed telling you until now—though you may already know; *they* are writing to you at the same time I am—is that I have surprise visitors at Raven's Wing. From London! MOTHER! and UNCLE ASH! Imagine!? Out of the blue! They just appeared. (I won't tell you *how* they looked; their condition was simply *ghastly*! I won't even begin now to tell the story of their voyage; it would take a two-volume novel to do that.) But they do both want to see you and Robbie, and love you. They love you every bit as much as I do, my darling. It's terrible that they had to arrive at such a tragic time for you. But it's also wonderful that they *could* be here for you. It's better to have all your loved ones present in your time of grief. Absence makes the pain all the greater.

I have one last piece of news that I will only briefly advert to. But I must tell you the essence of it before you reach Raven's Wing lest it come to you as a total surprise. I'M IN *LOVE!* I'VE FOUND THE MAN I'LL MARRY!

He's wonderful! And you know him! But that's all I can tell you right now.

I'll stop here, my darling. Do come to us at the very soonest you possibly can, my darling dearest one! We miss you and need to be with you!

> Your Loving and Grief-Stricken Sister,
> Miranda

\* \* \*

*Big Black River, Mississippi*
*September 15, 1863*

During the greater part of the summer of 1863, Union General William Rosecrans and Confederate General Braxton Bragg maneuvered against one another with nearly equal forces across southeastern Tennessee and northwestern Georgia. By the first weeks of September, these maneuvers showed signs of turning into a major battle. On the eighth of September, because it was tactically indefensible, Bragg evacuated the town of Chattanooga, a vital east–west and north–south rail junction. On the ninth, Federal forces entered Chattanooga, while Bragg consolidated his own forces south of the town along the Western and Atlantic Railroad, which connected Atlanta with Chattanooga. The battle, when it happened, would take place near Chickamauga Creek in Georgia.

While the final maneuvers for this battle were taking place, Sam Hawken and Jane Featherstone were crossing Alabama. They reached Jackson on September 13.

During the course of their journey toward Mississippi, Sam had kept close watch on Jane. She was not, to put it mildly, well disposed toward him. As they traveled west by train and by stage, her loathing seemed to increase. In her current mood she was dangerous. He knew that the best solution to the problems she posed was to bring her safely to General Sherman's headquarters. From there, he hoped, she could be sent someplace far from the battle lines.

One consolation to Sam was that he was well aware that Jane Featherstone was not suicidal. She wouldn't risk her own life for the sake of some mad act like informing on Sam to the Confederate authorities.

The railroad station in Jackson was crowded when they arrived there. The depot itself, of course, was destroyed, and no effort had been expended yet to rebuild it. But the rail yards and tracks around where the depot had once stood were a huge bustle of activity.

The bustle suited Jane perfectly.

Soon after they had disembarked from the Meridian train,

she turned to Sam, removed her glove, and held out her hand. "This is the end of the line, Sam. This is where I leave you," she said.

He took the hand and held it in a firm grip. "Leave?" he asked, suddenly open-mouthed. She'd surprised him. The last thing he expected from her was to give up her chance to leave the Confederacy. In his mind, Jane was no more welcome there than he was. "Where did you get that idea, Jane?"

"I'm not going to stay with you any longer, Sam. I've got other things to do. Other people to see."

"What do you mean? Who?" His voice was calm, but he was anything but calm. She could make terrible trouble for him here in Jackson if she was willing to put herself at terrible risk. Perhaps she was furious enough to do that. . . .

"That's my business, don't you think, Sam? Actually, I'm going to see about the rest of my life."

"I can't let you go, Jane. You know that."

"I know you'd like to keep me with you. I know you've had your eyes on me all the way back from Georgia. But now that I've decided it's time to leave you, I'm going."

His grip on her hand strengthened, but it was not yet painful. "Come on with me, Jane. We'll talk about this when we've reached our own lines."

"Don't try to hurt me, Sam," she said, trying unsuccessfully to wrench her hand away. The movement excited some attention from people standing around, and Sam realized then that she had him. If she started screaming the words he knew were all too close to the surface of her mind, he would never leave Jackson himself. That meant she could walk away from here and he couldn't do anything about it.

She put words to what he was thinking. "I'll tell you what I'm going to do, Sam," she said. "I'm going to leave—calmly, if you'll have it that way. And I suspect you will." She looked at him with a tight but triumphant smile. "I promise you, if you don't make any fuss about me, I won't make any fuss about you."

"What do you mean?" he asked carefully.

"I mean I won't start screaming, and I won't tell anybody who or what you are."

Sam took a deep breath and released it slowly. Then he let go of her hand. "You win, Jane," he said. "Get the hell out of here."

"One more thing, Sam."

"All right."

"You're a pretty good spy. I'll have to give you that much. But if I were you, I'd refrain from that kind of work from now on."

"What do you mean by that, Jane?" he said evenly.

"I mean that your days of spying in the South are over. I'm going to make sure of that."

"Good-bye, Jane," he said.

"Sam," she said in acknowledgment.

She vanished into the crowd.

With luck, he thought, that will be the last time I see her.

Sam reached Major General William Tecumseh Sherman's summer quarters on the evening of the fourteenth. He briefly greeted the general then, and delivered his written report of his mission to Atlanta.

He was scheduled to deliver a more lengthy briefing for the general on the morning of the fifteenth.

When Sam entered Sherman's command tent that morning, he found the general on his knees, doing something to one of his son Willy's toys. A wheel had fallen off, and the general was trying to reattach it. Willy was on his knees, too, next to the general.

"Captain Hawken reporting as directed, sir," Sam said with a snappy, parade-ground salute. He didn't often have a major general on his knees in front of him, and he wanted to rub it in as much as a lowly captain could, under the circumstances.

"At ease, Sam," Sherman said without looking up. "You don't expect a salute from me, do you, Sam, when I'm down here in the dirt?"

"I did sort of expect it, sir," Sam said with a smile, "now that you mention it."

"Well, don't count on it," Sherman said, rising stiffly to

his feet. "Military decorum is all well and good in its place, but this boy has a broken toy, and his father had to fix it."

"It's still broken, Pa," Willy pointed out ungallantly.

"Never you mind, boy. My intentions were good."

"But it's still broken."

"What you need, Sergeant, is a blacksmith. Go find yourself a blacksmith and tell him to fix that thing. Tell him I said to."

"Yes, Pa," Willy said, a little reluctant to go. He wanted to hang around Sam, whom he had missed.

"Go on, Sergeant, get out of here. I need to talk to Sam. Go on. Git."

Willy backed away uncertainly through the open tent front, hoping for a reprieve. When none came, he turned and ran off.

"Do you hear the bugles sounding, Sam?" Sherman asked after both men were seated.

"The bugles, sir?" Sam asked.

"In the east, Sam. In Georgia and in Tennessee the bugles are blowing. There's a battle working its way to a head."

"There's a lot of talk about it, General," Sam said.

"There'll be a lot more talk over the next few days. It'll be a big one. We've got Chattanooga now. If Rosecrans wins, we'll have a clear path to Atlanta."

"And if he loses?"

"The war will last another year, at least."

"What does that mean, sir?"

"The Rebs are rushing reinforcements from Mississippi to Bragg. And from Virginia there, too." He cast a long glance out the tent opening, past Sam. "I should probably be packing myself and bringing this army east, but that's not in the cards, alas." Sherman looked back at Sam. After a time, he said, "I read your report on your trip to Atlanta. It's a fine report, Sam. Everything we could have possibly wanted from it was there."

"Thank you, sir."

"I'm so pleased with you, Sam, that I've put you up for a promotion. When all the paperwork's done, you'll be a major, and you're going to get a battalion of your own. It seems to me that you will conduct yourself splendidly in that command, and that, by the time this war is over, you'll have your first star.''

Sam was more than a little stunned to see that haggard, indomitable face break into a wide, warm grin. ''I'm most grateful, General,'' was all he could say, until he added, ''and overwhelmed.''

''Well, that's over with, Sam. And I'm glad I've done it—though I'll be lost without you on my staff. But I suppose,'' he added thoughtfully, ''that you've been off my staff for all practical purposes for a good part of the summer.''

''I have been busy doing a few other things,'' Sam agreed. ''But I wouldn't at all mind a command now. I've done all the spying I can handle.''

Sherman looked at him for a long moment from under hooded eyes. ''Anyhow,'' he said, ''you deserve your new command. And I'll be delighted to give it to you.''

''Thank you, sir.''

''Now,'' Sherman said, ''I'm going to drop the other shoe.''

Sam stared at him, waiting, and Sherman just sat there examining him. ''Should I be looking for cover?'' Sam asked finally when the general had made no move to break the silence.

''When the other shoe falls?'' Sherman asked.

''Yes, sir.''

''It depends, Sam. It depends.'' He smiled vaguely. Then he asked, almost casually, ''I take it that you would prefer not to be assigned to another spying expedition. Another trip behind the lines doesn't intrigue you?''

''To tell you the truth, General, not especially. I've had my fill of spying.''

''I can well understand that,'' Sherman said. He caught Sam's eye. ''I read in your report that you seem to have mislaid Miss Featherstone in Jackson.''

''That's a long story, sir,'' Sam said carefully. ''Long and complicated. . . .''

"And you are going to tell it to me, Sam. The whole sordid tale, in due course. But meanwhile, and unhappily, we're going to have to disregard your wishes about another spying mission."

Sam stared silently across at Sherman's gaunt eyes.

"We have another job of espionage for you, *Major*. And you've got to go on it as soon as you can make yourself ready."

Sam took a long breath. "All right," he said.

"Here's the thing, Sam," Sherman explained. "There were a pretty fair number of railway locomotives left behind in northern Mississippi after the Rebels retreated from there. From what we can tell now, there were maybe fifty or more."

"Were?" Sam asked.

"That's right, Sam. They're gone now. Though we gave orders to destroy everything useful to the Confederacy, somehow or other these were missed. Later Grenville Dodge's adjutant, George Spencer, discovered something like fifteen of these, and he had them brought north of Tupelo for safekeeping.

"What happened was that the Rebels somehow got word of not only those fifteen but all forty or fifty of the rest of them. You know how badly they need locomotives and other rolling stock, don't you, Sam?"

Sam nodded. "I've ridden on a good portion of what rolling stock they have," Sam said. "They could use all they can get hold of."

"Well, they went and got it. Took those fifteen or so right out from under George Spencer's nose, even though they were supposedly guarded by an entire regiment of volunteers.

"And they took the other ones, too, at the same time. And they did it all by means of a couple of artful feints and diversions."

"Whose idea was all this?" Sam asked.

"It appears that James Seddon sent somebody from their Railway Bureau by the name of Hottel to look after the locomotives. And Joe Johnston put a bright young engineer major in charge of his railroads. His name is Ballard."

Sam shut his eyes tight and pressed his lips together. "I know him," he said. "We were at the Academy together."

"Ballard?" Sherman asked, then answered his own question. "Of course. You would have been there at about the same time, wouldn't you?"

"We graduated the same day. We were friends before the war. It doesn't surprise me at all what he's done."

"Well, then," Sherman said with a sly twinkle, "that information should make your new job all that much more . . . interesting."

"I'm not sure I want another one of your interesting jobs," Sam said.

"But you'll take this one." He looked hard at Sam. "It's voluntary, like the others you've done for me. But you'll take it, Sam. You're the only man I know who can handle it."

"All right, General," Sam said, drawing in a deep breath. "I'll do it—*if*," he paused, "you still want me to after you've heard about my Atlanta trip. And about Jane Featherstone."

"I want to hear about both Atlanta *and* Miss Featherstone."

"I'm no coward, General," Sam said, getting immediately to the point.

"No, Sam," Sherman said firmly, "you're not."

"But Jane made threats."

"I'll listen, Sam. And then I'll make up my mind."

"All right, General, tell me what you have in mind."

Sherman resumed discussing the locomotives: "What they've done is they've moved the engines down to Mobile, where they're going to ferry them across the bay so they can transport them back up to Atlanta.

"We can't let them reach Atlanta. If they do . . ." He paused, then said thoughtfully, "Imagine fifty or sixty more trains of reinforcements and weapons and ammunition able to form up to give aid to Braxton Bragg. Imagine what could happen if twenty thousand men were moved in a couple of days from Virginia to northwest Georgia."

"I get your point, General," Sam said.

"Where this movement of locomotives is going to be most vulnerable," Sherman continued, "is in Mobile itself.

It's going to take them weeks to modify the ferries so they can get those engines across the bay.''

Sam nodded understanding.

"I want you to go down there, Sam, and stop them. Or at least stop as many of them as you can. Put them out of commission. Blow them up. Sink them. Do anything to them that your fertile and devious mind can devise.''

Sam shrugged. "All right," he said.

"Now," Sherman said, leaning back in his chair and relaxing, "you tell me all about your trip to Georgia. And I want you to leave out nothing—you hear that, Sam; *nothing*—about your escapades with the fascinating Miss Jane Featherstone.''

"Yes, sir," Sam said with a slow sigh. "You are aware, General, that there are parts of this story that I'd rather not tell you.''

"I know, Sam. I know. Those are the parts I'm most interested in hearing.''


*Mobile, Alabama*
*September 18, 1863*


As soon as Will Hottel passed through the door of Noah Ballard's borrowed office on Front Street in Mobile, Noah was yelling at him at the top of his voice. As he yelled he waved a paper over his head like a banner.

"Goddamn it, Will," he shouted, "how are you going to explain this? How can you do this to me? How can you do this to yourself?''

The paper in his hand was an order from Captain William Hottel, in his capacity as chief representative of the Confederate Railroad Bureau in Mississippi and western Alabama, authorizing the release of fifteen of the locomotives previously destined for Atlanta, Georgia, to the responsible officers of the Mobile & Ohio, the Mississippi & Tennessee, and the Mississippi Central railroads. Nine of these fifteen locomotives were to go to the Mobile & Ohio, and three apiece to the other two lines.

The paper had an effect on Noah nearly identical to his likely response to a message from his wife that she had found another man.

"Will," Noah continued without Hottel having uttered a word, "you've cut off my hand and my arm! And you've cut off your own hand and your own arm! Goddamn it!"

"Calm down, Noah," Hottel said quietly when there was a break in Noah Ballard's furious cascade of words.

"Calm down? Jesus Christ in heaven!" He released the paper, and it fluttered to the floor between the two men.

"That's right, Noah. You don't need to let off all that steam."

"It's nothing at all, is it?" Noah yelled. "nothing at all that we had sixty and some odd engines down there on the docks ready for shipment east, where they'd be the core of the Confederate railroad—*our* railroad. Now we have fewer than fifty. Why did you go and do that, Will?"

Hottel waited for Noah to let a few more salvos fly. Then he finally spoke. "You seem to think, Noah, that those locomotives belong to you and to you alone by virtue of some kind of divine right, if not because of lawful proprietorship. I don't think you'd ever claim those are your own machines, but you act as though they are."

Noah didn't answer. He stared, fuming.

"Well, they're not yours, Noah," he said softly. "Get that thought into your head. Nor are they mine. They are the responsibility of the Railroad Bureau. And therefore"—he paused to let what was coming sink in—"they are *my* responsibility. They are mine, Noah, to dispose of and dispense as I see fit, insofar as I judge they will be of use to the Confederate States of America. Your responsibility, Noah, lies solely in making sure that such locomotives as I deem are necessary will be transported to Atlanta."

"That's all double-talk, Will Hottel," Noah said. "And you know it. You're talking a load of shit."

"You're wrong, Noah. I'm doing what I think is best for the Confederacy."

"What do you mean, best? The Confederacy needs those engines in Georgia and Virginia. The Mobile & Ohio doesn't need nine of these locomotives. They have enough to suit their needs already.''

"You may not have noticed, Noah," Hottel continued coolly, "that Mississippi is still contested by us and them. The state has not been completely lost. And what's more, I for one do not intend to hand Mississippi to the Union on a silver platter. If we're going to prevent that, then we need functioning railroads."

"When do you think the Confederacy is going to mount a serious offensive in Mississippi? Do you have any idea about how long it's going to be before we give serious thought to retaking Vicksburg? Let's say, for the sake of discussion, two years. In two years, then, we might need those locomotives in Mississippi. Meanwhile we need them right now in the east on the seaboard. And we need them under central control. Sixty locomotives under the authority and direction of the Railroad Bureau might begin to make a real impact. But if you start giving those engines away to this little railroad and that little railroad . . ." Noah stopped, then dragged his hand through his hair. "Jesus, Will, it's the goddamned dumbest idea I've ever heard."

"I'm sorry, Noah," Hottel said, "that you don't see the logic of my decision."

"You're sorry? Shit. You're *sorry*," he repeated mockingly. "Well, how about that?" He stopped and shook his head. When he resumed, he restoked the fires of his fury. "There's another thing, Will. Another piece to all this rottenness."

Will looked at him, politely interested.

"You never once came to talk to me about any of this move of yours. Why didn't you do that?"

"You know as well as I do why I never came to you, Noah," he said quickly. "It's because it would have been a meaningless act. Nothing I could have said to you would have convinced you. So why should I bother?"

"I'd think common courtesy is a good enough reason," Noah said. "Not to mention what I took to be friendship gained out of a lot of hard times and shared dangers."

"The point remains, Noah, that you would not have listened to reason. I did what I had to do.

"Besides, it's already done. Colonel Sims backs me, and James Seddon backs him.

"So admit your losses, Noah. Be a man and live with them."

"You are a son of a bitch, Will Hottel."

"I don't want to leave here your enemy, Noah."

"That seems hard to prevent, Will."

Hottel started to leave. "I'm sorry about this."

"Yeah," Noah said as he turned away from Hottel. He wanted to avoid taking his hand or his salute, or any sign of recognition or farewell from the captain. As far as Noah was concerned, what Hottel had done was unforgivable.

It was not just anger that made Noah Ballard burn white hot; it was fear. Fear that this act of Will Hottel's, bad though it was, might be repeated. Other rail lines were desperate for traction. Would Hottel donate still more of the priceless engines to them?

If the woman who was the great passion of Noah Ballard's life had rejected and deserted him, he would have been less white hot with fury.

After Hottel left, Noah retrieved his copy of Will Hottel's order and tore it into small pieces. Then, clenching and unclenching his fists as he moved, he prowled around the office he was using while in Mobile. The building it occupied was on Front Street, and it belonged to a Mobile merchant and cotton shipper whose business had collapsed because of the war and Farragut's blockade of Mobile Bay. Since he had no immediate use for it, the merchant had offered to loan the building to the Confederate authorities. And they had taken him up on the offer.

The office, which was on the third floor of the building, presented a good view of the docks, Mobile River, and Blakely Island across the river channel. From his windows, Noah could see all the work going on. Three ferries were being altered so that they could carry his locomotives, but he was too jangled and dismayed to merely stand above the action and observe. He wanted to mix with other people. Better still, he required the reassurance of friends.

If Lam Kemble had been around, Noah would have gone

instantly to him. He could have unburdened himself to Lam, let off his rage, taken a drink or two, maybe even managed to laugh a little. But Lam and his cavalry squadron had been yanked out of Mississippi at the first intimation of a large battle shaping up in Georgia. That left Noah on his own now.

Restless and still angry, he left the office and the building, crossed Front Street, and personally inspected the day's work on the ferries that were being adapted to transport the locomotives.

The work that had to be done was substantial. In order to make room for locomotives, much of each ferry's super-structure and deck house was being ripped away. A pair of locomotives would then be placed on rails on the deck, one on the port side, and the other on the starboard.

Everything Noah saw he found fault with.

When he finally left the ferries and returned to his office, there was murder in the faces of the foremen and the workers.

"There's a lady to see you," the corporal who was acting as Noah's clerk and secretary announced to him as he passed through the outer office. "She didn't give her name."

"A lady?" Noah asked, puzzled.

The lady, he saw when he opened the door, was sitting erectly in a chair in front of one of the windows, gazing at the river. She was wearing something off-white, pale, and creamy. Because of the backlight, her dress seemed to glow with an inner illumination. But Noah didn't need to see her features in order to recognize her. He guessed who it was before he'd entered the room.

She was a most welcome sight, especially at this moment.

Even though he had innumerable questions for her, and even though prudence told him to treat her cautiously—she had after all vanished without a trace two months ago—he needed her very much now.

"Hello, Noah," Jane Featherstone said. Her voice was only a shade louder than a whisper.

"Hello, Jane," he said, wanting very much to offer her a smile and a welcoming look. He thought better of it.

Jane's head swiveled slowly so that she could face him. Her eyes and mouth were shadowed, but he could just discern the slightest hint of a smile.

"I'm glad to see you, Noah. It's been much too long. I missed you."

He stared at her. She was amazingly calm, and yet at the same time she was fragile and vulnerable. One yearned to come to the aid of this woman, but Noah had many questions for Jane Featherstone before he would let himself do that.

Some of his questions tumbled out as though from impulse, but none of Noah's questions was impulsive. They'd been on his mind for weeks. "Where have you been, Jane?" he asked. "What happened? You were supposed to meet me in Meridian. You weren't on the train. It's been two months since you missed that train, and now here you are." He stepped forward. "What am I supposed to think?"

Jane rose from the chair and for a moment stood silently, poised but unmoving. Then she approached him with her hands outstretched. She took his hands firmly in her own. "I know it's been two months, Noah darling," she said in her near whisper, her eyes locked on his, confident, reassuring, "and I've spent every day of those two months aching for you."

"I haven't been hiding from you, Jane. You could have come anytime." There was a chill in his voice, and anger.

"I haven't been hiding from you, Noah. Believe me, I wouldn't have stayed away from you for a second if I hadn't been prevented from joining you."

"You couldn't write, Jane? You couldn't telegraph? You couldn't have a friend carry a message?"

She shook her head slowly, solemnly. He paid her close attention, yet her voice was narcotic, addictive. She didn't lull him to sleep, but to belief. "No, Noah, I couldn't. That's just what I couldn't do."

"Why not?"

She raised her face toward the ceiling, then she turned toward the window, away from him, as though retreating from a shame she couldn't bear. "I have to tell you about a man . . . who forced his way into my life, Noah. He's a Union officer, and a master spy. As Joe Johnston was evacuating Jackson, this man infiltrated into the city—insidiously.''

"Go on."

"As I was walking to the rail depot that night in Jackson, the man stopped me in the street. He seemed pleasant and presentable and well-bred. He had a horse and carriage and offered to escort me to the train. I welcomed the offer, of course. That was no night to be a single woman on the streets of Jackson. I entered the carriage and sat down. We had hardly started up when he leapt upon me and held me tight. Before I could struggle or scream, he placed a cloth over my nose and mouth. The cloth was drenched with some kind of soporific. It was sweet and pungent—chloroform, I think. And I was quickly unconscious.

"When I woke, I was lying on a bed, bound hand and foot in a locked and darkened room. But I was not otherwise harmed."

"There was no . . . violation?" Noah asked cautiously.

"Oh, no. Nothing like that. The man might be a fiend, but not that kind of fiend."

"Go on," Noah said.

She nodded slowly, then continued with quiet intensity, "I was in the room for several days, I think. I'm not sure how long. I was fed and otherwise cared for. And I was not ill treated—except that my liberty was taken away.

"And then, finally, one day I was led blindfolded, with my hands bound, to a carriage. I was driven for miles. When I was released from the carriage, I found myself in General Sherman's camp on the Big Black River. And there standing before me, dressed in a Union captain's uniform, was the man who had abducted me." She caught Noah's eye. "His name is Hawken. Sam Hawken."

"Sam?" Noah said. "Sam Hawken?" he laughed nervously. "Jesus!" Then his shoulders sagged.

"You're acquainted with Captain Hawken, Noah?"

"I knew him a long time ago. We were friends then."

"I'm sorry, Noah. I'm sorry for what this man has

become. He's an evil man now. A master spy...as I told you." She stopped, then resumed in a grimmer voice, fluttering her eyelids just a little. "He was the one responsible for the tragedy on the night before the evacuation of Jackson. He caused the head-on train collision that night."

"Sam Hawken did that?" Noah asked.

She nodded gravely. "He was the one." She waited for a moment, watching the quiet fury kindle in him, then she resumed. "He was in Atlanta. Jackson. Montgomery. He was everywhere, Noah, finding our weaknesses, stealing our secrets, destroying what he could."

"It's hard to believe Sam Hawken would do that."

"People change, Noah."

Noah nodded, sadly agreeing. But the sadness was only momentary, for as Jane's words sank in, Noah's rage was reignited. The possibility that his friend of long ago might be the author of so many of Noah's miseries hit him hard, but it was credible. Noah Ballard knew in his heart that the Sam Hawken he'd befriended at West Point was capable of such things.

"What happened then, Jane?" Noah asked. "And," he paused, confused, "why did Sam Hawken choose to kidnap you, of all people?"

"I'll tell you, Noah," she sighed. "I'll tell you the whole thing. But it's a long story, and I'm exhausted from my traveling." She quickly added, "As soon as I could get away, I came directly to you."

"What would you like then, Jane?"

She smiled warmly, wearily. "Not a lot, Noah, really. First I want to sit down. And then I'd like a very small glass of whiskey, if you have it."

"Oh," he said, chagrined, "I'm sorry. I've left you standing."

He quickly led her to a heavily upholstered sofa where she could rest herself. After that he took a decanter from a sideboard and poured both of them something to drink.

Once he was sure she was comfortable, Noah pulled up a chair close to her, and she proceeded to relate for him the narrative of her captivity and escape.

She also had a number of ideas about the kind of mission that General Sherman might send Captain Hawken on next. His target was likely to be Mobile, Alabama.

On September 18, the battle that had been brewing in northwest Georgia finally broke out near Chickamauga Creek. After several days of hard fighting, Confederate General Braxton Bragg was left in command of the field. By the night of September 21, General Rosecrans, the Union commander, had retired to Chattanooga, defeated. Chattanooga was promptly surrounded by Bragg.

The Confederate victory could have been a rout but for the fortitude and steadfastness of Union General George Thomas, who held his own lines even when other Union forces were in fast retreat. And Braxton Bragg, it has been argued, could have deployed his forces to much better advantage, making a significant and lasting victory out of what turned out to be only a pause in the inevitable drive of the North into the heart of the Confederacy.

But it was a pause that the Confederacy very much needed. Bragg's victory at Chickamauga may well have kept the Confederacy alive for another year.

That victory would not have been possible without the railroads. As frail and fragile and worn to tatters as the southern railroads were by September 1863, the reinforcements that turned the tide at Chickamauga were transported on them.

And with Chatanooga, the Union was in possession of a city under siege for the first time.

Noah Ballard wired Atlanta on September 19, which was a Saturday. On Monday, the twenty-first, he received by wire confirmation of Jane Featherstone's story. A Federal spy had indeed been active in Atlanta two weeks earlier. He had, among other things, set fire to the arsenal there, killing at least two soldiers who had apparently tried to apprehend him. There was no description of the spy, but there was strong evidence that he had posed as a minister. And that man, from the description provided to Noah, could have been Sam Hawken.

Out of Jane's guess that Sam's espionage activities would soon bring him to Mobile—what better target than Noah's locomotives?—Noah formed the conviction that her guess was correct.

Noah made quiet preparations to deal with the arrival of his one-time friend. If Sam Hawken was indeed coming to Mobile, Noah wanted to be ready for him. At the same time, Noah did not want to give Sam any warning that he was expected. The preparations had to be discreet and cautious.

And then, once Hawken was identified, Noah planned to play out some rope for him. He wanted to see what Hawken was up to. He wanted to catch him in an actual act of espionage.

He informed Captain Hottel neither of the possible arrival of the Federal spy nor of his own preparations to defend against the spy's activities. As far as Major Noah Ballard was concerned, Captain Will Hottel was forever persona non grata. He had not only defected from what Noah Ballard thought was right, he had betrayed Noah, and he had betrayed his own integrity.

Although Noah kept well away from Will Hottel for the time being, Captain Hottel did have a significant impact on the events Noah was putting into play. What Noah Ballard took to be his defection added much fuel to Noah's rage and that rage was now directed toward Sam Hawken.

Major Ballard picked a quiet, soft-spoken captain named Peter Crandell to keep a watchful eye out for Captain Hawken. Every day Crandell made the rounds of the town of Mobile. He went to the hotels and rooming houses, the saloons and eateries, asking if a man meeting Hawken's description had made an appearance.

A possible suspect arrived in Mobile on the twenty-third, a Wednesday, and checked into a rooming house on Anthony Street. The man was tall, lanky, and sandy-haired, Crandell told Major Ballard, and maybe thirty or thirty-five years old. He went by the name of David Pickering.

Pickering claimed to have come from Galveston, where he'd worked as first mate on a blockade-running schooner that was sunk off Galveston in August. After the loss of the ship, he'd come east to find another ship, he said, or failing that, any work at all. He was accompanied by a younger man, one of the schooner's crew. The name the younger man gave was Tom Stetson.

On the twenty-third, church bells rang for what seemed hours, celebrating the victory at Chickamauga.

On the twenty-fourth, Pickering and Stetson asked for and were given jobs at the shipyards, working on the three locomotive ferries.

That evening, at the end of the workday, while Peter Crandell stood outside examining the men passing by, Jane Featherstone and Noah Ballard waited in a closed carriage on Front Street near the yards. Crandell had kept the man called Pickering under surveillance for the past day. When Pickering appeared among the other workmen, Crandell made a signal to Noah and Jane and the two of them opened the window curtains a crack to look at the man Crandell had identified.

It was, of course, Sam Hawken.

Major Ballard ordered Captain Crandell to place Hawken-Pickering under more careful surveillance—but still bearing in mind that it was crucial that the man not be made aware that he was being watched. One of Crandell's men booked a room at the rooming house where Hawken and his companion were staying. Another man was placed on their work crew. Other men, in relays, followed them—but from a distance. Noah believed that it was better to lose track of the two men now and again than to risk discovery.

On the night of the twenty-fourth, Hawken spent an hour strolling around the rail yards, carefully examining the forty-six remaining locomotives. He made no attempt to harm any of the machines; he simply poked around.

During the moves in the espionage and counterespionage game, Noah Ballard kept Jane Featherstone out of sight in a hotel room he provided her with. And he himself stayed confined to either his office or to his quarters, except during those times he was certain that Hawken was busy working on the ferries.

Meanwhile both Hawken and his companion acted above suspicion in every way. There were no more late night walks through the rail yards, and the work they did at the ship-yards was exemplary. They were both liked and trusted by their fellow workers.

The ferries were pronounced ready on the thirtieth of September. The sabotage attempt came that night.

It was past three in the morning, and Noah Ballard was asleep in his quarters when Peter Crandell entered his room without knocking, and with unusual excitement shook him awake.

After Noah was on his feet and had splashed handfuls of water on his face from the pitcher at the washstand, Crandell told him what the excitement was all about. Hawken and Stetson had slipped by the guards at the shipyards, boarded one of the ferries, and climbed down beneath the ferry's lowest deck into the bilge near the bow. As soon as the two men had left their rooming house late that night, word was sent to Crandell. He then ordered five armed men to join him at the yards.

Well over an hour after Hawken and Stetson had descended into the ferry's bilge, they emerged and looked furtively around. Seeing nothing disturbing, they proceeded to the next of the three ferries.

While they were inside that one, Crandell himself went down into the first bilge and examined the work the two men had done.

He found that a number of the crucial beams and structural supporting pieces of the bow framework had been cut through, after which the damage had been disguised with a mixture of wax and sawdust. It would take most diligent and careful observation to detect the harm. Once the ferry was under way, however, and up to speed, Crandell was pretty certain that the ferry's bow would cave in.

Crandell's orders from Major Ballard clearly stated that he was only to observe the activities of Captain Hawken. He was in no way to stop him or apprehend him unless Hawken was directly endangering someone else's life.

Captain Crandell went to wake the major.

When Noah Ballard arrived at the shipyards, Hawken and Stetson had not yet emerged from the second ferry. Noah ordered a guard placed at all the bilge exits. Then he himself descended into the bilge. He was armed with a Colt revolver.

He half crouched and half crawled noiselessly through the dark, dank muck in the bowels of the boat, his movements muffled by the slap of the waves against the hull, the creaking of the boat, and the slow, steady rustle of the bilge water itself. He'd considered but rejected a lantern. What he intended to do, he wanted to do in the dark.

The two men, lit by dim candlelight, were intent on their work when Noah got close enough to make his move. They seemed indifferent to the possibility of their being caught.

And then Noah considered that they realized that the bow itself was such a trap that they would never stand a chance, so their best security was fast work.

Despite the bodily contortions forced by the cramped space, they were both working swiftly, efficiently, and surely.

Noah was perhaps fifteen feet away from the two men. He wiped droplets of sweat from his forehead and around his eyes, drew his revolver, and slowly, carefully cocked it.

He drew in a breath and spoke: "How are you, Sam? It's been a long time."

"Jesus!" Sam Hawken breathed, and then moving almost too fast to see, he dropped the tool that was in his hand, snatched at the candles to put them out, and started to dive for cover.

Noah fired a warning shot before Sam's hand reached either of the candles. "Don't, Sam," Noah warned.

"Who's there?" Sam asked warily. "I know the voice."

But Noah didn't want to satisfy his curiosity yet. "Both of you take what weapons you're carrying and drop them." The two men carefully lifted their revolvers from their belts, and then the younger man looked doubtfully at the bilge water. "That's right," Noah said to him. "Drop it into the water." There were two splashes.

There was also the noise of other men arriving, signaled by Noah's earlier warning shot. These men came with lanterns.

"Now put your hands on the tops of your heads," Noah said. By the time they had complied, the men with lanterns had reached Noah, and his face was now illumined enough for Sam Hawken to see it.

"Jesus Christ!" Sam said, shaking his head with angry resignation. The anger was aimed at himself. "Noah Ballard! I should have known!"

"It's been a long time, Sam," Noah said. There was anger in Noah's voice as well, but his anger was directed not at himself but at Sam Hawken. "And from the looks of things, Sam, you've changed more than I have."

"I knew you were in Mobile, Noah," Sam said, still shaking his head slowly. "I shouldn't have risked coming near you."

"But you did, didn't you, you bastard?"

"Yes, Major Ballard, I did." Then drawing himself as erect as the situation allowed, Sam Hawken spoke formally to Noah Ballard: "Major Ballard, sir," he said, offering some semblance of a salute, "I, Captain Sam Houston Hawken of the United States Army, respectfully submit my surrender to you, effective immediately. I expect to be treated in accordance with the rules governing the treatment of prisoners of war."

"You can go fuck yourself, Sam Hawken," Noah Ballard said.


Noah Ballard did not imprison Sam Hawken and Tom Stetson in the Mobile town jail; he had available a much more secure place of captivity. The building on Front Street where Noah maintained his offices contained a large storage cellar, part of which was divided into strongrooms for the safekeeping of especially valuable merchandise for import or export. The dimensions of these rooms were approximately eight by twelve feet; they were windowless, with brick walls, flagstone floors, and double-thick oak doors.

Two of these storerooms were converted into cells for Hawken and Stetson. They were each allowed a blanket to sleep on, a pail for bodily wastes, one meal a day, and a separate pail of water. Except for a very brief meeting with Sam that Noah Ballard allowed himself, the two prisoners were forbidden visitors, and they were not allowed lamps or candles, reading material, writing material, or conversation with one another or with their guards.

In that one meeting, Major Ballard was rigidly cool, calm, and factual, never once alluding to his one-time friendship with Sam Hawken. And Hawken, for his part, granted Noah the distance that Major Ballard clearly wanted to maintain.

Major Ballard explained to Captain Hawken that he intended to make Hawken's and Stetson's imprisonment in Mobile as severe as he could devise. And he further intended to personally supervise their transport to Atlanta; there they would be placed on trial. He had no doubt about the verdict and the punishment.

Captain Hawken replied that he accepted his own situation, but that he hoped the authorities would be lenient with Lieutenant Stetson. Major Ballard made no comment to that request.

Even though conversation between guards and prisoners was officially denied, that prohibition did not reckon on the presence of Sergeant Jimmy Sutton as chief warder. Sergeant Sutton and Captain Sam Hawken were longtime friends. In the past Lieutenant Hawken and Sergeant Sutton (he was Sergeant then too; and the word was that he'd always been a sergeant, spilled out of his mother's womb with stripes on his arms) had served with then Colonel Robert E. Lee in South Texas before the war.

Sutton was lean and bearded, with dark eyes and thick, bushy brows. He had never been known to stand crisply and militarily straight, yet somehow he contrived to look taller that his actual five feet ten. He had likewise never been know to obey with anything approaching diligence or alacrity most military rules and regulations, yet somehow he was the one sergeant that officers most depended on to take on and handle (or subdue, if that were required) their hardest troops. It was his reputation for toughness that had recommended Sutton to Noah Ballard for the job of supervising his star prisoners.

It was a job, in fact, that Sergeant Sutton handled superbly. There was no danger that the prisoners would do anything that they were not supposed to. But at the same time, Jimmy Sutton wasn't going to lose the chance to chew the fat with a man he had ridden with for many hot days and many thousands of miles all over the near desert between San Antonio and the Rio Grande.

When no one else was around to bother them, Sutton would take a jug of Havana rum and a candle into Hawken's cell, and they would trade tales together about the times they'd spent riding with Bobby Lee.

By an unspoken but mutual compact, they did not talk about the war—a compact that Sutton violated slightly when he asked Sam at one point why he'd chosen to fight against his home state. Sam had sidestepped that question, and Sutton had wisely decided not to pursue it. Sutton would never in a million years have asked about the charges that had brought Sam into the cell. Neither would Sam in a million years have granted him the slightest hint of an answer.

Partly because of Sutton's now and again blindness to rules, and partly because the visitor was who he was, the general prohibition against visitors was violated sometime during Hawken's second day of captivity.

The bolts outside the heavy oak door were shot, the door swung open, and Hawken blinked his eyes rapidly as he adjusted to the sudden light.

"We've got a visitor for you," Jimmy Sutton said to him. Sutton moved aside, revealing behind him Jane Featherstone. Jane stood quietly there for a moment, then walked through the doorway. She carried a lamp in one hand and a small, paper-wrapped package in the other. Once she was safely inside, the sergeant swung the door shut. "I'll be right outside, Miss Featherstone," he said with a wink and an almost imperceptible nod toward Sam. "If you need me, knock."

"Thank you, Sergeant," she said.

After she entered the room, she placed the lamp and the package on the floor, never taking her eyes off of Sam. She was acting now very much as he remembered from their first meeting in Jackson—calm, self-possessed, intensely quiet.

While Jane went about her business, Sam remained seated in a corner with his bedding arranged under him and his back against the wall. His face was without expression, and he made no move to speak. Nor did he try to rise—which would have been difficult; his ankles were linked by leg irons. But he kept his eyes intent on Jane as she spent several long moments looking him up and down.

"You aren't surprised to see me, Sam?" she said at last.

"Surprised, Jane?" he asked, soft voiced, controlled. "Why do you say that?"

She smiled a coy little smile. "You didn't really expect to see me here, did you?"

"You have a talent for the unexpected, Jane. I've learned not to be surprised by you." He breathed a slow, regretful sigh, then resumed. "It's taken some effort and experience, but it's a lesson I've learned." He paused, then caught her eye. "Actually Jane, I am surprised that they don't have a cell here for you. A well-deserved captivity, no?"

"Sam!" she cried softly, with mock anger and petulance. "You don't mean that, do you?"

When he didn't answer her, she switched to another track. "I've brought you something to eat," she said, and indicated with her eyes the package beside the lamp.

He shot a brief look at the package, but otherwise ignored it.

"I wanted you to know that I don't bear you any ill will . . . now."

"Why should you bear me ill will, Jane?"

"Oh, Sam! Don't be so thick!"

He looked at her impassively.

"Why are you here?" he asked, changing the subject.

"I wanted to see you."

"Then by all means look, Jane. It's the same Sam Hawken that you've seen many times before. A little worse for wear, maybe."

"Don't be sarcastic, Sam. I'm here to help you."

"What kind of surprises are you planning for me, Jane," he said quickly, "at the end of your help?"

"Don't be this way, Sam, please. I've brought you some food, and I can come to see you now and then. We can talk. I can make your imprisonment more comfortable." She stopped, grew more grave. "I might be able to help you beyond that."

"What are you doing in Mobile, Jane?" he asked ignoring her last hint.

"I'm the guest of Major Ballard."

Sam cocked his brows at that. This was the first he had heard about a relationship between Noah and Jane. "Well," he said, "that comes as no surprise, either."

"I've known Noah for quite some time. He's offered me help and protection. And I've provided him with information that is important to him."

"I can well imagine," Sam said. "Is it safe to guess that certain pieces of information you provided concerned a certain Union captain named Hawken?"

"I told him what you are, Sam," she admitted quietly. "It's the truth."

"I'm sure he believed what you told him. You are a very convincing woman, Jane. You didn't by any chance tell him the truth about yourself, did you?"

"I'm not sure I know what you mean, Sam," she said innocently.

"Well, Jane," he said, "I won't waste effort trying to enlighten you . . ." He paused significantly. "Or him. He's not likely to believe what I tell him anyhow."

"No, he's not, Sam," she allowed.

She moved a few steps closer to him. "May I sit, Sam?"

"By all means," he said in a mocking, sarcastic tone. "Do sit down; I won't force you to stand. Be my guest. The

flagstone is pretty much equally soft anywhere you choose."
As he said these words, however, he half rose and pulled his
bedding out from under him, then threw it across to her.
"Better still, Jane, sit on this. It's softer than the stone."

"Thank you, Sam," she said, arranging the blankets on
the floor and then sinking down on them. "You *are* a
gentleman, you know."

"That doesn't seem to be an opinion that's generally
shared in these parts," he said. "My old friend Major
Ballard, as a case in point, thinks I'm some kind of
monster. I personally think he's wrong, but still, Jane, I
somehow trust his opinions more than I trust yours." He
sighed again. "It puts me into sort of a quandary, doesn't
it?"

"Please, Sam," Jane said, "there's no requirement that
you be cynical." Then she moved on before he could come
up with another mocking reply. "But there is one thing I
think we both agree on: Noah Ballard is a very good man,
Sam."

Sam nodded. "It's a shame we're on opposite sides," he
said in a low, gentle voice. "I miss his passions and his
enthusiasms." Then he added crushingly, "But those qualities make him vulnerable to people like you, don't they,
Jane?"

"You may not know it," she said, ignoring his last
remark, "but he still thinks the world of you."

"Evidence to the contrary notwithstanding."

"No matter what the evidence seems to be, he still loves
you. But," she went on quickly, "that doesn't mean he will
not do to you what he says. As you said, he's a man who's
prone to strong convictions. He's ardent and passionate. He
gives everything he has to what he does."

"You must need to use him very much to praise him so
highly, Jane," Sam said.

"Sam Hawken! God*damn* you!" she cried, her control
finally snapping under his sarcasm. "Don't you believe I
ever tell the truth? Do you think I can never be sincere?"

"How long have you known Noah, Jane?" he asked,
pointedly avoiding her questions. "Where did you meet?"

"You didn't answer me, Sam."

"No, I didn't. Now tell me when and where you met Major Ballard. And I *may* believe that."

"Goddamn you!" she said in a near whisper.

He waited expectantly.

Finally she spoke, but her voice was still scarcely audible. "I met Noah in Jackson. He was in charge of designing and building the fortifications there for Joe Johnston."

"Were you already spying for Grenville Dodge then?"

"Yes," she said.

"Did you like him then? Or was he just useful?"

"Of course I liked him. I still like him."

"But you passed on his information to General Dodge, and later to me?"

She gave him a slight nod.

"What's he useful for now, Jane? Is it because you want to get revenge against me?"

"If you're trying to make me cry, Sam Hawken, you won't have any luck. I'm going to give you no rewards."

"You tell me you're sincere, Jane. I'm curious as to the limits of your sincerity."

"I came here because I wanted to help you, Sam Hawken! Goddamn you! I wanted to show you compassion because of our past . . . friendship, and all you do is throw every word I say back in my face!"

"You came here because you wanted to gloat over how successfully you've managed to betray me, Jane. You're jealous that I've rejected you, aren't you? You're jealous because of Miranda Kemble. You'd have her in the cell with me if you could, as long as that meant she'd be executed along with me. But at the same time you thought you'd try a little kindness with me, for the sake of the possibility that I just might forget what you are, and maybe even forget Miranda Kemble, too, and that I just might show you that I really want you and not her." He looked with infinite coldness at Jane. "You told Noah Ballard I might come to Mobile, didn't you, darling Jane?"

"I'm glad of what I've done," she snapped.

"That's exactly my point, Jane. I know it." He pressed

his lips into another grim smile. "And there, Jane, for once you're sincere."

"Why is it, Sam Hawken," she said, lifting herself slowly to her feet, "that you provoke in people who care for you a burning desire to see you dead?"

"You're leaving, are you?" he asked.

"Civil conversation with you is impossible." She bent down to retrieve the lamp.

"Good," he said. "This is a delightful time for you to go."

She made a move for the door, then paused and turned back to him. "I do wonder about you and the Kemble girl, Sam. I wonder if you would be able to make a life with her—providing that you have a life at all, a doubtful outcome as matters now stand. But I do wonder whether you wouldn't drive her away just as you've driven away everyone else who has tried to love you."

"One thing about you, Jane. You never lose hope. You still want me to throw myself at you, don't you?"

"I told Noah Ballard you are a fiend. I was right to do that. You're truly a creature from hell, Sam."

"I could change your mind about that, dear girl, if I told you that Miranda Kemble doesn't mean anything to me. If I told you that it was really you I want, you'd probably find some way to help me out of this place."

"I'm leaving, Sam."

"Is that why you came to see me, Jane?"

"Go to hell, Sam Hawken," she said as she rapped sharply on the door.

"Go to Noah Ballard, Jane Featherstone," Sam said. "But a note of warning. You keep too many balls in the air, and you put more in the air all the time. You're a skilled juggler, but you can't keep them up forever."

"Go to hell, Sam," she said. "Stew by yourself in the dark."

The door opened, and without looking back, she left Sam's cell.

After she'd gone, he left untouched the package she'd brought for him.

Later he gave it unopened to Jimmy Sutton. "I'd test it for poison if I were you, Jimmy," he said, "if there's food inside."

"A woman scorned, is she?" Sutton asked.

Hawken gave him a wry smile.


While the two bow-damaged ferries were repaired, the one Hawken and Stetson did not sabotage shuttled locomotives between Mobile and the connection with the Mobile and Great Northern Railroad. For five days *The Fair Hope* made daily trips from Mobile to the Tensaw River across the bay, and then five miles up the Tensaw to the railhead, a total distance of twenty-five miles. On Monday the sixth of October, the other two boats were ready to sail.

That night Dart and Javelin were loaded on one of the two, *The Bay Queen*, and Perseverance and another locomotive were boarded onto the second, *The Mobile Star*.

That same evening the fishermen who worked the Gulf outside the bay all returned to port. Though these men usually spent several days out at a time, they were troubled about the weather. The sky that Monday was cloudless and the breeze was mild, but there was a chop in the water they didn't like, and the frequency of the waves had picked up in a disturbing way. Normally in that part of the Gulf, something like eight waves passed any given point every minute, but as that Monday wore on, the waves speeded up to nine, then ten, then twelve per minute.

What that meant, they knew, was that somewhere in the Gulf a big storm was brewing. The Gulf was a big sea, and chances were that the storm—at least the worst of it—would miss Mobile, but fishermen in small boats don't get to be old fishermen without treating the evidence of chop and waves with respect. They pulled in their nets and headed for home.

Early Tuesday morning, Sergeant Sutton and a team of guards gathered Sam Hawken and Tom Stetson and led them at gunpoint, their hands and feet in irons, up the cellar stairs and out into Front Street. From there, the two men were paraded to the ferry slip, and then escorted aboard *The Bay Queen*.

Major Ballard himself greeted them on the rear deck, while Jane Featherstone stood quietly several feet behind him, carefully avoiding any glance in the direction of Sam Houston Hawken. It hadn't been hard for her to conclude by this time that Sam was everything evil that she had told Noah he was.

Jane was elegantly and fetchingly dressed; she'd made herself into a fine lady for the occasion. And that elicited a number of stares and comments from soldiers and deckhands.

Dart and Javelin were forward, chained to the deck— powerful, monstrous black machines that seemed to dwarf the little bay ferryboat.

Indeed, with the two large engines aboard, the distribution of weight on the ferry was not all her captain desired. They made the boat top-heavy, a potentially serious problem in rough weather.

The ferry captain was aware that a storm might be on the way. He knew the fishermen had come into port last night, and he was aware of its significance. The summer hurricane season was just about over, but it was not so late in the year that he could rule out a big, rough tropical storm. Still, the bay seemed quiet enough today, and save for high bands of wispy clouds, the sky was blue. Furthermore, he knew his exposure on the bay would be scarcely four hours, enough time to allow him to avoid any serious weather.

"Good morning, Sam," Noah said, as Sutton led Hawken and Stetson aboard. Noah almost granted Sam a smile when he made the greeting. He was feeling a degree more mellow and generous toward Sam than he had a few days earlier. This greater benevolence did not owe anything to a change in Sam, nor to any change in Noah's attitude toward him, nor especially to any change of opinion about Sam expressed by Jane Featherstone. Rather, it was a consequence of Noah's growing certitude that he'd at last reached the frontiers of his one, totally consuming goal: the delivery of his large herd of Mississippi locomotives to Atlanta.

And of the herd, Dart, Javelin, and Perseverance, the

engines he was about to ship across Mobile Bay, were the best of the breed. The mellowness and generosity Noah displayed that morning sprang out of the pride and satisfaction he felt as he personally escorted them through their difficult voyage.

It would be a misrepresentation, of course, to claim that Noah Ballard's pleasure that morning was absolutely unmitigated. He was still deeply troubled by the defection of Will Hottel, but Will was already in Atlanta, and that absence was most welcome. It set Noah's elation free to swell all the more luxuriantly.

At the same time, no small part of Noah's pleasure was owed to the presence of Sam Hawken in chains to witness his success. That was a consummation he devoutly prized.

"Good morning, Noah," Sam answered cautiously, noting the change in Noah's bearing toward him, but not knowing what to make of it. Sam had no illusions about reconciliation between himself and his old friend, but he hoped for an opening to at least communicate with him.

"I wanted you to be with me when we crossed the bay," Noah said. "You'll be with me," he added pointedly, "all the way to Atlanta."

I've always treasured the companionship of close friends, Sam was about to say, but he thought better of it. Noah never found great delight in Sam's ironies. Instead he said, "Perhaps we'll have a chance to talk during that time. I'd like very much to share words with you, Noah."

Noah waited a long time before he replied. "That's not impossible," he said finally, in slowly measured tones. Then he went on more rapidly, making a fluid gesture in the direction of *Javelin*, which was up ahead of him on the deck, just behind the port sidewheel, flanking and nearly overshadowing it. "What do you think of my engines, Sam?" he said without trying to muzzle his pride.

"I think they're great beauties, Noah."

Bells rang, announcing the imminent departure of *The Bay Queen*.

"I have nearly fifty," Noah said, "not as lovely as the two aboard here, and the other one across the way"—he pointed to Perseverance, which was aboard *The Mobile Star* in the next slip over—"but they're good, solid machines, all of them."

"And all quite a feather in your cap," Sam said with genuine admiration.

"The South needs them desperately," Noah said diplomatically. "And I'm glad I could do my part in delivering them where they are most desperately needed."

Sailors cast the lines off, and the last bells sounded. The twin sidewheels turned slowly, driving the boat into the river.

Noah left Sam in order to settle Jane near the bow in a chair under a wide awning. Before he left, he ordered Sergeant Sutton to chain Sam and Lieutenant Stetson to the drive wheels of Javelin. "You won't be more uncomfortable here than you deserve, Sam," Noah said as he left.

"I've always counted on the kindness of friends," Sam replied, unable to resist the crack.

Noah gave Sam a pained look and shook his head, then walked away to deal with Jane.

"How are you bearing up, Tom?" Sam asked after they were both fastened to Javelin. The two men had scarcely spoken since their capture nearly a week earlier.

"I've been happier," Tom said.

Sam smiled. "Me, too."

"What's likely to happen in Atlanta?"

"For you and me?"

Tom nodded.

"There'll be a trial," Sam said evenly, "a large trial for show. I'll be found guilty of all the vilest crimes ever imagined by mankind, and you may be found an accomplice or an accessory or whatever it's called." He breathed in deeply. "My guess, if we reach Atlanta, is that once they've satisfied themselves of my guilt, they'll lose interest in you and send you to prison."

"*If* we reach Atlanta?" Tom asked, picking up on what sounded to him like hopeful words.

"We'll do our best, Tom, not to reach Atlanta," he said as coolly as he could manage.

Sam had very little hope of achieving that goal, and even less hope that the result of the trial would be as fortunate for Tom as he was suggesting. Sam's actual expectation was that they would both be shot, but he wasn't about to tell Tom that.

"I heard you talking to Sergeant Sutton," Tom said. "I thought that maybe you were cooking up something with him."

Sam shook his head and gave a roll of his eyes. "Jimmy Sutton and I go back to the far distant past," Sam said. "We rode with Bobby Lee between San Antonio and Laredo, and we chased Coahuilan cattle rustlers across the Rio Grande together." He smiled almost in spite of himself. "You've never had a true experience with inebriation until you've been drunk with Sergeant Sutton. And if you're ever in Laredo with him, he'll find you a girl who is not only beautiful beyond your wildest imaginings, but who even likes gringos. He speaks their language like he was born to it.

"I like Jimmy Sutton about as well as any man I know. And he'd probably give up his life for me, except if doing that caused him to violate his oath to his nation."

"So he's going to do nothing for us."

"Not Jimmy Sutton, Tom."

"He wouldn't even turn a blind eye to give us a chance to run for it?"

"Not even that."

"Well, goddamn," Tom said, screwing up his face. Then, "Let me know what you want me to do, Captain, and when you want me to do it. I'm here whenever you want me."

"Yeah," Sam said quietly, "I've noticed."

There was a stiff breeze from just south of east when *The Bay Queen* sailed out of the Mobile River into the bay itself. The early fluffy, high banded clouds had firmed up and grown dark purple and heavy with rain. And there was a snapping chop to the water. It made for discomfort among the travelers and concern in the ferry's captain. *The Bay Queen* was overloaded, and the weather was turning unkind to an overloaded ferryboat.

The captain ordered more steam, and *The Bay Queen* surged ahead a bit faster. The wind was veering more and more to the south, and its speed was picking up.

An hour and a half out into the bay, the rain started. It was slow and soft at first—but it grew heavier fast. And the wind was still picking up, veering ever more from east to south, crowding more and more heavy Gulf waves into the narrow funnel of Mobile Bay.

The captain had to slow the ferry down, but he kept pushing it to attain whatever headway he could. He wanted to reach what was ahead of him fast, because what was behind him was swiftly turning monstrous and black, whipping the water into a fury of power beyond the strength of mere steam, muscles, wood, and iron.

The rain was now falling at the rate of two or three inches an hour, the winds were gusting toward the upper end of gale force, and the sky was murky and twilit—not dark as night, but a frightening amber gray.

It was not yet noon. *The Bay Queen* struggled forward, barely halfway across Mobile Bay.

The deck heaved and lifted and slewed drunkenly this way and that, and the twin giant locomotives showed signs of breaking loose.

Sam Hawken and Tom Stetson, chained to Javelin's drive wheels, stayed curled up, huddled compactly, insofar as that was possible, into the protection offered by the locomotive.

Sam was growing alarmed. Javelin was chained to heavy deck rings, but it strained and groaned fiercely against its chains. If the machine had possessed sentient intent one would have said it was struggling to be free of its fetters.

Jim Sutton appeared out of the dark and the rain, his face, beard, and hair wind lashed, streaked with blood. Some wind- or wave-driven object had smashed into him. The wound was clearly painful, but not disabling.

He put his mouth to Sam's ear. The wind howled, screamed, and thundered, its voice many octaved, loud almost beyond the limits of flesh. "How are you making out?" he yelled.

"What's happening?" Sam yelled back.

"We're floating . . . which is as much of a miracle as I want to ask for."

"Any sign of shore?"

"No."

Javelin shifted and groaned, and then a huge wave wiped over the deck, lifting Jim Sutton up, threatening to sweep him away. Almost before he'd noticed it, Sam's hand had found Sergeant Sutton's grasping and steadying him.

"Thanks, Sam," Sutton mumbled after he regained his feet. Sam's grip was on his belt now. Sutton said, "Why don't you keep your hand right where it is for the time being. I need to have a steady hand for what I came here to do."

"What are you about to do?"

"Get you two men out of these chains. This boat's in deep trouble, and you're not going to want to be fastened to this locomotive fifteen minutes from now."

"It's that bad?"

"A couple of minutes ago the steam died; the waves or the rain or some damn thing smothered the fire. And when that happened, the captain just seemed to give up trying to run the ship. The last time I saw him, he was standing by the wheelhouse, and he'd tied himself to a cork ring. He looked like he was only waiting for the boat to sink out from under him.

"And he's probably right," he continued, working on Sam's locks as he did. "The wind's caught us and it's driving us broadside. God only knows why we haven't broached and flipped over, or why we're even floating at all."

"And nobody has tried to get the boiler lit again?"

"In this weather? There's more time left for me to learn to swim than to do that."

"You don't swim, Jimmy?" Sam asked, as Sutton unlocked the chains that held Sam to the locomotive.

"You bet I don't swim. I'm a horse soldier."

Sam was free. He glanced at Tom and then he and Sutton made their way over to him.

"And, Tom, can you swim?" Sam asked.

"I can swim as much as anybody can who gets out of the Military Academy."

"All right, Sergeant Sutton," Sam yelled above the howling, "you'll stay with me and Tom, just in case swimming gets necessary."

"I don't take orders from Federal officers," Sutton said.

"Shut the righteous fuck up, Sergeant. You'll take orders from me."

"I have men out there on the deck somewhere I have to take care of."

"And you will. But by staying with me. Come on, we're going to try to restart the engine."

They met Noah Ballard on the stairway down to the boiler room. He was coming up, holding tight to the stair rail, swaying against the movement of the ferryboat. It was evident he'd already failed to do what Sam intended to try. His face was indomitably intent, driven.

When he saw Sam, Noah gave a slight start, as though he didn't quite recognize the man facing him. He pulled himself to a halt, then said vaguely, "I have to save Dart, Sam. And Javelin. Will you help me?"

"That's not possible, Noah," he said gently. "There's not enough time."

"There has to be," Noah insisted. "Has to be! They're the best of the lot!"

"We're wasting time here, Noah," Sam said, still kindly. But then with greater urgency: "What I want to know is whether there's any chance of getting the boiler fire lit again."

"No, Sam," Noah answered, his voice drained of hope. "There's too much water down there."

"Then come on with me, Noah," Sam said. "We'll do what we can to save ourselves."

Noah's eyes grew suddenly wide, then filled with fury. "Where the hell are your chains, Sam?" he said loudly, to make himself heard over the screaming wind. Then he noticed Jim Sutton behind Sam and Tom Stetson. "There, you, Sergeant. These men are in your custody. How come they're loose?"

"Noah, for God's sake," Sam yelled. "This is a damn-fool poor time to worry about chains and custody."

"You're wrong, Sam. You're absolutely mistaken. All of that still stands." He turned again to Jim Sutton. "Sergeant, how do you explain it that they're free?"

"Come up on deck," Sam broke in, shouting. "There's a chance for us up there."

Noah continued working on Sutton, speaking loudly and urgently. "Sergeant, I want these two men confined in chains. And," he added angrily, "you've got a lot of explaining to do once we are back on shore, Sergeant."

"I can't, Major. Not while we might sink any second."

"What do you mean, 'can't'? That's a direct order, and I'm an officer."

"I still can't, Major. We get ashore, and I'll take care of them for you. But while this boat's about to break up or sink or turn over . . . goddamn it, Major, I can't let any man die that way!"

"You're going to be in chains, too, once we make it to shore! And I'd shoot you right now—along with Sam Hawken and the kid that's with him—if I had a pistol."

"Noah!" Sam yelled. "You're a damned fool! And I'm just as much a fool as long as I stand arguing with you! All of us are here below decks on a boat that doesn't have more than five minutes' life left in it. You can argue with yourself all you want, Noah, or you can argue with the wind and the waves, but I'm going up and see about saving myself and maybe a few others. And you're coming with me, Sergeant Sutton. And so are you, Tom." Sam surged rapidly up the stairs past Jim Sutton and Tom Stetson.

Noah watched him until he reached the exit to the deck. Then he ran up the stairs as far as Sutton. "You're not to obey that man," Noah said, grabbing his shoulder. "Not if you don't want to be shot with him."

Sutton shook himself loose. "What's got into you, Major? You crazy?"

"Just do what I say," he said.

"You don't know this, Major, and I don't have a lot of time to give you a patient explanation, but I've known Captain Hawken since both of us served with Colonel Bob Lee. He and I have been in hard situations before, and we got out of them with skins intact. If anybody can get up out of this here situation, I'd bet on him."

"Even though he's your enemy?"

"He ain't *my* enemy, Major."

Noah stared at him, furious, silent. When words finally came, his voice was strange, calm, threatening. "All right, Sergeant, do what you want. Get the hell out of here."

"You know something, Major?" Jim Sutton asked before he left. "You and Bob Lee have the same steel rail up your asses. And it's going to be the death of both of you."

When Sergeant Sutton rejoined Sam Hawken on deck, he found Sam at the starboard rail, his hand pointing hard over the water. Sam's face was full of amazement and awe. Not three hundred yards away, a piece of shore was visible through the rain and the dark. *The Bay Queen* was being driven in the direction of the starboard side. Somehow, despite that, and despite the presence of the locomotives on deck, the incredible waves had not tipped the little vessel over.

"What do you think?" Sutton asked.

"I think I'm hoping," Sam said.

"What are you going to do?"

"I'm going forward."

"Why?"

"I don't know. Seems the best place to be—as far away from those engines as I can get."

"Sounds good to me," Sutton said. "I'll meet you there. I want to gather my troops there, too, if they aren't already up forward."

"Right," Sam said. "You do that." He turned to Stetson, who was standing next to him, clutching the rail as if it were his last hope.

The boat heaved and dropped, made a corkscrew motion, and righted itself miraculously. The three men were momentarily plunged underwater. Then, sputtering and shaking their heads, Sam and Tom moved forward while Sutton made his way to the rear to pick up any stragglers who might still be there.

Sam found Jane Featherstone a few feet behind the bow. She was seated on the deck, her hands firmly gripping an iron deck ring. Sometime earlier she had stripped off her heaviest clothes—the hoop, the petticoats, the jewelry, the fashionable traveling coat—and changed into a simple cotton dress. Also sometime earlier she had slipped a cork ring over her head; she now had it under her arms. Sam even noted with interest that she was barefoot.

Our Jane is never at a loss when it comes to survival, Sam Hawken thought to himself with admiration.

When she turned and recognized him, though, her face was rigid with fright. For Sam, that was gratifying.

He glanced in the direction of the patch of shore he'd seen earlier. To his relief, it was maybe fifty yards closer.

But he also saw something low and dark in the water ahead. Its shape was jagged and irregular, but it was hugely solid and threatening.

Jim Sutton reappeared, trailed by a pair of troopers carrying Noah Ballard. One held his left shoulder, the other his right. He was unconscious, and his right foot dangled from his ankle at an unnatural angle.

"What happened to him?" Sam asked when Sutton and the others reached him.

"He was trying to do some damn thing to one of his engines, and the fucker like to jumped and flicked him in the foot. Maybe it's crushed, but I can't tell for sure."

"Jesus!" Sam said, but his mind wasn't totally on Noah's injury, because his eyes had been pulled toward the object he'd seen earlier in the water. It now squarely blocked their passage toward the shore.

Now he realized what it was. He was looking at the top of a locomotive—the funnel, the domes, the cab.

It must be, he guessed, one of the two on *The Mobile Star.* The *Star* must have sunk there and tipped sideways, and the engine must still be attached to it.

And they were closing on it fast.

*The Bay Queen* surged, rose, and fell. Surged again, then slammed sideways into the half-submerged locomotive. *The Bay Queen* shuddered, lurched, cracked, began to break up. . . .

"Get into the water!" Sam screamed unnecessarily. There was little choice. "And grab something that'll float as you go!"

He made his way—with supreme difficulty, as the deck angle was now close to forty degrees above the horizontal— to the place where the two troopers had deposited Noah. They themselves had already deserted the ship. Noah was now semiconscious, but he did not recognize Sam.

It's just as well that he's not conscious, Sam thought. That injury is going to feel painful—if I can get him to shore, where he can feel it.

He looked around for Jim Sutton, saw him, and motioned him over. He came. Sam looked around for Tom, too, but he was not visible. Tom would have to take care of himself.

From the place where Sam and the other two were perched, the deck sloped down into churning, sucking, deadly water. It was the windward side of the boat; it would be impossible to enter the sea there. There was a pause in the ferry's breakup, and Sam had time to consider another option or two.

He scrambled up the precariously pitched deck, grabbed a piece of rail, and stared over. It was comparatively quiet on the lee side of the ferry.

The calm wasn't all that Sam was offered. A number of heavy lengths of wood—railroad ties?—had collected next to the sides of the boat, caught in the leeward eddies.

That's where we'll go in, he decided.

He scrambled back down to Sutton and Noah Ballard, and explained to Jim what he wanted to do. Together they dragged Noah up the deck. Then Sam dropped into the bay.

He swam to one of the logs. His guess had been right. It was a tie. He grabbed it, then propelled it as close as he dared to the place where Jim waited with Noah.

He waved. Sutton maneuvered Noah over the side and

into the water. Somehow Sam managed to grab him before he lost him. Once he had Noah in a sure grip, he lifted him onto the tie, and though Noah was still only at best semiawake, he was aware enough to circle his arms around the tie and hold on.

Jimmy Sutton followed, and again Sam was successful. He caught Jimmy before he sank and placed his hands onto the tie. Sam had to do that for him, because Jim Sutton's eyes were closed tight. He looked again for Tom Stetson, and again he failed to see him.

Sam then started kicking his feet to propel them toward the shore.

After a time, he felt eyes on him. He twisted around and saw Noah watching him. He was staring at Sam, unblinking. Noah Ballard's eyes, for the first time since Sam had left him at the boiler room stairwell, showed consciousness and recognition. He knew who it was who had saved his life, but the eyes were at the same time vacant, hollow. Defeat had emptied them.

# ♦ TEN ♦

*Atlanta, Georgia*
*October 10, 1863*

A shrapnel burst gravely wounded Colonel Lamar Kemble during the Battle of Chickamauga. Within an hour of the event the colonel was transferred from the battlefield to a surgical station, where three large and several smaller shell fragments were removed from his body. The battlefield surgeons accomplished these delicate and excruciatingly painful operations without the aid of either morphine or chloroform, since both drugs were almost impossible to come by in Georgia. Confederate wounded were asked to substitute courage in their stead.

Colonel Kemble was transported by rail from the battlefield surgery to the large hospital complex recently constructed at the fair grounds in Atlanta. It was one of the many military hospitals that had sprung up in that city as a result of the war.

There he was expected to die.

His closest relatives, prominent Georgians, were so notified. The instant they received word, Ashbel and Miranda Kemble, Ariel Edge, and Colonel Kemble's mother, Fanny Shaw, sped from Raven's Wing to Atlanta to be with Lam during his last moments.

Colonel Kemble failed to die.

It wasn't just that his decline was slow—his condition actually improved. The wounds were clean and remained clean, his injured flesh quickly turned pink and healthy looking, and there was no evidence of gangrene or septicemia. He was feverish, which was only natural, but not alarmingly so.

Lam's change for the better did not actually astonish his doctors; they had much too much on their minds for that. And, more to the point, they had seen other young men beat the odds and triumph over wounds that would have felled ninety-nine other men. The one in ninety-nine apparently possessed some extra measure of will and vital energy, and perhaps the help of God.

Survival for Lam was not going to be an unmixed blessing, however. If he lived, Lam would have the use of only one eye, since a sliver of iron had punctured the other. There would also be terrible, disfiguring scars on his face, skull, and body, and it was doubtful that he'd have full use of his right arm.

Soon after Lam's family arrived in Atlanta, Ash Kemble obtained the loan of a lovely, substantial, and currently vacant house on Pryor Street next door to The Terraces, the most famous residence in Atlanta. As soon as the family moved in, Lam was transferred there from the military hospital.

"You don't want to stay in a hospital," Ash told him. "You can *die* in that damned place."

Lam put up no resistance to his uncle's suggestion. The surgical hospital was a human abattoir. Death bred there. The faster he escaped from it, Lam knew, the greater would be his own chance of living a normal life span.

Once he arrived at the house on Pryor Street, it was immediately established that the nursing chores for the recovering patient would be shared by his two sisters and mother. But most of these duties, as it turned out, fell on Ariel Edge and Fanny Shaw. This came about not because Miranda schemed to evade her responsibilities to her brother, but because she was the one woman in the family who could plausibly handle necessary functions outside the immediate household, and there were a good many of these. The Kembles were an eminent family, and Ash was a magnet of society. He received invitations as a flower receives bees—and for good reason. He was wealthy, he was handsome, he was a genuine adventurer, he was a sparkling conversationlist, and he was unattached. Whenever he accepted selected invitations, he took Miranda along as his companion. He did this partly to discourage attempts to set up a fresh attachment, but mostly because he liked having his niece along.

Ariel Edge was in mourning for her husband, Ben, and this limited her social life. And the mere presence in Atlanta of Fanny Shaw had to be kept quiet; she ranked near Harriet Beecher Stowe as an object of southern hostility. It was hard to imagine propaganda more abhorrent to the Great Cause than her published journals.

It was, needless to say, impossible to keep Fanny's presence anywhere secret. She could be kept behind the doors of the borrowed house on Pryor Street, but she could not be made invisible.

As it turned out, however, when word was whispered around Atlanta that Fanny was in residence for the sake of her wounded hero son, she was not driven out of town.

On Sunday, October 10, Miranda accompanied Ash to an outdoor gathering—a late afternoon buffet followed by dancing—at The Terraces. It was an event aimed at raising funds for the hospitals, and everyone who was anyone in Atlanta attended. The suggested door offering was a hundred Confederate dollars, and there were contests, raffles, and prizes as well. Ash gave twice the suggested donation for himself and Miranda.

To Miranda's eye The Terraces' reputation as Atlanta's finest dwelling was well justified. Not only was the mansion itself lovely and graceful, but it was surrounded by splendid gardens and lawns. It wasn't merely a plot with a house and a border of grass and flowers; it was a sprawling Provençal villa nestled in a botanical park. Even so late in the season, there were blazing flowers still in abundance. This impressive establishment was owned by a hardware man from Vermont, Edward Rawson, who was somehow able to live down his Yankee origin.

Among the notables present were the mayor, James Calhoun, and his brother Ezekial, a physician; Captain Lemuel Grant, an engineer, who was in charge of building the extensive fortifications that were rising at the peripheries of the city; John Neal, a real estate entrepreneur and the richest man in Atlanta; John Ballard, the president of the Atlanta and Western Railroad; Jabez and Samuel Richards, who ran a book and stationery store; the plantation owner Thomas Maguire; Captain William Hottel of the Railroad Bureau; Colonel Marcus Wright, commander of the city's defense force; and the Reverend Charles Todd Quintard, Atlanta's leading clergyman—and the man who was truly Atlanta's heart and soul, the city's propagandist, for courage, self-sacrifice, and honor.

It was a glittering affair. The air vibrated with laughter and graciousness and celebration. The South had won a great victory at Chickamauga, Union-held Chattanooga was under Confederate siege, and Atlanta was safe from the Yankee invaders—at least for the time being.

The joy was not without its edge, however, though few chose to recognize it. The laughter and the gaiety were brought forth by dint of no little effort. Gaudy holiday clothes only barely covered the fears of doom that festered within most of these illustrious Atlanta hearts.

"Do you see all those people out there?" Ash said to Miranda soon after their arrival. "They're wearing happy faces, but there's panic in their eyes. Don't you see it?" She told him she did, and he went on, "You'll meet about as much real pleasure here as you'd have found at one of those wild carnivals nobles threw while plague spread through the countryside."

"Do you blame them for it?" Miranda asked.

"No, of course not," Ash said with a smile. "Eat and be merry, darling." *Cras moriemur.*

Though Miranda couldn't find it in herself to blame her Atlanta neighbors for trying to find pleasure in a dark time, she didn't look forward to a long evening of gaiety. She could put on her party clothes easily enough, but she could not so easily make herself glitter or be gay.

Especially when she ached so terribly for Sam Hawken.

What was the use of dancing or chatting charmingly when she wasn't doing it with Sam?

As things turned out, Miranda's fear of a long and boring evening turned out to be unjustified.

To accommodate the diners, a constellation of over fifty white wicker tables with matching chairs had been arranged all about the great lawn of The Terraces. This meant there were seating accommodations for more than three hundred people. Scattered among these tables were dozens of flambeaux on poles, and many-colored Japanese lanterns were hung in the trees. It was indeed a splendid gathering.

When the dinner bell was rung, Ash Kemble tracked down his niece, who had wandered off when he had settled into business gossip with the owner of a rolling mill. He found her making conversation with a flock of sixteen- and seventeen-year-old girls. Ash had few words for her when he fetched her; he looked thoughtful, preoccupied, and distant. She knew her uncle well. She could discern urgency under the preoccupation, and that unsettled her.

After he filled a plate for himself and for her at the long, wide buffet boards, Ash maneuvered Miranda toward a table near the edge of the lawn. John Ballard and Captain Will Hottel were seated there.

"I was talking to Mr. Ballard and the captain earlier this evening," Ash explained as they made their way through the tables. "You'll be interested in them."

"He's Noah Ballard's father, isn't he?" Miranda said.

"That's right," Ash said. "And he's the chief of the Atlanta and Western Railroad. Hottel," he went on to explain, "is with the Railroad Bureau. He's just returned from Mississippi, where he and Noah worked together."

Miranda had by that time related to Ash and her mother the story of her renewed relationship with Sam Hawken. Miranda's mother and her uncle approved of what they heard, as she knew they would. More than that, they were both richly delighted at the prospective match, even though it was on its face an unusual one.

Neither Ash nor Fanny had forgotten Sam from those June days at West Point long ago.

Sam Hawken was a far cry from the ordinary "nice" young gentleman who offered himself to Miranda. He was the very rare and special young man who could act, and he could act with powerful effect. Once the war was over, they both saw a brilliant future for him.

"Noah has also returned to Atlanta," Ash went on. "He arrived yesterday evening after some sort of injury—nothing so serious, I take it, as Lam's." He paused, gravely thoughtful. "And he's brought news that concerns you, Miranda."

Miranda's brow furrowed. "What do you mean?" she asked.

"You'd best hear it from John Ballard," Ash said. "And later, probably, from Noah himself."

"Tell me now," Miranda insisted, sensing the ominous edge in his tone.

"I can't yet, darling. Listen to what the other people have to say first."

"It's about Sam?" she asked, beginning to guess why Ash was avoiding her questions.

He nodded a slow, grave acknowledgment.

"What's happened to him?" she asked with growing alarm. "Has he been captured? Or"—she managed to keep from choking it out—"killed?"

He looked at her, pursing his lips thoughtfully. "I'm in the dark about Sam's exact situation. Truly I don't know... but," he added, reassuring her, "he's in Confederate custody, and he's alive."

"That's consolation," she said, not especially consoled. "But you know more than you're saying, Ash. I can see it in your face. Tell me now. I don't want to hear it from people I don't know."

He looked at her again. "Let's go talk to Mr. Ballard and the captain. Then we'll discuss it afterward, all right?"

"All right," she agreed reluctantly.

"And a word of serious caution, my dear," he went on. "Don't blurt anything out. Let me do the talking. Play the belle. If the subject of Captain Sam Hawken comes up, you don't know him." He stared hard at her. "All right?"

"All right."

Will Hottel was a large, portly man, with a smooth manner and an air of crisp competence. It wasn't any of these qualities however, that most struck Miranda Kemble. It was his eyes. They blinked continuously and distractingly. That peculiar flutter gave the big man a strangely abstracted look that disturbed Miranda.

Noah Ballard's father was a pleasant-talking, good-looking, confident man in his midfifties. He was of slightly less than medium height, with a full, rich head of curly silver-gray hair, and he had a sliding eye. It didn't take Miranda long to recognize that he was attracted to her. The slide almost always ended on some part of her body. That kind of attention normally gave her pleasure; she was delighted when men delighted in her. But from this man, the attention left her cold. It was not delight she saw in John Ballard's eye, but a will to possess and control.

During the progress of the meal, Miranda left most of the talking to the men, as Ash had suggested.

Both railroad men, she could tell from the first, were eager for admiration. And Ash Kemble doled admiration out—though never so copiously as to seem false or sycophantic. As a result, they both seemed to like Ash; he was a man after their own hearts, one of their own kind. And so they both loosened up and talked freely.

During the chitchat and male gossip the three men produced, she smiled agreeably. Now and again she batted her eyelashes in the manner prescribed for single women of her class, and she managed to look ever so slightly bored with the masculine talk of railroads and locomotives and rolling stock.

Miranda was actually more interested than she appeared to be, and she was especially interested when Ash steered the conversation to a topic the three men had apparently discussed earlier, before Miranda had joined them.

When Ash broached it, the two other men instantly filled with self-approval. Wide, satisfied smiles spread across their faces, and Hottel actually speeded up his rapid-fire blinking.

"The two of you were talking to me before my niece joined us," Ash said to them, "about—what was it, three score?" He looked at John Ballard for confirmation. Ballard gave him a nod. "Right, three score locomotives in top condition that Captain Hottel and your son"—he paused to glance at Ballard—"have caused to be brought all the way to Atlanta from northern Mississippi."

"In point of fact," John Ballard corrected him, "the total number that has reached Atlanta is forty-two. We had originally slightly over three score. But there were casualties and other,"—his lips formed a sober smile—"losses."

"Anyhow," Ash said graciously, "there were—and are—a goodly number of locomotives." He caught Miranda's eye. "You'll be fascinated at the story of how they got from there to here, Miranda. It's an amazing tale, darling, every bit as fabulous and full of adventure as an old epic." He laughed, "Ulysses voyaging on great and powerful machines instead of sailing ships."

"How right you are!" Will Hottel exclaimed. "Just so! It *was* an epic journey! What a splendid concept!"

"And my niece," Ash sailed on smoothly, "had some previous acquaintance with your son." He glanced again at John Ballard.

"So you said earlier," John Ballard replied, beaming a

radiantly golden smile in Miranda's direction. "I'm positive he would be most delighted to see you again," he continued.

"And I would adore seeing Noah," Miranda said sweetly.

"We'll arrange such a meeting at the soonest possible moment," Ash said, then turned to Will Hottel. "Meanwhile would you be kind enough to regale Miranda with the odyssey of the locomotives?"

Miranda batted her eyes and smiled, then opened her mouth in the tiniest of yawns, a yawn that she instantly concealed with her fingertips. "I'd just love to hear about all those great and powerful machines," she said.

Inside she was churning. What has all this got to do with Sam Hawken? she asked herself.

Will Hottel launched with happy gusto into the tale of the travels of the locomotives. He, of course, had a great part in the success of the adventure, and he did not minimize his role, but he didn't fail to give John Ballard's son credit for his part, either. The whole operation would have fallen to pieces, Hottel maintained magnanimously, were it not for Noah Ballard's cleverness, bravery, and daring.

John Ballard took up the narrative at the point when the locomotives reached Mobile. He started by describing how the bay ferries were reconstructed to accommodate the locomotives—which elicited more discreet yawns from Miranda.

But he suddenly managed to catch her attention—almost beyond her ability to hide it.

"Do you know what happened then, Miss Kemble?" he asked her, knowing that she didn't.

"Why, no," she said with a delicate quiver of lashes.

"All those big, beautiful locomotives just sitting there naked and defenseless turned out to be an irresistible temptation to our Yankee friends. Those of us who've been engaged in this business didn't expect it—and why we didn't I'll never figure out—but the Yankees saw how valuable the engines will be to us, and they did what they could to keep us from enjoying them."

"And what was that?" Miranda asked, afraid that she knew what his answer would be.

"They have a spy—or, I should say, had—" Miranda shot Ballard a look, but she didn't say anything, so Ash's barely lifted restraining hand proved unnecessary. "A spy who was maybe just about their main spy. We've had experience of him even here in Atlanta—bad experience."

"Oh, *my*!" Miranda said, managing to make her reaction sound like wonder at the effrontery of a spy who'd even attempt to insinuate himself into the heart and hub of the South.

"They sent him down to Mobile, and his mission was to do what he could to stop or destroy the locomotives.

"But we caught him. Or rather, my son did."

"Oh, *good*!" Miranda exclaimed, clapping her hands. "How splendid!"

"Isn't it?" Ash said with raised brows.

"What's this man's name?" Miranda asked, as casually as she could.

"Sam Hawken," Ballard said. "He's a turncoat Texan who went with the Union. A profoundly evil man."

"Sam Hawken?" Miranda blurted, as though she were amazed to hear that name. She turned to her uncle, reaching out for his hand. "Uncle Ash," she said, wide-eyed, "I think I've met this man Hawken. And you met him, too, if my recollection serves. Do you remember years ago at the Military Academy?"

"I remember some such name," Ash allowed.

"He graduated with Noah and Lam," Miranda continued, "didn't he?"

"I believe he did."

"Imagine *that*!" she breathed. "That nice boy that I met up there . . . turning into such a *monster*!"

"There's no explaining the human heart," John Ballard said.

"No, there isn't," Ash agreed.

"So tell me," Miranda continued breathlessly, "where is this man now?" She opened her mouth, then shut it. "They haven't shot him yet, have they?"

"Oh, no. Not yet," Will Hottel said. "But shoot him they will." He smiled benignly, then added, "After a fair and proper trial."

"Where is he?" she insisted.

"Why, he's right here in Atlanta," John Ballard said.

Miranda took a long, deep breath. "In *Atlanta*!" she said. "Oh, *my*!"

"It's the proper place for his trial," Ballard said.

"Was he the one who burned down the arsenal?" Ash asked.

"That's the one," Ballard agreed. "Killed two soldiers in there, too. Shot them both in the head in cold blood."

"Amazing!" Miranda said. "Will they try him soon?"

"As soon as my son's well enough to testify against him."

"Oh." Miranda asked. "What happened to your son?"

"His leg was broken in four places by one of the locomotives. It was during a storm on Mobile Bay. An amazing thing, in fact."

"How so?"

"Noah was taking Hawken and two locomotives across the bay. From there they'd go on to here, but a big, late season storm blew up, and the ferry started to sink. During all the confusion despite his wounds, my son saved this man Hawken's life. Carried him to shore."

"Kind of a surprising thing for a man with four breaks in his leg to do, don't you think?" Ash observed drolly. "Especially for a man who's such a reprobate." Neither Hottel nor Ballard paid notice to the drollery.

"Noah is a man with strong attachments to his obligations," John Ballard said. "He has the soul of a crusader. He felt it was his holy mission to return the man for trial."

Miranda gave Ash a questioning look, but his only reply was a small negative shake of his head: keep quiet.

"I guess you're right that there's no explaining the human heart," Ash said.

"Now I remember how I met him," Miranda said, as though summoning up with great difficulty a distant fact out of the depths of her memory. "The three of them were friends at the Military Academy—my brother Lam, and Noah and Hawken."

"Well, they sure aren't now," Ballard said with a dismissive shrug. "At least not Hawken and my son. Noah *does* say good things about your brother. Lam actually helped Noah in Mississippi with those locomotives; he gave him some cavalry support."

Miranda nodded. "I didn't know that," she said.

"But Noah just can't forgive Sam Hawken for what he has done to our nation. Taking arms against your own land and people is bad enough, but spying against them is indefensible and unforgivable. And, like I said, Noah has the soul of a crusader."

"An admirable quality," Ash said quietly, after which he turned to Miranda. She saw a new light in his eyes. He was on to something he hadn't been before, and that gave her sudden—though still faint—hope.

She saw warning there, too. Let me keep doing the talking, he was telling her.

Ash turned then to Noah's father. "Say," he said, as though struck by a sudden, vagrant thought, "where is your son these days? In one of the hospitals?"

"Oh, no," John Ballard said. "Not on your life. He's at home now. I'd never have him condemned to one of those charnal houses."

"Smart man," Ash said, nodding his agreement. "And he's doing well there?"

"As well as you can expect for someone who's fractured his leg in four places."

"What I was thinking," Ash said with a sage inclination of his head, "is that he might do better with more company."

"What do you mean?"

"Well, you see," Ash said, "Your son's friend Lam—

my nephew—was hit at Chickamauga, and we have a big house here that we're using and two perfectly lovely and competent nurses who could use more work." He leaned toward Miranda. "My niece and her sister, Ariel, would adore taking care of another handsome and unmarried young man, especially one who doesn't suffer the stigma of being their brother."

John Ballard tipped his head back and laughed hard. "That's quite a fascinating idea," he said, obviously liking what he was hearing. He gave a concerned toss of his head. "Poor Noah has fallen into a melancholy mood I'd very much like to see him out of. All the inactivity of an invalid, I suppose, distresses him. Friends would do him good."

"So then, let's do it," Ash said, beaming. "I'd be proud to have him in my house."

"By all means. Consider it done. Noah would love the companionship, I'm certain of it."

"Tomorrow?" Ash asked.

"Tomorrow," John Ballard agreed. "We'll ship him over in the morning."

"We'll pick him up," Ash said. "Let us do that."

"Fine," John Ballard said, "if you insist."

"Don't you think," Miranda asked, "that we ought to ask Noah first? Not," she added, "that I don't want him to stay with us. I'd adore it. But . . ."

"You're right, my dear," Ash said, laughing. "Some of us have the bad habit of arranging people without consulting them."

"I don't think that's a bad habit," John Ballard said. "Not when we know what's best for them."

"Of course you're right," Ash said, laughing. Then to Miranda, "Come on, my dear, you and I will pay a visit to Major Ballard. Let's see if he's up to a change of venue." Then to Will Hottel, "It was a pleasure, Captain." Ash rose and extended his hand. Hottel rose and grasped it.

"The pleasure is mine," Will Hottel said.

John Ballard was by then on his feet, too. "We'll be seeing you again tomorrow, Mr. Kemble. It has also been *my* very great pleasure to meet you, and I hope to be seeing you at much greater length in the future."

Ash smiled. "By the way," he said, as an afterthought, "just out of curiosity, what's going to become of all those locomotives your son and the captain brought back here?"

"They'll be used for the cause," Ballard answered quickly. "Split up among various rail lines, where they can do the most good."

"I see," Ash said.

"They're much needed here," Captain Hottel added. "We left a few back in Mississippi; it was only just. But the real need in coming months is right here in Georgia. Mississippi . . ." He shrugged, holding his hands away from his body. "That state's lost to us."

"Split up?" Ash asked, curious. "Does that mean that your line will receive some of them?"

"That's right," John Ballard said guilelessly. "I expect we'll receive something in the neighborhood of eighteen or twenty of them."

"That should be a great relief," Ash said.

"Oh, it is."

Ash looked at Miranda, and she bowed slightly to each of the other men and extended her hand.

"It was so nice to see you," she said.

Miranda was able to hold back her tears until she and Ashbel were seated in their carriage and he was driving them to the Ballard house, which was a large double-brick home on the corner of Washington and Mitchell. But when her tears started, they flowed like a river. She cried as she had never cried before; her crying was even more forlorn than it had been when her father died.

"Your Sam is in deep trouble," Ash said, acknowledging her distress. "That's for sure." With the arm that was not holding the reins, he reached over and clasped her, drawing her closer to him. "I'm sorry, darling, though I know that's no comfort."

"It isn't," she agreed.

"But it's all the comfort I have to give you," he said.

"'I know," she choked. "Thank you, Ash. You've been lovely."

Then, releasing the reins for a moment, he took her face in his hands and brought her close to him. "There's one other thing I want you to know," he said. She looked at him through tear-filmed eyes. "It's important. Listen carefully."

"All right," she nodded.

"There's not nearly enough for me to go on yet for you to get your hopes up, or to take any comfort." She nodded. "But the thing is, girl, I think there's a chance to pull your Sam out of this."

"What chance?" she whispered through clenched lips. Her tears, which had partially let up, started to flow copiously again. "Tell me about it, Ash!" she demanded.

"I told you, it's not a clear notion yet. I can just tell you that I'm thinking about it, and that my idea may develop. Take it as a sign of my love for you, girl, and as a sign that I'm working for you. When I'm surer of myself, I'll talk to you about what's on my mind."

"You don't need to hide things from me, Ash. I'm a grown woman."

"It's not you that worries me. It's me. As I said, I'm not sure of myself. When I start getting sure of myself, then I'll tell you what I'm thinking."

"All right," she said doubtfully.

"When we get to Noah Ballard," he added, "let me keep doing the talking. I want to stay off the issue of Sam Hawken for now."

He released her face then, and she sank back into the seat, slumping abjectly, until the carriage reached the Ballard home.

A servant escorted Ash and Miranda Kemble upstairs to Noah Ballard's room. They found Noah lying on his bed, his leg encased in a heavy cast, his back supported by pillows. When they entered the room, they found him staring into half-darkness; there was only one lamp lit, and it was turned down low. He did not look especially pleased to receive a visit by Lam Kemble's sister and uncle.

Before he had left the party at The Terraces, Ash had thought to pack up in a linen napkin a few inviting delicacies for Noah. After he'd introduced himself and Miranda, he opened the napkin and spread the food out on it.

"I don't know if you've seen anything so nice in a while, Major," Ash said. "We've come from the party at The Terraces. I thought you might be hungry for food that doesn't taste of sawdust."

"Thank you," Noah said without much interest.

He was thinner than Miranda remembered him, more gaunt and hard. Of course not many people added on flesh these days, and John Ballard was right about him; he was melancholy and morose. But what surprised her about Noah Ballard was that he had lost none of the boyishness she remembered from the time they'd first met. Some of the flame had faded from his eyes, but the flame was still there.

"We dined with your father," Ash said, "and your friend Will Hottel."

"My friend?" Noah asked with evident distaste.

"So I was led to believe," Ash said, then sailed on after a quick questioning glance at Miranda, which she quickly returned. "And we discussed you and your many courageous exploits. And, realizing that you were all alone tonight, Miranda suggested we pay you a visit."

"In order to cheer me up?" Noah asked.

"You *are* alone," Ash reminded him. "It's not a pleasant way to spend your days and nights."

"It's good enough for me," Noah said, trying, and succeeding, to be rude.

"Well," Ash replied, undaunted, "here we are. And I'm glad to see you."

"Thank you for coming," Noah said. "But I'm terribly tired. Perhaps," he added vaguely, "some other time."

"Not so fast, son," Ash said. "I'm not done with you yet."

Noah looked at him without interest, impatient for Ash to get on with his business.

"You know my nephew, Lam, don't you, Major?"

Noah allowed him a slight assenting tilt of his head.

"Have you heard he was injured?"

"Lam? No. Was he?"

"A shrapnel burst. Did him a lot of damage."

"I'm sorry to hear that."

"He's in town here, recovering."

"I'd visit him," Noah said, "but as you see, I'm pretty much out of action myself." His tone made his words sound like an excuse, but Miranda knew he was telling the truth.

"Your father told me your leg was smashed up in four places," Ash said, giving him some commiseration. "Quite an injury!"

"It'll do until something better comes around."

Ash nodded vacantly, then grew intent. "I came to talk about you and Lam."

What is there to say?"

"Just that tomorrow we're going to move you two together. We've got a house over on Pryor for the time being, and some of the best and most beautiful nurses you could hope to have to minister to you. So tomorrow you're going over there."

"That sounds like an order," he said with resentment in his voice. Miranda could tell, though, that he was interested.

"It is an order."

"What if I'd rather stay here?"

"You wouldn't."

"You can see inside me? You must be quite a perceptive man."

"No, I can see your face and your eyes. That tells me what I need to know. They tell me you could do with some companionship. And that's just what I have a surplus of."

Noah just stared, which was probably a victory, Miranda thought. At least he didn't continue to deny that he wanted to go. And he held off on his petulance, too.

"So," Ash said, rising to his feet, "that's settled. We'll take our leave now. You said you wanted to rest."

"Thanks for coming," Noah said. His voice was not unfriendly now, but it was still distant and uncertain. "And thanks for the food."

"You're quite welcome, Major."

"Noah," he corrected. "Call me that."

"All right," Ash said, "Noah." He offered Miranda a hand. "Come on, my dear, we'll be off."

"Good-bye, Noah," she said, as she came to her feet. "I hope you are more rested tomorrow."

She started for the door, but as she did, she felt a restraining pressure on her hand. "By the way," Ash said to Noah, almost as an afterthought, "your father was saying to me that you had quite an adventure down on Mobile Bay."

"There was a storm," Noah allowed.

"I've been in bay storms. They can be wild and dangerous."

"Yeah," Noah said.

"He told me the ferry you were on sank out from under you after your leg was busted, and that you managed to save the skin of that man—what's his name, Miranda?"

"Hawken."

"That's it, Hawken. Even with your busted leg, you pulled him off and saved his skin so that you could bring him to justice here in Atlanta."

"My father told you that?"

"That's what he told us," Ash said. "And he was damned proud of you when he said it. And he should be."

"That's not what happened."

"Oh?"

"It was the other way around," Noah said. "Sam Hawken saved me. Sam and Jim Sutton, who's an old cavalry sergeant friend of his from Texas."

"Sam! Miranda choked, then sobbed. Her hand, she realized, was still encased in Ash's. She realized it when he tightened his grip on it to keep her from saying anything.

"Is that so?" Ash asked mildly. "I was sure we heard it the other way. Right, Miranda?"

"Yes," she said, her mind churning.

"It happened the way I told you. I was hurt bad, and unconscious, and the two of them pulled me off the boat."

"I wonder why they told us the story that other way," Ash asked innocently. But his mind was churning, too. Miranda could tell from the tension of his hand.

"Well," Ash went on, as elaborately casual as a country lawyer, "that being the case, I wonder about your current opinions of Sam Hawken."

Noah's eyes grew pained, confused. "Why do you ask that?" Then the eyes grew narrow, suspicious.

"Just curious, is all," Ash said. "It's just that your father and Captain Hottel had nothing positive to say about Captain Hawken."

"I'm grateful to him," Noah admitted.

"I recall that you and Lam and him were friends once, way back when."

"We were."

"But that's all changed."

"I don't know."

"It's pretty damned confusing, isn't it?"

"You can't deny that we're enemies."

"You *are* fighting on opposing sides," Ash said.

"And you can't deny the harm that he's done to us." Noah's voice caught.

"I guess you can't."

"But . . ." Noah's voice trailed off into uncertainty.

"But Sam Hawken did save your life, and you're grateful. And you don't know what to make of all the evidence you see with your mind and feel with your senses."

"Yeah," Noah said. "That just about sums it up."

"So what do you think, Noah, is going to happen to Sam Hawken?"

"He's a spy. He'll be tried."

"And shot?"

"Looks like it." Noah said that slowly, in a near whisper.

"But if you had your way. . . ?" Ash asked gently. His hand was like a lock around hers, though. It was almost painful.

"I don't know. I don't know what I'd do," Noah said with a deep sigh. "He didn't just save me. There's another thing."

"Uh-huh."

"After Sam and his sergeant got me to shore, Sam stayed there until the sergeant could bring help back. To make sure I was all right."

"He did?"

"He could have run off. Escaped."

"But he didn't."

"That's right, Mr. Kemble. He stayed with me."

"Your father told me they're going to put Sam Hawken up for trial as soon as you're well enough to testify."

"I guess that's so. I'm the chief witness against him."

"Well," Ash said with easy good humor, "that sure makes a fascinating tale." Then to Miranda, "I told this young man a while ago that we were going to let him rest. And here we are keeping him up with uncomfortable questions. Let's get us gone, my dear."

"No, wait," Noah said. There were questioning furrows on his forehead. "Before you all go, tell me what makes Sam Hawken so fascinating to you."

"Oh, nothing much, Noah. It's just a good yarn, and I'm overendowed with curiosity. Tell him good-bye, Miranda."

"Good-bye, Noah. We'll be seeing you tomorrow."

"Good night, Miranda. Thank you for coming." This time he meant it.

"Oh, yes," Ash said when the two of them reached the door, "there's one more thing."

"All right," Noah said.

"Your father was just sky-high proud of you for bringing back those locomotives. Captain Hottel obviously had a large hand in all that, but I could tell that it was you your father was proudest of."

"Well, I am his son."

"Yes, there is that," Ash said. "And I'm sure that's a big part of it." He paused, took a breath. "But there's also the fact that you've delivered a splendid benefit to the family business."

"Huh?" Noah asked, genuinely baffled by that remark.

"You've probably done the best thing you've ever done for him. You've brought him a big slice of those engines."

"Him?" Now Noah was not only confused, he was disturbed.

"Well, to be accurate, you provided them to the Atlanta and Western Railroad, but it's all the same. The point is he's about to accept about eighteen or twenty of those locomotives you brought here."

Noah didn't say anything. His eyes filmed over, then refilled with cold, intense fury.

While that was going on, Ash looked at Miranda.

*We've hit gold!* his look told her.

After that, she trembled; all that was happening this evening was almost more than she could handle.

Ash's hand found hers again and steadied her.

Then he led her out and quietly shut the door behind him.

On the stairway downstairs she stopped and turned to him. "What was going on in there?" she asked.

"I'm not completely sure," he said. "But I'd be willing to bet that that boy has been betrayed by his father. And we carried him the first news of it."

"Betrayed?" she asked, leaning against the banister. She needed all the support she could find. "How?"

"Maybe about Sam. Certainly about those engines. I don't know how all."

"How did you know to ask him about those things?"

"I didn't. I threw bait on the water and waited to see if I got any bites. I got more than I expected."

"What are we going to do next?"

"Think some more. Get that boy with Lam. It will do both of them a world of good. And tomorrow I'm going to see your man, Sam Hawken."

"You know where they're keeping him?"

"It won't take long to find out."

"What are you going to say to him? What will you ask him?"

"I don't know. I'll play it by ear, the way we've been doing so far."

"And then what?"

"And then I think I might go see Mr. Calhoun, the mayor, and maybe Colonel Wright, the military commander. And maybe after that, Sergeant Sutton—if he's still around."

"I want to go with you to see Sam."

"You can't, baby," Ash said quickly. "That just wouldn't work." He bent down and gave her an affectionate kiss on the forehead.

"I still want to see him."

"You just can't, Miranda," he insisted. "And besides, I've got a more important job for you."

"What's that?" she asked, curious but also reluctant to let go of her need to see Sam.

"It has to do with your brother."

Just then a servant appeared and approached the foot of the stairway. "Can I help you find the doh, Mistah Kemble," he said.

"Why, thank you," Ash said, and he and Miranda walked out to the carriage.

The night was brilliant, starry, and lonely as infinite space.

"What about Lam?" she asked.

"I want you to work on him. I'll tell you how later."

"I probably know how already."

"You probably do," he said. Then, under his breath, "I hope it works out."

## *October 11, 1863*

Captain Sam Hawken was confined in a building just north of Walton Street, where the garrison of the Military Post of Atlanta was headquartered. His cell was larger and more comfortable than the one Noah Ballard had devised for him in Mobile. He was given better food, better bedding, a pen and paper, a Bible, and a lamp to read and write by.

As in Mobile, the authorities forbade him visitors. As in Mobile, this rule was not enforced.

Sam's first visitor was his sergeant friend, Jim Sutton.

Sutton was currently assigned to the fortifications around the city. He was in charge of half a dozen work crews.

"I can't stay long, Sam," Sutton said. "I just wanted to look in on you to see how you were. And to see if there was anything I could do for you."

"It's hard to think of anything you can do for me, Jim," Sam said. "Or at least anything they'd let you. But I'm looking all right—at least for a man who's got nothing better to do than to read the Bible. It's a weight on a person reading that. It sets your mind too much on the afterlife."

"Thinking about the afterlife doesn't yield much pleasure," Jim agreed wryly.

"Oh, I'd be willing enough to give the afterlife a try," Sam said, "after I've exhausted all the other possibilities...."

"Maybe I could find you something else to read," Sutton offered.

"I'd appreciate that."

Sutton grinned. "Myself, I'd rather read a pretty girl," he said.

"You and me both," Sam said with a rueful shake of his head. "There's one in particular..."

"I sort of sensed something like that."

"She's a good one."

"You wouldn't take less than the best, Sam Hawken,"

Sutton said. "Where'd you find her?" he continued. "Up north?"

"No, as a matter of fact, she's living not far from here." His face grew suddenly animated. "And there *is* something you can do for me, Jim."

"You want to get a message to her?"

"That's it! Her name's Miranda Kemble, and she lives at a place called Raven's Wing. It's about thirty miles northeast of here."

"Write something, and I'll make sure she gets it. I'll come back for it this evening, if I can. Then you can tell me all about her."

"Thanks, Jim," Sam said. "And I will."

"I've got to be goin' now."

"Sure," Sam said, rising to shake Sutton's hand. "But before you go," he said, as their hands both clasped, "tell me. Is there any word on Tom Stetson? Was he drowned in the storm? Did they catch him?"

"There's no word, Sam. Nothing."

"Damn!" Sam said. "What about you? Are you all right? My old friend Major Ballard looked like he was planning to throw the book at you for insubordination and all kinds of terrible shit."

"He decided to forget all that, it looks like, after his life got saved."

"That's good. He can be a horse's ass sometimes."

"Most of the time," Sutton said. "You'd think he'd be grateful to you for being alive, and consider returning the favor."

"There's nothing he could do even if he wanted to," Sam said.

Sutton shook his head. "I'm not so sure," he said, moving to the cell door. "Well, I've got to go."

"I'll see you, Jim."

"Yeah."

Then he gave a holler for the guard and was let out.

Sam's second visitor was Jane Featherstone.

When she appeared at the cell door, he laughed. "Well,

congratulations, Jane. I knew you would make it. It would take more than a storm and a sinking boat to snuff out Miss Jane Featherstone.''

"Try to be civil this once, Sam," she said. "I haven't much time. I have to catch a train."

"Be my guest," he said civilly. "How's Noah?"

"I haven't seen Noah. And I won't see him."

"What did you do to him that made him see the light?"

"Sam, goddamn you!"

"My apologies, Jane. My mouth runs away from me sometimes. I have a will to prevaricate, but somehow or other the truth gets blurted out."

"I'm going to ignore your taunts and your mocking, Sam," she said. "I'll never get out of here if I don't."

"Please continue."

"What I've come to tell you, Sam," she said, pressing on, "is that I'm going to California."

"That *is* good news—and smart, Jane. Traveling away from this place is a brilliant move. There's danger you'll be recognized here. And if they do, I imagine they can find one more cell. It only has to be a small one."

"I'm not going to try to keep on with Noah," she said, continuing to ignore his sarcastic comments. "I'm not good for him."

He started clapping. "Good for you."

"But you could have come with me," she said seriously.

"Unfortunately, I'm already engaged."

"I can't do anything here. I could have gotten you out of Mobile, though. You knew that. And we could have been halfway to San Francisco by now. I have money there, and you could have turned it into much more."

"The dream is staggering, isn't it?"

"Why didn't you come with me when you had the chance, Sam?"

"The truth is, Jane, that all the other alternatives looked more inviting."

"You can't be serious."

"I guess I am."

"Well, then, I'm sorry, Sam." She rose to leave. "Good-bye again. It's a shame..."

"You know something, Jane? I have a dread suspicion that we'll keep on running into one another, even after I leave Atlanta."

"I'm not going where you're going."

He shrugged.

Sam Hawken's third visitor was Ashbel Kemble.

"You're not someone I expected to see in a cell in Atlanta, Mr. Kemble," Sam told Ash after introductions were taken care of. "But it's a pleasure to see a friendly face, that's for sure."

"I'll only stay a few seconds now, Captain," Ash said. "I hope to be able to spend much more time with you later."

Sam looked up at Ash sharply at the remark, but he didn't attempt a response.

"But we have a few, quick matters of business to take care of now."

"You didn't come...?" Sam stopped himself. He was about to say "from Miranda," but he realized that she may not have told this man about him, that she may not have wanted to admit to her connection with a spy who was close to being executed.

"You were about to ask if Miranda sent me?" Ash said with a broad, warm smile. Sam liked this man.

Sam nodded, just a little sheepishly.

"She's told me all about you," Ash went on. "And in so doing, she has given me considerable reason to think well of you, and to wish to see the two of you together in a more lasting way. And yes, she's most of the reason why I'm here. And yes, she sends you her love. And yes, I had to fight her off in order to keep her from coming with me. It simply wouldn't do to bring her—though I know how much you both want to be with one another." He smiled again. "Is that good enough, son? Is that what you want to hear?"

"It'll do until something better comes," Sam said. "You'll tell her that I miss her. And that..."

"I know what you'll want to say to her, and you can be sure I'll give her the message. Meanwhile I told you I have business with you."

"I'm not sure there's any business I'm in a position to transact."

"You leave that to me to decide, son."

"All right," Sam said with an amazed shake of his head.

"But you have managed to put your finger on the heart of the problem we have to face," Ash said wryly. "Your reputation in these parts right now could hardly be lower, and your prospects are pretty dismal, too. However, I think there's a chance we can do something about that. And without," he added when he saw the look Sam was giving him, "having to bring in a Federal army corps to break you loose."

"I can't say I'm not eager to hear what you have in mind," Sam said, unable to contain his smile.

"All in due time," Ash said. "All in due time. The first thing we have to do, though, is make sure that there's no trial any time soon. Once the trial has happened," he shrugged, "well, that's it."

"I'd prefer not to go through that trial."

"So what do you think about Noah Ballard?" Ash asked, abruptly changing the subject. "Do you think he will testify for you or against you?"

"I think Noah Ballard will try to tell things the way they appeared to him. He won't lie."

"So part of him is going to say that you did all those bad things they say you did, and part of him is going to want to say that you saved his life."

"I imagine that's the way he'd like to testify."

"He *will* testify that way," Ash said, "unless he decides to forget some of the bad things."

"The truth is, Mr. Kemble, that most of the things they say I've done, I did do. Whether or not what I've done is bad or not is the point at issue. And that depends on where you stand geographically."

"You should have been a Jesuit, son, and not a soldier."

"Then I wouldn't have been able to court your niece."

"Not officially, no," he laughed. "But consider this, Captain. Last night I sought and obtained the permission of Noah Ballard's father to bring him over to stay with my nephew, Lam."

"Noah is all right, then? I haven't heard."

"He's all right—except that he'll probably go through the rest of his life with a gimp leg and a rolling walk. It's Lam that just missed the big one. But he's apparently going to be fine, too."

"I'm glad of that."

"So, like I said, I brought the two boys together. I thought they'd both recover easier together than all alone. And I had other ideas, too."

"I'm beginning to see that."

"But before I did that, I went to see Noah last night, and I took Miranda with me. I learned some things then that I hardly expected to learn." He looked at Sam. "Are you familiar with the story of how and why Noah brought his locomotives to Atlanta?"

"I know he wanted to do it badly. And I know how desperately his people need them. It's why I was sent to stop them."

"Right. Well, one small addition to that: Noah was given the impression by Captain Hottel that the locomotives would be kept together and placed into a kind of Confederate military railway corporation. You've got something like that in the North. They can take what rolling stock and equipment they need—expropriate it—and use it for as long as they need it.

"He thought they were going to get that kind of thing here." Ash paused for a long breath. "But he was lied to. The locomotives are going to be divided up among various rail lines in Georgia and Alabama. His own father looks to be getting something like twenty in the deal."

"How did you find out all this?"

"Part of it came out last night, and the rest of it came out this morning. We sent a carriage over to pick Noah up.

What we found out when we got there was that Noah and his father had fought all night. One of them would probably have killed the other if Noah had been able to walk.''

"Yeah," Sam said. "I know Noah."

"What came out of it is that Noah and his father aren't likely to be friendly for the rest of their lifetimes. And the other thing is that Captain Hottel was paid twenty-five thousand dollars in gold to oversee transferring the engines to Atlanta."

"Jesus!" Sam said.

"And both Hottel and John Ballard knew that Noah was the best person on the scene in Mississippi to bring the locomotives through."

"But they didn't tell him the real reason he was doing it?"

"John Ballard couldn't trust Noah *not* to be virtuous."

"It's a hell of a thing," Sam laughed, "when a father can't trust his own son to be bad. Noah just resists being bad. When Noah Ballard joins a crusade, there's no turning him."

"That's just what John Ballard said."

"Well, he should know," Sam said.

"The point about all this, son," Ash said, moving on, "is that your old friend Noah Ballard is a very confused young man. His whole world has been thrown into violent and, I suspect, terrifying disorder. If things don't look totally topsy-turvy to him right now, I'll be very˙ much surprised. And my guess is that even as we talk, he's lying in his bed asking himself hard questions about what makes him tick—about loyalty, and trust, and betrayal. And what will happen next is that he's going to have to reassess a lot of things.

"And you're going to be one of the chief things he's going to reevaluate—not that you're going to suddenly become an exemplar of virtue and right thinking—don't get me wrong about that. But you are just not going to look as bad as you once did.

"And that means he will probably be persuaded to speak

up on your behalf—at least to the extent of disposing the people in charge to delay your trial.''

"I won't dispute that delay," Sam said. "But what good will it do me?"

"That you'll have to leave to me, son," Ash replied. "But believe me, a lot can be changed in two weeks—if we can put together a two-week delay."

"Well, I'm at your service," Sam said with a smile, beginning to think that he liked this man very much.

"There's one thing you can do for me," Ash said. "You can tell me about your sergeant friend Jim Sutton."

"What do you need to know?"

"Can I trust him? Will he help me if I ask him?"

"Depends, I guess, on what you want him to do. But he's a good man. You can believe him if he says he'll help you."

"You know where to find him?"

Sam told him.

"I'll be in touch with you, Sam," Ash said.


For the rest of the day Ashbel Kemble held delicate and very unofficial talks with the great powers of Atlanta—with James Calhoun, Colonel Marcus Wright, the Reverend Charles Todd Quintard, a doctor by the name of Meade, who was in charge of the hospitals, and one or two others. Despite the many tactical difficulties involved, the talks moved satisfactorily. He felt by the end of the day that he was making good initial progress.

While Ash was occupied, Miranda had at some length bared her soul to her brother. For the first time she opened up to him about her love for Sam Hawken.

When she first began to bare her soul before him, she expected a battle to follow. And she was prepared to be bruised in the fighting, for she was convinced Lam would be nearly impossible to win over. How could a passionate and convinced son of the South like Lam ever approve of her Yankee spy lover?

But the battle she expected failed to occur. She had not reckoned on Lam's love for her—or on Lam's own good sense and hard-earned experience. It turned out that Lam did not hate Sam Hawken. He even doubted that Sam had actually committed crimes against the South.

To Lam, Sam's original choice of loyalties was questionable, but his acts following from that were not. Indeed, Sam's spying and his destruction of property were the equivalent of the kind of long-range cavalry raids that he himself had taken part in, and for which he had been decorated.

And besides, for Lam his family came before his country. As long as Miranda wanted to unite herself with a gentleman, then he would do everything in his power to help her.

Thus Lam proved to be anything but an obstacle to Miranda. It was almost disarmingly easy for Miranda to enlist him in the campaign to handle the problem of Noah Ballard.

Uncle Ash made a brief, rushed appearance at suppertime. He ate a hasty meal with Miranda, Ariel, Robbie, and Fanny Shaw. Much to Fanny's chagrin, the meal had all the leisure and grace of a rest stop at a station during a rail trip. After supper, Ash led Miranda up to Lam's bedroom, and the three of them held a fast strategy session.

During the session he declined either to tell them anything at all concerning the talks he'd held all day, or to answer any of Miranda's or Lam's insistent questions about them.

"Privacy is the first requisite of diplomacy," he explained. Neither accepted his explanation, and neither succeeded in prying anything out of him.

The one piece of news he allowed them was the hopeful and disturbing fact that Noah Ballard was the crucial link in the effort to save Sam Hawken's life. Ash needed two weeks, he told them, to activate the plan he believed could save Sam. The great powers of Atlanta were willing to give him his two weeks—provided they could put forward a plausible excuse to do it.

That meant the trial had to be delayed, and that meant

that the key witness must be persuaded to offer some mitigating reasons to delay it. The great powers had agreed to accept the reasons, Ash explained, but Noah had to come up with them.

"So how are we going to deal with him?" Lam asked. "Noah is not well disposed to help Sam Hawken."

"No," Ash admitted, "and in his current frame of mind, I don't expect he's going to move easily off the position he's occupying."

"I think we're just going to have to do the best we can with the cards we've been dealt," Lam said. "We'll sit with him this evening, and we'll chat about old times together, and we'll play the difficult part by ear."

"I'm going to leave you young people to yourselves," Ash said. "That's the best way to handle things. You aren't going to want an old man spoiling your fun, and innocent pleasure," he grinned. "But I will add something special to the mix. I have a quantity of very old, private-reserve, single-malt whiskey that I picked up sometime ago in Aberdeen. I'll decant enough of it to lubricate the affair."

"You know what I think?" Miranda said quietly, almost timidly. "I think we're going to have to tell the truth."

The four of them—Miranda, Ariel, Lam, and Noah—gathered that evening on the second-floor gallery of the house on Pryor Street. The gallery was just off the rooms that Lam, and now Noah, as well, used for sleeping, so it was a hardship for neither man to hobble out to it. Chaise longues had been set up for them, and rocking chairs for the women. A crystal decanter and four glasses had been placed on a small table. The decanter contained Ashbel Kemble's single malt whiskey. There was also a lamp, more for comfort than illumination.

A light, misty rain was falling, and it was cool.

But it was not so cool as to drive the young people inside. Light shawls on the women's shoulders took care of their comfort, and Ariel draped woolen throws across the legs of the boys.

Miranda decided to pass up her rocking chair. Instead she placed herself next to a column on the porch railing, which was wide enough for her. Ariel moved her own chair very close to Noah's chaise, for she spent the greater part of her energies that day devoting herself to him. The effect of her devotion had been to drive out the worst of the demons that had encamped in him after his battle with his father.

Miranda noted with interest Ariel's position beside Noah, and she noted with even greater interest Ariel's evident dedication to caring for him. Her concern obviously went beyond mere nursing.

Ariel had not been brought into the conversations between Miranda, Lam, and Ashbel. The three feared that her grief over the loss of Ben would color her judgment. But when Miranda became aware of Ariel sitting next to Noah, with all her concern directed so sweetly toward him, she began to wonder if the three conspirators wouldn't have served their cause better by telling Ariel the truth—just as they planned to reveal it to Noah.

Well, Miranda thought, she's going to hear the truth soon enough. If all goes as I hope it will. . . .

Meanwhile she continued to be astonished at Lam's remarkable recovery. He was by no means out of danger yet, but the sheer fact that he'd been able to make his way under his own steam from bed to gallery was an exciting development. Did the energy he was putting into the plot to save Sam also have a beneficial effect on his own recovery? she wondered.

The whiskey relaxed Noah and Lam, as Ash had designed it to, and it lubricated their conversation—not that either of them required help from chemical intoxicants to talk rivers of words to one another. But each of them had come through difficult times. The single malt was calming, with a taste that was deliciously smoky.

The talk in the gallery that evening started out light and airy, yet they were also warm and affectionate to one another. By common and mutual, though silent, consent none of them brought up any of the matters that gnawed at their hearts. It was enough that all four of them were together. Their warm communion was sufficient reason for rejoicing.

Even Noah Ballard managed to talk and smile with relative ease. And that meant that no one had cause to worry about him. He wasn't his old, whole self, but he wasn't sullen and miserable and full of self-contempt, either.

When Ash and Lam agreed with Miranda on a course of truth-telling with Noah, the three of them fully expected that Miranda and Lam would be able to choose the best moment to act on the course they'd chosen.

So it came as a surprise to both of them when Noah forced matters before either of them could do it.

"You all are holding back something from me," he said out of the blue in a soft but firmly insistent voice. "What are you holding back?"

"I'm sure I don't know what you mean," Ariel said quickly and truthfully, since she had not been privy to the private conversations.

At the same time Ariel was no fool, and she had already made some guesses about what was going on, some guesses that proved to be in the main accurate.

So when she saw the flash of consternation on her sister's and brother's faces after Noah dropped his bombshell, she decided she would do the only right thing—she would give them time.

"I'm not hiding anything from you, Noah. And I can't imagine that Miranda or Lam would, either."

"I believe you're innocent, Ariel," Noah said. "Truly I do. But I've been used by so many people over the past months that I've grown cautious. Before they hauled me over those rocky places, I'd given my respect to the people that did the hauling. And one or two of them were even family.

"So tell me, Lam," he said, staring hard at his friend, "what are you keeping from me? And," his voice dropped an octave, "how are you trying to use me?"

There was a long, nervous silence, which Miranda was the one to finally break.

"Tell him, Lam," she said. "Tell him the truth."

"I need some more whiskey," Lam said. "A good deal more. Would you pour it, Ariel? I'd much appreciate that." Ariel rose to comply, "And you better give Noah a large splash as well."

"I'm doing fine," Noah said with a negative shake of his head.

"All right," Ariel said, tilting the decanter over Lam's glass.

"You better take some for yourself, too, Ariel, and give some to Miranda."

"We both told you we don't want any whiskey," Ariel said.

"You've had enough time, Lam," Noah said. "Why don't you tell me the truth, the way Miranda said?"

Lam drank close to three of his four fingers of scotch whiskey, then said, "Well, it's like this, Noah." He stopped, drew in a deep breath, and continued, "My sister Miranda ran into Sam Hawken in Atlanta last month. They'd met and liked one another when the three of us graduated from the Academy, and they wrote a few letters back and forth after that, but the war came, and they lost touch.

"Anyway, last month Sam was on his way out of town, and she saw him and offered to help."

"Stop," Noah said. "Wait." He turned to Miranda. "You knew he was a Federal spy when you took him in?"

"Yes," she said softly.

"You knew you were helping an enemy of your country?"

"This is not my country, Noah. I just live here. The United States is my country."

"You own land here," Noah announced quietly, without apparent rancor. "You were born here."

"All the same . . ." she said. "I didn't take Sam in *because* he was a Federal spy. I took him in because he was *Sam* and he was—is—my friend."

"He's more than a friend, isn't he?" Noah asked, still thoughtful.

"Yes, Noah," she whispered. "Much more."

"God!" Noah sighed, shaking his head slowly.

"I can't say I'm sorry," she said.

"I won't ask you to say that, Miranda. It's just that ... goddamn! He's a goddamned Union *spy*!"

"He's also a friend, Noah, and he did save your life."

"I know that. I won't forget it. And," he muttered bitterly, "nobody else I know will let me forget it."

"We want to save him," Lam announced cautiously. "That's the other thing we've waited to tell you."

Noah gave him a short nod. "I thought so; that makes sense." He smiled sadly. "You know something, all of you? I was ready to pin on that man every piece of hatred and rage I'd saved up for the entire North—and I have not a few pieces of hatred saved up. His being a friend is probably what made it so easy to blame him, to make him the chief symbol of all that I despise.

"And he's not innocent, either—not by a long shot. Just for one instance: on the night of the fourteenth of July, a train carrying hundreds of women and children and old people collided head-on with a locomotive going at full throttle. Sam was the one who set the locomotive running toward that train."

"I know about that," Miranda said.

"He told you about it?" Noah asked.

"He told me," she said. "He also told me that he never knew there were women and children on that train."

"And you believe him?" Noah asked, still soft voiced, without visible anger or hostility.

"I do, Noah. How could he have been aware of what any of those trains were carrying? He didn't make the schedules. He's not God. He's not omniscient. He was just doing what he was sent to do."

"But that's just it. That's what bothers me most of all about Sam, or at least that's what bothers me now. No gentleman, in fact no man who professes to be civilized, would allow himself to be sent on the missions Sam Hawken went on. It wasn't just that he wasn't forced to commit the crime of espionage, Sam put all of his energy and intelligence to the task of doing it well. He has more of both than most men, and the job that bastard did was superb—but goddamn!''

"You're right," Lam said. "I agree with everything you've said, except for one thing. Sam Hawken has done nothing that I can see that is criminal. He's done what every soldier does—unless his crime consists in doing it on the other side of his enemy's battle lines. Is it the line that makes the criminal, Noah? Is it all right to smash up a train on the line, but not across it?

"Would a southern gentleman be justified in taking a shot at President Abraham Lincoln across the battle lines?'' He looked at Noah, then answered his own question. "Of course,'' he said with certainty. "Would the same gentleman be justified in putting the same bullet into the same gentleman on a street in Washington?''

"I can't answer that,'' Noah said, staring off into the light misting rain. He looked empty, depleted.

"I can't either,'' Lam replied. "And if we asked Sam, I bet he couldn't answer it any more than the two of us.''

"But there are rules of war, laws, conventions to follow,'' Noah insisted. "And there has to be, or else we are all barbarians. Sam broke the laws of war, and he knew he was breaking them.''

Lam fell silent, then turned and locked his one good eye on Noah's. "And your own father . . . ?'' he asked. "What rules has he kept sacred?''

"He wasn't . . .'' Noah stammered. He finally managed to say, "He's not the same as Sam. They're different. It's not fair to speak of them in the same breath.''

"That's exactly what I'm trying to get through to you. Sam may or may not have failed to observe the laws you hold so dear. But he never betrayed you, Noah.''

"I've thought about that all day,'' Noah sighed.

"Tell me, Noah,'' Lam said very slowly, very softly, "what are you going to do about your father?''

"Do about him?'' Noah said, his voice a controlled sob. "Now? Nothing. Later? I don't know. He and Will Hottel have won for now. There's not a goddamned thing I can do to change that. The thing's done, and I'm a goddamned fool to have let Will Hottel have his way with me." Then he added bitterly, "To have let both Will Hottel *and* my father have their way with me. I believed Will Hottel when he told me he had secret orders from James Seddon to do with those engines exactly what I wanted done with them. He had secret orders all right, but from my father."

"I think you're right," Lam agreed. "It looks like the two of them have got you where they want you, and there's not much you can do about it." Lam caught Miranda's eye and gave her a compelling, confident wink. "I guess what's left for you to do is slink back to Mississippi once your leg heals, and bury yourself in your work."

Noah did not, could not respond to that. Finally he looked at Ariel. "You better pour me some more of that whiskey," he said.

"Your father's been passing it around that you saved Sam's life in the storm."

"That's the story my father's giving," Noah agreed.

"What do you think he's doing that for?" Lam asked cautiously.

"I don't know," Noah answered, confused and uncertain. "I guess it makes him look good when I look good."

"Yes," Lam replied, "it does. But it also gives you something to be in complicity with him about, doesn't it?"

"What do you mean?" Noah asked softly.

"It means that if you go along with that lie, you put yourself—partly at least—on his side."

Noah gave a nod. "Yes, I guess that's right."

Lam didn't add to what he had already said. Ariel sat on the edge of her chair, having returned there after filling Noah's glass. And Miranda sat on her rail, her hands gripping it; they were white with tension.

"What do you want me to do, all of you?" Noah asked, looking at each of the Kembles in turn, his eyes lingering longest on Ariel.

Ariel was the first to respond to him. "How about telling the truth?"

"What do you mean?"

"Here is the thing, Noah. I wasn't in on the talking Lam

and Miranda were doing all afternoon. And I wasn't in on any of the conversation the two of them had with Uncle Ash, either. So in a lot of ways I'm as much in the dark as you are about what they're up to. What I know—and believe—is just what you've heard this evening. I think you've heard the truth—or at least as much of it as they know. I trust my brother and my sister, and I trust my uncle, too. And I think you ought to do the same. There's more reason to trust them than there is to trust most of the other people we've talked about this evening.''

Miranda felt at that moment more grateful to her sister than she had ever felt before.

''So what should I do?'' Noah asked.

''Do as she said,'' Lam answered. ''Tell the truth about Sam. Do it so you won't be in complicity with your father. Do it knowing it's not a big victory against your father—but it's a victory for you.

''We need you to help us delay the trial. Ash thinks he has a way to save Sam, but he needs a couple of weeks to carry it off. If we can delay the trial, Ash will have time to put through his plan.''

''And me?'' Noah asked.

''You write a deposition in which you state the truth about Sam's saving your life, together with a few other mitigating circumstances in Sam's favor that you and we can probably come up with. Such a deposition, coming from you, ought to give us our two weeks.''

''Why does it have to come from me?'' Noah asked.

''You're the chief witness against Sam, aren't you? Don't you think the people who are about to stand in judgment of him will listen to you?''

''The case doesn't depend on me,'' Noah said. ''There's already plenty of evidence to justify executing him.''

''The case doesn't depend on you, that's right,'' Lam said firmly. ''But the delay does.'' He lifted himself up as much as his wounds would allow, and leaned toward Noah, bringing himself as close to his friend as he could. ''Well, Noah?''

Noah closed his eyes and then covered them with his palms. He remained that way for several minutes.

"Yes," he said finally, his voice a whisper. "I'll do it tomorrow."

Lam sank back into his cushions. "Good man!" he managed to say.

"Oh, Noah!" Miranda said, as tears formed in her eyes.

A moment later she realized that someone was standing beside her, and an arm had grasped her about the shoulders. She looked, and it was Ariel.

"I'm glad for you," Ariel said.

"I'm sorry Lam and I kept you in the dark," Miranda said, "about all this. But we thought that you . . . because of Ben . . ." She stopped, her words failing her.

"I understand," Ariel said. "Don't worry."

There was a silence, and then Noah said, "I'm glad you told me this, Lam. In fact, it's because of all of you, I think, that I'm going to do this thing for Sam. If it were just Sam and not you, I don't think I'd do it."

Later that evening Uncle Ash met with Lam, Miranda, and Ariel. They told him how the meeting with Noah had gone, and he told them he was as satisfied with the outcome as they were.

"You've all done wonderfully," he said. "But that comes as no surprise," he added generously.

"Thank you, Uncle," Lam said.

"Now I want all of you out of here," Ash continued, astonishing them.

"Out of Atlanta?" Miranda cried.

"That's right," Ash said firmly. "Tomorrow. It's important. I want you all in Raven's Wing. Even your friend Noah. And your mother, of course."

"But . . ." Lam said.

"I have to stay with Sam!" Miranda cried.

"No, you don't," Ash said. "We'll take care of Sam, don't you worry. But all the Kembles, meanwhile, have to be out of town, off of people's minds. I don't want tongues wagging.

"You can travel, can't you, Lam? You're well enough for that," Ash questioned.

"I can travel," Lam allowed.

"Then that's it."

And so it was. They all boarded carriages as soon as Ash had read and approved Noah's deposition on Sam's behalf.

## Raven's Wing
## October 30, 1863

By the time the little caravan reached Raven's Wing, even Fanny Shaw had been fully brought into the secrets that had made the move necessary.

She had by then pretty much sniffed out the nature of the mystery; yet when it was at last revealed to her, she hit the roof. She was, in her words, "terribly hurt and miffed that not one of my children trusts me." With her actress's sense of timing, she knew enough to keep her anger to herself until the proper moment to indulge it.

When the moment came, her fury was withering.

The children of the great actress, however, did not seem to be as devastated by her rage as she intended. She found it hard to believe that they knew her too well to be affected by the demonstrations of her greatness.

The two weeks of anxious waiting passed, and still there was no word from Ash about the disposition of Sam Hawken.

Fanny Shaw turned out to be a great comfort and solace to Miranda during those two terrible weeks. She did not give her daughter a performance, but her own genuine caring and concerned heart; Miranda saw that and appreciated it.

Miranda also kept herself going with the help of the nearly boundless support her brother and sister gave her, and with the help of Noah Ballard. The communion the four of them had joined in during that misty, rainy night two weeks before on the gallery grew more solid at Raven's Wing.

But the communion didn't start then, Miranda realized; it started years earlier at West Point, New York, on a June day during graduation time. On that June day she had glimpsed bright, radiant possibilities for that glowing company.

The war had seemed to crush all chance that those possibilities could be fulfilled.

But now . . . well, who could know? Here four of them were together, wounded, stripped of their sails, but afloat. And somehow they'd managed to reunite themselves into something resembling the company that had shined so irresistibly seven years before.

But the fifth . . . ?

The first hint that a resolution to Miranda's anxieties was nearing came from a totally unexpected source. On the morning of Friday, the thirtieth of October, the Reverend Charles Todd Quintard arrived by horseback from Atlanta. The Reverend Quintard was paunchy and florid faced, but he was tall enough to cut an impressive figure. And though he was an Episcopal priest, his manner was austere and fearsome enough to frighten small children.

Robbie Edge, who was playing outside when Quintard arrived, was duly terrified when the reverend descended from his horse and made as though to approach him. Robbie fled into the house screaming and calling his mother.

Robbie's mother gathered him up and gave him comfort while Miranda Kemble walked out to see about the apparition that had so filled her nephew with dread.

She was acquainted with Reverend Quintard, but only in a passing way. She had not felt eager to prolong her previous meetings with him. As it happened, though, he turned out to be more uncomfortable introducing himself than she was in receiving him.

"I've come here to Raven's Wing at the urgent request of your uncle Ashbel Kemble," he told her, implying that he would not have traveled to Raven's Wing on his own account. "He believes that you will have need of a clergyman out here very shortly, and he felt that I'd be the best man to perform the necessary services under the circumstances. He's a most persuasive man, your uncle. I saddled my horse the instant he asked me to ride out."

"Services?" Miranda managed. "What kind of services?" The services that flashed into her mind were the services for the dead.

Reverend Quintard was disinclined to explain himself further.

"Your uncle wrote a message for you, Miss Kemble," Quintard said, plucking a sealed envelope out of an inside pocket of his long, black frock coat. He handed the envelope to her, and she tore it open.

The note read:

> My Dearest Miranda,
>    Please be so kind as to take in this gentleman for a while—it may be only a few hours, or as long as a day—until I can come to see you myself.
>    He's a good man underneath his dark, gaunt, lonely exterior and his sometimes rabid enthusiasms. Be kind to him.
>    I'm sure your kindness will be repaid. You're going to need this man very soon.
> > As ever, your loving Uncle,
> > Ashbel

The note from Ash did nothing to calm Miranda's fears. But she did as she was told. After she read the note, she led Reverend Quintard into the house, gave him a meal, and showed him to a spare room. During all this, he was silent about the nature of his visit.

Two hours later Sergeant James Sutton made his appearance—another complete surprise to those residing at Raven's Wing.

Sutton also arrived on horseback, and Robbie was again playing outdoors. To Robbie this visitor was as much a stranger as the reverend had been, but this man failed to frighten him—though Sergeant Sutton was much more grizzled, scruffy, and raffish looking than the well-tailored, well-barbered, and well-shaved minister of God. Robbie led him graciously by the hand to Miranda and introduced him to her.

Miranda had by then heard something of Jimmy Sutton from Noah, but she had never met him. He, too, handed her a message from Ash. It came without an envelope this time, and it was even shorter than the minister's:

> Miranda—
> You're going to have to put Jim Sutton up, too. You'll like him. And besides, he's a hero.
>                                   Ash

"I don't know why I'm here, either," Sutton said to her after she'd had a chance to glance at the note. "Ash Kemble sent me a message to come here, and here I am." He produced another piece of paper and showed it to her. "I'm even legal," he said. The paper was a three-day leave, and it was granted by Colonel Marcus Wright.

"Well, you're most welcome here," she said.

But beneath her gracious behavior she was upset and baffled. Why Sutton? she kept asking herself. And why the Reverend Charles Todd Quintard? Why here?

No other sudden and unexpected arrival rode in to Raven's Wing that day. Sutton proved to be a hit with all the residents of the plantation. Quintard kept to himself. He was hostile and resentful but polite.

Miranda went to bed early that night, but her sleep was fitful and troubled.

She woke once, hearing what might have been hoofbeats. She listened intently. The sound was gone.

She then tried unsuccessfully to untangle the hopelessly knotted bedclothes. After she gave up on that, she returned to her fitful sleep, sprawled on her back with her arms flung over her head.

She was on her back that way when she felt Sam's kiss on her mouth. It was full and deep and long. At first, of course, she didn't realize it was Sam kissing her—or even that she was being kissed. But she started to respond even before she was fully awake.

And then she gave a full-throated cry, "Sam!" for she knew then that it was indeed he.

"Sam!" she cried again. Then she launched herself into his arms, pressing herself against him fiercely as in a physical attack. It was an attack Sam was prepared to endure.

"Hi there, darlin'," he spoke softly in her ear. "It looks like you're glad to see me."

"Glad!" was all she could say.

"It's good to see you, too, darling," he said. "Truly!"

"I thought I would never . . ."

"I thought you would never, either," he said with a faint smile.

They continued that way, holding one another, telling each other the words of love and concern until another voice interrupted them.

"All right," Uncle Ash said; he'd been watching their reunion from the shadows. "Enough! Up, both of you. Out of bed, and dress properly! We don't have much time."

"Uncle Ash," Miranda managed. "I didn't know you were here!"

"I'm sure you didn't," he said. "But quick! Up with you. There's little time. You're going to have to travel."

"Wait, wait," she said. "I'm not . . ." She fell silent, then slowly flailed about on the bed, searching for something. Somehow she managed to lay her hands on her robe and slipped it over her gown.

"It's all right, darling," Sam whispered in her ear, at the same time gathering her again in his arms. "It's all right, truly." Then he turned to Ash. "Explain to her."

"We only have an hour or two," Ash insisted, his voice full of urgency. "At most we have until dawn, and then we have to get you moving."

"What's happening? What are you doing? Where am I going?" Miranda asked, still confused.

"It's all right, darlin," Sam said. "We'll clear all this up in a minute."

Ash lit a lamp, then pulled up a chair, took out a cigar, and lit it from the lamp. "You do it," he said to Sam. "But hurry. You've got three minutes. And then she has to get herself dressed and packed and into the parlor. They'll be waiting for her."

"Dressed? Packed? Parlor?" Miranda said, wide-eyed, swinging her startled gaze back and forth between Sam and Ash.

"All right," Sam said, rubbing his head as though he wasn't sure where to begin. But then she realized that wasn't the real reason he was doing it. His real reason was that he was nervous. She soon found out why. "You know, Miranda, I never thought I'd say this to a woman in her own bed, but here goes." He put his hands on her shoulders. "You know I love you, don't you?"

"Of course I know that," she said.

"I'd like you to marry me, too. Do you want that?"

"Of course I want to marry you," she said. "I want that very much." Her eyes misted over, and she might have trembled, but his hands on her shoulders steadied her.

"Will you do it tonight, darlin'?"

"Tonight!"

"Right. We have to do it now or else we have to wait for the end of the war."

"Tonight? How?" she asked.

"I commandeered the Reverend Quintard yesterday for that purpose," Ash said, interrupting. "The Reverend Charles Todd Quintard is the most ferociously ardent and single-minded advocate of slavery and secession you're likely ever to run into in a reverend. He was most unhappy at the prospect of officiating at the wedding of a soon-to-escape Yankee spy. But I still had a few chips to cash in here in Atlanta, and I cashed them, and he agreed to do it. He's a real reverend. He'll do the job the way it should be done."

"And besides," Sam muttered under his breath to Ash, "you thought it would serve him right to marry Miranda and me."

"That thought did pass across my mind," Ash admitted with a sly, wicked smile.

"What chips?" Miranda asked. "What did he know about a soon-to-escape spy? How did he know about that?"

"All in due time," Ash said. "You'll have it all explained. But not now."

Sam took her hand in his. "You haven't said yes yet," he said.

"Yes," she said.

"Then get dressed,"Ash ordered. "And get packed."

"Wait," she said.

"What now?" Ash asked impatiently.

"I still want to know what happened," Miranda demanded. "You haven't told me that. How did Sam escape?"

"You can learn all about that on the road," Ash said. "Come on, girl, move!"

"Move? Where?" she cried, confused again. "What am I doing?"

"If you marry him now," Ash said, "you're going to have to go with him. He can't hang around Atlanta or stay here, that's for sure. And they've only given us until tomorrow until the alarm goes out and they start looking for him. We've got to have both of you miles away from here by then."

"Let me finish telling her what happened," Sam said. "I didn't have a chance to finish."

"Do it fast," Ash said.

Sam began, "When the ship your uncle and your mother were on went aground last month, they managed to salvage a quantity of drugs and medical supplies all together worth over half a million dollars, and almost impossible to get here in Georgia. A lot of pain and death could have been prevented in Atlanta if there'd been enough of those kinds of drugs. Both Lam and Noah suffered because they didn't have them."

"I know," Miranda said. It hurt to think about it.

"After Ash salvaged the drugs," Sam continued, "he buried them on an island that's part of the Kemble Altamaha plantations. The idea was that he'd retrieve them when he could do it in safety.

"When I got into trouble, it occurred to him that he might be able to work a deal with the people in Atlanta. So he and Jim Sutton took a train to Savannah, and from there they took a fishing sloop down the coast. They picked up the chests of drugs and brought them back to Atlanta."

"You mean he traded over half a million dollars' worth of medicine for you?" she asked, amazed, her eyes fixed in wonder and gratitude on her uncle. "You did that for him?" she asked Ash.

"And for you," he said simply.

"Ash!" she cried, leaping off the bed and launching herself at her uncle with the same loving ferocity she'd showed toward Sam ten minutes before. "You're absolutely wonderful!"

"Tell me later, darling," Ash said, trying and failing to peel her gently away from him, but adoring at the same time her display of affection and thanks.

"So your uncle talked to six or seven of the leading lights of Atlanta," Sam said, finishing his story as Miranda finished smothering Ash with kisses, "and they agreed to trade me for the drugs—or at least they agreed to unlock the prison doors and look the other way for a time."

"But only for a time," Ash said impatiently. "We've got to *move*, girl. I can't tell you that often enough."

"But wait," she said.

"Oh, God," he said, drawing deeply on the cigar which had somehow survived her recent assault. "What now, darling?"

"What will we do about Raven's Wing?" And then the answer came to her. "Ariel! She can do it!"

"That's a good idea, darling," Ash said, shaking his head no, "but uh-uh. It won't work."

"Why not?"

"In a very short while, the war is going to pass through these parts. When it comes, it's going to cut a terrible swath. I don't want her here— or you, for that matter. Ariel and Robbie are going to London with your mother until the war is over. Raven's Wing will just have to survive on its own.''

"You don't mean that, Uncle Ash!" Miranda said, her voice catching in her throat.

"I'm afraid I do," he said. "They have to go to London. It's the only safe thing for them to do.

"This land will survive the war, darling. Lots of land has survived lots of wars.'' He stood up suddenly and glared at her, then at Sam. "All right, both of you, you'll have a lifetime of one another, but now you're going to be apart for about twenty minutes. Sam, get out of here. And, Miranda, if you own something white, put it on. Then pack light. The bulk of your things your mother and I can deal with later."

"Yes, Uncle," she said.

Sam and Ash left her to prepare herself for her wedding. It was half past three on Saturday morning.

Soon after Sam and Uncle Ash departed, Miranda's mother appeared in her room, offering her help, comfort, and advice. Miranda sent her off, though, with thanks and blessings. She had to be by herself right now; she needed to gather her own forces. And as helpful as Fanny could be, she could also be meddlesome.

The dress she chose was not white, but creamy silk, with lace around the neck and a wide, lovely V of lace down the front. After she laid the dress and its attendant petticoats across her bed, she poured water from the pitcher into her basin and scrubbed her face, and then her neck, chest, and arms until her flesh glowed. After that she tried to make something of her hair—a near impossibility at such short notice. She managed in the end to devise a simple-looking but ingeniously flowing piece of architecture that she tied artfully together with ribbons. The result left her looking fresh and youthful, and at the same time graceful and elegant.

Not bad, she thought, admiring herself in her mirror. And all done in less than twenty-five minutes.

When she left her room and started to make her way to

the parlor, where the marriage would be performed, she was met by Ash, who was dressed in a dark suit, gray waistcoat, and silk tie. Ash led her to the wide, double doorway of the parlor entrance, and the pair of them waited there.

Everyone else was in the parlor and dressed for the occasion. Fanny was in sumptuous silks, standing near the makeshift altar, apparently eager to break into song. Noah and Lam were in their uniforms, and each reclined on one of a matching pair of love seats. Ariel, in a plain but richly beautiful indigo dress, sat in a wide armchair next to Noah's love seat. She held Robbie asleep in her arms. Jim Sutton wore a white shirt and gray uniform trousers; he was freshly shaved, and his hair was brilliantined and glossy. The Reverend Quintard wore clerical black with a white, priestly stole over his shoulders. He held a well-used Bible in one hand, and a carefully manufactured smile was on his face.

The smiles on the other faces were real.

Sam stood to the side and just behind the reverend. He was wearing the dress blues of a major in the United States Army.

When she saw him, Miranda let out a sudden, involuntary cry. Ash touched her arm to catch her attention.

"You're wondering about the uniform, I take it?" he asked.

She nodded.

"It was one of the pieces of business I managed to finish while I was still in Atlanta. In fact," he smiled, "it was not terribly difficult to procure, since the market for Federal uniforms is depressed in these parts."

"You'll notice from the insignia and badges of rank," he went on, directing his gaze at Sam, "that the wearer of that uniform has achieved his majority. That part is correct, Sam assures me. Or at least it will be by the time he rejoins his companions in blue.

"You've found yourself a handsome young man, my darling, who possesses other more valuable qualities as well. And he's going to go far. He won't stop at army major, that's for sure.''

"I keep having to thank you, Uncle," she said, dewy-eyed.

"Well, I'll just have to keep accepting your thanks, niece," he said.

At that moment Fanny Shaw launched into a fervent, swelling rendering of the Allelujas from Mozart's *Exsultate Jubilate*. The high notes were a struggle for her, and many of them eluded her, but Fanny, as always, was game. What she lacked in accuracy, she made up for in energy. Miranda thought her mother sang beautifully.

After that, Ash led Miranda to the altar—a small, round, marble-topped table. And she and Sam pronounced their vows. Then he slipped the gold ring on her finger.

"Where did you find the ring?" she whispered to him as the bride and groom kissed. "It isn't another gift from Uncle Ash?"

"It was your mother's," he said.

She smiled and gave herself up to the kiss.

When the ceremony was over, Ash stepped forward and made an announcement. "The happy couple are required to make a hasty departure," he said in a big, booming voice. "Their wedding journey will be more rushed and hectic than is usually the case with such things," he added in a stage whisper. "And unhappily," he continued in his normal voice, "there is no champagne to toast them with. . . ." He paused, then resumed a bit louder, "However, I have prevailed upon the powers that rule this place to put together a perfectly satisfactory substitute punch. We can't let these two innocent young people ride off into the sunrise of married bliss without toasting them."

"Here, here," Lam called out.

A pair of servants appeared bearing pitchers full of strong brandy punch and crystal cups. The cups were filled and distributed, and everyone waited for Ash to deliver the first toast.

But the first toast didn't come from Ash Kemble; it came from Noah Ballard. Noah struggled to his feet and propped himself up on a pair of crutches. He raised his cup and waited dramatically, searching out and finding Sam Hawken's eyes.

"Major Hawken," he said slowly, gathering himself. "Mrs. Hawken—I have to make a confession to you. I know it's an extraordinary thing to do at such a moment, but this is an extraordinary occasion." He paused, staring at the two of them. "May I?" he asked in a whisper.

"Yes, Noah," they said as one.

Noah went on slowly, deliberately, "If a silver-winged angel of the Lord had dropped out of the sky three months ago and handed me a golden scroll announcing this marriage at this time in this place, I would have had that angel placed under arrest as a messenger from the enemies of the Lord. If that angel had dropped out of the sky three weeks ago and handed me the same scroll, I would have shot him. His message would have appeared not just unthinkable to me, but evil, a vile obscenity.

"And now here you both are, married, and here I am joined with you in friendship.

"I'm truly glad that I'm here, Sam and Miranda. I'm awed and humbled to be with everyone here—but especially with you, Major Hawken, and with you, Colonel Kemble. I never imagined that the three of us would serve in the same unit together.

"And here we are." He raised his cup. "To Sam and Miranda." His voice rose, surged. "You are both magnificent!" He touched the cup to his lips.

"And finally," he said quietly, "to absent friends."

"Absent friends," Lam replied. He was the first to respond.

But Sam was not far behind. "Absent friends," he said . . . choked.

"Absent friends," everyone else in the room chorused.

There were other toasts; but it was Noah's that Sam and Miranda remembered for the rest of their lives.

Miranda went to her mother after the toasts and embraced and kissed her. Then it was Ariel's turn. And then Ash's. "Where are we going, Uncle?" she asked him. "You never told me where Sam and I are off to next."

He laughed. "What an extraordinary oversight, darling," he said. "Of course you should know your next move." He looked at her. "It's Kemble Island," he said. "From there you'll go to Saint Simon's, to the Federal installation there—I've sent someone ahead to warn them to expect you, by the way.

"From there it'll be a sea journey north."

"And you?" she asked.

"To London," he said.

"With Mother?" she slipped in.

"What do you mean?" he asked sharply, evidently flustered.

"Certain words and glances between you two have not gone unnoticed."

"Meanwhile," he said blithely, avoiding her eyes, "I'm off to London with your mother... *and* your sister."

"Then I won't see you until the war is over."

"I fear not," he said. "But that won't be long. I'm sure of it."

"Yes, Uncle," she said.

"Go change," he ordered. "You must be off."

"Not yet, Uncle, please. I have to talk to Mother and Ariel just for a minute."

He gave her a smile of impatient but fond acquiescence.

While she was engaged with her family, Sam and Noah and Lam were locked in vigorous and animated conversation. Though Miranda was desperately curious to hear that conversation, and desperately eager to take part in it, she held herself back. This was their moment, she knew. They deserved it. She had already had her time of glory.

Before she went to her room to change, she approached Reverend Quintard to thank him.

She was surprised to see when she drew near that much of his hostility seemed to have deserted him. The hostility was replaced by amazement.

The reverend gave her his blessing, and promised to keep her in his prayers. Then he grabbed her hands, and holding them tight, he looked soulfully into her eyes. "I've *never* seen anything like this! Never in my life! And I hope to

God, dear girl, I never have to face anything like it again!''

Within the hour the sun had started rising, and Sam and Miranda were both on horseback on the road that would eventually take them to Saint Simon's Island.

"What did you and Noah and Lam talk about after the toasts?" Miranda asked him when they were well away from Raven's Wing. She was unable to hold back her curiosity any longer.

"Don't you want to guess?" he asked playfully.

"No, I don't want to guess. Just tell me."

"If you insist," he said.

"I do insist. I'm burning up with curiosity."

"We were discussing a proposition," he said.

"A proposition?"

"Right. A proposal that your uncle put forward to me during our trip to Raven's Wing."

"Well?"

"He told me he has a mind to get into the railroad business after the war, and he wants the three of us to come into the business with him. There's going to have to be more than one line out to the West and the Pacific, he said. And he wants to set up the corporation that will build one of them."

*A Pacific railroad!* she thought to herself, liking that. From the moment that the flaming brand had fallen on her through the train window, she knew she was fated to be linked with railroads. So Sam might as well make that link official and permanent—and mighty. *A Pacific railroad!*

"And what did you tell him?" she asked. "What did the other two say?"

"What do you think?"

"I think you all said yes."

"That's right. That's what we said."